Broken Prey

JOHN SANDFORD

POCKET
BOOKS

LONDON • SYDNEY • NEW YORK • TORONTO

First published in Great Britain by Simon & Schuster UK Ltd, 2005
This edition published by Pocket Books, 2006
An imprint of Simon & Schuster UK Ltd
A CBS COMPANY

1 3 5 7 9 10 8 6 4 2

Simon & Schuster UK Ltd
Africa House
64-78 Kingsway
London WC2B 6AH

www.simonsays.co.uk

Simon & Schuster Australia
Sydney

A CIP catalogue record for this book is available from the British Library

ISBN 0 7434 8417 7
EAN 9780743484176

Printed and bound in Great Britain by
Bookmarque Ltd, Croydon, Surrey

For Barb Farmer and Sally Shannon

CHARLIE POPE TRUDGED down the alley with the empty garbage can on his back, soaked in the stench of rancid meat and rotten bananas and curdled blood and God knew what else, a man whose life had collapsed into a trash pit—and *still* he could feel the eyes falling on him.

The secret glances and veiled gazes spattered him like sleet from a winter thunderstorm. Everyone in town knew Charlie Pope, and they all watched him.

He'd been on the front page of the newspaper a half dozen times, his worried pig-eyed face peering out from the drop boxes and the shelves of the supermarkets. They got him when he registered as a sex offender, they got him outside his trailer, they got him carrying his can.

Pervert Among Us, the papers said, *Sex Maniac Stalks Our Daughters, How Long Will He Contain Himself Before Something Goes Terribly Wrong?* Well—they didn't really *say* that, but that's exactly what they *meant*.

Charlie tossed the empty garbage can to the side, stooped over the next one, lifted, staggered, and headed for the street. Heavy mother-fucker. What'd they put in there, fuckin' typewriters? How can they expect a white man to keep up with these fuckin' Mexicans?

All the other garbagemen were Mexicans, small guys from some obscure village down in the mountains. They worked incessantly, chattering in Spanish to isolate him, curling their lips at the American pervert who was made to work among them.

CHARLIE WAS A LARGE MAN, more fat than muscle, with a football-shaped head, sloping shoulders, and short, thick legs. He was bald, but his ears were hairy; he had a diminutive chin, tiny lips, and deep-set, dime-sized eyes that glistened with fluid. Noticeable and not attractive. He *looked* like a maniac, a newspaper columnist said.

He *was* a maniac. The electronic bracelet on his ankle testified to the fact. The cops had busted him and put him away for rape and aggravated assault, and suspected him in three other assaults and two murders. He'd done them, all right, and had gotten away with it, all but the one rape and ag assault. For that, they'd sent him to the hospital for eight years.

Hospital. The thought made his lips crook up in a cynical smile.

St. John's was to hospitals what a meat hook was to a hog.

CHARLIE PUSHED BACK the thought of St. John's and wiped the sweat out of his eyebrows, wrestled the garbage cans out to the truck, lifting, throwing, then dragging and sometimes kicking the cans back to the customers' doors. He could smell himself in the sunshine: he smelled like sweat and spoiled cheese and rotten pork, like sour milk and curdled fat, like life gone bad.

He'd thought he'd get used to it, but he never had. He smelled garbage every morning when he got to work, smelled it on himself all day, smelled it in his sweat, smelled it on his pillow in that hot, miserable trailer.

Hot and miserable, but better than St. John's.

EARLY MORNING.

Charlie was across the park from the famous Sullivan Bank when the chick in the raspberry-colored pants went by. The last straw? The straw that broke the camel's back?

Her brown eyes struck Charlie as cold raindrops, then flicked away when he turned at the impact; he was left with the impression of soft brown eyebrows, fine skin, and raspberry lipstick.

She had a heart-shaped ass.

She was wearing a cream-colored silk blouse, hip-clinging slacks, and low heels that lengthened her legs and tightened her ass at the same. She walked with that long busy confident stride seen on young businesswomen, full of themselves and still strangers to hard decision and failure.

And honest to God, her ass was heart shaped. Charlie felt a catch of desire in his throat.

Her hips twitched sideways with each of her steps: like two bobcats fighting in a gunny sack, somebody had once said, one of the other perverts at St. John's, trying to be funny. But it wasn't like that at all. It was a soft move, it was the motion of the world, right there in the raspberry slacks, with the slender back tapering down to her waist, her heels clicking on the sidewalk, her shoulder-length hair swinging in a backbeat to the rhythm of her legs.

Jesus God, he needed one. He'd been eight and a half years without real sex.

Charlie's tongue flicked out like a lizard's as he looked after her, and he could taste the garbage on his lips, could feel—even if they weren't there at this minute, he could feel them—the flies buzzing around his head.

Charlie Pope, thirty-four, a maniac, smelling like old banana peels and spoiled coffee grounds, standing on the street in Owatonna, passing eyes like icy raindrops, looking at a girl with a heart-shaped ass in raspberry slacks, and telling himself,

"I gotta get me some of that. I just gotta . . ."

2

THE MIST CAME IN WAVES, now almost a rain, now so light it was more like a fog. Across the Mississippi, the night lights of St. Paul shimmered with a brilliant, glassy intensity in the rain phases, and dimmed to ghosts in the fog.

After two weeks of Missourilike heat, the mist was welcome, pattering down on the broad-leafed oaks and maples, gurgling down the gutters, washing out the narrow red-brick road, stirring up odors of cut grass, damp concrete, and sidewalk worms.

A rich neighborhood, generous lawns, older houses well kept, a Mercedes here, a Land Rover there, window stickers from the universities of Minnesota and St. Thomas and even Princeton . . .

And now the smell of car exhaust and the murmur of portable generators . . .

.   .   .

SIX COP CARS, a couple of vans, and a truck jammed the street. Light bars turned on four of the vehicles, the piercing red-and-blue LED lights cutting down toward the river and up toward the houses perched on the high bank above it. Half of the cops from the cars were standing in the street, which had been blocked at both ends; the other half were down the riverbank, gathered in a spot of brilliant white light.

People from the neighborhood clustered under an oak tree; they all wore raincoats, like shrouds in a Stephen King chorus, and a few had umbrellas overhead. A child asked a question in an excited, high-pitched voice, and was promptly hushed.

Waiting for the body to come up.

LUCAS DIDN'T WANT to get trapped, so he left his Porsche at the top of the street, pulled a rain shirt over his head, added a green base-ball cap that said *John Deere, Owner's Edition*, and headed down the side-walk toward the cop cars.

When he stepped into the street, a young uniformed cop, hands on her hips, maybe twenty-three or twenty-four, in a translucent plastic slicker said, "Hey! Back on the sidewalk."

"Sloan called me," Lucas said.

He was about to add "I'm with the BCA," when she jumped in, sharp, officious, defensive about her own inexperience—part of the new-cop scripture that said you should never let a civilian get on top of you: "Get on the sidewalk. I'll see if Detective Sloan wants to talk to you."

"Why don't I just yell down there?" Lucas asked affably. Before she could answer, he bellowed, "HEY, SLOAN!"

She started to poke a finger at his face, and then Sloan yelled, "Lucas: Down here!"

Instead of shaking her finger at him, she twitched it across the road and turned away from him, hands still on her hips, shoulders square, dignity not quite preserved.

A PORTABLE HONDA GENERATOR had been set up on the street, black power cables snaking down the riverbank where a line of Caterpillar-yellow work lights, on tripods, threw a couple of thousand watts of halogen light on the body. Nobody had covered anything yet.

Lucas eased down the hillside, the grass slippery with churned-up mud. Twenty feet out, he saw the body behind a circle of legs, a red-and-white *thing* spread on the grass, arms outstretched to the sides, legs spread wide, faceup, naked as the day she was born.

Lucas moved through the circle of cops, faces turning to glance at him, somebody said, "Hey, Chief," and somebody else patted him on the back. Sloan stood on the slope below, leaning into the bank. Sloan was a narrow-faced, narrow-shouldered man wearing a long plastic raincoat, shoe rubbers, and a beaten-up snap-brim canvas hat that looked like it had just been taken out of the back closet. The hat kept the rain out of his eyes. He said to Lucas, "Look at this shit."

Lucas looked at the body and said, "Jesus Christ," and somebody else said, "More'n you might think, brother. She was *scourged*."

SCOURGED. The word hung there, in the mist, in the lights. She'd been a young woman, a few pounds too heavy, dark hair. Her body, from her collarbone to her knees, was crisscrossed with cuts that had probably been made with some kind of flail, Lucas thought: a whip made out of wire, maybe. The cut lines were just lines: the rain had washed out any blood. There were dozens of the cuts, and the way they wrapped around her body, he expected her back to be in the same condition.

"You got a name?" he asked.

"Angela Larson," Sloan said. "College student at the U, from Chicago. Worked in an art store. Missing since yesterday."

"Cut her throat like she was a goddamn beef," said one of the cops. A strobe went off, a flash of white lightning. Lucas walked around the body, down to stand next to Sloan.

Because his feet were lower than the victim, he could get closer to her face. He looked at the cut in the throat. As with the wire cuts, it was bloodless, washed clean by the rain, resembling a piece of turkey meat. He didn't doubt that he could have buried a finger in it up to the knuckle. He could smell the rawness of the body, like standing next to the meat counter in a supermarket.

"The neck wound's what killed her, I think," Sloan said. "No sign of a gunshot wound or a stab wound. He beat her, whipped her, until he was satisfied, and then cut her throat."

"Ligature marks on her wrists," said a man in plainclothes. His name was Stan, and he worked as an investigator for the Hennepin County Medical Examiner, and was known for his grotesque sense of humor. His face was as long as anyone's.

"We got a call last night when Larson didn't get back to her apartment," Sloan said. "Her roommate called. We found her car in the parking lot behind Chaps; she worked at a place called the MarkUp down the block . . ."

"I know it," Lucas said. Chaps was a younger club, mixed straights and gays, dancing.

". . . and used to park at Chaps because the store didn't have its own parking, the street is metered, and the Chaps lot has lights. She got off at nine o'clock, stopped and said hello to a bartender, had a glass of white wine. Bartender said just enough to rinse her mouth. Probably about twenty-after she walked out to her car. She never got home. We found her car keys in the parking lot next to the car; no blood, no witnesses saw her taken."

Lucas looked at the ligature marks on her wrists. The rope, or whatever she'd been tied with—it was rope, he thought—had been a half inch thick and had both cut and burned her. There were more burns and chafing wounds at the base of her thumbs. "Hung her up," Lucas said.

"We think so," Sloan said. He tipped his head down the bank. "Give me a minute, will you?"

THEY STEPPED AWAY, twenty feet down the bank, into the privacy of the darkness.

Sloan took off his hat, brushed his thinning hair away from his eyes, and asked, "What do you think?"

"Pretty bad," Lucas said, turning back to the circle of lights. Even from this short distance, the body looked less than human, and more like an artifact, or even an artwork. "He's nuts. You've checked her friends . . ."

"We've started, but we're coming up empty," Sloan said. "She was dating a guy, sleeping with him off and on, until a couple of months ago. Until the end of the school year. Then he went back home to Pennsylvania."

"Didn't come back to visit?"

"Not as far as we can tell—he says he hasn't, and I sorta believe him. He was there when she disappeared, we talked to him ten hours after she dropped out of sight—and the Philadelphia cops called a couple people for us, and he checks out."

"Okay."

"He said they were a little serious, but not too—she knew he planned to go in the army when he got out of school, and she didn't like the idea. Her friends say he's a pretty straight guy, they can't imagine that he's involved. They don't know she was involved with anyone else, yet. And that's what we've got."

Lucas was still looking at the body, at the rain falling around the cops. "I'd put my money on a semistranger. Whoever did this . . . This guy is pushed by brain chemistry. He's got something wrong with him. This isn't a bad love affair. The way she's displayed . . ."

Sloan half turned back to the lights: "That's what I was thinking. The goddamned display."

THEY JUST STOOD AND WATCHED for a minute, the cops moving around the lights, talking up and down the bank. The two of them might have done this two hundred times. "So what can I do for you?" Lucas asked. Lucas worked with the state Bureau of Criminal Apprehension. Minneapolis had its own murder investigators, who would tell you that they were better than any BCA cherry who ever walked the face of the earth.

Lucas, who had been a Minneapolis cop before he moved to the state, mostly bought that argument: Minneapolis saw sixty or eighty murders a year; the BCA worked a dozen.

"You agree he's a nut?"

Lucas wiped his eyebrows, which were beading up with rain. "Yeah. No question."

"I need to talk to somebody who is really on top of this shit," Sloan said. "That I can get to whenever I need to. I don't need some departmental consultant who got his BA three years ago."

"You want to talk to Elle," Lucas said.

"Yeah. I wanted to see if you'd mind. And I wanted you to look at the body, too, of course. I'm gonna need all the brains on this I can get," Sloan said.

"Elle's an adult," Lucas said. "She can make up her own mind."

"C'mon, man, you know what I'm saying. It's a friendship thing. If you said not to call her, I wouldn't. I'm asking you."

"Call her," Lucas said. "I would."

. . .

SLOAN CALLED ELLE—Sister Mary Joseph in her professional life. She was the head of the department of psychology at St. Anne's College and literally Lucas's oldest friend; they'd walked to kindergarten together with their mothers.

When Lucas became a cop and she became a teacher, they got back in touch, and Elle had worked on a half dozen murders, as an unofficial advisor, and not quite a confessor. Then, once, a crazy woman with a talent for misdirection caught Elle outside at night and had nearly beaten her to death. Since then, Lucas had shied from using her. If it happened again . . .

Elle didn't share his apprehension. She liked the work, the tweezing apart of criminal psyches. So Sloan called Elle, and Elle called Lucas, and they all talked across town for two weeks. Theories and arguments and suggestions for new directions . . .

Nothing. The murder of Angela Larson began to drift away from them—out of the news, out of the action. A black kid got killed in a bar outside the Target Center, and some of the onlookers said it had been a racial fight. Television news pushed Larson back to an occasional mention, and Sloan stopped trudging around, because he had no place farther to trudge.

"Maybe a traveler?" Elle wondered. She had a thin, delicate bone structure, her face patterned with the white scars of a vicious childhood acne; Lucas had wondered if the change from a pretty young blond girl in elementary school to a irredeemably scarred adolescent might have been the impulse that pushed her into the convent.

She'd known he'd wondered and one time patted him on the arm and told him that no, she'd heard Jesus calling . . .

"A traveler? Maybe," Lucas said. Travelers were nightmares. They might kill for a lifetime and never get caught; one woman disappearing every month or so, most of them never found, buried in the woods or the mountains or out in the desert, no track to follow, nobody to pull the pieces together. "But real travelers tend to hide their victims, and that's why you never hear much about them. This guy is advertising."

Elle: "I know." Pause. "He won't stop."

"No," Lucas said. "He won't."

A WEEK AFTER THAT CONVERSATION, a few minutes before noon, on a dry day with sunny skies, Lucas sat in a booth in a hot St. Paul bar looking at a lonely piece of cheeseburger, two untouched buns, and a Diet Coke.

The bar was hot because there'd been a power outage, and when the power came back on, an errant surge had done something bad to the air conditioner. From time to time, Lucas could hear the manager, in his closet-sized office, screaming into a telephone, among the clash and tinkle of dishes and silverware, about warranties and who'd never get his work again, and that included his apartments.

Two sweating lawyers sat across from Lucas and took turns jabbing their index fingers at his chest.

"I'm telling you," George Hyde said, jabbing, "this list has no credibility. No credibility. Am I getting through to you, Davenport? Am I coming in?"

Hyde's pal Ira Shapira said, "You know what? You leave the Beatles out, but you got *folk* on it. "Heart of Saturday Night"? That's folk."

"Tom Waits would beat the shit out of you if he heard you say that," Lucas said. "Besides, it's a great song." He lifted his empty glass to a barmaid, who nodded at him. "I'm not saying the list is perfect," he said. "It's just an attempt—"

"The list is shit. It has no musical, historical, or ethical basis," Hyde interrupted.

"Or sexual," Shapira added.

· · ·

LUCAS WAS A TALL MAN, restless, dark hair flecked with gray, with cool blue eyes. His face was touched with scars, including one that ran down through an eyebrow, and up into his hairline; and another that looked like a large upside-down apostrophe, where a little girl had shot him in the throat and a doctor had slashed his throat open so he could breathe. He had a chipped tooth and what he secretly thought was a pleasant, even pleasing smile—but a couple of women had told him that his smile frightened them a little.

He was wearing a gray summer-weight wool-and-silk suit from Prada, over black shoes and with a pale blue silk golf shirt, open at the neck; a rich-jock look. He'd once been a college jock, a first-line defenseman with the University of Minnesota's hockey team. Lucas was tough enough, but he'd picked up six pounds over the winter. They'd lingered all through the spring and into the summer, and he'd finally put himself on the South Beach Diet. An insane diet, he thought, but one that his wife had recommended, just before she left town.

He leaned back, chewing the last bite of cheeseburger, yearning for the buns. He hadn't had a carbohydrate in a week. Now he held his hands a foot apart, and after he'd swallowed, said, earnestly, rationally: "Listen, guys. Rock and its associated music divides into two great streams. In one, you've got Pat Boone, Doris Day, the Beatles, Donny and Marie Osmond, the Carpenters, Sonny and Cher, Elton John, and Tiffany, or whatever her name is—the chick with no stomach. Anybody that you might snap your fingers to. In the other stream, you've got Chuck Berry, Elvis Presley, the Rolling Stones, Tina Turner, Aerosmith, Tom Petty. Like that." He touched himself on the chest. "That's the one I prefer. I guess you guys are . . . finger snappers."

"Snappers?" Hyde shouted. A couple of guys at the bar turned to look at him, the bored, heavy-lidded howya-doin' look. In the back, the manager screamed, "I don't give a fuck what's happening on Grand Avenue, I want a fuckin' truck outside this place in three minutes . . ."

"If you're so much against snappers, how come you got the fuckin' *Eagles* on your list?" Shapira demanded. "I mean, the *Eagles?*"

"Only 'Lyin' Eyes,'" Lucas said, looking away. "I feel guilty about it, but how can you avoid that one?"

Hyde sighed, nodded, took a hit on his drink: "Yeah, you're right about that. When you're right, you're right."

"A piece of country trash, if you ask me," Shapira said.

"About the best song of the last fifty years," Lucas said. *"Rolling Stone* had a survey of the best five hundred rock songs. They had 'Hotel California' and 'Desperado' on the list, and not 'Lyin' Eyes.' What kind of shit is that? Those guys have got their heads so far up their asses they can see their own duodenums."

"Duodeni," said Shapira.

"You ever hear 'Hotel California' by the Gipsy Kings?" Hyde asked. "Now there's a tune . . ."

"Goddamnit," Lucas said. He took a black hand-sized Moleskine notebook out of his pocket. "I forgot about that one. I got too goddamn many songs already."

LUCAS WAS LOOKING for the barmaid, for another Diet Coke, when his cell phone rang. He fished it out of his pocket, and Hyde said, "They ought to ban those things in bars. They distract you from your drinking." Lucas put the phone to his ear and stuck a finger in his opposite ear, so he could hear.

His secretary said, "I've got Gene Nordwall on the line, and he wants to speak to you. He says it's urgent. I didn't know what to tell him: You want me to put him through?"

"Put him on," Lucas said. He sat through a couple of clicks, and then a man said, "Hello?" and Lucas said, "Gene? This is Lucas. How's it going?"

"Not going worth a good goddamn," Nordwall said. He sounded angry and short of breath, as if he'd just been chased somewhere. Lucas could see him in his mind's eye, a tall, overweight chunk of Norwegian authority, a man who'd look most natural in Oshkosh bib overalls. Nordwall was sheriff of Blue Earth County, fifty or sixty miles southwest of the Twin Cities. "Can you come down here?"

"Mankato?"

"Six miles south, out in the country," Nordwall said. "We got a killing down here like to made me puke. We called in your crime scene crew—but we need *you*."

"Whattaya got?"

"Somebody killed a kid and tortured his dad to death," Nordwall said. "Tortured him and raped him, we think, and maybe cut his throat with a razor. I ain't seen anything like it in fifty years."

Sloan's case popped into Lucas's head: "You say it's a *guy*?"

"Yeah, local guy. Adam Rice."

"It's not a gay thing? Or did he screw around with bikers or . . ."

"He was absolutely straight," Nordwall said. "I've known him since he was a kid."

"And he was raped?"

"Jesus Christ, you want a photograph?" Nordwall said, the anger flashing again. "He was fuckin' raped, pardon my French."

Lucas waited for a second, until Nordwall got himself back together. "Are you right there, Gene?"

"I'm out in the side yard, Lucas. Came runnin' out of there, like to strangled myself to death on this old clothesline."

"Was the guy's body, you know, *arranged*? Or was he just left however he died?"

A pause, and then Nordwall asked, "How'd you know that? What they did with him?"

"I'll be down there in an hour," Lucas said. "Don't let anybody touch anything. Get out of the house. We're gonna work this inch by inch."

"We'll be standing in the yard, waitin'," Nordwall said.

"Gimme your cell-phone number, and tell me how I get to this place . . ."

"WHAT'S GOING ON?" Hyde asked when Lucas punched off.

"Got a bad killing down by Mankato," Lucas said. He finished his Diet Coke in a single gulp, dropped a twenty on the table. "Pay this for me, will you, guys? I gotta get my ass down there."

"Too bad," Hyde said. "I've got a closing on a shopping center at two o'clock. I thought you might want to see it."

LUCAS GOT SLOAN on his cell phone as he went out the door: "Where you at?"

"Sitting at my desk reading a British *Esquire*," Sloan said. "They got nudity now."

"You might want to spend some time looking at the clothes . . . Listen, get a squad, lights, and sirens, get down to the top of the Twenty-fourth Avenue off-ramp to the Mall of America. I'll be down there fast as I can make it: twelve minutes. You gotta run."

"Where're we going?"

"Mankato. It's weird, but we might have something on your nut case."

OFF THE PHONE, Lucas jogged down the street to the Marshall Field parking ramp. He'd taken the Porsche to work that morning, which was good. He had a new truck, but the truck was awkward at speed and he was in a hurry. He wanted to see the scene in the brightest possible daylight, and he wanted to see neighbors, rubberneckers, and visitors as they came by the murder scene.

Rubberneckers.

"Goddamnit," he muttered to himself. He slapped his pockets as he jogged, found the slip of paper with Nordwall's number on it, and called him back.

"Gene, this is Lucas again. I'm heading for my car. Listen, put a guy down by the road . . . How far is this house from the road?"

"Couple hundred feet, maybe. Old farmhouse."

"Put a guy down by the road and have him take down the license number of every car that comes along. Don't stop them from coming. Let them go by, let'em rubberneck, but I want all the numbers. Put your guy where he can't be seen."

"How about a photographer?"

"That'd be good, but don't put somebody out there who'll screw it up, so we get a bunch of out-of-focus pictures we can't read. Better to write the numbers down."

"We'll do both," Nordwall said.

THEN LUCAS WAS INTO THE RAMP, into the car, out on the street, slicing through traffic in the C4, to the I-35E ramp, down the ramp and south, running fifty miles an hour above the speed limit, across the Mississippi to I-494, west on 494 across the Minnesota River, and up the Twenty-fourth Avenue ramp.

The Minneapolis squad was sitting at the top of the ramp, lights flashing into the sunshine. Sloan got out of the squad, jogged around the back end of the truck, and said, "The all-time speed record from the airport to Mankato is an hour and one minute."

"Must have been an old lady in a Packard," Lucas said.

"Actually, it was myself in a fifteen-year-old bottle green Pontiac LeMans my old man gave me," Sloan said as he strapped in.

"Do tell."

Lucas blew through the red light and down the ramp and they were gone west and south into the green ocean of corn and soybeans of rural southern Minnesota.

3

THEY WERE SLOWED BY ROADWORK north of the city of Mankato, where one side of the divided highway had buckled, and traffic was switched to the east lane.

"Wonder if they bother to put concrete in the fuckin' roads anymore," Sloan grumbled. "Everything falls apart. The bridge over to Hudson was up for what, six or seven years, and they're tearing the whole thing apart again?"

"Thinking about it will drive you crazy," Lucas said. When he had a chance, he pulled the Porsche onto the shoulder of the road, hopped out, stuck a flasher on the roof, and used it to jump the waiting lines of traffic.

On the way down, Lucas told Sloan what Nordwall had said about the killing, and Sloan had grown morose: "If I'd just gotten a break. One fuckin' thing. I couldn't get my fingernails under anything, you know?"

"Maybe it's not your guy, or it's a coincidence. The victim this time is male," Lucas said.

"Seen it before, nut cases who go both ways."

They talked about serial killers. All major metro areas had them, sometimes two and three at a time. The public had the impression that they were rare. They weren't.

"I remember once, I was in LA on a pickup. The *L.A. Times* had a story that said that the cops thought there might be a serial killer working in such-and-such a neighborhood," Sloan said. "The story just mentioned it in passing, like it was going to rain on Wednesday."

THEY CAME UP BEHIND a pickup struggling through the traffic, and flicked past it. A woman's hand came out of the passenger-side window and gave them the finger. Lucas caught it in the rearview mirror and grinned. Generally, he felt some sympathy for women who'd give the finger to cops, especially if they were good-looking. The women, not the cops.

"ONE THING ABOUT THIS GUY—he's leaving the bodies right in our faces. He took Larson somewhere to torture her, killed her somewhere else, and then brought her back and posed her almost in her own neighborhood . . . the neighborhood where we're most likely to take a lot of shit, where it'd get the most attention," Lucas said. "This guy, this Rice guy, he tortures and leaves in his own house . . ."

"He's probably scouting locations, putting them where they attract attention, but he feels safe doing it."

"For sure," Lucas said. "None of this feels spontaneous."

BESIDES THE SERIAL-KILLER TALK, they argued a little about Lucas's rock 'n' roll list. Lucas's wife, Weather, had given him an Apple iPod for his birthday and a gift certificate for one hundred songs from the Apple Web site. He'd taken the limit of one hundred songs as an invitation for discipline: one hundred songs, no more, no less, the best one hundred songs of the rock era.

Word of the list had spread through the BCA, and among his friends, and after a month of work, he had a hundred and fifty solid possibilities with more coming in every day. He still hadn't ordered a single tune. "What bothers me is, I think I'm just about set, and then I'll hear something I completely forgot about, like 'Radar Love,'" he told Sloan. "I mean, that's *gotta* go on the list. What else did I forget?"

"One thing, since you're mostly making it for road trips—it can't be all hard stuff. It can't be all AC/DC," Sloan said. "You've got to have some mellow stuff. You know, for when you're just rolling along. Or at night, when the stars are out and it's cold. Billy Joel or Blondie."

"I know, I know. I got that. But right now, the way I'm thinking, you're going on a road trip—you start off with ZZ Top, right? Gotta start off with ZZ. 'Sharp-Dressed Man,' 'Legs,' one of those."

"I can see that," Sloan said, nodding. "Something to get you moving." He turned away, stared at the acres and acres of corn. "Jesus Christ, if I'd just gotten a single fuckin' break."

"COULD BE DRY OUT THERE," Sloan said, as they came down on Mankato. "Hot and dry."

"We'll stop," Lucas said.

Mankato was the site of the largest mass hanging in American history, thirty-eight Sioux Indians in a single drop. The Sioux said that thirty-eight eagles come back to fly over the riverbank site every year on the anniversary of the hanging. Lucas didn't believe in that kind of thing, but then, one time he'd been in the neighborhood, on the anniversary, and he'd seen the eagles . . .

"There," Sloan said. "Holiday store. They got Krispy Kremes."

They picked up twenty-four-packs of Coke, Diet Coke, and Dasani water; a throw-away Styrofoam cooler and a bag of ice; a couple of hot dogs; and a couple of Krispy Kremes.

"I thought you South Beach Diet guys weren't even supposed to eat the buns, much less a doughnut," Sloan said through a mouthful of hot dog, as they headed back into the country.

"Fuck you," Lucas said. The Krispy Kreme tasted so good that he felt faint.

THEY FOLLOWED HIGHWAY 169 for three or four miles south of town, turned east across a thirty-foot-wide river, took a narrow black-topped road out a mile or so, then jogged onto a gravel lane. As soon as they got onto the gravel, they could see a covey of cars, mostly cop cars with light bars, arranged under an old spreading elm tree next to a white clapboard farmhouse.

The farmhouse, with a detached one-car garage on its east side, sat on an acre of high ground. A grassy lawn supported a dozen old elms and oaks and two apple trees. A tire swing hung from one of the oaks, and bean fields crept right up to the unfenced lawn. A hundred feet out behind the house, a series of old sheds or chicken houses were slowly rotting away, slumping back into the soil. *Not a working farm*, Lucas thought, *just the remnants of one*.

"How'd he find them?" Lucas asked, as they came up. "How'd he pick them out?"

THEY WENT PAST a mailbox that said RICE, in crooked black hand-painted letters, and spotted a cop up on the lawn, looking at them through a camera lens. Four cops, including the sheriff, were standing on the lawn, just as Nordwall said they'd be. Four more people, including three women, civilians, and a cop sat in an aging Buick on the grass beside the driveway. A red-eyed woman drooped in the backseat, the door open, and looked toward them as they came up.

"Relatives," Sloan said.

Lucas pulled onto the lawn next to the end cop car, and he and Sloan got out.

"Davenport, goddamnit, you got the crime scene coming?" the sheriff asked. He was a tall man, and wide, with white hair, a red-tipped button nose, and worry lines on a head the size of a gallon milk jug; he was anxious.

"You call them?"

"I called them, and they said they were rolling."

"Takes awhile," Lucas said. He turned to the house. "You shut everything down?"

"Everything." Nordwall was looking at Sloan. "Who's this guy?"

Lucas introduced them, and Sloan told him about Angela Larson. "Ah, jeez, I saw that in the paper," Nordwall said. "But I don't remember . . . you must not have given them all the details."

"No, we didn't," Sloan said. Sloan dropped the cooler on the ground, and said, "Cokes, if anybody's thirsty," and started passing around the cans.

"Might get some to Miz Rice and Miz Carson," Nordwall said to one of the deputies. He looked past Lucas at the Buick and said, "Rice's mom, and her sister, and a friend. Miz Rice wants to see them, but I ain't gonna allow it. Not until after they're bagged. She'd have that picture in her head until she went to the grave."

Lucas nodded and gestured toward the farmhouse. "Who found them?"

"One of my deputies, George," Nordwall said.

One of the deputies, a thin man with shaggy black hair and a ricocheting Adam's apple, lifted his Coke.

"Me," the deputy said.

"Tell me," Lucas said.

The deputy shrugged. "Well, Rice didn't come to work. He's the manager of a hardware store in Mankato, and he has the keys to the place. Today he was supposed to open the store. When he didn't show, the gals who worked there called the owner, who came down to open up. He tried to call Rice, but got a phone out-of-order thing. When he still didn't show up by ten o'clock, the owner got worried and called us."

"And you came out?"

"Well, first Sandy, she takes our calls . . ."

"Yeah . . ."

"Sandy's chatting with the store owner, and he says Rice had a boy in grade school. So Sandy called over to the elementary school and asked if the kid showed up. They said no, and that Rice hadn't called in an excuse. I was down this way patrolling, and they asked me to swing by. I come up, saw a car around back, but nobody answered. The doors were open and then, uh, I went around back and looked in through the back door and I saw the boy lying on the floor, and man, he looked like, you know, he was dead. He looked like a rag doll. Then I come in and found him and I got the heck out of there and alerted the sheriff."

"Didn't touch anything?"

"I been trying to think," the deputy said, looking over at the house. "The door handle, for sure. And I think I put my hand on the door frame on the way out. The main thing was, I didn't know if somebody was still in there, and I wanted to get outside where I could see somebody running, if they were. Then I stood here until everybody come in."

"Sounds like you did okay," Lucas said, and the deputy bobbed his head, taking the compliment. Lucas said to Nordwall, "We gotta have your guys figure out if they touched or moved anything. It'll make things easier. We're gonna be looking for DNA, and that's a touchy thing."

"I figured," Nordwall said. He looked up at the house. "You gonna go in?"

"Just for a quick look," Lucas said.

LUCAS HAD LITTLE FAITH in crime-scene analysis as a way of breaking a case, but it often came in handy after they caught somebody. He got thin vinyl throwaway gloves from his car, handed a packet to Sloan. They went in through the back door, since that entry route had already been contaminated, trying not to bump anything, or scuff anything. The door opened into a mudroom, six feet square with coat hooks on the wall, ancient linoleum flooring, then through a glass-paneled door into the kitchen. The boy was lying in the kitchen, a pool of dried blood around his head; he was wearing pajamas.

"Been there awhile," Sloan said. He stepped closer, squatted. "He was hit on the head with something. Something crushed the skull."

"He never moved, the skid marks lead right into the blood," Lucas said. Lucas had a toddler at home, and swallowed, the bitter taste of acid in his throat. "Must have killed him outright."

Sloan sighed, put his hands on his thighs, and pushed himself back up. "I'm gonna quit," he said.

"Yeah, right." Lucas led the way toward the next room, a hall. They could see the living room beyond it.

"I'm serious," Sloan said. "I got the time in. I'm gonna put this guy away, and then I'm gonna do it. That dead kid is one dead kid too many."

Lucas looked at him: "Let's talk about it later."

"Fuck later. I'm gonna quit."

ADAM RICE WAS IN THE NEXT ROOM. He was naked, kneeling, his hips up, his head on the floor. He had duct tape on both wrists, as though they'd been taped together, and then cut loose. His body was a mass of blood, a hundred bloody stripes across his chest and stomach and thighs. *Scourged*, Lucas thought. Blood spattered the walls, a round oaken dinner table, two short bookcases full of books and china; and splashed across the faces of a dozen people smiling down from pictures on the living-room wall.

Sloan looked at him and said, "That's our guy. No question about it."

"No question."

"None."

RICE'S CLOTHES HAD BEEN flung in one corner, and were rags. The killer had cut them off with some kind of razor knife or box cutter or scalpel. He'd brought it with him, Lucas thought, and had taken it away with him.

"He's got some muscle," Sloan said, looking at the dead man. "The killer must have had a gun on him. Doesn't look like he fought back much."

Lucas nodded. "The guy comes in, he has a gun, points it at Rice, tells him it's a robbery and that there'll be no trouble if he cooperates. Rice is worried about the kid, who's up in bed. He cooperates. He gets his hands taped up and then the shit starts. They're struggling, knocking around, maybe, the kid hears it, comes down, sees what's going on, and runs for the door. The killer gets him in the kitchen. Maybe whacks him with the butt of a shotgun."

Sloan nodded: "I'll buy that, for a start."

"The thing is, the killer came for Rice, the father. He wasn't pulled in by the kid. The kid looks like an accident, or an afterthought. Maybe the killer didn't even know he existed."

"Huh." Noncommittal.

"Look, if he'd known about the kid, he'd have put the old man on the ground, then he'd have gone up to the bedroom to take care of the kid, to make sure that he didn't get out somehow. Instead, he has to go after him in the kitchen, whack him with something."

"Okay . . ."

Rice made an awkward pile in the middle of a large puddle of blood. The light fixture on the ceiling was bent, cocked far off to one side: a lot of weight had been put on it.

The weight had been Rice: he was a slender blond man, maybe a hundred and sixty pounds. The killer had taped his wrists, then put a rope through them, and hung him from the light fixture. Rice had tried to twirl away from him when the beating began, and his blood sprayed in an almost perfect circle. When the killer cut him down to pose him, he centered Rice's body in the blood puddle.

Rice's eyes were open, blue now fading to translucent brown; his palms were facing up, his fingers crooked. Lucas looked at one hand, then the other, and squatted as Sloan had squatted next to the boy.

"Got some blood here, under his nails. Maybe some skin . . ."

"Could be something," Sloan said. "All the other blood on him is running *down* his body—he hung him up like he hung up Larson. Wonder if he tried to fight at the last minute, and scratched the guy?" He squatted next to Lucas, then bent to look at the fingernails. "Skin, for sure, I think. Your guys gotta be careful or they could lose it."

"They'll get it," Lucas said. He stood up and made a hand-dusting motion. "What do you think? Look around, or wait for crime scene?"

Sloan shook his head. "I don't think we'll find anything looking around. I've done everything I could think of with Angela Larson— went over her apartment inch by inch, the place she worked, did histories on her until they were coming out of my ears. I don't think this has much to do with the victims. They're stranger-killings. He stalks them and kills them."

"Trophies?"

"I don't know. We never found Larson's clothes or her jewelry, so maybe they were taken as trophies . . . but then . . . Rice's clothes are right here."

"Never found out where he killed Larson."

"No. Probably a basement. The soles of her feet were dirty, and there was concrete dust in the dirt. So . . . could have been a basement."

THEY STOOD NEXT TO THE BODY for a minute, a strange comradely cop-moment, their shoes just inches from the puddle of blood, a half dozen fat lazy bluebottle flies buzzing around the room; bluebottles, somebody once told Lucas, were actually blowflies. One landed on the far side of the blood puddle, and they could see it nibbling at the crusting blood.

"You can't really quit," Lucas said.

"Sure I can," Sloan said.

"What would you do?" A fly buzzed past Lucas's head, and he swatted at it.

"Ah . . . talk to you about it sometime. I got some ideas."

Lucas got up, looked around: a pleasant, homey place, the house creaking a bit, a sound that must have seemed warm and welcome; a glider-chair lounged in one corner, comfortably worn, facing a fat old Sony color TV with a braided rug on the floor in front of it. A couple of nice-looking quilts hung from the walls, between yellowed photographs of what must have been grandparents and great-grandparents.

"YOU KNOW THE PROBLEM," Lucas said softly. He was looking at a log-cabin quilt; he didn't know anything about quilts, but he liked the earth colors in it. "We're not going to pick up much here, not unless we get lucky. Maybe DNA. But where's that gonna get us?"

"A conviction when we get him."

"The problem is getting him. That's the fucking problem," Lucas said. "A conviction . . . that can always be fixed, when we get the right guy. Getting him . . ."

"Yeah . . ."

"I want all the paper from Minneapolis," Lucas said.

Sloan nodded. "I'll get Anderson on it."

"And I'll get the crime-scene guys to copy everything to you, from here. You got nothing off the Larson killing?"

"I got names. That's one thing I got."

"Okay. That's a start. I'll get a co-op center going, get them to set up a database. We'll pipe in everything from here, from Nordwall's guys."

"There's *gotta* be more from here. There's gotta be," Sloan said, looking around, an edge of desperation in his voice. "If we don't get anything, then we won't get him before . . ."

Lucas nodded and finished his sentence: ". . . before he does it again."

OUTSIDE ON THE LAWN, Nordwall and the other deputies were sitting on the grass, in the shade of an elm, looking like attendees at the annual cop picnic. The summer was at its peak, the prairie grasses lush and tall, just starting to show hints of yellow and tan. A mile or so away, across a wide, low valley, a distant car kicked up a cloud of gravel dust.

Nordwall was chewing on a grass stem; when they came up, he stood and asked, "What do you think?"

"Same guy," Sloan said.

"Sloan did a lot of research on the first one, up in Minneapolis," Lucas said. "We're gonna set up a co-op center out of the BCA. We need a complete biography on Rice and the kid—who did they know, who had they met recently. The guy knew about him—something about him. He didn't come out here by accident. And he knew about

29

the first one, too. Maybe the two of them, Rice and Larson, intersect somewhere."

"You think . . . maybe some kind of boy-girl romance thing?" one of the deputies suggested. "A jilted lover? Rice's wife got killed in a car accident a couple years ago, he might have been looking around."

"You get a jilted lover, you get a gun in a bedroom or a knife in the kitchen, but you don't get the boyfriend raped," Sloan said mildly.

Nordwall swiveled and looked at another of the deputies and said, "You get right on this biography, Bill. Don't hold back, and don't worry about the overtime. I'll cover anything you need." To Lucas, he said, "This is Bill James. I'll get his phone number for you."

The deputy stood up and dusted off the seat of his pants with a couple of slaps: "I'll go right now. Get started."

"What happened with the wife?" Lucas asked. "A straight-up accident, no question?"

"In the winter, winter before last," said Nordwall. "She came around a snowplow, didn't see the pickup coming the other way. Boom. Died in the ditch."

"So . . ."

"Whole goddamn family up in smoke," a deputy said.

"Here comes a truck," somebody else said.

A white *Mission Impossible*–style van was rolling down the gravel road toward them. "That's the crime-scene guys," Lucas said. "Why don't you guys get them inside? Me and Sloan'll go talk to Mrs. Rice."

LAURINA RICE WAS IN HER SIXTIES, with white puffy grandmother hair and a round, leathery face lined by age and the sun. She was too heavy, too many years of potatoes and beef. She wore a dress with small flowers on it. Her sister, Gloria, was perhaps three or four years older, and the friend about the same.

Laurina Rice struggled to get her feet on the ground and get out of the car as Lucas and Sloan walked over to it. On the other side of the car, a hundred and fifty yards out over the bean field, a flock of red-winged blackbirds hassled a crow, diving on the bigger bird like fighters on a bomber.

As had happened on other crime scenes, Lucas was for a second struck by the ordinariness of the day around him: nature didn't know about crime, about rape and murder, and simply went on: blue skies, puffy clouds, blackbirds hassling crows.

"You're the state man, Mr. Davenport, and Mr. Sloan from Minneapolis . . ." Rice said. Her eyes were like a chicken's, small and sharp and focused.

"Yes. I'm terribly sorry about what happened, Mrs. Rice."

She twisted the fingers of her right hand in her left, literally wringing them. "I need to see my boy, to see that it's him."

Lucas shook his head: "I'm afraid we have to process the scene first. We have to try to catch this man—he killed a young woman up in Minneapolis a few weeks ago, and he's going to kill more people if we don't catch him. We can't move the bodies until we have the crime scene processed . . ."

"Like on the TV show?" Gloria suggested.

"Something like that, but better," Lucas said. "These people are real."

"How long?" Rice asked.

Lucas shook his head again. "I can't tell you. It depends on what has to be done. It would be best if you went home and rested. The sheriff will call you before they move the bodies. That would be the time."

"I'm not going anywhere," she said.

Sloan smiled at her, his best sympathetic smile, and said, "We understand. If you need anything, ask the sheriff. And would you . . . we have some questions about your son."

"Okay," she said. She sniffed. "We knew there'd be questions."

They did the routine biography—who might not like him, whom he had arguments with, debts, women, jealous husbands, where he spent his nights, what he did for entertainment.

Lucas asked the hard one: "Mrs. Rice, as far as you know, did your son have any homosexual friends, or acquaintances?"

She looked to Sloan, then back to Lucas. "Are you . . . he was married. He didn't hang around with homosexuals." She started to tear up.

"This is routine," Lucas said. "We have to ask. There was a good deal of violence here, which sometimes characterizes homosexual murders, especially murders of passion."

She knew what he was asking. "My boy was not a homo," she snapped. The women behind her all nodded. "He was married, he was widowed, he would have remarried someday, but he just hadn't got started since Shelly was killed. He was *not* a gay person."

"But did he know any gays?" Lucas persisted. "Somebody who might have built up a fantasy about him? He was a good-looking man."

Laurina looked at Gloria, and they simultaneously shook their heads. "I don't think he even knew any gays," she said. "He would have mentioned it. We had supper together once a week, we talked about everything."

"Okay," Lucas said.

THEY CHATTED A BIT LONGER, then moved back into the house, leaving Rice and the others in the car.

The next four hours were taken up with the technicalities and legalities of murder: the crime-scene technicians worked the murder scene, the medical examiner came and went, leaving behind an assistant and two men to handle the bodies. A state representative, who lived ten miles away, stopped and talked to the sheriff, said something about the death penalty, wanted to look inside but accepted the "no," and went on his way.

"Dipshit," Nordwall said, as the legislator's car trundled down the driveway.

When the crime-scene techs had decided that the murders took place pretty much in the area of the two bodies, Lucas and Sloan began working through the small intimacies in other parts of the house, looking at bills and letters, collecting recent photographs, checking the e-mail in the five-year-old Dell computer, stopping every now and then for a Diet Coke. They didn't know exactly what they were looking for in the house, but that was okay; they were impressing images and words on their memories, so they would be there if anything should trip them in the future.

"He has a Visa card about due," Sloan said at one point. "We oughta get the bill and see where's he's been."

"I looked at his Exxon bill out on the kitchen table. He hasn't been far away, not for the last year or so," Lucas said. He was digging through Rice's wallet. "One tank of gas every Friday or Saturday."

"Had the kid in school," Sloan said.

"Yeah . . ." He flipped through the register in Rice's checkbook. "Four hundred dollars in checking, seventeen hundred in savings. He didn't write many checks . . . mostly at the supermarket, and bills." He found an address book, but nothing that looked like a particularly new entry, but Lucas set it aside for the database they'd be creating.

A cop stuck his head in: "They're picking up the kid."

"All right."

Two minutes later, the same cop came by: "One of your crime-scene guys says to stop by for a minute."

They were upstairs, in Rice's bedroom. They followed the cop down and found a technician working with a small sample bag and some swabs. He looked up when Lucas and Sloan stepped into the room:

"Thought you'd want to know. The fingernail blood, I'm almost sure it isn't Rice's. There's skin with it, and a little hair follicle that's darker than Rice's. I think."

"Anything else?"

"The usual stuff—lots more hair around. We're picking it up, but who knows where it came from? And the guy took a trophy—he cut Rice's penis off, and there's no sign of it around here. Just the penis, not the testicles. The anus seems to have some lubricant still on it, so I think the killer or killers used a condom. Probably won't be any semen."

Lucas looked at Sloan, who shrugged. "Hard to tell what that is," he said. "Maybe he didn't want there to be any DNA, so maybe he knows about DNA and worries about it. Maybe he's afraid of AIDS, which might mean something if we could show that Rice had some homo-sexual contacts."

"The sexual . . . um, aspects . . . really look like a gay thing to me," the tech said. "The violence and the sexual trophy-taking."

Lucas and Sloan nodded. "But why was the first one a woman?"

"Maybe there was a gay thing, then Rice went after the woman, and his gay partner blew up," the tech said. "Maybe he was punishing them, and that's what all this whipping stuff is about."

"Maybe," Lucas said doubtfully.

"It's a concept," Sloan said. He didn't care for the idea either. "We need to get this biography. I need to see if I can link Angela Larson to anything down here."

"You said she was a student; there's a state university branch down here."

"I'll look," Sloan said. "But I did all that background on her, and no-body said nuthin' about Mankato."

WHEN THE CRIME-SCENE PEOPLE were done, the medical ex-aminer's assistants came in and picked the body up, zipped it into a bag, and carried it out. The blood splotch on the floor, which retained the impression of the kneeling body, looked like strange black modern art.

They stood over it for a moment, and then Sloan said, "I don't think there's much more here." They'd been inside, looking for something, anything, for five hours. If they'd found anything useful, it wasn't apparent.

"This guy . . . ," Lucas said. He took a deep breath, let it out as a sigh. He was thinking about the killer. "This guy is gonna bust our chops."

4

HE WAS SHORT, big nosed, red haired, pugnacious, intense, loud, never wrong, willing to bend any ethical rule, and three years out of journalism school. He had a facility with words admired by some in the newsroom. The admiration was offset by the undeniable fact that he was an ambitious weasely little asshole; and saved, to some extent, by the additional fact that at the *Star-Tribune*, being an ambitious weasely little asshole was not a distinguishing characteristic.

Ruffe Ignace stood on the corner, talking to himself—nothing in particular, snatches of old songs, possible story leads, bits of internal dialogue, comments on the passing cars and the women inside them. He bounced on his toes like a boxer, and talked to himself, all the time, like humming, or buzzing. He called the ongoing dialogue Ruffe's Radio, and he played it all the time.

Boy in a Bubble, maybe there's something there; Mmm, Lexus GX470, you old fart; hey, look that, look at that ass. Yes, Pat, there he is, Ruffe Ignace, sup-

posedly the richest man in America. He was with the Special Forces before that, you know, a war hero, in Afghanistan, killed twenty-four Afghanis with a Bowie knife. He's got more money and had more supermodel pussy than any other six guys in the country. Say, I'd like to get that jacket—that's a good-looking coat . . .

Like that.

All the time.

A co-worker once complained that sitting next to Ignace was like sitting next to a bad-tempered bee. Ignace ignored her; and now he stood on the corner, bouncing, waiting, and buzzing.

HUBBARD CAME DOWN the other side of the street, bright blue double-knit blazer from JCPenney, gray slacks, brown shoes. From a hundred yards away, he held Ignace's eyes, then turned and went into the front doors of the public library. Ignace waited through another light, then followed him.

RUFFE IGNACE HATED HIS NAME. Both first and last, but especially Ruffe. Ruffe—Roo-Fay—came from a French word meaning "red haired." Since he was red haired, and since his parents had been French, he could hardly deny the truth of it. The newsroom people learned early in his career that Ruffe hated being called Rufus, which also meant red haired, so they called him that at every opportunity. A few people even tried Iggy, but that drew a response so violent and poisonous that they decided to leave it alone.

Ignace barely tolerated the *Star-Tribune*, which he considered next of kin to a suburban shopper. He looked forward to his career at the *New York Times*, where virtually all reporters had weird names, and where Ruffe Ignace would be considered distinguished, rather than an occasion for jokes.

To get there, he had to do something *good*. To do something really good, you needed luck and talent.

Ignace had the talent. In addition to his writing ability, he had a nice sense of drama and, more important, knew how to suck when he needed to. As a member of the paper's Public Safety Team, he applied the suck liberally around the Minneapolis Police Department.

A part-time homicide cop named Bob Hubbard was Ignace's best inside source. Hubbard wanted a full-time homicide desk, instead of being shuffled off to Sex or Property Crimes whenever they needed more people. Ignace promised, and delivered, attention to Hubbard's crime-solving talent. Hubbard delivered the goods from the inside.

Luck was an entirely different matter. Luck either kissed you on the ass, or it didn't. Not much you could do about it but get ready in case it happened.

IGNACE SLIPPED INTO THE LIBRARY two minutes behind Hubbard. They met at the library because Hubbard had never seen a cop there, and back in the Female-Problems stacks, you might go decades without seeing one.

Hubbard was peering into a book called *The Vaginal Perspective* when Ruffe turned the corner. The cop slipped the book back on the shelf and asked, shocked, "You ever see what's in these things?"

Ruffe looked at the ranks of books and shuddered. "No." To Hubbard: "Whatcha got, Bob? I got that thing on the Mikasa shop and the Mini-Cooper . . ."

"This ain't funny," Hubbard said urgently, pitching his voice to a near-whisper. He was a blond, fleshy man with pink cheeks made rosier by booze. He was holding a manila envelope. "You gotta, gotta, gotta cover for me. Honest to God, I don't even think I oughta be here."

Now Ruffe was interested. Hubbard was sweating.

"So whattya got?"

"You owe me big for this one," Hubbard said.

"What is it?" Ruffe pressed.

"You owe me, and you're gonna pay," Hubbard said. "I get to name a story."

"Whoa, man. That'd depend. What story you want . . . what story you *got*."

"The story I want is just a nice story for a lady I know. The story I got . . ."

"What?"

"We got a serial killer," Hubbard said. "You know Sloan?"

"Yeah." They were close enough that Ignace could smell the afternoon martinis on Hubbard's breath, and maybe something else—peanut-butter cheese crackers? With martinis? "He thinks I'm an asshole."

"You are an asshole, Ruffe."

"Yeah, yeah . . ." Ignace didn't mind what the small-towners thought, if it got him to the *Times*; he made a keep-rolling motion with his finger.

"Sloan caught this killing a couple of weeks back," Hubbard whispered. "It was really fuckin' ugly, but everybody chilled on it, because we don't want a lot of shit from the TV stations."

Ignace thought for a second, his eyes narrowing: "Angela Larson, from Chicago. Everybody thinks it's a boyfriend problem."

"Well, it wasn't. It never was. She was tortured, raped, and displayed . . . you know what displayed is?"

"Yeah." Ignace was hooked now. He could feel Lady Luck puckering up. "But how do you know it was serial?"

"Because this morning, this old buddy of Sloan's from the BCA calls him up, and they haul ass down to Mankato. The word is—and the word is good—that it's an identical killing, except for one thing. The victim was tortured and raped, just like Larson. Only it was a *guy*. Then they were both killed the same way: their throats were cut."

"Throats?" Ignace whispered. They both turned and looked up and down the stacks. "You mean, like with a razor?"

"Just like with a razor," Hubbard said. "To top it off, the killer also killed the second victim's child. Swatted him like a fly. Killed the kid, then went ahead and raped and killed the father."

Ruffe was impressed. "Jesus. You got something from the scene?"

"Not from that one—but I got the inside shit from the Larson case, what they never told anybody. And I got a Xerox of a crime-scene photograph. You can't use the picture. In fact, I'm not even gonna give it to you, come to think of it. I'll let you look at it."

Ignace wet his lips. "I promise you I wouldn't put it in the paper. Especially not if it was a Xerox."

"Uh-uh. I can't take the chance," Hubbard said, shaking his head. "The thing is, what I'm giving you could have come from lots of people, but the picture had to come from Homicide. They'll know it was me. You can look at it so you can write up the crime scene. I figured you'd want to do that."

"Bob . . ."

"You swear to God you'll cover me."

"Yeah, yeah, yeah. Let me see the goddamn thing. And who do I talk to for on-the-record?"

"Okay. The sheriff down in Blue Earth County. His name is Nordwall. And Sloan, I guess. I'd stay away from the BCA guy, his name is Lucas Davenport. He's got better sources at the *Star-Tribune* than you do. He'd find out in two minutes who you were talking to."

"He couldn't, because I've never told anybody. I never will," Ignace said. "I only use you for the tips."

"Some of the guys have noticed I get a little print on my cases." He was carefully holding the manila envelope out of reach.

"Well, tough shit. You can either have it or not," Ignace said. "Let me see the fuckin' photograph. Give me a couple names . . . I can always pin it on somebody else."

"You owe me a story," Hubbard repeated.

"Yeah, yeah . . ."

HUBBARD SHOOK THE XEROX out of the envelope and passed it over. Ignace looked at it for a moment: the photograph was harshly lit, in the night, giving it a garish vibe. The woman looked like she'd been crucified in the dirt, her body bright white against the short spring foliage. He said, "Huh. Horseshit photo."

"It wasn't a goddamn portrait studio," Hubbard rasped.

"I can tell. Focused right on her pussy. Photo guy probably peddled it out to the Internet."

"Rufus . . ."

"Fuck you, Bob," Ignace said. He pulled a narrow reporter's notebook out of his back pocket, looked at the photo for a few more seconds, then made some rapid notes in perfect Gregg shorthand. When he was done, he said, "Give me some names. I need to start at the bottom and confirm some of this shit from outsiders, before I go to Sloan."

Hubbard nodded. "Okay: the new victim's name was Adam Rice, the kid's name was Josh, and Adam's mom's name is Laurina Rice. She's listed . . ."

"What about a wife?"

"I heard she died a while back, but I don't know the details . . ."

THEY TALKED FOR ANOTHER two minutes, and then Ignace folded the notebook and said, "Bob, I owe you. I truly do."

"Well, I'll tell you what I want. Write this down in your fuckin' notebook. There's a new restaurant named Funny Capers in Uptown. I want a story about it. A good story. What a happenin' place it is. Like that. They got music on Friday and Saturday nights."

"Girlfriend? Or investment?" He'd opened the notebook again and was taking it down.

"A friend of mine," Hubbard said. His eyes flicked away.

"If I need some last-minute comments on the place, can I call you at home?"

Hubbard flinched. "Jesus Christ, don't do that."

Ignace said, "One more thing. We got no art for this murder. Suppose we went with a graphic of a straight razor. I mean, would that be fucked up? Are they saying razor, or could it be a box cutter or something?"

"Fuck, I don't know, I guess a razor would be all right," Hubbard said. He ducked down a bit, to look through a bookshelf, looking for anyone who might know him. "Do what you want—and give me that Xerox." He took the Xerox back, stuffed it into his jacket pocket. "Wait five minutes before you come out. Read something, or something."

"It's a library, Bob, they might get suspicious."

"Okay, go look at blow jobs on the Internet. Just give me five minutes."

RUFFE'S RADIO WAS RUNNING hard on the way back to the paper: *I shall not be moved; that's what Ignace said, just before he led the attack on the hijackers. Tragically . . . Is that a cashmere sweater? It's eighty degrees out here . . . Wonder if alpaca comes from alpacas? Four-wheel drift; could you do that in a Jeep? . . .*

He took the elevator up to the newsroom, bustled back to his desk. Most reporters dreaded calling survivors in a murder or tragic accident. Ignace didn't mind. He called Laurina Rice first, got a sober, cold-voiced woman, and asked, "Laurina?"

"Laurina is . . . indisposed," the cold-voiced woman said. Ignace recognized her immediately: the officious neighbor or relative who was "protecting" somebody the media might want to talk to. "May I tell her who called?"

"I just heard about Adam and Josh, and I really need to talk to her," Ignace said. Then he pulled out a reporter's cold-call trick, an implication of intimacy with the target. "Is this Florence?"

"No, no, uh, just a minute."

Most people involved in tragedies want to talk, Ignace had found, if only you could get through to them. He waited ten seconds, and then had Laurina on the line: "Laurina: I'm terribly sorry about Adam and Josh . . ."

"Oh, my God, oh, my God, they wouldn't even let me see them . . ."

"Do they know when it happened?" Ignace asked.

"They think yesterday . . . uh, who is this?"

"Ruffe Ignace from the *Minneapolis Star-Tribune*. We're alerting people around the state that we have this monster loose . . ."

"He is! He is! He's a monster."

She began sobbing and Ignace noted in Gregg, "Weeping, sobbing, disconsolate . . ."

"People tell me that Adam and Josh were wonderful people, no bother to anyone," Ignace said. "They can't figure out who would do this. Do the police think anyone he knows . . . ?"

"No, they told me this man is a monster, that he killed a woman in the Twin Cities . . ."

"A beautiful young girl named Angela Larson from Chicago," Ignace said. "She was just trying to work her way through college."

"Oh, God. And with Adam, after the tragedy last year . . ."

"Tragedy? The police didn't tell me about a tragedy." A disapproving tone, as though secrets had been withheld.

"His wife was killed in an awful, awful accident," Rice said. "Adam was a widower and poor little Josh lost his mother . . ."

"Did little Josh ever talk to you about her?"

"You know, just last Christmas, he said that he would give up every gift he had if he could have Mommy back. He was so sweet, and smart! He was my only grandchild, I'll never have a grandchild now."

She was rolling. Once you got an interviewee rolling, you tried not to interrupt. With an occasional prompt, or short sympathetic question, Ignace had pumped her dry in twenty minutes. He even had the detail about the tire swing hanging from the oak tree out on the lawn.

"But they didn't let you see them . . ."

"Only their faces. The sheriff told me I didn't want to, but they came out with him in that black bag and I marched right up and I said, 'I want to see my grandson!' I wouldn't take 'No.' So they unzipped it and let me look at his face . . ."

"What did you think when you saw his face? What was your reaction?"

"Oh my God . . ." The bawling started again, and Ignace took it down in Gregg . . .

HE WAS BUZZING when he hung up, Ruffe's Radio: *There you go, Ooo, the thing about Ignace is, he's smarter than any reporter in the Twin Cities. You know he used to be an Olympic acrobat . . . Wait, do they have acrobats in the Olympics? Maybe it's gymnastics. Some hot chick with the big boobs on ESPN: Tell me, Lord Ignace, how does it feel to be knighted by the queen . . . ?*

He was buzzing because he had the story. Whatever else might happen, he had the basic facts, he had the color. He didn't even need the cops, but he'd have to call them anyway. Because Sloan thought he was an asshole, and Hubbard had warned him away from Davenport, he started with the sheriff.

Nordwall didn't want to talk, but Ignace said, "First of all, Sheriff, this is public record, the basic facts. You really do have an obligation to warn people about this guy."

That got him the basics. Then he said, "The stuff that I got from the survivors, let me just give it to you quick, just to make sure there isn't anything terribly wrong. I want this to be accurate—you don't even have to tell me anything else, but just if this is right."

He then gave Nordwall everything that Hubbard had given him, plus everything that Laurina Rice had given to him, plus some bullshit that he made up. That got the sheriff rolling, and when they were done, he had a front-page story nailed down.

He talked to his team leader, who in olden says would have been called an assistant city editor, and *she* talked to the metro editor, and then the team leader came back and told him they would take everything he had, don't worry about length.

A photographer was dispatched to Mankato to get a shot of an empty tire swing, and a graphics artist starting pulling up Internet images of straight razors. Ignace spread his notes over his desk, marked some of them with a red felt-tip.

Hubbard: he owed him. No question about it.

HE COULDN'T FIND SLOAN. He had stolen an internal police department phone book, with home phone numbers for all the cops, but nobody answered when he called Sloan's home. He left a message with the answering service, said briefly what he wanted, and hung up. He toyed with the idea of calling Davenport, thought about Hubbard's warning, and decided against it.

Besides, there was an old newspaper maxim that he was happy to honor: too many facts could ruin a perfectly good story. Nobody could complain that he hadn't done the work—he'd talked to the principal law-enforcement officer of the county where the murder happened, he had talked earlier in the week to Sloan about the Angela Larson murder, he had comments from survivors. He didn't need Davenport.

He settled in behind his computer, webbed his fingers together, cracked his knuckles, and started typing.

A serial killer is loose in Minnesota, a sexual predator armed with a razor, a man who tortures his victims before raping them, male and female alike, and cutting their throats . . .

Another reporter passed by Ignace's cubicle as he passed a thousand words, and thought, *Jesus: the guy really does buzz.*

AND WHILE IGNACE WAS BUZZING, Millie Lincoln was . . .
Well.

MILLIE LINCOLN WAS SHORT and blond and liked men; always had. She liked her father, she liked her uncles, she liked all four of her brothers, and they liked her back.

Men liked her back.

Millie gave up her virginity when she was sixteen, fumbling around in her boyfriend's parents' bed. By twenty-two, she'd had four additional lovers. She spent her senior year in high school with the second one, after the fumbler, and then messed around with a college kid, an affair begun with another freshman during the first long Mankato winter, then got into a more serious thing that lasted almost two years.

Then, finally, Mihovil Draskovic.

MIHOVIL WAS SEVEN YEARS OLDER than she. A strong, ropy *man,* slightly mysterious; and a doctor.

Mihovil had made his way from his native Serbia to the United States as a fifteen-year-old, had enlisted in the marines when he was seventeen, became a medic, got out of the crotch, as he called it, went to med school on a marine corps scholarship. He had marine tattoos and now wore his hair long and loose over his wide shoulders, like Jesus. He always had a smile on his face, he was a man perpetually amused, a man with Gypsy eyes . . . a man of slightly fractured English, a crazy mixture of broken grammar and cutting-edge slang.

Mihovil had spent much of his young life in a refugee camp, where the children slept on one side of the hovel and the parents made love behind an army blanket that hung from the ceiling. Since they didn't have a TV, they were behind the blanket almost every night, and the activity was almost uncommented-upon. Natural.

Mihovil and Millie met in the Mankato hospital emergency room. Millie had dislocated a finger playing football, and he'd popped it back in place. They'd talked a little before and after, had bumped into each other in the bagel place a couple of days later, and one thing led to another . . .

Led to another all over the place.

Inside, outside, on hospital beds, floors, lawns, under apple trees, standing up, lying down, now one on top, now the other.

Mihovil taught her to say things like "Wait. Do this—here, move your head right over here and now lick slower and shorter . . . Oh, my God, that's almost right. Wiggle your finger down . . . Oh, my God . . ."

He'd gone into instructional mode the second time they slept together. Why was she moving around aimlessly, he wanted to know. Why didn't she have an orgasm and beat her feet on the sheets? Why was she treating his dick like a shovel handle?

He was nice enough about it, but blunt. She didn't think it was a language barrier; he was just a blunt guy.

For example, they'd gone to an arty party, and a woman had been holding forth on Diverse Ways of Meaning, the Science of Signs and the Clash of Cultures. Millie spotted her for a poseur: not only did she smoke, but she held her cigarette upright, between her thumb and forefinger, like some kind of Russian film director or maybe a Nazi. She made no bones about edging in on Mihovil. After delivering a nearly incomprehensible spate on the Evils of American Cultural Imperialism, she asked Mihovil what he thought.

He said, "I think what you said is bullshit. No, wait—it's worse than that. We talk about the black people in Uganda and the brown people in New Guinea, and you say that we push our cultural artifacts upon them . . . You mean, medicine? You mean, TV? You mean, cars? Those people are just as smart as we are. They'd love to sit around a swimming pool and drink lemonade and listen to Eminem and get flu shots when they need them.

"You want to keep them in some kind of crazy zoo, hunting with spears, so we can look at them and study their culture. That's bullshit. I've done that. I lived in a zoo, I lived in a tent when I was a kid and drank sewage and had the shits for six years in a row. I'd kill somebody to keep from going back to that. I can goddamn well guarantee if you took one of those guys out of the jungle in New Guinea and gave him some jeans and T-shirts and a good pair of shoes, he'd cut your heart out before he'd let you send him back.

"I'd bet you anything that they'd rather live in a nice apartment with a stereo and a toilet and running water that you can drink. So what I think is, you're arguing that you have to allow the niggers to stay in their place. That's about half a step from we gotta *keep* the niggers in their place. Simple racism is what it is."

ANYWAY, HE WAS A BLUNT GUY. She wasn't the least embarrassed by any of his blunt sexual suggestions, except for the suggestion of ignorance.

"If you'd tell me what to do, I'd do it," she said.

"I don't *know* what *you* want, I only know what I want. You have to tell me what to do, and I tell you what to do, and we're both happy."

"That sounds kind of . . . icky."

"No, no, no," he said, moving his index finger like a windshield wiper, a gesture she'd only seen from people who'd grown up outside the U.S. "Not icky. *Icky* is the wrong word. *Dirty*, maybe. Like Catholic dirty. Or . . . I don't know. But not icky. Icky is like when somebody sneezes and blows snot on your croissant."

So she started telling him what she liked.

She found out that she liked telling him.

ANY OTHER TIME, she'd have been nothing more significant than a college girl discovering sex. Not this time. This time, there was a predator hovering next to her.

She was the most vocal woman he'd ever encountered, talking, analyzing, demanding—a long-running commentary that might have been a template for an advanced version of *The Joy of Sex*.

All that turned him on. But what really got to him, on an emotional level, something that went beyond any simple erotic twitch, was her orgasms. They started with a growl, a sound that was almost doglike, and proceeded up in pitch and intensity until she was screaming like a cat; yowls that must have woken half the building.

If he had ever sat with her, and told her what he really felt, how he wanted to go a step beyond anything she'd ever contemplated, wanted to go there with steel and rope . . . then they'd lock him up. They'd know that he'd already been there with other women, and they'd put him next to the Gods Down the Hall, and they'd come and look at him like a goldfish in an aquarium.

But God, he'd like to talk about it; just to tell her how her howls were tearing him apart. To go just one more step with her . . .

5

LUCAS WAS HALF AWAKE when he heard the *whap* of the *Pioneer Press* hitting the front porch, and the deliverywoman reversing her car out of the driveway. Ten minutes later, as he was about to go under again, having punched his pillow flat, the second deliverywoman came in, with two *whaps*: the *Star-Tribune* and the *Wall Street Journal*.

He tried to get back to sleep but was only marginally successful, slipping in and out of confused dreams that sometimes seemed like memories, sometimes like fantasies.

His problem was the empty bed. He'd slept by himself for years, and now, groaning through his later forties, he couldn't sleep without Weather beside him.

On the other hand . . .

The house was certainly neater than when the family was home.

. . .

THE FAMILY WAS IN LONDON. Weather had gotten a prestigious fellowship in maxillo-facial surgery, and had first thought to go alone. But she hated the idea of three months away from Sam, the baby. And Letty, their ward, started whining around about never getting to go anywhere, and the housekeeper wondered what she'd do if everybody left . . .

Finally, Weather decided to pick up the whole bunch of them and transplant them to London for the summer. "We don't have a money problem, so why not?" she asked.

"I'd be happy to take care of everybody, and you'd have the time to yourself," Lucas had said. She was suspicious—he got along quite well on his own and often seemed to pull a loneliness around himself. And she *really* didn't want to be away from Sam . . .

So they packed it all up, everything they would need for three months, surgeon, baby, ward, and housekeeper, and at enormous cost, left for London, leaving him alone in the house.

He'd cluttered the place the first few days the family was gone. Then he'd picked it up and resumed his bachelor ways: he'd never been exactly tidy, but he kept things in their places. When the family was around, nothing was ever where it was supposed to be. The amount of junk that came in the door was befuddling: new clothes and electronics and DVDs and school supplies and Pampers and snack food and medical journals and what seemed like an endless pile of cardboard boxes and wrapping plastic and empty bottles.

That all stopped.

Still. The hole in his life seemed to be getting larger; and he waited every morning until she called from her office in London, to tell him about the day she'd had, and what the kids were doing.

WHEN THE PHONE RANG, he sat up, groggy, looked at the clock: too early. She never called this early. He picked up the phone, and Rose Marie Roux said, "Your secret serial killer is all over the front page of the *Strib*."

"What?"

"This guy really *is* a monster," she said, conversationally. She sounded as though she had a cup of coffee in front of her and a cigarette in her hand, which she probably did. Rose Marie Roux was the commissioner of public safety, and, indirectly, Lucas's boss. "Cutting their throats with a straight razor and scourging them with a wire whip? Where do you even *get* a straight razor these days?"

Lucas said, "Shit," scratched under his left armpit, and said, "They get straight razors from the same place they get lead pipes. The cliché mine. What else do they say?"

"Pretty well-written piece, if you have a taste for the Gothic," Rose Marie said. "You're still in bed, right?"

"Right."

"I'll read it to you." She did; and when she finished, she said, "This is gonna be trouble for my favorite cop. The newsies are in it now."

"I better call Sloan," Lucas said.

HE DIDN'T CALL SLOAN RIGHT AWAY. He went back to sleep, and the next time he cracked his eyelids it was two minutes to eight o'clock. He fumbled past the lamp, through the pocket junk that he dropped on the bed stand each night, past watch and wallet and lucky stone and cash receipts from the gas station, a small wad of currency and two dollars in change, and finally dug out the cell phone, turned it on, and lay with it on his chest.

Two minutes later, right on time, it rang.

"Do anything good today?" he asked.

"Gave a lecture on the . . . on a facial muscle and the nerve that operates it," Weather said.

"I wish I'd been there. Did you show slides?"

"You're pulling my weenie."

"You don't have a weenie, unless you've grown one in London."

They talked for fifteen minutes: she told him about the work; he told her about the story in the *Star-Tribune*.

"The thing is, you like that," she said. "You like being in the newspaper."

"Only when I'm standing over the bad guy's body with my gun in my hand, wearing a new gray suit with a thin chalk stripe, and the Porsche in the background."

"You'll take it any way you can get it, buster. Maybe I should worry about you hanging out with newspaperwomen, again."

"Ah, I'm too pussy-whipped to do anything questionable."

"I *beg* your pardon . . ."

AS SOON AS THEY BROKE OFF, he said, "Sloan," and punched in Sloan's office phone from memory.

Somebody else answered. "Where's Sloan?" Lucas asked.

"Who is this?"

"Davenport."

"Hey, Lucas. This is Franklin. Sloan was talking to Anderson out in the hall a minute ago, let me go look. He's been calling you at the office and on your cell phone . . ."

Franklin dropped the phone and went away. Lucas looked at his cell phone's screen: sure enough, three missed calls. Then Lucas heard Franklin's voice again but couldn't make out what he said, then Sloan picked up: "We got some ink. This little fucking weasel from the *Strib* picked it up."

"I know," Lucas said. He yawned. "What do you think?"

"Are you still in bed? You sound like you're in bed."

"Yeah, yeah, so what do you think?"

"The chief is jumping up and down, which is what you get when you hire a small-town guy. He's scared to death that the city council might pee on him. Or even worse, the TV people," Sloan said.

"You worried?"

"Not yet. Not as long as he doesn't kill another one in town. I suppose you're gonna have the governor on your ass."

Lucas yawned again. "Don't know yet," he said when he had the yawn under control. "Dead people don't have any political clout, but it could come from somewhere else, I suppose."

"How about a sense of moral obligation?" Sloan said.

"Ah, you fuckin' Republicans, nothing ever makes you happy."

"Fuck a bunch of Republicans," Sloan said. "Anyway, I had Anderson send a whole book over to you by e-mail. You could have your secretary print it out for you before you get there. It's everything we got, plus some medium-rez pictures from the Larson scene. You can have your co-op guys put it all in the database."

"All right. I'll be over there by ten. Want to hook up, say ten-thirty?"

"You got the case now?"

"I'm giving it to myself," Lucas said. "If they want to put somebody else on it, too, that's okay."

"See you at ten-thirty," Sloan said. "By the way, I got my papers."

Lucas didn't immediately track the reference. "Huh?"

"My retirement papers. I got them. I'm filling them out," Sloan said.

"Ah, for Christ's sake, Sloan, you aren't gonna quit."

"Yeah, I am. Talk to you at ten-thirty."

. . . .

LUCAS CALLED HIS SECRETARY and told her to print out Sloan's murder file, and get it to the co-op group. Then he dressed, went downstairs, into a silent house, sat at the bar in the kitchen, and ate cholesterol-free, fat-free, carbohydrate-free, salt-free, puffed oatmeal air with a splash of fat-free milk. Still hungry, he went, feeling furtive, even though Weather was six thousand miles away, into Weather's home office, opened the file cabinet, picked up a stack of medical reports, found the gold box of Godiva birthday bonbons hidden under them, stole the two he figured would be least conspicuously missing, and let them melt in his mouth as he headed for the door.

The second one had a maraschino cherry in the center: excellent. Feeling much better and hardly guilty at all, he wheeled out onto Mississippi River Boulevard, over to Cretin, and down to I-94, playing with the Porsche's engine as he went.

CAROL WAS POKING FRANTICALLY at her computer when Lucas arrived at the office. Lucas ran the BCA's Office of Regional Research, a bullshit title invented by Rose Marie Roux created to cover up the fact that he did what he wanted, or what the governor wanted him to. A fixer, in some ways.

He had two full-time investigators, and since the office was so small, Carol, technically a secretary, was effectively the office manager. She was a cheerful young woman with auburn hair and blue eyes and freckles, black plastic glasses, a little too heavy, and sometimes a little too loud. Despite her cheerful personality, she'd had a reputation around the Department of Public Safety for ruthless efficiency. Lucas had stolen her from the Highway Patrol, in a transfer arranged by Rose Marie Roux as a payoff for solving a series of horse shootings.

She propped herself in the doorway as Lucas hung up his jacket: "You didn't sign the overtime."

"You sign it," he said. She'd have to forge his signature.

"I did. I'm just saying. You gotta start signing it, or someday they're gonna put me in jail. Also, Lanscombe called and said that Del put eight hundred miles on a state car last weekend."

"Ah, jeez, could you handle that? Make up some shit and tell him I said it."

"You want me to kick Del's ass?"

"Find out what he was doing, anyway. You get that stuff from Minneapolis?"

"Yup." She'd bound the paper into a blue report cover. "Photos are in the back. I borrowed the photo printer down in crime scene. You should buy one for us. You're rich enough."

He ignored the suggestion. "Is Del coming in?"

"He *was* in. He went back out on the Ransom thing. Dannie's with him. Husband and wife."

"Christ, like Jack Sprat and his old lady."

She smiled, a white-tooth Wisconsin dairy smile as Lucas headed into his office: "But who'd suspect they were cops?" she called after him.

Ransom was not a payoff. Ransom was a man who'd run a series of home-improvement scams with the help of a local lawyer and an out-state bank. Del and Dannie Carson were about to take out a second mortgage on a house they supposedly owned, to pay for a new roof, windows, garage door, and driveway, work that would never be done, even though the money had been paid. When the bank came around to foreclose on the mortgage, two or three months down the road, the governor would hold a press conference. Ransom would go to jail, the bank would cough up a few million dollars, and the governor would be hailed as the champion of the poor and benighted . . .

With any luck.

But why had Del driven eight hundred miles over the weekend? That was as far as Kansas City and back . . .

LUCAS WAS HIGH ENOUGH in the BCA hierarchy to get an extra seventy square feet of office space and rich enough—Carol was right about that—to buy two comfortable chairs to fill it with. He got a steno pad from his desk, dropped into one of the chairs, and started reading through the bound murder file: much of it he already knew from talking with Sloan and Elle the week before.

And he thought, "Elle." He should give her a call.

He made a note to do that and pushed farther into the file. Made another note: Larson worked in some kind of artsy-crafty store, and Rice worked in a hardware store. A craft connection? Weak. A retail connection, people whom a killer might see in the routine course of business? Also weak. Larson was single, just breaking off a relationship, maybe. Rice was out looking?

He was poring over the photos when Carol came to the door: "There's a parole officer on the phone for you. About the case. He says it might be urgent."

Lucas nodded: "Put him through."

HE STEPPED OVER to his desk and when the phone rang, picked it up. "Davenport."

"Mr. Davenport, agent, uh . . . Yeah, this is Mark Fox down in Owatonna. I'm a parole officer. I just read the *Star-Tribune* story about this serial killing and I called Gene Nordwall and he said I should call you . . ."

"What's up?"

"There's this guy . . . A few weeks back a guy named Charlie Pope was turned loose from St. John's," Fox said. "He was a Level Two, convicted in St. Paul of raping a woman and trying to strangle her. There was evidence that he might have killed another woman or maybe two, way back."

"I don't remember the case."

"It was years ago. And he didn't kill anyone in the case he was convicted on." Fox spent a couple of minutes outlining Pope's career and added, "Frankly, he's nuts. He doesn't say much, but he's crazier than a loon."

"They let him go?"

"He was only convicted on the one rape, and he was coming to the end of his sentence. They couldn't hold him. They decided the best thing to do was to let him go a few months early—he was pretty desperate to get out—and make a long-term ankle bracelet a part of the deal. A few weeks back, he cut the bracelet off and split. He was staying in a trailer down here in Owatonna. When I went over to look for him, there was no sign of him."

"Trailer still there?"

"Yeah. I sealed it and told the manager to keep an eye on it," Fox said. "I didn't know what had happened to him. I still don't. Anyway, I thought this might have something to do with your problem."

"Good call," Lucas said.

"I would have gotten in touch after the Larson thing, but I didn't know about it until I saw the Star-Tribune story."

"Bureaucracy," Lucas said. "Give me a number—I've got a meeting with the Minneapolis homicide people in about ten minutes, but I might come down there and bring some guys with me. Do we need a warrant to look at that place?"

"Not if you're with me. I'd be happy to meet you there," Fox said.

"I'll get back to you within the hour, tell you one way or the other," Lucas said.

"One last thing," Fox said. "He's in your DNA database. They made damn sure of that before he left St. John's."

SLOAN CAME IN, with Elle Kruger trailing behind, looking a little abashed. She was wearing street clothes, as she had started to do more often: the full traditional nun's habit, she said, had started to feel too much like an affectation. "I wasn't sure I should come," she said, near-sightedly peering around, checking out Carol. Elle came to dinner twice a month, had become tight with Weather, but she'd never been to his new office.

"Glad to have you, as long as I don't have to put you on my budget," Lucas said. He put them in the soft chairs and dropped in behind his desk. "I just got a call from a parole officer . . ."

He filled them in on what Mark Fox had said, and Sloan said, "So Pope disappeared just before Larson was killed? That's the best lead we've had so far. Why didn't we hear about it?"

"Usual BS. He didn't know about Larson, nobody knew to ask about Pope, time passes," Lucas said. "Anyway, I'm getting Pope's file sent up from St. John's." To Elle: "Sloan has you all filled in on the Rice killings?"

"Not so much on the detail, as on the behavior," she said.

"One important detail," Lucas said. "Adam Rice apparently tried to fight the guy off, and there was blood and skin under his fingernails. If it's not his own blood . . . well, we have Pope's DNA in the database here. We oughta know tomorrow if we've got a match."

"We're looking for him now?" she asked.

Lucas nodded. "Yes. There's a bulletin out, I'm sending it to Iowa and Wisconsin, too. We've got a six-week-old picture from St. John's. They took it just before they let him go."

"Gonna be a black eye for the state, letting him go," Sloan said.

Elle said, "Could I see Pope's file?"

"Sure. Don't tell anybody. It's supposed to be a confidential medical file . . . I'll get Carol to make a copy for you. What about behavior . . . ?"

Elle had a simple nylon briefcase with her and said, "I've got a note . . ." As she dug into it, it occurred to him that the old nun's costume, by isolating her face, had kept her young even as she aged. Now, dressed in the gray-and-black garb of her order, she looked like a thin, middle-aged woman who'd lived an ascetic, but sedentary, life. Her hair, which he hadn't seen for twenty years after she'd gone into the convent, had turned steel gray, and her wrists and ankles seemed frail.

Then she looked over the note at him, and her eyes were as young as a kindergartener's: "There are some interesting aspects to the behavior of this man. I think, after looking at the material that Mr. Sloan gave me, that he is probably intelligent. A planner. Nothing spontaneous or extemporaneous about this—he chose his victims, he knew when they would be alone and when he could get them without being interrupted. He knew where to leave Angela Larson's body where it would have the greatest impact, but at a place where he could stop, take a little time to arrange her, and then leave, without being seen or noticed or monitored in any way. That's not necessarily easy to do in a large city. Security cameras are everywhere, and as far as we know, he has not been seen by a single one."

Lucas pointed a finger at Sloan: "Security camera at the store where Rice worked?"

"I'll call."

Elle continued: "There's also something interesting in the way he tortures his victims. He's methodical. I pointed this out to Mr. Sloan . . ."

"She won't call me by my first name," Sloan said to Lucas, grinning at Elle. Then, "Sorry, go ahead."

"He beat both of them with some kind of whip, but not in an uncontrolled frenzy. If he were in a frenzy, he would keep hitting them in the same place, but these victims look like they had been put through a mechanical shredder—some of the slashes cross each other, but most of them are carefully laid in, proceeding down and around their bodies, as though he's being . . . careful. Thorough."

"Nuts," Lucas said.

"He's crazy, but it's not an uncontrollable frenzy. Not mechanically uncontrollable, at any rate. He's like a punisher: remote from his victim. Like a paid torturer in a prison."

"Is he taunting us? Is he going to call somebody? Will he look for publicity?" Lucas asked.

"He could very well," she said, nodding. "He's intelligent, but the way he displays the bodies, he's looking for attention. I don't think he'll call the TV stations—he'll call a newspaper, if he does call."

Sloan asked, "Why not TV?"

"Because they would record him, and he wouldn't want his voice on tape. He will be careful."

"What else?" Lucas asked.

"He's strong. Probably attractive. Quite likely charismatic—a person who might attract his victims' attention in some way. Not necessarily a pleasant way, but somebody they would notice."

"You think they knew him?"

She considered it for a moment, then nodded: "Maybe. That's a hard call. These two people were unattached—it's possible that he seduced them in some way before the attack. Or he might simply be visually appealing to them. That would get him close without a fuss. They may have welcomed his attention—he could very well be soft-spoken, somebody you would trust."

She looked up at Lucas. "One thing I would do is this: I would check on current and previous relationships that the victims had, and see if the men with whom they were involved are similar in some ways. The same appearance, somehow, the same attitude, or some particular status. Did they both like tall, dark men? Then the killer may be tall and dark . . ."

"You're assuming . . . a sexual connection with Rice. The sheriff says Rice was absolutely straight," Lucas said. "A widower with a kid. Nothing we've got would suggest that he had any homosexual contacts ever, even as a boy. We've talked to people who have known him for his entire life."

Elle pulled at her lower lip, and Sloan said, "Yeah, but . . . in that culture down there, out in the countryside, an interest in homosexuality might be pretty well hidden."

Elle nodded: "Very much hidden, especially if a man were essentially bisexual—he would always have his relationships with women as a cover. Even if somebody else knew about it, about any homosexual impulses that Rice might have had, that man might not admit it because of the implication that *he* might be gay . . ."

Lucas to Elle: "One of the crime-scene guys said he'd seen similar violence and it was usually gay, and the specific sexual mutilation usually came from a former lover, a jilted lover . . ."

"This is not like that," she said quickly. "I know precisely what your technician was saying, but as I said, this was not done in an emotional frenzy. This was cold and calculated and, I think, enjoyed. This does not seem to me to have been done in anger." She paused: "I could be wrong. Nothing is for certain."

"Good." Lucas made a note.

Carol knocked and stuck her head into the office: "The stuff from St. John's is here, on the Pope guy. You want paper or electronic?"

"Paper. Three copies," Lucas said. "Right away."

Carol's eyes involuntarily ticked over to Elle, raised perhaps a millimeter, and then she said, "Three copies," and left.

THEY TALKED FOR ANOTHER twenty minutes, then Elle looked at her watch and said, "I've got a seminar."

"Pick up the copy of the Pope file on your way out," Lucas said. "I'll be on my cell phone."

"I'll read it right after the seminar," she said. "I'll call this afternoon."

WHEN SHE WAS GONE, Lucas asked Sloan, "Are you going to Owatonna with me?"

"Absolutely, but we got some bureaucratic shit to figure out first," Sloan said. "Pennington absolutely doesn't want to be the media face on this. And he doesn't want me involved. He says you guys gotta do it."

"Ahhh . . . ," Lucas said. Pennington was the Minneapolis chief. Lucas didn't like him. "Nordwall didn't want to do it, either. Maybe Rose Marie could do it. She can screw something out of Pennington in trade."

Lucas got Rose Marie on the phone, outlined the problem.

"I'm not going to do it," she said. "I'm trying to pull the string on this special session. Either you or McCord can do it. I'll talk to McCord this afternoon and figure it out. I'll talk to the governor, too . . . Be helpful if you could get the guy before he kills anyone else."

"We might've had a break," Lucas said. He told her about Pope. "If it's him, we'll look pretty good. Otherwise . . . right now, we don't have anything that would point at anybody in particular."

"So he's going to do somebody else; if he's not this Pope guy."

"If he's careful, he could do a few," Lucas said.

"Goddamnit, we don't want that. I'll talk to the governor, I'll talk to McCord, and we'll figure something out and get back to you."

"I'm on the cell," Lucas said. He hung up and said to Sloan: "Let's go."

OWATONNA WAS AN HOUR south of St. Paul, straight down I-35, back in the sea of corn and beans. A few miles out of Owatonna, they took a phone call from Nordwall. "Where you at?"

"In my car, on the way to Owatonna." He told Nordwall about Charlie Pope.

"Okay, that's something," Nordwall said. "I got something else for you. Bill James, the guy I got doing the biography you wanted? He says that Rice was almost perfectly straight."

"Almost," Lucas said.

"Yeah—almost," the sheriff said. "There's a bar in Faribault called the Rockyard. Country bar, bunch of shit kickers, fights in the parking lot, Harleys and trucks, and so on. Live music Fridays and Saturdays. Anyway—a friend of Rice's named Andy Sanders said there's a bartender there, named Carl, who everybody calls Booger. If you talk to Booger, he can introduce you to some young ladies who will fall in love with you, if you've got the money. Sanders said Rice had been going up for the girls."

"Hookers."

"We just have girls down here, Lucas," Nordwall said mildly. "Some of them have hasty love affairs."

"But straight: male on female."

"Straight. Sanders says no-way, no-how would Rice ever have gotten friendly with a gay guy. But I figure, you could meet some bad people at the Rockyard. There's always a little shit going through there, a little cocaine, a little meth, and you could probably buy yourself an untraceable pistol if you asked just right."

"All right. We just went past there. We'll hit it on the way back."

"Good."

"Anybody gonna give us shit?" Lucas asked.

"No, no, it's not *that* tough. It's just a little . . . sleazy."

"With some guys who like to fight."

"Occasionally."

6

OWATONNA IS A SMALL CITY known to a few architecture buffs for a Louis Sullivan jewel-box bank. They got lost for a while, running down edge-of-town streets, and finally found Charlie Pope's trailer in a weedy mobile-home park down a dead-end road.

Pope's trailer was a mess. An aging Airstream travel-trailer, once silver, it had been hit by something—a falling tree?—that had put a dent across the top; the whole thing sat maybe five degrees off level, the tires shot, steel wheels visible through the rotting rubber. Weeds grew window-high around it, and a box elder tree flaked bark, leaves, and red bugs onto it.

As they pulled into the trailer park's visitor parking lot, a blade-thin black cat ran out from one of the other homes, paused, one foot in the air, to look at them, and then disappeared into the brush behind Pope's place. Some of the mobile homes in the park were well kept, with neatly cut yards; most were not. Either way, Pope's place was the neighborhood slum.

. . .

MARK FOX WAS SITTING on the hood of his Jeep, which was tucked in an overgrown parking slot next to Pope's trailer. Fox was a tall, thin, cowboy-looking guy with a weathered face, black roper boots, a black T-shirt, and a denim jacket and jeans. He was smoking a cigarette when they pulled up. He crushed it into a rust spot on the hood of the Jeep as they got out of the Porsche.

"Must've been more money coming out of the legislature than I thought, cops riding around in a Porsche," he said as they shook hands.

Lucas shrugged: "Guy's gotta have a four-wheel drive to get around in, this part of the country."

Sloan rolled his eyes and said, "We know the guy for three seconds and the bullshit starts . . . This is Pope's place?"

Fox looked at the trailer and said, "Yup. Such as it is. Come on in."

"I sorta know why he ran for it," Sloan said. "If I lived here, I'd run for it, too."

"Ah, it's different inside," Fox said. "It's worse."

HE TOOK THEM INSIDE. A sour odor of human dirt hung about the place, with a underlying tone of sewage: there might be a cracked sewer pipe somewhere, or something wrong with the septic system. Sloan said, wrinkling his nose, "Smells like an armpit with an onion in it."

Fox: "Or an asshole."

"Hold that thought," Lucas said.

The three of them were too much for the tiny kitchen, and Fox continued six feet down the trailer into a nominal living room. The kitchen was made of dented metal cupboards, a stove the size of a breadboard, and a yellowed microwave. Fox said, "When he cut the bracelet off, he left it here on the floor. No sign of him. I put out a bulletin but never heard back from anybody."

"Nobody's seen him here in the park?"

"I checked, nobody's seen him—and if he'd been here, they would have. He was a hard guy to miss."

"And the park's about the size of my dick," Sloan said.

"Everybody assumes he took off," Fox said. "But, as far as anybody knows, he doesn't have a car."

"No car," Lucas said. He glanced at Sloan, who shook his head. If he didn't have a car, how was he moving around?

"Not as far as I know," Fox said. "He rides the buses. Charlie hasn't made enough since he got back to buy much. Last time we talked, he said he was spending everything he made on clothes and food. That looked about right to me."

"How much does a beat-up car cost?"

"You might get something for a grand, but he didn't have it."

"Relatives?"

"His mother's still alive, but she's poor as a church mouse herself," Fox said.

"He just walked off the job."

"Yeah. That's the story. I went down to see his boss—he worked with a garbage hauler—and he said Pope finished up one day, said, 'See ya,' and never came back."

"They owe him money?" Lucas asked.

"Three days," Fox said, nodding.

"Huh." They took their time poking around the trailer. Some clothes must be missing, they agreed, because there was almost nothing left. They did find an open three-pack of black Jockey shorts under the pull-out bed, with one pair left inside, along with a dozen DVDs. Lucas flipped through them: *"Strokemaster Finals, Fantasic Facials, Best of Anal Adventures 24 . . ."*

"There's a violation for you," Fox said.

"*Strokemaster* could be golf instruction," Sloan said.

LUCAS TAPPED A CHEAP color TV and an even cheaper DVD player that sat on a cardboard box across from the bed. "He didn't take his movies, his new shorts, or his TV. Maybe he was thinking of going out for a run, but coming back."

"Maybe he fucked something up and figured he couldn't come back," Sloan said.

"What'd he fuck up?" Lucas asked. "He was absolutely clean on the Larson killing, if he did it."

"Maybe something we don't know," Sloan said. He looked at Fox: "Was he smart? Good-looking? Controlled-crazy?"

Fox snorted. "Charlie? Charlie was a pervert. He looked like a pervert. If you saw him walking down the street, you'd say, 'There goes a pervert.' Didn't you get that file from St. John's? There're pictures . . ."

"We just got it; haven't had time to think about it," Lucas said. "How about smart? Is he smart?"

"He got arrested a block from the Target Center trying to anally rape a screaming woman, two feet from the sidewalk that ten thousand basketball fans were about to walk down. He just grabbed her and started whaling away. Charlie is a dumb motherfucker. He just blew off the best job he ever had."

"As a garbageman," Lucas said.

"An apprentice garbageman."

Lucas and Sloan looked at each other for a moment, then Sloan wagged his head and said, "That ain't the picture Elle was painting."

THEY EXPLAINED ELLE to Fox and the image she'd constructed of the killer. "That's not Charlie. If she's right, we're looking for the wrong guy," Fox said.

"Maybe something snapped when he was in St. John's," Sloan suggested.

"I didn't know him before he was in St. John's," Fox said. "I know him now. He's stupid and ugly now."

MOST OF THE TIME, thoroughly shaking down a house or an apartment would take hours. With Charlie Pope's trailer, they were done in half an hour —not only was there not much to look at, there was hardly any paper. They could find no checkbook, no credit cards, no computer, not even a notepad. The state paper he had, involving his imprisonment and parole, was in a state file folder under a six-year-old phone book.

"Nothing here but a bad smell," Sloan said.

WHEN THEY LEFT, Fox locked the door, and Lucas shook his head: "I had my hopes, but I don't think so. I can't get around the car thing."

"You can steal cars," Fox said.

"But would you steal a car to transport a bloody body, and then keep it?" Lucas asked. "I haven't heard about anybody finding a stolen car full of blood. I suppose he could have abandoned it, but it's been weeks since Larson was killed. Somebody should have seen it by now, if it was stolen."

"Could be parked out at the airport for a month," Fox suggested.

"Not with the new security," Lucas said, shaking his head. "Their surveillance system takes your tag number when your car comes in, runs it right there. And if you're out there for more than a week, they'll take a look at your car."

"Could be at one of those twenty-four-hour Sam's Club places," Sloan suggested. "Might go unnoticed for a while."

They all thought about it for a minute, then Fox said, "I don't know. There are some possibilities, but Charlie isn't a master criminal."

THEY WERE STILL STANDING in the parking lot, scuffing gravel, talking about possibilities, when Elle called.

"Lucas, I've been reading about this man Charles Pope," she said. "He is nothing like I expected."

"I know. We've been talking about that. We just went through his trailer . . ." He recapped the search, and then said, "This wasn't a sure thing, anyway. Just a guess. I wouldn't be surprised if the dumb shit caught a bus for California." He winced: "Sorry about the language."

"That's . . . never mind," she said. "Anyway, I'm skeptical. I'm very interested in what the DNA brings back. I would predict that we don't have a match. Will you call me when you know?"

"The minute I hear," Lucas said.

AND TEN SECONDS AFTER ELLE rang off, as they were saying good-bye to Fox, Carol called from Lucas's office. "Rose Marie wants you to call her," Carol said. "Right now. She's going to a music thing tonight so you won't be able to get her later. And about twenty reporters called."

"I thought they might. I'll get back to you," Lucas said.

FOX AND SLOAN WANDERED OFF, chatting, while Lucas poked in Rose Marie's number. When she picked up, Lucas told her about the trip to Owatonna, and the bad news: "We came up empty."

"I talked with the governor and McCord," she said. "The governor doesn't see anything in it for him, and McCord said he's too busy to front for the media. You're gonna have to do it."

He looked at his watch: "Ah, man . . ."

"Hey. You're good at it. Do it."

"All right. I'll do it. But I'm laying down some rules, and you have to back me up. I'll hold a press briefing at five o'clock, but that's it. Nobody goes around me."

"Make it four o'clock or they'll all be yelling at me about missing the early news."

"Fuck 'em. I got another stop to make. Five o'clock—maybe we can change it to four o'clock on other days."

"If you gotta—I'll pass the complaints along to Carol. She's probably gotten some calls already."

"About a million of them."

"So—handle it."

LUCAS CALLED CAROL BACK, told her to set up the press conference and to call Nordwall and invite him to make a statement. "He might want to get his picture on TV. He's running this fall."

FOX LED THEM BACK to the I-35 connection, waved good-bye out the window, and Lucas spun down the ramp and they headed back north. "Sorta like the old days when we were operating in Minneapolis," Sloan said. "The old days were sorta fucked up, you know? Looking back?"

"You're just getting cranky," Lucas said. "What could be better than chasing assholes like Pope? Think of all the guys who never get to do anything. You can't sit on your ass until you die."

Sloan cleared his throat. "I'd thought maybe . . . I'd buy a bar."

Lucas looked at him for ten seconds, then said, "You're kidding me."

"I'm not kidding. I've been looking into it. Seriously," Sloan said.

"When did this come up?" Lucas asked. "You don't know anything about running a bar. That's a complicated business."

"Hey, I took a small-business class last semester at the community college," Sloan said. "The situation I'm looking at, it's not a big deal. The owner's getting old, wants to retire, but he'd work with me as long as it took. You know Bernie Berger . . ."

"The Pine place? Out by Golden Valley?"

"Yeah. Don't piss on it; it's not that bad a place."

"I wasn't gonna piss on it. It *is* a likeable place. Other than the fact that it's called the Pine Knot. But even if you got a deal, you're a cop, Sloan . . ."

"I'm tired," Sloan said.

"Ah, for Christ's sake." Lucas took his hands off the wheel and rubbed his eyes with the heels of his hands. "If you quit . . . who's gonna chase the assholes with me?"

THE NEXT CITY NORTH was Faribault. The Rockyard was just outside the city limits on a county frontage road that ran parallel to the interstate. A yellow sign that said TOPLESS faced the highway, a beacon to truck drivers, but the paint was coming off the sign and it might not have been current. The bar itself had a gravel parking lot, fake yellow-log siding with a simulated hitching post, and a wooden boardwalk. A barbeque sign flicked an orange BBQ-BBQ-BBQ out toward the county road, and a Coors sign said COORS-COORS-COORS.

Four pickups sat in the parking lot, with an Oldsmobile with hand-sized rust spots down the sides and across the trunk. The Olds's license plate hung off the bumper on wire loops.

"Good-looking place," Sloan said, as they got out of the Porsche.

"Ah, if I were seventeen . . ."

"And stupid . . ."

THE SALOON WAS COOL INSIDE, smelling of beer and fried hamburger. A woman bartender in a white blouse, black vest, and ribbon tie was wiping down the bar. A couple of guys were shooting pool in the back, nine ball, and three more watching, all of them with long-necks in their hands. Everybody turned their heads when Lucas and Sloan stepped inside. Sloan muttered, looking at the bartender, "That doesn't look like a Booger."

"C'mon," Lucas said; he'd been checking faces in the back.

They went on to the bar, and the bartender asked, "Gentlemen? What can I do you for?" She was a sturdy dark-haired woman, about fifty, with too-red lipstick and too much rouge. A cigarette was burning in an ashtray next to the cash register.

"Carl around?" Lucas asked.

"Can I tell him who's calling?"

"Yeah, the cops," Lucas said. He held out his ID. "We need a little help."

She looked at Lucas, then at Sloan, and asked, "Is he in trouble?"

"Can't tell yet," Lucas said.

"I'll see if I can find him," she said. She walked down behind the bar and out, and into a back room. The pool watchers were now all watching Lucas and Sloan, and Lucas smiled at them. Ten seconds later, the bartender reappeared. A fat man, with hair like a haystack, and who might have described himself as muscular, shambled along behind.

"Hi, I'm Carl," he said. "You're police officers? Is there a problem?"

"You know a guy named Adam Rice?" Lucas asked.

Carl blinked rapidly, then said, "Jesus. He *was* the guy. We weren't sure."

"Yeah, he was," Lucas said. Everybody in the bar was listening now. "You gotta place where we can go talk?"

CARL HAD A SMALL OFFICE, a cherry-laminate desk with a swivel chair, and two formed-plastic chairs for visitors. The desk was piled with paper, a well-used desk calculator to one side. Carl leaned back in the chair, which squealed under the load, and said, "I know the guy. He'd come in, have a few beers, cry a little, listen to music. He was a sad guy. How'd you know he came in here?"

"Heck, everybody's been calling us," Sloan said. "You ever see him with a guy . . ."

Carl's eyes got thin: "The way you said that—you mean, a gay guy?"

"Yeah."

Carl snorted and leaned farther back in the chair. "A gay guy would not come in here. Or if he did, he'd sure as shit not let anybody know he was gay. I only saw Rice talking with a couple of guys, and then it was just random guy-shit, sitting at the bar, drinking beer."

"What about the girls?" Lucas asked.

Carl's eyes involuntarily wandered. "He'd come in alone . . . ," he began.

"Don't bullshit us, Booger," Lucas said, scuffing his chair an inch toward the fat man. "We know about the girls, we know you introduced them. We need your help, and we're gonna get it one way or another. Now . . . was there one girl, or more than one? And where could we find them?"

After a moment of silence, Carl said, "They're gonna give me a ton of shit about this."

"We're talking about a serial torture killer. If there's any hint that he somehow met Rice here, through the girls, they'd want to know about it," Lucas said.

Carl sighed, put his hands over his belly, twiddled, then said, "He'd try to get Dove, a blondie. If she was busy, he'd take one or the other. But he'd usually ask if anybody had seen Dove."

"But he hooked up with some of the others, too."

"Yeah, he did," Carl said. "They'd go over next door, the girls got rooms. He'd get his blow job, and he'd come back here all weepy, have another beer, and then go on home."

"How often?" Sloan asked.

"Twice a week, maybe," Carl said.

"How much?"

"For a blow job? Fifty if you wear a rubber, or seventy without," Carl said. "The extra twenty is, like, AIDS insurance."

"That's a good idea," Sloan said. "Nothin' like AIDS insurance."

"Hey, it's not me, the girls don't work for me," Carl protested. "They come in here, but what am I gonna do? I'm not a cop. I'm not their guardian. They don't do any business on the premises, and some of the guys . . . like to have them around."

Lucas: "Their names are Dove and . . . ?"

"Andi and Aix, right now. The one girl's name is pronounced X, but it's spelled A-I-X, as she'll tell you every chance she gets. She thinks she's speaking French because she once went there with her boyfriend. There were a couple more girls, but they moved away, I couldn't tell you where. They come and they go."

"Dove is still here?"

"Should be right next door, unless they're shopping." He looked at his watch. "Mornings, lots of times, they run up to the Mall of America, but they're usually back by two—guys get off work a couple hours early, they like to stop by for an afternooner. You know, before supper."

"Wouldn't want a blow job on a full stomach," Sloan said.

"What rooms?" Lucas asked.

"Usually twenty-three, twenty-five, and twenty-seven, down at the end of the hall. Close enough that they can scream for help."

"They ever scream for help?" Sloan asked.

"Not lately, but who knows?"

"We may come back and talk to you some more," Lucas said, standing up. "Don't call the girls, huh?"

THE Y'ALL DUCK INN'S parking lot was separated from the Rockyard's lot by a fringe of grass. A shabby two-story building, it showed two long rows of gray-green doors facing the highway, with a small window next to each door. The parking lot was gravel, the stairs and walkways were concrete and outside in the weather: a fifteen-dollar-a-night motel used as a crash pad by truckers and refugees from the Rockyard who were too drunk to drive home.

They didn't bother with the office; they climbed the stairs and walked south until they got to twenty-five and knocked. They were lucky the first time: Dove answered.

She probably looked good in a bar, in the evening, Lucas thought. During the day, and outside, she wasn't quite pretty. Twenty years old, maybe, with a pasty face that didn't like the light, and hips that already ran to wobbly fat. She answered the door wearing a yellow halter top, white shorts, three-inch-thick platform flip-flops, and too much makeup; she was chewing gum.

She saw Lucas first, and a frown flitted across her face: "You don't, uh . . ." Then she saw Sloan and blurted out, "Jesus Christ, don't arrest me. My mother doesn't know I do this."

"Your mother," Sloan said.

Lucas stepped toward her, and Dove backed into the motel room, and Lucas stepped in after her. Sloan followed and pushed the door shut. A soap opera was playing on the TV. A furry moose doll with crooked velvet horns sat on top of the TV. Lucas found the remote control, pushed the power button, and the noise went away. "Do you know Adam Rice?"

"Ohmagod," she said. She looked from Lucas to Sloan, chewed once on her gum. "I wasn't sure it was him." She sat on the bed, picked up a pillow, and squeezed it around her chest, looking up at them, eyes big.

"We're running down everything we can find," Lucas said. "We understand you were his favorite date."

She stared slack mouthed into the open bathroom. "We were wondering today if it was him in the newspaper."

"Anything unusual about him?" Lucas asked. "Strange sex stuff . . ."

She shook her head. "Nope. Always the same. Wanted me to get naked and go down on him. He'd watch. I mean mostly people watch, but he was like, you know, *curious*."

"Never pushed you around, never wanted you to push him around . . ."

She shook her head, her hair bouncing around her shoulders. A dark streak ran down the middle of her part: she needed a new blond job. "Nope. When he was finished, he'd tip me, and then he'd wait until I got dressed, and if there was nobody else ready to go at the bar, he'd buy me a beer. He was a sweet guy, sort of. Maybe a little corny."

Lucas spotted her purse, picked it up. She said, "Hey," but he ignored her, took out her wallet, looked at her driver's license. It said Bertha Wolfe.

"Bertha—did he ever talk about friends, ever come in with friends?"

"C'mon, man, don't mess with my stuff . . ."

Lucas put the wallet back in the purse and tossed it back on the dresser.

"Friends?"

"Just one guy, he came along two or three times," she said. "The friend never went with one of us guys—Adam said he was an old school buddy, they knew each other for years."

"A name?" Sloan prompted.

She squinted, rolled her eyes, thinking, then, "Larry Masters? That's not right, but it's something like that."

Sloan suggested Andy Sanders, and Dove pointed her finger at him and said, "That's it. Exactly."

"Nobody else."

She turned down the corners of her mouth and said, "Nope. Not that I can think of."

"Think harder."

She tried to put a thinking look on her face, but shook her head. "Do you guys . . . I mean, do you think whoever did it comes to the bar? This girl up in the Twin Cities, was she working?"

"We don't know any of that," Lucas said. "You might think of taking a vacation for a couple weeks, though. Until we get him."

"You're sure you're gonna get him." A small edge of skepticism?

"We'll get him," Lucas said. "We just don't know how many more people he'll kill before we do."

She shivered and said, "The paper said Adam was mutilated."

WITH LUCAS PUSHING HER, Dove took them down to the next two rooms, rented by Andi and Aix; both, like Dove, were thin, a little flabby, and unnatural blondes. Andi claimed that she hardly remembered Rice and wasn't even sure she'd had sex with him.

Aix had had sex with him, twice, she thought, and with some prodding, said, "I did see him talking to a pretty strange guy, once. Kind of a snaky guy. He looked like a pool hustler, or something, somebody who works at night or maybe was in prison, because he was like dead white. Adam didn't know him, but he was teasing Adam about being such a fresh-faced guy hanging around with the likes of me . . . this guy knew, I guess, you know, even though I never went with him or anything."

"How often did you see the guy?"

"That was the last time," Aix said. "I might have seen him once before, shooting pool. He said he used to be a sailor, and sailed yachts. I'm like, right, a yachtsman right here at the Rockpit."

"Rockyard," Sloan said.

Her little joke: "Pit. You look at the place?"

"Their idea of culture is a wet-T-shirt contest," Dove said, snapping her fingers, as though flicking a flea off her shirt.

"This guy, this sailor . . . you said he was snaky. How? What do you mean?" Lucas asked.

"Like he was thin, but he looked strong, wiry, you could see these muscles working in his arms. Black hair but really pale white. Oh: he had a tattoo, one of those barb-wire dealies that go around your biceps."

"A biker," Lucas suggested.

She nodded and wrinkled her nose: "He might've known his way around a Harley," she said. "But he never mentioned anything."

They all sat looking at her for a moment, then Sloan said to Lucas, "Not much."

"No."

Aix shook her finger at him: "But it was something. You know? There was something going on. One of those things you think might go on and be a fight. The guy kept teasing Adam about his fresh face . . . This newspaper story made me think there might have been something gay going on . . ."

"What made you think that?"

"Just . . . something. You know how you can tell sometimes? And the thing is, the thing that was going on with the snaky guy . . . there was something a little gay in that, too. Neither one of them looked gay, or talked gay, but there was something there."

A FEW MORE MINUTES of pushing got them nothing. Lucas turned to Sloan and said, "You happy?"

"I guess."

Dove said, "You're not going to arrest us, are you?"

Lucas shook his head. "Nah. But really—maybe take a vacation?"

And to Aix: "If you see the snaky guy again, call us. And if you see him, get somebody to walk you out to the parking lot. Somebody you know."

Andi, shivering: "You really think he's around here?"

Sloan stood up and said, "Listen, if any of you'd seen the woman up in Minneapolis, you wouldn't want to take any chance. *Any* chance."

THEY ALL NODDED, and Lucas and Sloan backed out of the room. As they walked down to the car Sloan said, "If you wind up in Room twenty-seven at the Y'All Duck Inn, you probably made a bad career choice somewhere."

"What if everybody in three counties calls you Booger?"

"Another bad sign," Sloan said. "A bad sign."

7

THE PRESS CONFERENCE was held in a beige-walled, tile-floored, odor-free, windowless meeting room with a podium and rostrum at one end, in front of a blue Minnesota state flag that hung slightly askew on the wall behind the rostrum. The room was full of cheap Chinese plastic chairs with loud steel feet, which scraped and squealed when they were pushed around.

Reporters started drifting in a half hour before the press conference, led by the TV cameramen, who pushed the chairs around to make room for themselves and their lights. The newspaper guys, scruffy next to the TV on-air people, pushed the chairs around some more, the better to bullshit with one another. They were a little noisier than usual, a combination of off-camera cheer and on-camera solemnity, because the story was a good one.

All of it was enhanced in the eyes of the attendees by an entertaining spat between Sloan and Ruffe Ignace.

. . .

AT FIVE, THE TV PEOPLE brought the lights up, and Lucas did the intro:

"We have two murders. As you may have read in the paper, there is a possibility that the two are related. Representatives of the two jurisdictions in which the murders occurred are with us today and will describe the murders and the scenes . . ."

Nordwall, large and intense in a jowly, paternal, slow-moving way, said that his men were following several leads in the most recent murder but that overall coordination had been moved to the BCA. Then Sloan stood up and said that Minneapolis was coordinating with Nordwall and the BCA and that Minneapolis also had several investigators running down leads, which was a bald-faced lie but was not contradicted.

Lucas, following Sloan, said that the BCA had established and staffed a co-op center to coordinate information on the case.

Some of the reporters had started looking at their watches when he announced that they were looking for Charles "Charlie" Pope, a convicted Level-2 sex offender who had been recently released from the St. John's Security Hospital and who had cut off a leg bracelet and disappeared.

The reporters stopped looking at their watches.

"At this point, we have no reason to believe that he is involved, except for general proximity and the fact that he has violated parole," Lucas said. "We'd like to know where he is and what he's been doing. If he sees this, we urge him to call us. If anybody has seen him, please call. Photographs are available and are being distributed. They were taken at St. John's before his release and are only about two months old."

Channel Three's principal talking head, self-assigned to his semiannual story, one that wouldn't wrinkle his shirt, jumped up and demanded, "Are you telling us that the state of Minnesota recently released an insane sex offender who immediately went into the community?"

That got it going; Nordwall, improbably, kept it going when he said, gruffly, "We don't have lifelong preventive detention in the United States, and we won't get it, no matter what the media wants, because we're not Nazis."

Lucas winced, and a happy *Pioneer Press* reporter, jabbing a yellow number-2 pencil at Nordwall, asked, "Are you implying that Channel Three in some way supports the tenets of National Socialism . . . ?"

AFTER BLEEDING OUT all the details on Charlie Pope, Lucas was pushed into admitting that the details in Ignace's story were generally accurate. "They weren't disclosed at the time of the murders to spare the victims' families the trauma of seeing these brutal murders used as entertainment on television," Lucas said.

Channel Eight's weekend fill-in talking head leaped to his feet: "Are you trying to imply . . ."

Well, yes. Lucas's implication pissed a few people off, in a pro-forma way, but since they all knew that the story *would* be used as entertainment, and *were* hoping that it might be used for several days if not weeks, the irritation was more about the public rudeness of mentioning the fact than because of any inherent unfairness. They wouldn't use the clip of Lucas's comment anyway, so no damage would be done.

Besides, Lucas knew most of the reporters, including the talking heads, and got along with them. He hadn't met Ruffe Ignace, though, and when Ignace asked the predictable self-aggrandizing question "Would you say the recent *Star-Tribune* story on the murders spurred this sudden effort to track down Pope and create this so-called co-op center?"

Sloan jumped in. "Well, uh, Rufus . . ."

"Ruffe," Ignace snapped, looking up at him suspiciously.

"Roo-fay? Okay. Roo-fay. Sorry. No, I don't really think that the story got us moving any faster on anything, to tell you the truth. We were already pounding on it. This killer is a monster. We know that. We're working on it as hard as we can, including using civilian experts to advise us. Your story was okay. Some of your details of the supposed display in the Larson case weren't exactly correct, but I really can't go into the precise problems . . ."

"They *were* exactly correct," Ignace said. He added something under his breath, which might have been, *You fucking twit,* or something close to that.

Sloan stepped away from the microphone, as if to have a personal word with Ignace, but he spoke loud enough that everyone could hear. "Not exactly," he said. "You weren't at the scene, and I was. That whole thing about the way, *mmm* . . ." He glanced at the TV cameras. ". . . about the sexual aspects of the arrangement of the body, were not exact. I don't know where you got your information, but you have to be more careful about hearsay . . . or maybe the way your imagination works."

"It wasn't hearsay, and it was exact," Ignace insisted.

"I won't argue," Sloan said, and he stepped away from microphone, turning it back to Lucas.

"It's not right for you to stand up there and suggest that I wrote something that was incorrect when both you and I know it was correct," Ignace said.

"I won't argue," Sloan said again, dismissively.

The other reporters were enjoying the show, a little hand-to-hand combat at Ignace's expense. They would all mention in the report that Sloan suggested that some of Ignace's details were incorrect, revenge for his having beaten them.

At the end of the press conference, with all questions repeated three times so the various media representatives could be shown on tape asking them, Lucas, Sloan, and Nordwall moved off the podium and out through the conference room's back door.

Ignace followed them through the door and said, "Wait a minute."

Lucas turned: "Uh, you're not supposed to be back here . . ."

"Yeah, yeah." Ignace went after Sloan: "What was that all about? About my details being wrong? You know that's not right."

"I know," Sloan said. "I'm trying to figure out where our leak is. If all the details were right, and they were, and you insisted on it, and you did, then you probably saw photographs. There are about six people who could have made copies for you. I didn't, so that gets it down to five. I'll figure it out."

Ignace stared at him for a moment, then turned, shoved his notebook in a hip pocket, walked back out the door, and as he went through it, said, "Fuck you."

"Talk to you later, Rufus," Sloan called back, adding, in a slightly lower tone, "You little asshole."

THE INFORMATION ABOUT POPE, and the press conference, froze the investigation: the routine continued, but there weren't a lot of decisions to be made until the DNA came back. Lucas talked to the BCA director about space and personnel for the co-op center, then went home and ate a microwave dinner. He reread the murder file as he ate, talked to Elle by phone: she had no more suggestions.

"I saw you on television," she said. "This will add pressure to find somebody."

"Yup."

"And it might also put pressure on the perpetrator to act again—when the attention starts to fade away in a day or two, he may move to get it back."

"Thanks for the thought."

He read the file some more, he went out to a used bookstore, then on to a movie, a spy thriller about an assassin who'd lost his memory. None of it seemed likely, but it had a decent car chase involving BMWs and Mercedes Benz Yellow Cabs.

The next morning, at eight o'clock, Weather called, and he told her about the press conference.

"Has there ever been a crime solved by matching DNA from a scene to something that was already in the bank?" she asked. "I mean, the primary solution, rather than an after-the-fact thing?"

"Yeah. A couple of times. But it's rare."

AFTER CLEANING UP, he took 35E to the BCA headquarters, settled into his office, signed papers that Carol put in front of him, and then checked with Bill James, who was doing the biographical research on Adam Rice and who'd uncovered Rice's connection to the hookers.

"Not getting much more," James said. "I'm doing background on the people he worked with, neighbors, like that, you know, but nothing is popping up. The hookers thing was . . . way out of control. If you knew everything else about him, you never saw that coming."

"Maybe just sex," Lucas said.

"I think it was. But it's the only point where he sorta connected with the underworld . . . the Minnesota underworld. If you're doin' hookers, you're not too far from the drugs and all the rest of it. So if he knew the killer, a sex killer, where'd he meet him? Those hookers seem like a possibility."

"Exactly. Keep digging. Look for a snaky guy, real white complexion, with a barbed-wire tattoo around his biceps."

"Who'd that be?"

"Maybe just a fantasy," Lucas said. "Good job on the hookers."

. . .

HE CALLED MARK FOX, Charlie Pope's parole officer: "Could you ask the people Pope worked with, if he ever hung out at a place called the Rockyard, in Faribault? It's not too far . . ."

"I know it, and it's Charlie's kind of place," Fox drawled. "I'll ask around and get back to you today. Still haven't found a car, have we?"

"No. I worry about that."

LUCAS TALKED TO SLOAN. Sloan said, "I can't get Angela Larson and Adam Rice together, except for one thing and it's weak."

"What?"

"If you look at the transcript of Nordwall's interview with Rice's mother, they talk for a minute about Rice's wife. Laurina Rice says, quote, 'She liked doing artistic things,' unquote. Larson worked at an art-supply store . . ."

"So your theory is . . ."

"No, no, no, it's not a theory," Sloan said. "It's not that strong. But maybe . . . they could have met? Like on an art-supply buying trip up here? And after his wife dies, when he starts thinking about companionship, he remembers Larson. That they hit it off a little, so he drops by."

"Then what?" Lucas asked.

"I don't know. Maybe some sort of kinky artist guy is fixated on her, and sees them together . . ."

Lucas: "That's not weak—it's just not quite ridiculous. Why don't you get one of your millions of investigators and see if he can make the link?"

"Ah, jeez, they'd think I was crazy."

"Get a young one," Lucas said.

. . .

WHEN HE GOT OFF THE PHONE with Sloan, Lucas went down the hall and bought a pack of almonds from a snack machine: they were his permitted midmorning snack. He was back at his desk, counting out the allotted fifteen almonds, when John Hopping Crow stuck his head in the door and said, "They fuckin' match."

Lucas sat up, astonished: "They fuckin' *match*?"

"They fuckin' *match*," Hopping Crow repeated, stepping inside. He was wearing the largest smile Lucas had ever seen on him, big white teeth like Chiclets. "How about that for a little *CSI: Minneapolis* bullshit, huh? We're going network."

"You got enough goop to repeat the procedure?" Lucas asked.

"We don't have to . . ."

"For the trial? For the defense, if there is one?"

Hopping Crow caught on: "Yes. We've got the evidence chain nailed down, everything passed hand to hand and signed for, and we've got enough for three or four more tests."

"I'd French-kiss you if you weren't married," Lucas said, picking up the telephone.

"It's always something," Hopping Crow said.

SLOAN WAS AS ASTONISHED AS LUCAS.

"Got him. Goddamn it, Lucas. Got him." Lucas heard him turn away from the phone and shout to somebody, "They matched it. We got him." Then, back to the phone, "If you get the media hooked up, we can have his face all over five states by six o'clock."

"I'm going down to St. John's today, talk to the people who worked with him. If you're loose . . ."

"How soon?"

"I want to make those media calls, set up a four-o'clock press conference. Say, an hour?"

"Pick me up at the Mall of America. I'll go down there now, I wanna buy some shoes."

LUCAS TOLD CAROL, his secretary, to set up a press conference for four o'clock; called Nordwall and told him.

"Goddamnit, that's wonderful," Nordwall said, his voice warm with relief. "But why four o'clock? Why wait?"

"I've got stuff to do. We need more background on the guy, we should organize some more pictures, and besides, it doesn't matter—we can't do it in time for the noon news, and at four o'clock they'll have it in time for every single evening news program, and both papers."

"I'll see you at four," Nordwall said.

THE NEXT CALL WAS to St. John's. A secretary told him the administrator, Dr. Lawrence Cale, was fishing in Bemidji, but would be on his cell phone. Lucas called and found the guy in a boat.

"Haven't caught a goddamned thing," he grumbled. "I'm saying it loud enough for the guide to hear me."

Lucas explained about the DNA: "I need to talk to the people in St. John's who were the closest to Pope."

"That'd be his treatment team," Cale said. "My second's name is Darrell Ross. I'll call him and tell him to hang on to the team until you get down there. They normally get off at three o'clock . . ."

"No problem, we can be down there in an hour and a half. We've got to be back here by four, anyway."

"Wish I could be there, especially since I'M NOT CATCHING ANY FISH," Cale said. "Charlie Pope, huh? I'll tell you what—we're not taking the fall on this one. We saw it coming from a long way back, and we told everybody who'd listen."

LUCAS GOT OUT OF THE BUILDING, cut across town, and found Sloan, with a shoe bag, standing on the sidewalk outside Nordstrom's. They headed south down the Minnesota River again. "Pope's face will be all over the Northern Plains. He won't be able to stand outside his car to take a leak without somebody recognizing him," Lucas said. "That's one good thing about a really ugly murder; people pay attention. Maybe we oughta make all murders ugly."

"All murders *are* ugly," Sloan said. He was trading his old shoes for the new ones. Both pairs were nearly identical black wingtips. "If they were pretty, I wouldn't be quitting."

"Aw, man . . ."

THE RICE MURDERS had taken place just south of the city of Mankato; St. John's Security Hospital was located eight miles to the north, in a red-brick riverside hamlet originally built around a grain elevator and a creamery. Now the town was mostly a bedroom community for hospital employees.

The hospital sat in the hills west of the town and came in two parts. A reception center for new inmates and visitors sat down a short access road; the road continued through the parking lot and farther up the hill, to the main hospital.

The reception center was a new, low, brick building that looked like an elementary school, except that the back side had a chain-link prison pen attached, with glistening concertina wire looped through the fence. The main hospital was an older brick-and-concrete-block building that was just Gothic enough to scare the shit out of people who saw it.

THEY CHECKED IN at the lower building, and a chunky young woman named Nan escorted them up the hill. The hospital was set up like a prison: an outer area for administration and support, a hard wall running through the center of the building, with confinement areas behind the wall.

From an earlier visit, Lucas knew that the level of confinement varied from section to section: the worst sexual psychopaths were kept in hard cages under twenty-four-hour surveillance, while the inmates of other areas, where there was no immediate threat of violence, had a good deal of freedom. Some sections housed both men and women, which had caused some problems with sex and even the occasional pregnancy, but which also gave those areas a greater feeling of normal human society.

"Most of the people here really are . . . a little lost," Nan said. "They're not bad people. Most of them aren't stupid. The world is just a little too much for them."

"Most of them," Sloan said. "There are a few . . ." He shook his head.

"Sure," she said.

THEY SIGNED IN AND LEFT their weapons with a security officer. Entry to the confinement area went through twin electronic barred doors, with a hardened guard's booth between the two doors. The booth was called "the cage" and was made of concrete block up to waist height, and from there to the ceiling with thick armored glass set into concrete pillars. The people inside the cage controlled the entry, the locks in the confinement blocks, and monitored the cameras that were spotted through the hospital.

Nan took them as far as the first barred gate, pointed out a man leaning against the wall in the confinement area, behind the second gate. "That's Harvey Bronson. He'll take you to your conference."

They said good-bye and stepped through the first door, which slowly closed and locked behind them. They then walked through an airport-like metal scanner, emptying their pockets and removing their shoes. When they were through and had their shoes back on, one of the men in the cage opened the second door, and they stepped through into the secure area.

"Gives me the creeps, being inside," Sloan said, looking back at the doors.

"Never get used to it," said their new escort. He pointed down the hall. "You're down this way."

The inside of the hospital reminded Lucas of an aging high school. Bronson took them to a conference room where a principal's office should have been, popped open the door, said, "Have a seat—I'll see what happened to the team."

They dropped into the chairs and looked around: the place had the same architectural neutrality as the press-conference room back at the BCA, except for a dark glass plate in one wall, which hid a camera and microphones; they both looked at it, and Lucas said, "Big Brother."

A few seconds later, the door popped open, and a guy stuck his head inside: "Davenport and Sloan?"

Sloan raised a hand: "That's us."

The man said over his shoulder, "Here they are," and then, as he stepped inside, "They told us the wrong room."

TWO MORE MEN and a woman followed the first man inside. They were dressed casually, in white staff coats and pastel shirts, tan slacks, pens in their breast pockets. All four wore the masked expressions Lucas recognized as Prison-Guard Face: tight, watchful, controlled. There was always an edge of fear, held in a mental fist, never allowed to leak out when there was a prisoner around. Fear in a prison was like blood in a shark pen. The four of them shuffled around the conference table, put papers on the table, files. Two of the men had coffee cups. The first man said, "You guys want coffee?"

"We're okay," Lucas said. He said, "I'm Lucas Davenport, with the BCA, and this is Detective Sloan from Minneapolis PD. You guys are . . . ?"

They introduced themselves: three were psychologists; the fourth, the woman, was an M.D. She was pretty in a careful way, slender, with brown hair, brown eyes, short nose, and a few freckles. She held Lucas's eyes for an extra second, and he thought, *Hmm.* Then one of the men said, "Charlie Pope?"

"Yeah. We got this DNA result . . ."

Lucas spent ten minutes outlining the details of the case, both of the killings and the DNA match. Prison people liked that—to be treated like brother cops—and they got on a first-name basis.

One of them, a burly, crew-cut guy named Dick Hart, kicked back from the table and said, "I'll tell you what, Lucas, you ask me if Charlie could do this, I'd say, 'Absolutely.' He was crazy enough. They should never have let him out of here. I knew something would happen. I said so before they let him go."

Karen Beloit, the M.D., agreed: "We'd take him for treatment—he had stomach and hemorrhoid troubles—you could watch him watching the women. The doctors and the nurses, watching them. You knew what he was thinking."

"But one of the victims was a man," Sloan objected.

Leo Grant said, "I was one of his therapists, and, uh, *mmm* . . ." He glanced at Beloit, grinned, and said, "Put your fingers in your ears."

"Spit it out, cowboy," she said.

"You know that movie, *American Pie*, where the guy puts his dick in the pie 'cause it's kinda warm? Charlie was like that. But with a mean streak. He'd just go around and he needed to *fuck* something. You'd see one of the younger guys go by, and Charlie would kinda look at his ass . . . Charlie'd do that. He wouldn't even consider it gay."

Hart agreed with Grant. "It's pretty common in here for the dominant member of a homosexual couple not to consider himself gay. The, *mmm*, receiver, everybody agrees that he's gay. I wouldn't have been surprised if Charlie had a sexual relationship of that kind. I'm a little surprised by this beating, this methodical torture you're talking about. Charlie might enjoy hurting people but didn't seem to me to be the kind who'd be methodical about it. To plan it. He might beat somebody to death or strangle somebody—hell, we're pretty sure he *did*—but this is a little different. With Charlie, sex was the thing, the violence was the way he got it. With these killings it seems like the violence is the thing, the sex is an afterthought."

Leo Grant was shaking his head, said, "Nah, nah, Dick, that's not right. The sex is central. The sex is central. The torture is part of the sex act; the actual penetration is the culmination. I wouldn't be surprised if the moment of murder, the throat cutting, comes simultaneously with orgasm."

"Jesus." Sloan stroked his throat with his fingers.

"You're saying the torture is the foreplay," Lucas said.

Grant nodded: "Exactly."

Sam O'Donnell, the third psychologist, said, "We tried everything we could to hang on to him. I would . . . there's a way of getting to a guy sideways. I'd read a newspaper report to him, a sex crime somewhere, and get him to imagine how they would track down the criminal. He had the reticence of a longtime prisoner, but when you went at him sideways, got him thinking about it, you could watch the control slip away. In the end, giving him potential access to sex would be like putting an ounce of cocaine next to somebody just out of rehab."

Sloan said, "Okay. So . . . where did he go?"

Hart glanced at the others, then shrugged and said, "Fuck if I know."

Beloit said, "He shouldn't be too hard to find. I'd start by looking in strip bars and topless places. Someplace where there's alcohol and women."

Grant was shaking his head again. "He isn't as dumb as he looks. He'll stay away from those too-obvious places. He might try for, like, a college place. Someplace where there are a lot of targets. I'm not sure he'd go for an obvious place like a strip joint. Not if he thinks somebody might be looking for him."

"We're already looking at a bar in Faribault," Lucas said. "They've got some hookers working out the back door."

O'Donnell looked at Grant: "That might be something he couldn't stay away from. Get off, and nobody to talk about it."

Grant seemed skeptical: "Maybe."

Lucas: "Now that we're gonna put his face all over the place, he won't be able to hang out in any bar. Where would he hide?"

"Someplace close," Hart said. "He's a homeboy. Even Iowa scares him."

"I can see that," Sloan said. "Iowa scares me a little."

"He's been out for what? Couple months? I'd bet you dollars to doughnuts that he has a beard and maybe has dyed his hair," O'Donnell said. "Maybe even gotten a toupee somewhere. What's he driving? He didn't have any money when he left here. Have you looked for stolen cars? Or friends who might loan him a car?"

"That's one of our biggest questions," Lucas said, tapping his finger on the tabletop. "How's he getting around? He had to get a car from somewhere. Do you have any records of him talking about friends? Or did he have any friends here who might have hooked him up?"

"There were a couple of people he sort of hung with," Hart said. "But they're all still here, as far as I know."

"Mike West," Beloit said.

Grant snapped his fingers: "I never thought of him." To Lucas: "West is a schizophrenic personality who can't stay on his meds. He'd get freaked out, you know, sometimes life would get on top of him, and he'd get violent—though it was aimless, more like excitement than rage. He never hurt anyone, maybe a couple of cut lips, but he scared people. Anyway, he knew Charlie on the outside, when they were growing up."

"That's good," Lucas said. "We need to talk to him."

"He's right in Minneapolis, at a halfway house," Hart said. "We can check before you leave. I'm not sure, but it seems to me he might've gotten out a couple of months before Charlie did."

Beloit said, "That's a possibility, I guess. But you know what bothers me?" She paused, getting her thoughts together, and then again held Lucas's eyes. "When Charlie was out in the population, sometimes he'd stop and talk to the Big Three. They were friends, I think. Much as those people can be."

Lucas: "Big Three?"

Hart: "Chase, Lighter, and Taylor. Lawrence Chase, Benjamin Lighter, and Carl Taylor. We think he killed at least two women, Charlie did, so they had something in common."

Sloan said, "Ah, shit. *Biggie Lighter* was a friend of his?"

Lucas leaned back and grinned at him. "Your old buddy." To the others: "Sloan's the guy who put Biggie away."

"I'd be more worried about Carl Taylor," O'Donnell said. "He's the one who spins out all these theories about why women need to be killed. He's the preacher. And some of these guys . . . I mean, some of them, go along."

But Sloan looked at Lucas: "Biggie Lighter used to cut the . . ." His eyes flicked sideways at Beloit, then back, ". . . penises off his victims, after he raped them. I don't know if he posed them."

Hart said, "Rice had his penis cut off?" When Lucas nodded, he said, "That does sound like Biggie. His files say that he . . . there was some cannibalism involved."

Beloit: "Oh, yuck."

"He's not a guy you mess with," Grant said. "When we're dealing with him, we use full protective restraints."

. . .

THEY ALL SAT AROUND silently for a moment, looking at one another, until Hart picked it up again.

"But you know, when it's all said and done, none of this really sounds much like Charlie Pope. He's a crazy killer, but he was clumsy," Hart said. "Sam is right: that first one, the woman, sounds more like Carl Taylor. He's the one who goes on all the time about punishment. He told me once, in a therapy session, that if he had to do it all over again, he'd punish the women before he killed them so that they'd have a taste of hell before they went there. He said he'd hang them up naked and whip them like Jesus was whipped. He's welded together sex and punishment like . . ." He shrugged. "Listening to him is like reading the Marquis de Sade."

"Hang them up naked," Lucas repeated.

"Yes. You know, so they were dangling and he could whip them all around . . ."

"God*damnit*," Sloan said.

Lucas: "Do you guys think Taylor and Lighter could be operating Pope by remote control?"

Dick Hart jumped in: "Couldn't really be remote control, because they can't talk to him. These are the most highly restricted prisoners in the state. They have no contact with the outside."

"Not even their families?" Sloan asked.

"Their families have disowned them," Beloit said. "Chase's sister said we should kill him if we ever got the chance. She was serious. Nobody in any of their families has ever come here or even called, except Taylor's, years ago. He was left some property, and his brother came in here to get him to sign it away. But that's been five or six years."

Grant said, "We know everything that goes in and out of their cells. We have people comb through their *food* before it goes in."

"Do they have access to TV news?" Sloan asked.

"Well, sure . . . They have TVs in their cells."

"So, if they programmed him, they could be getting off on it by watching the news."

O'Donnell nodded: "They could. Maybe that would be enough . . . to get them off, anyway."

"If Pope's a robot," Lucas asked, "do you think they sent him out there deliberately, or he just went?"

"Charlie was going after women no matter what," Grant said. He was the skeptical one: "But this? Robots? I don't know."

"Let's talk to Taylor and Lighter and Chase," Sloan said to Lucas. "What have we got to lose?"

Lucas looked at the others: "What do you think?"

They all shrugged or nodded. "Really don't have anything to lose—but don't go making any deals with them unless you get an okay in advance," Hart said. "They're gonna want something for talking."

Beloit looked at Grant, who showed a small smile and said, from the corner of his mouth to Hart, "Better read them the semen warning."

Sloan bit first: "What's that?"

"Lighter tends to hide semen around his cell. Or just keep it in his hand. We have a screen we keep up most of the time, but when we need to talk to him . . . Well, when you're least expecting it, zip, it's all over your face."

"That's why prison guards carry clubs," Lucas said.

"Yeah, clubs," Hart said. He stood up and stretched. "We'll keep him under control. But if the worst should happen . . ."

"Yeah?"

"There's a reflex to lick your lips. Don't do that."

THEY HAD TO GO BACK to the unsecured side of the administration building to arrange the visit to Taylor, Lighter, and Chase. Darrell Ross, the assistant administrator, was a friendly codger with a ring of white hair around his bald pate and a pipe rack on his desk. He leaned back in his leather chair and said, congenially, "There's a question here of whether you're investigating them for a crime. If you're investigating them for a crime, you'll have to read them their rights. Then they've got a right to an attorney."

"They're *nuts*," Lucas said. "They're locked up in a nuthouse."

Ross frosted up: "We don't use that language here. It's a little like referring to a paralyzed person as a crip. Most of them are harmless, and their problems are not of their own making."

Lucas held his hands up: "Sorry. I know that."

Ross nodded at him, laced his fingers over his ample gut, and twiddled his thumbs for a second. "Anyway, the Supreme Court says they get a lawyer. So if they ask, they get one. There are ways to work around that, and we'll try, but I'm just letting you know that there could be a hangup."

"What ways to work around it?" Lucas asked.

"We'll tell them that if they want a lawyer, we'll have to isolate them for a few days before we can bring them up to the visiting room. Just to make sure that they don't have any contraband concealed inside their bodies. They hate the isolation. That might convince them that they don't need an attorney."

"Is that legal?" Sloan asked.

"Supreme Court says we can use reasonable security measures." The friendly old codger smiled a smile that suddenly looked a lot like a prison guard's smile. "We get to say what's reasonable. Anyway—we'll try to get you in."

8

ROSS TALKED TO ALL three inmates personally, through the intercom system, told them what Lucas and Sloan wanted, recited their rights, and offered them privileges if they agreed to be interviewed. All three agreed to talk.

On the way to the security unit, Hart, who was escorting them, said, "The main thing to keep in mind, these guys are desperate for company. Except maybe Chase; we're losing Chase. His personality is coming apart. Anyway, they'll *want* to talk, if you handle it right."

The unit was separated from the hospital by a locked security door; Hart pushed a call button, a monitor looked at them, and the door lock released. "They monitor us from the cage," Hart grunted.

"How did Charlie get down here, with this door?" Sloan asked.

"Most of the inmates have duties. Charlie worked as a janitor," Hart said. "He was suited for it. He could lean on a broom with the best of them."

. . .

TWENTY CELLS LINED the hallway, ten on each side. The walls were steel, with a steel door to one side and a barred window inset in the wall. A flat fluorescent light shone from each window, like a line of exhibits in a museum. They could hear inmates talking back and forth as they went in, and could see silhouettes in most of the windows. Hart called, "Temporary shutdown," and groans and shouts rang along the hall. Hart punched a code into a wall phone, another camera looked at them, and Hart waved at it. Heavy plastic panels slid down across the windows.

"They can't talk with the windows down," Hart said. With the windows shut, they could still hear a few of the inmates shouting.

"Didn't seem to shut them down," Sloan said.

"Yeah, they can still hear each other, but they have to yell. Can't keep it up," Hart said. "If you keep your voice down when you're talking, the rest of them won't be able to hear you."

THE CELLS WERE NOT LARGE, but they were more spacious than typical prison cells. Each was equipped with a bed, a sink, a toilet, a chair, a desk, all bolted to the floor; fixed lights overhead, and a two-by-three-foot steel dining table that folded down from the wall. A television was built into a wall and covered with security glass; two glass-covered ports on opposite sides of the cell showed video camera lenses.

Of the twenty cells, fifteen or sixteen had men in them.

CARL TAYLOR WAS A TALL MAN, thin, square shouldered, with high cheekbones, pale blue eyes, and closely cropped hair; he looked like a retired air force major. He was neatly dressed in jeans, a T-shirt, and plastic slip-on shoes. He sat at the desk, reading a Bible. He looked odd, Lucas thought, and it took him a moment to put his finger on the oddness. Then he had it: Taylor looked rugged, trim, outdoorsy—but his skin was bone white from a lack of sunlight.

He was waiting for them: Lucas could sense it. He was too studied in his disregard to be really engaged with the Book. Hart glanced inside the cell, then pushed a metal plate six feet away from the cell window. The outer glass window slid halfway back. "Carl . . . ," Hart said.

Taylor turned, raised his eyebrows, as if he were a little surprised to see them.

"Dr. Hart." His forehead wrinkled. "I've been thinking about it, since Dr. Ross called. I'm no longer convinced I should talk to these gentlemen."

"It's up to you," Lucas said. "If you don't want to chat, we'll go away."

Taylor stood and stretched. "I think we might negotiate some ground rules."

"There aren't any ground rules," Lucas said. "We ask questions, you answer. If you don't want to answer, we go away. It's that easy."

Taylor stood up and lounged over to the window. "Nothing's that easy. I—"

"This is exactly that easy," Lucas said.

Sloan held up a hand to Lucas, then looked at Taylor: "My friend is in a hurry, because we've got a real mess on our hands," Sloan said. "We need your help with this, and we hope you can give it to us. But we're not here for chitchat. We're here on a mission."

"I see," Taylor said. He was gravely polite. He stood behind the glass, with no place to sit that was close enough to talk comfortably. He put his hands in his jeans pockets, shrugged, and said, "I'm happy to do what I can—I understand from Dr. Ross that I will receive some slight benefits."

Hart said, "The dinner extras, the movies. That's all he was willing to give."

Taylor nodded: "What can I do for you, then?"

. . .

SLOAN ASKED, "Have you heard about the killings of Angela Larson and Adam Rice and his son?"

"Yes." And now, weirdly, he smiled, a thin smile. While he'd seemed neat and trim and military in his bearing, his teeth were yellowed and ratlike against his pale lips. Lucas felt a crawling sensation along his arms; not fear, just the creeps. "You've got a real bad boy there, as much as I could tell from the TV."

"Do you think Charlie Pope could do that?" Lucas asked.

Taylor looked up at the ceiling, then back, and said, "You know, Dr. Grant asked the same thing. I've been thinking about it. To me, it sounds too . . . artistic . . . for Charlie. Charlie was a simple fool. He killed a couple of girls because he didn't want to get caught for sexing them. He couldn't figure out any other way to do it. To shut them up."

"There's been a suggestion that he might be taking after one of you guys, one of . . ."

Sloan looked at Hart, who grunted, "The Big Three."

Taylor's eyebrows went up: "Is that the case? Well, well." He cocked his head, showed his ratlike teeth again. "Tell me about this Larson girl. I understand he punished her."

"He goddamn near beat her to death," Sloan grated.

"But not with his fists," Taylor said, looking concerned.

"With some kind of whip," Lucas said.

"How'd he whip her?" More concern. "I mean, on her back, or her legs . . ."

"All over," Lucas said, incautiously.

Hart said, "Hey, huh . . . ," and Taylor's tongue touched his upper lip and his eyes glowed through the glass and he stepped closer to the window and asked, "How about on the titties? Did he get her titties?"

Lucas involuntarily took a step back, and Sloan said, "Fuck you."

Taylor reached out with the flat of his hand and screamed, "BIGGIE. BIGGIE. OUR BOY WHIPPED HER ON THE TITTIES, HE GOT HER ON THE TITTIES . . ."

"Jesus Christ," Lucas said, and Hart slapped the plate that pushed the glass up; inmates were screaming up and down the hall, wanting to know what Taylor had said, or screaming disapproval. Taylor now pressed against the window, banging on it with the flat of his hand. "Did he eat that cock? Hey, did he eat that cock? Hey, he did, didn't he? HEY, BIGGIE, HE ATE THE COCK . . ."

And from down the hallway, more window slapping, and a high whinnying laugh. "That'd be Biggie," Hart said. Hart's eyes looked frightened.

Taylor had gone berserk, now pounding on the window with both hands. "BIGGIE . . ."

"You want to talk to Biggie?"

"I want to look at him, but I don't think there'd be much point in talking," Lucas said. Sloan was white-faced. Lucas had to suppress an urge to run.

"They did it to him," Sloan said to Lucas. "They wound him up like a fuckin' toy and sent him out there to kill people."

BIGGIE LIGHTER WAS STANDING at his window, a wanna-be fat man, skinny from years of hospital meals, pale as the moon, with round lazy eyes that sparked hatred out at them. His eyes flicked over Lucas and fixed on Sloan: "I know you!" he shouted through the raised glass. "I know you!"

"Want me to drop the glass?" Hart asked.

Lucas shook his head. "He can hear me . . ." He looked at Lighter. "Did you send Charlie out to kill people?" Down the hall, Taylor was still slapping the glass, and two or three other inmates had started again.

"You'd like to know, but you can go fuck yourself," Lighter said, not taking his eyes off Sloan. To Sloan: "You were the guy who came to my house and talked to my mother while I was gone."

Sloan nodded. "How's Mom?"

"The old bitch is dead," Lighter said. "Good riddance. I thought maybe you were dead, too. If I knew you'd come here, I would have told Charlie to carve your name around this Rice guy's asshole. A big Sloan right around his asshole while he was going in and out. That'd be pretty good, huh? One asshole for another asshole . . ." And now he reached out and slapped the glass.

"Can you . . ."

"I can't fuckin' anything," Lighter said, eyes snapping over to Lucas. "Get the fuck away from me. I want a lawyer." Back to Sloan: "I'd like an hour with you."

Sloan stepped close to the glass: "I wish I could give it to you. I wish I could get one fuckin' minute alone with you. I'd put a fuckin' bullet right in your fuckin' brain, and then I'd spit on your fuckin' body."

Lighter recoiled, looked at Hart: "He can't talk to me like that. I want a fuckin' lawyer . . ."

"Ah, for Christ's sake," Hart said.

Lucas: "Let's go. We're done."

As they got to the outer door, Hart slowed and looked back down the hall and said, "Goddamnit."

"What?"

"They call them the Big Three. You didn't even talk to Chase—but Charlie did."

Lucas looked back down the hall: the glass slapping continued and Taylor was still screaming, but the screams had gone incoherent and his voice was beginning to break. They sounded, Lucas thought, not unlike what happens when a kid throws a rock in a monkey cage. "Two minutes," Lucas said, stepping back down the hall. "Let's give him two minutes."

. . .

LAWRENCE W. CHASE was so thin he might be anorexic. His cheek bones pushed through his skin, his hands trembled. "Don't call me Larry, 'cause that's not my name. My name is Lawrence."

Sloan: "Okay, Lawrence."

Chase said through the open glass, "You gotta get me out of here."

"Can't do that," Sloan said.

And Chase started to weep as he stood in front of the window. "I can't stay here. I ask them to put me at Stillwater, but they won't do it. I ask them to let me work, but they won't do that, either. I ask them to kill me, and they say they can't. They won't even let me kill myself. There are cameras in my room."

Hart said, "We don't want you to hurt yourself, Lawrence. Maybe you'll get better."

"There's nothing *wrong* with me, except that I'm in here."

"You killed nine people, Lawrence," Hart said. "Nine that we know of. You hunted them down and shot them."

"They were . . . I was being . . . Paleolithic. I was just . . ."

"Lawrence . . ."

"I don't want to argue," he whimpered. "I just want you to kill me clean." To Lucas: "I haven't seen the sky in two years."

"Shouldn't have killed those people."

"I had to; don't you see? You get out there, the Paleolithic rises up in you. Man is a hunter. I hunted. You must know that—you're a cop. You hunt people."

Lucas had to look away: "If you can help us, maybe you could look out the window."

A sly look crossed over Chase's face: "Biggie said he was going to get extra desserts all week. Could I look out the window *and* get extra desserts?"

Hart nodded. "But that's all. We'll take you down tomorrow where you can see out."

Chase started to weep again. His eyes reddened as the tears leaked out, and against his pale skin they looked like the eyes on a white rabbit, all pink and shot through with blood. He finally wiped his eyes with the heels of his hands and said, "I don't know what I can tell you, but I'll help if I can."

"Did you talk to Charlie Pope about kidnapping women? About keeping them?" Lucas asked.

And suddenly, everything about Chase seemed to tighten, and his face flooded with color. "I told him what they said I done. I didn't ask him to do it."

"What do you think about it . . . what he's doing?"

"Taylor says he's doing the Lord's work."

"But Taylor's full of shit," Lucas snapped. "What we want to know is this: Did you talk to Pope specifically about what you did? Exactly what you did? The details? Or did you just talk . . ."

"He pretty much knew all about it," Chase said. "That kind of thing comes out. They say if you don't get it out in the open, you can't deal with it. That's what they say. I don't remember what they said I did . . ." He scratched his head and then began leaking tears again. "I gotta get out of here."

"Did you tell him how to hide out? Do you have any idea where he might go? What he was thinking about?"

"No. He wanted to get a job in meatpacking. He said there was good money in it. He said he almost got a job at Hormel, but they turned him down because some old bitch didn't like him." His lips picked up a little curl, not quite a smile, something with a sneer in it. "I bet she . . ."

Then, just as quickly, the expression flicked away. "But where he went, I don't know. He never seemed to think about it too much. He just wanted to get out. He was desperate. They used to let him look out the window, though. He could see the driveway and people coming and going."

"Did he talk about razors? Did he talk about whipping women? Did he talk about hunting them?" Lucas asked.

"He didn't talk about it so much." Chase started squirming, wrapping his ankles together, like he had to pee, and again, Lucas had to look away. "But he *listened* to it. He liked to hear about it."

"I think you might be projecting, Lawrence," Hart said.

"I'm *not* projecting," Chase said. "He used to listen real close."

They talked for a few more minutes, but Chase had nothing more. Lucas finally shrugged and said to Hart, "Let's go."

THEY STEPPED AWAY, and then Sloan stepped back to the window and asked, "Hey, Larry . . . what'd Charlie Pope do to the woman from Hormel?"

Chase turned at the "Larry," to protest—but when the question got to him, he tried to rearrange his face into an expression of puzzlement, like a child trying to come up with another reason why his hand was in the cookie jar.

"Why . . . why . . ."

"What was her name, Larry?" Sloan asked lazily. "I mean, we're gonna find out. If you don't tell us, they could give you another twenty years for being an accomplice after the fact. You'd *never* see the sun."

"I didn't have nothing to do with it, I don't know . . ."

"Larry, what the fuck was her name?" Sloan asked. A little steel now.

Chase looked into himself for a moment, and Sloan said, "Lawrence?" and tears came to Chase's eyes again and he sobbed, then said, "I don't know, but her first name might have been Louise."

"When was this?"

Chase couldn't look at them. "Maybe, maybe in ninety-five."

"Sonofabitch," Hart said, peering at Sloan. "Did he just tell you what I think he did? Did you just solve a murder?"

HART WALKED THEM BRISKLY back through the hospital to the administrator's office and told Ross, "We had something come up with Chase."

He explained in a few words, and Ross said to Sloan, "My assistant has all those numbers. Would you like her to call around down there? We could probably get you something before you're back home."

"Sure," Lucas said. "And we need an address for this Mike West guy, the guy Pope used to hang with."

They got the address, and on the way out, the administrator said to Sloan, "This thing you did with Chase . . . You have a nice talent. Maybe you should have been a psychologist."

Sloan almost blushed. "Ah, it might all be bullshit."

IT WASN'T.

Ross called back when they were halfway to Minneapolis. Sloan took the call on his cell phone, listened for a minute, and then said, "Let me take that down." He took a pad and a mechanical pencil from his coat pocket, jotted down a name and number.

"Could you call him back? Tell him I'll get in touch in an hour or so—when I'm back in the office. Okay."

He punched off and said to Lucas, "A woman named Louise Samples, who worked in personnel at Hormel in the city of Albert Lea, was killed in her house in November of ninety-five. The cops say it looked like she walked in on a burglar. He hit her with a hammer and then raped her at least a couple of times, once anally. She was probably dead for most of it. They never got a break on the case."

A car in front of them suddenly slowed for a left turn, and Lucas swung around it, a quick brake and a quicker acceleration. Then he looked at Sloan: "How the fuck can you talk about quitting when you pull off something like this?"

"For all the good it did Louise Samples or anybody else," Sloan said.

"Man, you gotta take a couple of aspirin and lie down," Lucas said. "I'm really startin' to think you're losing it."

"That's what I've been telling you, dickweed," Sloan said. He looked out the window as they crossed the river: "When I get my bar, I'll want your list of songs. I'll put them on the jukebox."

"No Beatles."

"No Beatles. But how about a couple of Tom Joneses? 'Green Green Grass' or something."

"Sloan—you *gotta* get help."

JUST OFF THE SOUTHWEST corner of the metro area, Lucas called his secretary and was told that he had two dozen phone messages, one each from Rose Marie Roux, the commissioner of public safety; from John McCord, the superintendent of the BCA; and from Neil Mitford, the governor's top political operator. The rest came from various members of the media asking for interviews and updates.

He answered the first three immediately: all three wanted updates, and he gave them a quick recap of the trip to St. John's.

To McCord: "I got an address for a schizophrenic guy, a Mike West, that we need to talk to. He's an old pal of Pope's."

"Shrake and Jenkins are sitting on their asses; I could send them," McCord said.

"Okay, but for Christ's sake, tell them to take it easy."

"We got a charge?"

"Just hold him for questioning; have them bring him in, we'll get him a public defender if we need to, and see if we can work something out," Lucas said. "But if we do find him just sitting around, then maybe he's clear. If he's gone, if he's skipped, that'd be a little more interesting."

"I'll send them over," McCord said.

"Tell them to leave their goddamn saps in their car, okay?"

"I don't know about any saps," McCord said. "Saps would be against policy."

"Then tell them to follow policy."

"All right. If you need anything else, let me know."

"Mitford and Rose Marie called, and I told them I'd be doing another press conference this afternoon," Lucas said. "Same deal as yesterday, except we've probably made Pope for another murder."

He explained, briefly, and McCord said, "Put Sloan in the press conference. Spread the publicity around. We'll make some points with Minneapolis."

The publicity cut two ways: by putting Sloan out front, some of the glory was reflected onto the Minneapolis police department; and if they didn't catch Pope fairly quickly, some of the blame, as well.

"Press conferences are like fuckin' the neighbor lady," Sloan said, as he dialed up his own chief after Lucas finished with McCord. "Feels good at the time, but you're gonna have to pay in the end."

THEY GOT BACK AT three-forty-five and went to Lucas's office, where Carol had piled up everything that had come in from Albert Lea and the Freeborn County sheriff on the Louise Samples killing. They read through it, looked at everything else they had on Pope, and then walked down to the conference room.

The press conference itself was the same routine: scraping chairs, posturing TV people. Ruffe Ignace was in the front row, but his story that morning had been anticipated by the TV news the night before. He was now behind in the cycle, had lost his edge, and wasn't happy: he snapped questions out at Lucas, thrashing around, looking for something, anything. Lucas was polite.

Lucas described how Sloan picked up on the Samples killing, outlined what had happened, and what they believed. The Albert Lea cops were going through the retained evidence from the case, he said, looking for anything that might have a dab of Pope's DNA on it. When he finished, the reporters gave Sloan an only moderately sarcastic round of applause. That was a first, ever.

Sloan said, "It really was nothing much," but Lucas said, "It was amazing."

WHEN THEY WERE FINISHED, they headed back to Lucas's office. Halfway back, they bumped into Shrake and Jenkins, the BCA's designated thugs, who'd been sent to Mike West's designated halfway house to pick him up.

Jenkins was a square man who smoked too much; Shrake was tall and thin, and smoked more than Jenkins. They both wore sharp, shiny European-cut suits that had fallen off a truck somewhere; Shrake referred to them as quasi-Armanis.

"Fuckin' waste of time," Jenkins said. He habitually walked around with his hands in the pockets of his jacket, so all his jackets had stretched-out pockets. "The guy's been gone for a month. We talked to the administrator over there. He said West's meds were fogging him up so bad that he couldn't stand them. The house rules are that you have to take your meds—and since he couldn't stand doing that, he took off."

"Any idea where he might be?"

"Doc says he's probably on the street. His parents live in Arizona—they're retired. We could check with the Scottsdale cops."

"Do that," Lucas said. "See if they could have somebody stop by. And get a bulletin out to the local uniforms, get them to poke around. We really would like to talk to him."

AT LUCAS'S OFFICE, they found a note from Carol: "Dr. Grant called from St. John's and asked that you call him back. He's on his cell phone."

"Grant was the shrink," Sloan said.

Lucas called him, and Grant answered on the third ring: "Listen, I don't know if you're interested, but I pulled out all my session tapes on Pope," he said. "There're five or six hours of material. Most of it was just talk. How was he feeling, what was he doing. But there's an hour or so when he's talking about getting out, what he'll do, about the women he attacked. I edited down to the good stuff, an hour or so."

"I need that," Lucas said. "Can you messenger it up?"

"I'm coming up there tonight. If you want to tell somebody that I'm coming, I could drop it at the BCA office . . . it's just a regular cassette tape."

"Where're you going in the Cities?"

"Downtown Minneapolis."

"Why don't you drop it at my house? That'll save you a half hour, and it's easy to find."

LUCAS WENT HOME, ate a steak-and-onions low-carb, low-fat, low-protein microwave meal that had apparently been made purely from coal tars and goobers, perhaps seasoned with industrial phlegm; watched the television news; thought his suit looked pretty good but that his face looked too harsh—maybe from the diet? He looked at himself in the mirror, wondered if he should use a moisturizer—

Weather's solution for anything that didn't involve bleeding or broken bones—but was embarrassed by the thought and eventually went out to the garage.

When Grant showed up, a few minutes before eight o'clock, Lucas was lying in the driveway, his head under the ass end of his Lexus, trying to rewire the trailer harness. The harness hung in an exposed position and had gotten trashed while he was dragging a boat around Wisconsin. More fine auto design.

"You under there? Lucas?"

"Yeah." Lucas turned his head, saw a pair of cordovan loafers, and pushed himself out. "Just a minute. I almost got it."

He didn't, though. After fooling with the inadequate male-female connection for a moment, he decided he'd have to readjust the wiring distance between a support bracket and the connection. That would take more light than he had. He pushed himself out again and got to his feet.

"How's it going?" Lucas hadn't paid special attention to Grant at St. John's, but now he looked him over. He was about Lucas's height, but maybe fifteen pounds lighter, with edges. He didn't look like he worked out, but there was a feral toughness about him.

Grant fished a tape cassette out of his jacket pocket and handed it to Lucas. "There's not really anything *hard* on it; it just sort of shows you what he thinks about."

"That could help," Lucas said. "I'll listen to it tonight . . . I hope you didn't come all the way up to bring the tape."

"No, there's not much to do down by St. John's, so I hang out up here. I'm too old to chase college girls."

"Especially Lutheran college girls," Lucas said.

"Especially intellectual Lutheran college girls," Grant said. He drifted over toward the Porsche, which was crouched in the garage. "Of course, if I had a car like this . . . this is the wide one, right? Wide enough for Lutheran girls?"

"I'm a happily married man," Lucas said.

"Yeah . . . And if you happened to be unhappily married, I can tell you that Karen Beloit liked your looks. She was sort of bubbling about you."

Lucas laughed and said, "*Hmm* . . . Listen, you want a beer? What do you think about the Big Three? Is that just bullshit, or did they really do something with Pope?"

LUCAS GOT A COUPLE of beers and a step stool for Grant to sit on, and while Lucas hauled some work lights and tools out to the truck, Grant unwound a tangled coil of orange extension cord, plugged it into a garage outlet, and trailed it out to the truck. Lucas crawled back underneath and went to work on the wiring harness, while Grant sat on the stool, handed him tools, and they talked about Pope, the Big Three, and Mike West.

"I was pretty skeptical about Charlie, when I heard about it. But then, I heard about the reaction from Lighter and Taylor, and I thought—okay, I'll buy that, somewhat. But Charlie might tend to drift. They could wind him up and send him out, but after a while, he'd sorta . . . run down. So I wouldn't be surprised if there's somebody else involved. A battery kind of guy. Somebody to provide the energy."

"Mike West?"

"I don't know. I mean, I really don't know—I didn't have much contact with him."

"But two guys makes sense to you."

"More than Charlie by himself. You need something or somebody to provide the intensity. If you had that, I don't doubt Charlie would go along. These murder scenes you laid out for us . . . I can see Charlie enjoying all that."

"Hand me that small Phillips." Grant handed him the screwdriver, and Lucas asked, "But if Pope is doing all of this, with or without the West guy, and if one or both of them were programmed by the Big

Three . . . why did they wait so long before they started killing? You think they'd come right out, when the programming was the strongest . . ."

"I don't know. To get organized? To locate targets?"

"Mmm."

"We don't even know if they were programmed. *That* might all be bullshit," Grant said.

Lucas tightened the last screw and pushed out from under the car. "That's not bullshit. They did *something*. You had to be there to see it—those motherfuckers are involved," Lucas said.

THEY PUT THE TOOLS AWAY, and Grant handed Lucas his empty beer bottle. "Give me your bottom line," Lucas said.

Grant shrugged: "Something's wrong. Something stinks. For one thing, you should have caught Charlie by now. He's the kind of guy who would flee on a Greyhound bus."

"You worry me."

"I'm not a cop, so I don't know how you work, or how, *mmm*, efficacious your methods are. But if I were you, I'd at least consider the possibility that Charlie Pope is working with somebody. That there's a second man out there."

"A second man."

"Or woman." Grant touched his chin with steepled fingers, as though he'd surprised himself with the thought. "A *woman*. A woman adds a sexual element to the equation."

"You think . . ."

Grant said, "Listen, Lucas: the right woman could do anything with Charlie Pope that she wanted. Anything."

LATE THAT NIGHT, Lucas sat in a pool of light in his study, eyes closed, listening to the tape Grant had brought with him. Grant had a sly interviewing technique. He would profess ignorance of some point, or some event, or make an assertion that was clearly faulty, and then he'd let Charlie Pope straighten him out.

Charlie Pope said:

". . . They tease you all the time. They drive you out of your mind. I used to try to take care of myself, I'd get all cleaned up and shaved and put on new shoes, but nobody would ever go out with me. A man's gotta have some sex, and what was I supposed to do? Was I supposed to go hire a hooker somewhere? That's how you get AIDS, all the hookers in the Cities got AIDS or some other disease.

". . . It's like advertising, they wear these skirts and these tight pants and these see-through blouses and show off their legs and their asses and their tits, and then what? They don't think a guy is gonna want what they're advertising?

". . . I whacked her around a little bit but I didn't plan to kill her or nothing, that's just what the cops said. I mean, I did fuck her, but I was just trying to hold her down on her chest and the cops said it was around her neck. I didn't want her to scream . . .

". . . I tried to talk to her, and she didn't want to talk to me. I mean, look at me. I'm not a good-looking guy. When I was a kid I'd look in the mirror and try to make myself good-looking. I'd think, well, you're not *bad*-looking, there are lots of guys not as lucky as you were, but I always knew that I'm not a good-looking guy. I mean, not like Tom Cruise or anybody. I got okay teeth, though, and that's important . . .

"I thought maybe a truck would be a big idea, and maybe it would be. I got an eighty-six Ford F-one-fifty. It'd been wrecked but it'd been fixed, a cherry red color, best truck I ever had. I was working at an assembly plant building computer cases and making good money, six bucks an hour, nine bucks on overtime, pretty good job but it was all piecework, some weeks I'd work six days and some weeks I'd work two days . . .

". . . Women, you know, they're the big shots in the courts now, judges and lawyers and everything, they don't know about blue balls, because they don't have them. So how can they know about it? They don't know that you're *forced* to get some sex. Have you ever tried coke? I tried some once and the thing I thought was, it's like getting the blue balls. It makes your head different. I'd get me some sex and then my head would be all right, but if I'd go awhile without it, and get the blue balls, my head would get all weird and I'd have to get some.

". . . Okay, I paid a couple of times, but it was just a couple girls in Rochester that you sorta knew were okay. What's the difference between that and maybe taking some chick out to TGI Fridays and maybe blowing twenty dollars, just to try to get some, and then you don't get it. Maybe if you know a couple of girls it's better just to give them the money . . .

"I wouldn't ever go with a colored girl, their pimp'd catch you and he'd cut your nuts off. I seen some good-looking colored girls, though. If I thought, you know, they could go for me, and if they didn't have a boyfriend around . . .

". . . I don't remember strangling her. I don't think I did. I think the cops just made it up. I just whacked her a few times. I wouldn't do it again, you know, unless it was self-defense or something. Okay, so it probably wouldn't be self-defense, but some of these chicks, they can really fight . . ."

LUCAS LISTENED FOR ALMOST two hours, running the tape back and forth, made a few notes. Charlie Pope was afraid of big cities, he thought, and blacks and Latinos and Hmong. If he were hiding someplace, it would be in a small city or a town.

He would be looking for sex. The shrinks had been emphatic about it, and Lucas was convinced: sex seemed to soak through Charlie Pope's view of the world. A note should be sent to all the law-enforcement agencies to warn the local hookers against him, and to circulate his photograph where hookers would see it. In most smaller cities, that would be one or two bars.

Pope would definitely go for a car, Lucas thought, or most likely, a truck, and almost certainly already had one. Unless . . .

Could he be hiding out in the countryside? Literally living in the woods? Did he have that capability? He'd been working as a garbage-man and Lucas had known a couple of guys who'd lived on dumps, eating garbage and furnishing their hand-built hovels with whatever they could find on the piles of trash.

If not that, he must be disguised. At a minimum, he would have grown a beard. But what could he be doing? Stealing stuff to live on? How about just one holdup, where he scored a couple of grand, and continued to live on that? Lucas made a note to have the co-op guys check muggings and robberies by bearded men who fit Charlie's physical form.

WHEN HE FINISHED with the tapes, Lucas thought he knew Charlie Pope. But where was he? A Charlie Pope didn't hide well. Unless . . .

A second man or woman was hiding him. Was running him.

Or, maybe after the second killing he'd run so far that the news hadn't caught up to him. Maybe he was working as a janitor or a garbageman or an assembly worker in backwoods Florida.

That was possible, but Charlie was rooted in the Upper Midwest. He was nuts, but he was a small-town boy. He was afraid to go to big places, afraid of the people he might meet. And he didn't seem to be smart enough, or to have the will, to ignore those fears.

A village idiot.

Lucas sighed and put down his pen. A second man—or a woman. Something to lose sleep over.

10

RUFFE IGNACE WAS WORKING LATE. Not much to do, feet up on his desk, waiting for the paper to be put to bed. His latest triumph, the serial-killer story, cut no ice with the other reporters when it came to picking a replacement for the regular night man, when the night man went on vacation.

That occasion always started a newsroom dogfight. Ignace had been peremptorily ordered to take the job: "You have," his team leader said, "the requisite skills. What am I supposed to do, have the music critic write about fires on deadline? And you're single and you're not dating anyone."

"Is that why you asked me yesterday if I was dating anyone?" Ignace asked.

A muscle twitched in the team leader's jaw. "Well . . . yeah."

"You treacherous fuck."

The "treacherous fuck" line didn't do him any good, so here he was, eleven o'clock at night, waiting. He was the "just in case" guy. Just in case the president was assassinated, just in case terrorists took out the Target Center, just in case one of the Vikings was busted on cocaine charges. Nobody really wanted to tear up the paper when it was this close to the press turn.

SO IGNACE HAD HIS FEET UP, reading the *Idiot's Guide to Etiquette,* which he'd lifted off another reporter's desk. When the phone rang, he assumed it was the desk asking for a rewrite.

A voice in a harsh, rustling whisper inquired, "Is this, I don't know how you pronounce it, I apologize, Rough Ignacy?"

"That would be Roo-fay Ig-Nas," Ignace said. "Who is this?"

"This is old Charlie Pope, calling to thank you for the write-up."

Now Ignace sat up. "Who is this really? Is this Jack, you shithead?"

A whispery laugh: "Nope, it's me, old Charlie Pope."

Ignace had a notebook and a pencil out: "Okay, old Charlie Pope. Tell me something about the murders that wasn't in the newspaper."

A pause, then, "Wasn't in the newspapers that I cut Adam Rice's dick off."

"What?"

"I cut his dick off," the whisperer said. "You didn't put that in the paper."

"The cops haven't said anything about that—I don't believe it happened."

"Believe it, Ruffe." The whisper turned cold, ragged.

"We didn't say what you killed the kid with. What'd you kill him with?"

"He come down the stairs in his pajamas. I didn't even know he was up there until he started running. There was an aluminum baseball bat in the corner and when the kid went running into the kitchen, I picked up the bat and caught him right by the door and whacked him. Then I went back and finished with Daddy."

The ring of truth pushed Ignace back in his chair. "With a baseball bat."

"That's right. When I got outside, I wiped it down with Adam Rice's undershirt, so it wouldn't have no fingerprints on it. That's before I knew they were gonna pick up on me so fast. I threw it into that field of whatever-it-is off to the side of the farmhouse. Right by the driveway going up the hill."

"I'm going to check that."

"Check your ass off, Ruffe. By the way, you got something wrong in your story. I didn't have a straight razor to cut their throats. I used a box cutter. But. As soon as you wrote about the straight razor, I got a hardon. I said, I gotta get me one of those things. Now I got one. Got an old leather strop to sharpen it up, and I'm learning how to do that. Next guy I do, I'm gonna do with the razor."

"Jesus Christ." Ignace swallowed.

"He's not here. It's just me, old Charlie Pope."

"You gotta . . . let me, Jesus Christ." Ignace was flabbergasted. He'd never been at a loss for words, and now he floundering. "Are you . . . why did you . . . uh . . ."

"What do I want?"

"Uh, yeah."

"Mostly I just want to talk to somebody. I liked your story. And I tell you, I got this goddamn woman is driving me crazy. I don't know what to do about her. I don't want her to stop, but every time she starts to howl, I see blood. I want to take her, but . . . then she'd be gone. I like it when she starts to howl. I mean, she does me up like nothin' I've ever felt before. You know what I mean?"

"Not exactly." Ignace was scribbling like mad, taking it all down in shorthand. "Are you saying that you can't decide what you're going to do? I mean, Jesus Christ, don't hurt her. I mean how can you . . ."

"How can I do it?" The whispery laugh again, like a ripple of paper: "Because it feels good. I just ain't right, Ruffe. My head is fucked up. I know that. Everybody knows that. But what everybody doesn't know is how good it feels . . ."

"Jeez . . ."

"Hey, you ever see any of those terrorist guys on TV? Cuttin' somebody's head off or something? Everybody says it's because they're Moslems or something. I know better—I can tell by looking at them. They like it. They're having a good old time. That's what gets their rocks off—it ain't Mohammed. They like killing people. They're like me. They're like lots of us. And if you look at it that way, how many people are like us, it's really pretty normal."

Ignace was calculating now. Didn't Jimmy Breslin have something to do with the .44-caliber killer, the Son of Sam? Didn't he get more famous because of it? "Look: if you come in, I can cut a deal for you. I could cut a deal that would get you nothing but treatment . . ."

"Uh-uh. I ain't coming in, Ruffe. Never. I had treatment, remember? That fuckin' treatment . . . anyway, ain't you gonna ask me what I'm gonna do next?"

"Okay. What're you gonna do next?" Ignace was taking it all down in Gregg, word for word, trying to get it precisely right, every *ain't* and *nothin'* with a dropped *g*.

"I'm gonna hunt somebody down. Gonna take her out someplace, I'm gonna give her a head start, and then I'm gonna hunt her down. A woman this time. Take her out to the Boundary Waters, strip her out of her clothes, then turn her loose and watch her run. Give her a hope. A forlorn hope."

Ignace could feel the skin tighten at the back of his neck: there was no longer a question in his mind—he was talking to Charlie Pope.

"But what's all this bulls . . . What's all this stuff about hunting people? I mean, I'm sorry, but . . ."

"That's nuts." The whispery laugh again: "Of course it is. I *am* nuts. You seem to have a hard time getting over that. Write it down: N-U-T-S. The state says I'm nuts, and I'm nuts. What'd they think I was gonna do, lift garbage cans all the rest of my life? Fuck 'em." He laughed then, his ragged voice sounding as though a piece of paper were being torn through.

Ignace was writing frantically. "How did this get started? You never . . . I mean, your reputation wasn't for this kind of thing."

"There were some Gods Down the Hall from me, at St. John's. They made me see how much like God you can get to be, if you got the balls to go out and do it. I talked to them and they talked to me, and I can still hear their voices. They were right: it's just like being God."

"How are you staying ahead of the police?" A woman from the desk walked up, a piece of paper in her hand, and Ignace waved her away. She said, "We need . . ."

Ignace said into the phone, "Hang on just a second," turned to the woman and barked, "Go away. Go away."

She persisted. "We need . . ."

"Go the fuck away," he shouted and, as she stepped backward, he went to the phone again. "I'm back."

"Little trouble there, Ruffe?"

"I'm the night guy; they want me to do some horseshit. Listen, how'd you know I'd be here?"

"I didn't. I just kept calling your line every couple hours, until you answered."

"I can't hear you very well . . ."

Louder: "I said, I kept calling your line every couple of hours . . . that damn Rice tried to kick me, caught me one in the throat, I think he fucked me up. I can't hardly eat nothin'."

"You're hurt?"

"Yeah, I'm hurt. Nobody said this was gonna be easy," the whisperer said. "You can't believe the shit I go through. I gotta plan, I gotta find the right person. I'm already watching two or three of these chicks, now

I gotta decide which one to take. There are a lot of angles to figure out. You know, how much will they fight, will there be anybody around who might jump in to help them, maybe they got a gun, there's all kinds of shit to figure out. Makes my head hurt. Hard work. But I'm gonna do it soon. Maybe tomorrow, maybe the next day."

"What do you . . ."

"I gotta go. I can see a cop car on the next street. I don't want him looking at me. Maybe I'll call again, after I do the next one."

"Wait, wait. If you'd like to talk to a doctor, or a lawyer . . ."

The whispery laughter, then, "Too late for that. But I do got one more thing for you, a message for the cops. *I ain't gonna quit.* I'm gonna do twenty or thirty of them if I can. If they catch me, they better be ready for a fight, because I got me some guns and I know how to use them. They fucked with me all my life. Now I'm gonna fuck with everybody. I'm not going back to St. John's. I'm not coming in alive."

Click.

IGNACE PUSHED BACK from his desk, staring at the phone and his steno pad. A guy from the desk was coming his way, trying to assemble some authority, trailed by the woman Ignace had chased off: "Holy shit," Ignace said. "Holy shit!"

SLOAN AND HIS WIFE were in bed. Sloan had come down with a bug, and his sinuses felt like overinflated basketballs; his wife was asleep, but Sloan was rolling around restlessly, fighting to breathe, when the phone rang. His wife said, "What?" and groaned. The phone never rang at that time of night unless it was trouble: Sloan rolled over and picked it up. "Hello?"

"Sloan, this is Ruffe Ignace. Charlie Pope just called me."

"What?" Cobwebs.

"Charlie Pope just called me. I need you to call Davenport and have him call me back—I assume you don't have jurisdiction in the Mankato kill."

Sloan recognized Ignace's voice. "Is this a joke?"

"This is no fuckin' joke." Ignace was shouting into the phone. "I need to talk to Davenport right now or we're just gonna put this story in the paper raw and you can read it tomorrow morning when you get up."

SLOAN WOKE UP LUCAS. "Give him my number," Lucas said. Then he lay facedown on Weather's side of the bed, in the faint lingering odor of her perfume, until the phone rang again: "This is Davenport."

"Did the killer cut off Adam Rice's penis?" Ignace asked without preamble.

"What?"

"The guy who called me—I assume Sloan told you I was called by a guy who said he was Charlie Pope—the guy said he cut off Adam Rice's penis," Ignace said.

"Ah, man, are you going to use that?"

"That's negotiable—but did he? 'Cause if he did and if this was really Pope, I have some other information."

"What information?"

"Did he cut off Adam Rice's penis?"

Lucas thought for a moment, then said, "If you use that specific information, I will find some way to fuck you up. That's not fair to any of the survivors."

"So I was talking to Charlie Pope."

"I don't know, but that information is accurate," Lucas said.

"All right. He said he killed the kid with an aluminum baseball bat, wiped it with Adam Rice's undershirt, and then threw the bat into a field next to the house. Is that possible?"

"I don't know. Of course, it's possible," Lucas said. "We'll look tomorrow morning . . . Listen, I need to know exactly what this guy told you."

"Then you can either come over here and I can give you a transcript, or I can read it to you . . . Hang on, hang on."

Lucas could hear the phone being fumbled, then a woman's voice said, "Lucas, this is Sharon White."

"Hey, Sharon."

"You better come over here. We don't want to use anything that would mess anybody up or interfere with the investigation, but we're going to run something, and I would like to discuss it with you. And Ruffe. If you can get here in like, fifteen or twenty minutes?"

"I'll meet somebody at your door in fifteen," Lucas said.

WHEN LUCAS TURNED the corner in downtown Minneapolis, Sloan was already standing in the street outside the *Star-Trib* building. Thin, gray, unshaven, with hair sticking sideways out over his ears, he looked like a bum; and his nose seemed to be swollen. Lucas dumped the Porsche behind Sloan's Chevy, put a cop-on-duty sign on the dashboard—they were both parked in a no-parking zone—and got out.

"Gotta be the guy," Sloan said. He held a handkerchief to his face and coughed into it. "Man. I'm sick."

"What happened?" Lucas leaned away from him.

"I don't know. I was fine at dinner, and now I'm all fucked up. I took four green Nyquils, and my nose keeps getting bigger."

"Well, Jesus Christ, don't sneeze on me."

A YOUNG MAN WAS STANDING behind the *Strib*'s front doors. When Lucas and Sloan walked up, he lifted an eyebrow, and Sloan held up a badge case. The young man pushed the door open and said, "They're waiting."

They followed him into an elevator, then down through the cluttered newsroom to a cluster of people standing and sitting around a desk where Ruffe Ignace sat behind a computer, typing.

Lucas recognized Sharon White, the executive editor, and Phil Stone, the paper's attorney. White nodded and said, "It's a problem," and Stone said, "You guys look like I feel."

"I was sleeping like a baby," Lucas said. "What're we doing?"

"Ruffe is putting together the maximum story that we have," White said. "You have no approval over it at all. We decide what goes in and what stays out. We're telling you what we have in advance so we don't . . . *mmm* . . . step on some aspect of the investigation."

Lucas looked at Stone, who smiled the way an attorney smiles: with his lips.

"Good of you," Lucas said. "Could we get Ruffe to give us a couple of printouts of what he has?"

Ignace looked at White, who nodded, and he hit a button on his keyboard. A printer started humming in the quiet background, and Ignace said, "Fifteen seconds." The young man who'd brought them up said, "I'll get them." He headed for the printer.

Lucas asked Ignace, "What time did the call come in?"

Ignace, pitching up his voice: "I think there's a real question of how much cooperation we owe you guys . . ."

Lucas put his hands in his pants pockets, sighed, and said, "Ruffe, I've sat around with newspaper guys for years having philosophical discussions about this kind of thing, and I'd be happy to talk to you, but we, all of us . . ." Lucas gestured to White and Stone ". . . have sort of worked out an understanding. You don't help me investigate, so you stay pure, but you don't fight me on what might help catch a criminal, if I'm going to get the information anyway. If I have to, I can take you in for questioning, we can get lawyers and judges working on it, we can get the paper all kinds of bad publicity and maybe sued by some future victim, and I'll get the information anyway and all you'll have done is delay things in favor of the asshole who's killing these people. Is that what you want to talk about?"

"He's not talking about that," Stone said genially.

"Yes, I was," Ignace said.

"No, you're not," Stone said. The young man came back with copies of the story printout, and Lucas and Sloan took them. Lucas scanned it, then said, "What time did the call come in?"

"A few minutes before eleven o'clock," White said. "We don't know the exact minute."

Lucas to Ignace: "Was it direct-dial or did it come in through the switchboard?"

"Probably switchboard," Ignace said, with a show of reluctance. "We're not listed individually."

Sloan said to Lucas, "I'll get it." He stepped away and took a cell phone out of his jacket pocket.

Stone frowned and asked, "What's wrong with Sloan?"

"I don't know, but I wouldn't shake hands," Lucas said. To Ignace: "He said he might call back?"

"That's what he said." Ignace had gotten past his pro-forma objections and was enjoying himself now. He said to White, "I think we should get something for all this cooperation. Some kind of access."

White lifted an eyebrow, and Lucas said, "We'll take care of you, one way or another. You know."

She nodded, and Lucas asked Ignace, "How did he sound? He's supposed to be sort of a shit kicker . . ."

"His voice was weird. He says Rice kicked him in the throat, he didn't say when or how . . . so he whispered. It all sounded like . . . something you'd see in a movie. Hoarse whisper."

"How about his language?"

"I took it down verbatim," Ignace said. He took his notebook off his desk, and Lucas saw that it was covered with shorthand. Despite himself, he was impressed—the kid had some tools. "You want me to read it, word for word?"

"We don't have much time here," White said, looking at her watch. "You got a problem with the story?"

"If you want to print the penis thing, that's up to you," Lucas said. "I think it's in bad taste. The usual formula is 'mutilated,' but I don't see why you'd want to put this in so Rice's mother can read it, after she has lost both her son and her grandson."

White said to Ignace, "Change it."

"Man . . ."

"We've got no time," White said. "Change it."

Ignace's hand rattled across the keyboard, then he asked Lucas, "Do you have an official comment?"

"You can say, 'Davenport said authorities will immediately begin investigating the *Star-Tribune* report and indicated that there are aspects of inside information in the phone call that make it possible or even likely that the caller was Charles Pope.' That work for you?"

"That works for me," Ignace said, taking it all down.

"You can add this," Lucas said. He dictated: "Davenport added that any woman who feels that she is under surveillance, or might have been, or who has seen anyone who resembles Charlie Pope, should call her local police department and report it. Even a weak feeling—it's better to be wrong than to be dead."

Ignace's keyboard rattled along, keeping pace with the statement. "Good," he muttered. "That's great."

Sloan called, "Lucas," and Lucas stepped over to him. "Rochester pay phone."

"Call the Rochester cops. Get them out on the street, make stops on any single males, on foot or in cars. Give them a description. Tell them to be careful, he's probably got a gun. Tell them right now. *Right now.*"

"I better put that in," Ignace said.

SLOAN WALKED OFF, working the cell phone, and Lucas asked Ignace to read his shorthand notes, and Ignace did. Lucas stopped him once or twice: "You say he said, 'He come down the stairs . . .' He didn't say, 'He came down the stairs . . .'"

"Just like I've got it," Ignace said. He trailed his finger farther down the page of Gregg script. "And here he says, 'wouldn't have no fingerprints.'"

"Not grammatical," Lucas said.

"No, he wasn't. I picked it up a couple of times."

Then, a few seconds later, with Ignace reading, Lucas interrupted again, "He said he threw it into a field of 'whatever-it-is'?"

"That's what he said." Ignace nodded. "That's what *verbatim* means. It's *exactly* what he said."

One of the junior editors said, "He's gotta push the button on the story . . ."

White said to Lucas, "Do you have any other suggestions?"

Lucas shook his head: "You're gonna run it, so run it. I notice you shaded over the fact that he went out and bought a razor because of Ruffe's earlier story."

"I don't think that's essential to the thrust of the story," White said. "It confuses the issue."

"Besides, it's embarrassing," said Sloan, stepping up, wiping his nose. To Lucas: "Rochester's working it; and they're bringing in an on-duty Highway Patrol guy and the Sheriff's Department."

IGNACE PUSHED THE BUTTON on the story, sending it on its way, and said to Lucas and Sloan, "You guys owe me big."

"Bullshit. You're about one inch from being busted as a material witness," Sloan said. He sounded defensive.

Ignace smiled, calling the bluff: "So bust me. I might enjoy it."

"You wouldn't enjoy it," Sloan said.

"What, you'd put me in some cell with some big faggot?"

Sloan shook his head. "No, we'd put you in a locked room by yourself with a toilet and a sink and let you sit there. It'd be like taking a Northwest flight from Minneapolis to Duluth for three straight weeks. Except that the food would be better."

"Fuck you," Ignace said, linking his fingers together over his soft gut. "You owe me, and you know it. When you get this guy, I want a phone call. If you get him."

"We'll get him," Lucas said. "Maybe we'll call, maybe we won't."

THEY TALKED FOR ANOTHER ten minutes, going over the story. Ignace gave Lucas a shortened transcript of the conversation, only the material covered in the story. Lucas told Stone that the state would subpoena Ignace's shorthand notes. "Keep them safe."

"We'll probably fight the subpoena," Stone said.

"Probably—but don't lose the notes."

OUT ON THE STREET, Sloan said, "Ruffe is a noxious little motherfucker," and then, "Stand back, I'm gonna sneeze."

Lucas stepped away, Sloan sneezed, and Lucas said, "One good thing—Pope's staying in his home territory. He's not off in some goddamn weird place where nobody's seen the stories about him. He's hiding out. That means somebody has seen him, whether or not they know it, and all we have to do is find the connection."

"So now what?"

Lucas yawned and said, "I'm going over to the office to work the phones. I'll put together a meeting in Rochester, tomorrow morning. Everybody I can find."

Sloan looked at his watch: "It's way late."

"So I jerk a few people out of bed. Big deal. Uh—you personally might want to take some more pills."

"No kiddin'. My face is coming off. What about the baseball bat?"

"We can run down to Mankato early, check on the bat, then over to Rochester. We gotta find this woman he's looking at. That's the thing: if he's telling us the truth, we might not have a lot of time."

"I hope to hell he doesn't have anybody. I couldn't deal with another woman like Larson."

"Just . . . hold on, man," Lucas said. "You're going through a tough spot."

"It's all been tough," Sloan said. "Now, it's breaking me up."

THE MAN WITH THE throaty whisper felt better after talking with Ignace; more complete. Talking about what he was doing actually helped him to think through it, to appreciate it. Though . . . what a weird fuckin' name the guy had. Ruffe Ignace. Who'd name their kid something like that? Why not something decent, like *Bob,* or *Roy?* With a name like Ruffe, you were bound to grow up queer.

And it was nice to talk about Millie, even if just a little.

ONE THING MILLIE found out early was that sex in the shower sounded good in books but was less fun in real life. First of all, you were standing up, and you had to concentrate on not falling down. The way you did that was, you hung on the water faucet handles, and then just about the time you got a rhythm going, you pushed too hard on the cold handle and Mihovil got a shot of icy water down his back and his dick retracted like a snail in a shell. That wasn't good.

Then there was the drowning issue. Oral sex always seemed like a possibility in a shower, but that meant you had to rely on nose breathing to keep you alive, and with water pouring down on you, that wasn't as easy as it seemed.

They tried it in Mihovil's bathtub, but in a modern bathtub, there just wasn't enough room, and Mihovil cracked his head so hard on the water faucet that he actually bled from the cut.

In either the shower or the tub, soap was a problem in a number of ways . . .

They tried it standing up in the bedroom, but that was almost as awkward as the shower—something usually went wrong at exactly the wrong time. The pumping action would produce rude noises, or Mihovil would fall out and they'd lose the rhythm, and once he ejaculated on the shag carpet in Millie's bedroom, which had been a mess . . .

There were issues.

THERE WERE ISSUES, but they also made a lot of progress. She found that she could actually *learn* to have an orgasm. She could link a little fantasy with a little reality, she could get Mihovil to behave in certain ways to increase the sense of fantasy, get the physical part to match the mental stuff, and *Pop!* It worked almost every time, after she learned how to do it.

Like this. They were doing it doggie style, had just gotten started, and Mihovil asked, "How often do you masturbate?"

She was embarrassed by the question. That seemed a little private, and if she said something like "Every night," it might even seem to reflect on Mihovil's own sexual efficacy (in her case) so she temporized and said, "Well, I guess, you know . . ."

"No, tell me," he said. "You must (uh) do it all the time when you have no boyfriend."

"I do it (grunt) sometimes," she said. "I think it's (um) natural . . . I guess."

"Yes. It's natural. I do it all the time. Sometimes (ah) when I'm watching football. Okay?"

"Okay." But she was a little doubtful. Where was this going?

He cleared up that question right away: "Now. When we do it this way, it would work much better if you would just reach up and rub yourself a little, because I can hardly reach in there with my hands, and I know my cock doesn't rub you the right way . . . so just reach up there . . ."

So she did.

THE BEST THING, they discovered, with research, was to start in the shower, and then get toweled off, and then race into the playroom and do all the stuff in the bed that you imagined doing in the shower, but you let the bed hold you up. Since you were squeaky clean, there really were no limitations. The icky factor essentially vanished. And you didn't drown. And they only fell out of bed twice, which was actually, when you thought about it, pretty neat.

Falling out of bed, it felt so good . . .

11

THE MORNING WAS BRILLIANT, a bluebird sky with a breath of breeze from the south, and a lick of humid gulf air that meant there'd be thunderstorms in the afternoon.

Lucas woke at six, cleaned up, and went to the phones. Nordwall said he was moving people into the bean field even as they spoke; the Rochester chief of police said his guys had come up empty the night before. "You sure he was here?" the Rochester cop asked.

"Unless Ma Bell is lying to us," Lucas said. "You got a place for us to get together?"

"Yup. We're getting quite a few calls, too. The sheriff did some kind of District Six hot-line thing. You know where the government center is, downtown, right on the river? We're gonna use the boardroom."

"I know it. See you at ten. Get some coffee and doughnuts—the state will spring for it."

"Jeez—no wonder the legislature is back in session."

SLOAN SHOWED UP a few minutes after seven o'clock, dragging. He looked better than he had the night before, but only because he was standing in daylight. Lucas told him about Grant's visit the night before and their talk about the possibility of a second man. "A second man?" Sloan wondered.

"Or a woman."

"Could be a woman, I guess. Another nut. They had a problem at St. John's with male and female patients getting together . . ."

"We had a report on that: they keep the sexual predators away from the mixed-gender units," Lucas said. "Charlie wouldn't have met a woman there."

"But what if he knew a guy who knew a guy who knew a woman . . ."

They talked about inmates at St. John's, about the phone call from Charlie Pope, and about Mike West, the missing schizophrenic, as they finished the coffee. Lucas had decided during the night that he wanted to talk to Pope's mother, who lived in the town of Austin, south of Rochester.

"You're better at talking to old ladies than I am," Lucas said. "I thought as long as we were down there . . ."

"Yeah, sure."

When they finished the coffee, Lucas stood at the kitchen sink and rinsed the cups and said, "You don't look so good."

"Ah, I took about four orange Nyquils. I oughta be okay," Sloan said. He didn't look okay: his eyes were rimmed in red, and he occasionally gurgled. He'd brought a box of Kleenex with him.

"Your call," Lucas said.

"HOW ABOUT 'BEAST OF BURDEN'?" Sloan asked, on the way out of town.

"That's one too many Stones songs," Lucas said. "Besides, what's-her-name covered it, and I never liked the cover."

"How about Def Leppard, 'Rock of Ages'?"

"On the possible list, but down a way."

"You know what you oughta do? You oughta make a *worst* song list from the rock era. That's something nobody's seen before."

Lucas considered the possibilities for a second, then said, "Wouldn't work. You'd play 'American Pie,' followed by 'Vincent,' and then any normal human being would throw the iPod out the window."

THEY TOOK THE TRUCK, because the Porsche's paint job didn't like gravel, heading south again, down the four-lane to Mankato, through town, out to the Rice farm. They'd just gone through town when Weather called from London.

"You sound like you're up," she said.

"I just went through Mankato. I've been up since dawn."

"Something broke!"

Lucas told her about it, and about Sloan figuring out a murder, and the press conference. She told him about revising the burns on the face of a little girl who was messing around with the white gas in her brother's camp-stove set.

"At least we're both staying busy," Lucas said.

"What about the music list?"

"We were just talking about it. I've got about a million songs," he said.

"You know, for a few more bucks . . ."

"That's not the point. The point is the discipline. The best one hundred songs . . ."

"Have you considered 'Waltz Two' from the *Jazz Suite* by Shostakovich?" she asked.

He wasn't sure whether she was joking; sometimes it was hard to tell. "Uh, no."

"Well, I know you liked the music."

Lucas smiled into the phone. "Weather, I don't have any idea what you're talking about. I never heard of the thing."

"You know, it was the theme music in *Eyes Wide Shut*, when what's-her-face took her clothes off."

He remembered. Clearly. "Ah . . . that was a nice piece."

"I thought you'd remember . . ."

She said she missed him; he said that he missed her; Letty, their ward; and Sam, the kid; and even the housekeeper.

"Three more weeks," she said. "This is great, but I gotta get back."

WHEN THEY ARRIVED at the farm, they found two cop cars in the driveway, one of them just leaving. Lucas pulled onto the lawn and got out of the truck. Nordwall got out of the passenger side of the cop car that had been rolling down toward them.

"What happened?" Lucas asked, as they crunched toward each other on the gravel drive.

"Took about twenty minutes to find it," the sheriff said, hitching up his uniform pants, looking back over his shoulder at the bean field. "You see the tape over there? Right in there . . . Right where Pope said it would be. And exactly *what* he said it would be—an aluminum base-ball bat."

"You already pick it up?"

"Yeah. We had our crime-scene guy photograph it, and he's driving it up to your lab right now. He said there's some hair stuck to the end of it, gotta be the kid's, but we want to nail it down. We don't want some smart-ass saying it was a practical joke."

"It never felt like a joke," Lucas said. They both looked out at the field with the tape strung over the bean plants, the cops tromping up and down the rows. Then, "You coming over to Rochester?"

"Yeah—but that's not for a couple hours. I gotta stop back at the house. I haven't had breakfast yet." A man who didn't miss many meals.

"You see the paper?"

"Yes. Pope scares the shit out of me," Nordwall said. "I told my guys to shoot first, ask questions later."

"See you in Rochester."

THEY CUT CROSS-COUNTRY; the trip took an hour. They rolled down a long hill, the towers of the Mayo Clinic in the distance. Sloan sniffed and said, "Look at the fuckin' golf courses; just like a town full of doctors."

"Bigot."

"Ruin a perfectly good cornfield," he said. "What do you want to do? We got some time."

"Let's look at that pay phone. Maybe we can shake something loose."

"Like what?"

"Security camera?"

"Yeah, right," Sloan said. "Fuckin' waste of time."

"Hey, something could happen."

"And Snow White might come over to my house and sit on my face," Sloan said. His voice was nasal, stuffed.

"Okay. So let's sit around with some cops and drink coffee and talk about pensions."

Sloan sighed, pulled out a sheet of Kleenex, and blew into it. Lucas winced. "Okay," Sloan said. "We look at the phone. And don't look like you're trying to crawl out the side window."

ROCHESTER WAS DOMINATED economically and socially by the Mayo Clinic; but there was still a piece of the old downtown stuck to the south side of the hospital district—exfoliating brick and patched concrete block, halfhearted attempts at rehab, streets emptier than they should be in a town jammed with cars; streets from an Edward Hopper painting.

The phone was on a wall of an out-of-business gas station, the only outside phone they'd seen in the city. "Must've known where the phone was," Lucas said. He pulled into the parking area and killed the engine.

"Probably a doc at the Mayo," Sloan said. "Most docs are a little whacko." The words were just out of his mouth when he remembered that he was talking to the husband of a surgeon. "I hope you took offense at that."

"I didn't," Lucas said. "I tend to agree."

They got out of the truck and looked up and down the street. "Two slim possibilities," Sloan said. "The grocery store or the bookstore. Take your choice."

"I'll take the bookstore," Lucas said.

"Maybe they got some poetry," Sloan said. He looked across the street toward the grocery. "Park's Grocery. With any luck, Park is a Korean. They tend to stay open late."

SLOAN WALKED ACROSS the traffic-free street; Lucas headed down the sidewalk toward Krim's Rare and Used Books. The store occupied a twenty-foot-wide retail space with a single large window and a door to the side. The window was rimed with dust and showed two dozen fading hardback covers under an arc of hand-painted black letters: KRIM'S: THE COLLECTOR'S PLACE.

An overhead bell tinkled when Lucas went through the door, and he was hit by the odor of paper mold: not unpleasant, he thought, if you liked books.

Inside, two men huddled together over a book that sat squarely on the counter between them. The book's dust jacket was carefully covered with protective cellophane; collectors did that, Lucas knew.

"Can I help you?" The man behind the counter was overweight, blond, with smooth, ruddy cheeks. He filled a pink golf shirt as though he'd been poured into it; squinted at, he resembled a strawberry milk shake.

"Are you the owner?" Lucas asked.

"Mmm-hmmm." He nodded, friendly.

Lucas glanced at the second man, who was the physical opposite of the owner—reed thin with dark-plastic-rimmed glasses perched on a knife-edge nose, and under the nose, a mustache that looked like it had been sketched in with a pencil. He wore a seedy gray suit and yellow-brown shoes. A tie hung around his neck like a cleaning rag.

Lucas held up his ID: "I'm an investigator with the Bureau of Criminal Apprehension. Do you have a security camera in here?"

The owner's eyebrows arched, and he shook his head: "No. Not much to steal. Never had a break-in. What's going on?"

Out of the corner of his eye, Lucas saw the thin man casually lay his arm on top of the book that he and the owner had been looking at, then slip it off the counter and out of sight. "Just doing a check," Lucas said. "What time do you close?"

"Five, usually?"

"Yesterday?"

"Yeah, five o'clock. Nothing down here after five."

"Okay . . ." Lucas stepped back toward the door, then paused. Never hurt to ask the question. "What was the book you were looking at when I came in . . . if I might ask?"

The thin man was nervous. "Just a thriller." He flashed it up and down.

"Could I look at it?" Lucas asked. He put a little thug into his voice. "I like thrillers."

"Uhhh . . ." The thin man glanced at the store owner, who shrugged. The thin man said, reluctantly, "I guess."

He handed over the book: Lawrence Block, *The Burglar Who Met O*. "I read this guy," Lucas said, flicking a finger at Block's name. "Who's O?" He flipped through the book: Was there something hidden inside?

As he did it, there was a quick intake of breath by the thin man, who said, "Please . . . you'll break the binding. That'll cut the value in half."

"What's special about it?" Lucas asked, frowning at the book. "It's just a commercial—"

"Please." The thin man took the book back, closed it carefully. His glasses had slipped down his thin nose, and he pushed them back up with a forefinger. He nearly whispered it: "Printed in France. An edition of five hundred in English, five hundred in French. A hundred dollars a copy at the press, they go for a thousand dollars now."

"Well, maybe," the store owner said. He was skeptical. "If you can find somebody to pay the thousand."

"In a big metropolitan area . . ."

"There's one right up north of us," the owner said. "If you want to go try."

Lucas: "What? It's dirty or something?"

"No," the thin man said, offended. "It's *sophisticated*."

"Huh. Who's O?"

The thin man shook his head: "There was a famous book, *The Story of O*. If you haven't read it . . . well, I can't explain. You'd have to get into the literature."

The owner changed the subject: "So what's going on with the security camera?"

Lucas shrugged and let the book go. "We're trying to find somebody who might have taken a picture of that phone across the street. Guy we're looking for might have used it."

The owner snapped his fingers, then pointed a finger-pistol at Lucas: "I've seen you. You were on TV. You're looking for the killer, right? The crazy guy from Owatonna?"

Lucas nodded: "Yes."

The owner looked out the window, as though Pope might suddenly pop up in the window, like a Punch puppet. "You think he made a call from across the street?"

"We think he might have. Last night, about eleven."

The owner's eyes narrowed. "I wasn't here at eleven. Long gone. But have you talked to Mrs. Bird upstairs?"

"Mrs. Bird?"

"She sits up there and looks out the window all day and night," the store owner said. "Says she's waiting to die. If she didn't die last night, she might've seen something."

Lucas nodded: "Thanks. I'll go ask." As he went out the door, he looked back at the thin man with his *Burglar* book: "Sophisticated?"

The thin man nodded. "*European.*"

MRS. BIRD WAS TOO OLD to look thin—she looked wasted; she looked like she was going away for good. Lucas thought she might be ninety-five. She peeked at him over the chain on her door, pale blue curious eyes over lightly rouged cheeks. When Lucas showed her his ID, she opened the door.

"I don't believe I've ever spoken to a policeman . . ." She was a small woman with narrow shoulders, wrapped in a polyester housecoat printed to resemble a quilt, with peacocks and cockatoos on the quilt squares. She had short curly hair, like a poodle's, but silvery white, and looked at Lucas through cat's-eye glasses that might have been briefly fashionable in the fifties. A television rambled in the background, a shopping channel selling used Rolexes.

But she'd seen a man by the telephone. "I do remember that; yes. A man in a white shirt. That phone is not used very much."

"Do you remember what he looked like?" Lucas asked. He edged inside the door; she apparently had three rooms, a living room overlooking the street, a bedroom, and a small kitchen. Lucas couldn't see a bath, but he could see a half-open door in the bedroom, and thought that might be it. The place smelled of Glade deodorizer.

She frowned, was uncertain. "Well, I don't know . . . He was only there for a minute or two."

"Would you mind if I looked out the window?"

"Please do," she said. He crossed her living room in three steps, looked out the window. The phone was directly across the street and only fifteen feet from a streetlight.

"Did you see more than one man last night?" Lucas asked.

"No, not last night," she said.

"Did you see a car?"

Again she frowned. "Yes, I did. He got out of a car, he parked just over there . . ." She pointed a bony finger just up the street from the phone. "A white Oldsmobile."

"An Oldsmobile."

"I think so."

"New? Or old."

"New, I think."

"You say, you've said, *you think*. You've said it several times . . ."

"I was watching television. That's all I do now, watch television and look out the windows, except on Mondays and Wednesdays when the social lady comes and takes me to the store. But I wasn't paying too much attention to the telephone . . ."

"Okay . . . If we showed you some photographs, could you see if you recognize the man? Or the car?"

She smiled; she had improbably small, white, pearly teeth. "I could certainly try, but I'm pretty old."

"Mrs. Bird, I'll be back in a minute, okay?" Lucas said. "Just give me a minute or two."

"I'm not going anyplace. I hope."

WHEN LUCAS GOT back to the street, Sloan was just coming out of the bookstore, wiping his nose with a Kleenex: "They said you were upstairs."

"The woman upstairs said she saw a guy . . . I need your photo spread," Lucas said.

"What else did she see?"

"She said he's driving a white Oldsmobile. A new one," Lucas said.

Sloan's eyebrows went up. "That could be something."

Sloan got his briefcase from the car and together they went back up the stairs. As they walked up the stairs, Lucas said, "Try not to get too close to her. You give her that cold, you could kill her."

"Goddamnit." Sloan was offended.

"No, no—I'm not kidding."

MRS. BIRD OPENED THE DOOR for them. She was more animated now than when Lucas had first knocked; excited.

"We need a place for you to sit and look at these and see them all at once," Sloan told her.

They all looked around. In the kitchen, a single wooden chair faced a small oval table the size of a pizza pan, and on the table, a paper rose poked out of a glass bud vase. Lucas and Sloan wouldn't fit at the table.

"Could I move your end table around in front of the couch, maybe?" Lucas asked.

"Of course."

Mrs. Bird sat in the middle of the three-cushion couch. Lucas took some old *Reader's Digests* off the table and moved it in front of the couch. Lucas and Sloan sat on either side of Bird, and Sloan spread out ten five-by-seven color photographs. One of the men was Charlie Pope. The other nine, all of whom met the general description of Charlie Pope, were cops.

She looked at them for a moment, then said to Sloan, "I saw this on television once."

"It's pretty important . . ."

She looked back at the pictures, and then reached out and touched Charlie Pope's face. "This is the man, I believe."

THEY SAT LOOKING at the pictures for a few seconds, then Sloan said to Lucas, "We need to make out an affidavit and bring it back here." Unspoken: the old lady might die in the next fifteen minutes.

"We'll get somebody with Rochester to do it, and we can bring it back here after the meeting."

They explained the procedure to Mrs. Bird, who nodded and said, "I'll wait for you. I was just going to watch TV anyway." Then she did a little dramatic, girlish shiver: "You don't think I'll be in any danger, do you?"

Lucas thought, *Not unless you shake hands with Sloan.* But at the same time he smiled and shook his head, *No.*

12

ROCHESTER WAS A GOOD-SIZED CITY, built around a colony of doctors and wealthy patients, and probably had the highest per-capita income of any big city in the state. The money showed up in the government center, a modern red-brick, concrete, and glass building that sat on the Zumbro River a couple of blocks from the Mayo Clinic.

Twenty-nine sheriffs and police chiefs, or their alternates, along with a half dozen highway patrolmen, game wardens, and parole officers, got together in the boardroom, where the city council and county board met. Of the thirty-five, thirty were middle-aged men, most a little too heavy and going gray. The other five were women, all five tightly coifed and suited.

Lucas had talked to the Rochester chief about Bird; he would make arrangements for a formal statement. Then Lucas started the pitch to the gathered cops: "We know he's down here someplace. You've all seen this morning's *Star-Tribune*—he's going to do it again. He's probably already picked out somebody, and he's stalking her. Or him. We're looking for another guy from St. John's named Mike West. We're trying to keep this under our hats . . ."

They had questions, but Lucas had few answers: "Honest to God, we really don't know what he's doing, or how he's hiding. There's been a parole-violation bulletin out on him for a month, and we've got nothing. He's buried himself someplace. We need to pry him out of his hole."

He told them about the white Olds. They all made a note. One guy held up a hand: "A new white Olds . . . they stopped building Oldsmobiles . . ."

"I know."

"We should be able to track every one of them," the guy suggested.

"We're doing that," Lucas said. "The woman who gave us that information is elderly, really elderly, and we're not absolutely sure of its quality."

"You're not sure how he's armed?"

"No, but he says he is, he says he got some guns, and we believe him," Lucas said. "Rice was in pretty good shape. We don't think Pope would have taken him bare-handed. The medical examiner says all of the damage to Rice's body was inflicted either with the whip or a blade. He didn't show any signs of being beaten, or having been in a struggle before he was tied up. So there was probably a gun. If one of your guys even gets a whiff of Pope, he better be wearing a vest."

"Pretty goodamn hot out in the countryside right now," one of the cops said.

"Better hot than dead," somebody else said.

Another hand: "Where'd he get the guns?"

"Same place he got the Olds," Lucas said. "We don't know."

"We know he was in Rochester last night?"

"Three blocks from here," Lucas said. He gestured out the window at his back. "Right across the river."

And it went on for a while.

WHEN THEY BROKE UP, Sloan came over and said, "I'm feeling like shit, man. Bobby Anderson from Scott County's here. He said he'd give me a ride back home, if you're gonna go see Marcia Pope."

Lucas nodded: "You look bad. I can't believe the Marcia Pope thing is going anywhere, anyway. The Austin cops already talked to her twice."

Sloan took off, and Lucas, back in the truck, headed south toward the Iowa border, and the city of Austin.

MARCIA POPE LIVED IN a shingle-sided cottage on a tree-shaded street on the edge of Austin, in a subdivision built by meatpackers. The house was technically white, but probably hadn't been painted in forty years; the siding was grooved with dirt and mold, the ragged grass had only been fitfully mown, the narrow sidewalk leading to the front door was cracked and twisted.

Lucas pulled into the gravel patch that served as a driveway, and as he got out of the car, saw the curtains twitch. Until that moment, it hadn't really occurred to him that Charlie Pope might be inside. Could Charlie be stupid enough to hide out at his mother's? And here was Lucas going to the front door, no protective vest, his pistol tucked in a spot that might be a half second too slow, his mind working on other errands.

He slowed, scratched his face, miming a man who'd forgotten something, went back to the truck, pulled his gun out, and tucked it into his side pants pocket. The front sight had been smoothed to prevent hang-ups, and he kept the hammer and trigger assembly hanging out so his hand would fall on them.

Which wouldn't do him a lot of good, he thought, as he started back up the sidewalk, if Charlie was waiting behind the door with a shotgun stoked with double-ought buckshot . . . He saw the curtain twitch again and thought, *Why would he wait until I got to the door?*

GOOD THOUGHT. But nothing happened on the way up, and at the door he stepped to one side and rang the bell. A few seconds passed, and he rang it again; then the door jerked open an inch or two, and a woman asked, "Whattaya want?"

He felt like a Fuller Brush salesman, but put on his official cop voice: "Mrs. Marcia Pope?"

"Yeah?"

"I'm Lucas Davenport with the state Bureau of Criminal Apprehension." He held up his ID with his left hand. "We're looking for your son, Charlie. Is he here?"

"No, he's not here. I haven't seen him in more'n a month. I don't know where he is. I've already talked to the Austin police."

All he could see was one eye, a hank of steel gray hair, and the end of a short, pointed nose. "I need to interview you. Open up."

"You got a warrant?" The door opened two more inches, the better to argue.

"No, but I could get one. Then we'd come back, put handcuffs on you so all the neighbors could enjoy themselves, and take you to police headquarters to talk."

Silence, three seconds, five seconds. "You're not going to take me if I talk to you now?"

"Not if you tell me the truth," Lucas said. "Charlie's not here?"

The door opened wide enough that he could see her. She was a small, hatchet-faced woman wearing black slacks and a blue blouse that looked like a uniform from a chain restaurant. "I ain't seen that boy since the Fourth of July. He came down on the bus to see the fireworks. He always loved them."

Lucas nodded: "Can I come in?"

"The house is a mess," she said reluctantly. "I've been working all the time . . ."

But she backed up and he stepped inside.

SHE HAD A TV, a beat-up couch, a green La-Z-Boy, and a couple of end tables in the living room. Everything was stacked with magazines and tabloid newspapers; even more paper was stacked against the walls; decades of *Us* and *People*. The room smelled of fried meat and Heinz 57 Sauce.

Pope seemed to be looking for a place for Lucas to sit, but he said, "Never mind, I'm okay . . ." He eased toward the kitchen: more magazines, but no sound, or feel, or anything that indicated another person around. They stood facing each other and Lucas pushed her for names of friends, anything that might point to where Pope had gone.

"He had to have friends from high school . . ."

"He wasn't in high school that long. There was one boy, in grade school, but he drownded."

In the end, it seemed that she'd hardly known her child. When he was twelve, she said, he started skipping school. She didn't know where he spent his days; he simply went somewhere and hid. The school authorities hunted him down at the end of every summer, but as soon as his enrollment was counted for the state aid, they let him go. He was a pain in the ass, and always had been.

The high point of his teen years had come when he'd crashed his bike, hitting his head on a curb.

"They thought he was gonna die, but he didn't; goddamn brains almost squirted out his ear," his mother said.

In eleventh grade, Charlie Pope stopped pretending. He quit school, got a job at a McDonald's, was fired. "Never washed his hands after the bathroom, they said." He did some more time at a Burger King, was fired again, and then did whatever kind of pickup work he could get, lived however he could, Marcia said.

"His old man took off thirty years ago. Nobody knows where he is or what he's doing. He was a worthless piece of shit anyhow, but I didn't know that when I took up with him," Marcia said. "I was just a girl."

"So there's nobody—nobody ever talked to Charlie."

She looked away from him for a moment, her forehead wrinkling. Then, "You know, there was them brothers from over by Hill. He was talking about them on the Fourth, maybe they'd have a summer job for him. He didn't like hauling garbage . . . What was their name? I can't think . . ."

"What about them?"

"They're farmers. They got these big gardens, Charlie says. They live in the country somewhere by Hill, they sell tomatoes and corn and cukes and stuff down on the highway somewhere," she said. "One of them vegetable stands. They use to hire Charlie to work in the gardens . . . you know, pickin' shit and pulling weeds and they had one of those machines, like a lawnmower, but it plows . . ."

"A tiller?"

"That's it. They taught him how to run it and he'd help with the gardens. He did that for a couple of summers. He liked it."

A little tingle: "This was where? By Hill? That's a town?" Lucas asked.

"Yeah. Hill."

"You don't know their names?"

"No . . . I mean I used to. I seen one of the boys, once, he had one of those things on his face and neck, a raspberry thing, I think they call them? Or a strawberry thing? One of those like birthmarks, great big one on the side of his face . . ."

"A port-wine mark?"

She snapped her fingers: "That's it. A port-wine stain. Right on the side of his face."

He pushed her, but that was all she had. He left a card with her and said, "I need to tell you two things," he said. He crowded her a little, let her feel the authority. "If Charlie gets in touch, you call us. He's dangerous, and he's dangerous to you. He's completely run off the rails this time. You understand?"

"Yup. I'll call you, don't you worry." But her eyes slid away from his.

He got right back in her face. "You better, or you'll go inside with him, Mrs. Pope. You wouldn't like the women's prison. We're talking the worst kind of murder, now, and if you help him, you'll be an accomplice. So you call."

"I will." She looked at the card this time.

"Second, you don't talk to anybody about what you told me," Lucas said. "I need to go look up these garden guys, and we don't want anybody to know we're coming. So you just keep your mouth shut, okay?"

"Okay."

"I'm not fooling, Mrs. Pope. You mess with us on this, we'll put your ass in jail."

LUCAS FOUND HILL in his Minnesota atlas; more a crossroads than a town. The map showed two streets where a creek crossed a county road; the place might have a bar, maybe a gas pump. Still in Mower County, northwest of Austin. The sheriff had been at the meeting that morning . . .

. . .

LUCAS HEADED EAST out of town, on his cell phone as he drove. The sheriff was still in his car somewhere, and the Mower County dispatcher wouldn't give Lucas his phone number. "Then give him mine, call him and tell him to call me back," Lucas said.

Larry Ball got back five minutes later. Lucas could hear noise in the background, music and voices. The Rochester Mall?

"I just talked to Marcia Pope," Lucas told him. "There are a couple of guys just outside of Austin who hired Charlie Pope to work their gardens. They're truck gardeners, out by a place called Hill. You know a couple of brothers, one's got a port-wine mark on his face?"

"Huh. Yeah, I sorta know the guy. Don't know his name, but I talked to him once when I was campaigning. He was working at a roadside stand, *mmm*, I think where I-Ninety crosses Highway Sixteen near Dexter."

"Dexter. I saw that on my map."

"Yeah, listen, I'll tell you who'd know, is Bob Youngie," Ball said. "He's one of my deputies. He's working, I'll call him, and have him call you right back."

LUCAS COULD SEE the interstate up ahead. He was fairly sure he should go east but wasn't positive, so he pulled off to the side of the road, waiting. Youngie called a minute later. He had a gravelly voice, a whisky voice, and sounded like an older guy. "You're looking for the Martin brothers, Gerald and Jerome," he said, when Lucas answered the cell-phone call. "You going out there now?"

"Yeah. I'm just coming up on Ninety-four."

"You want to go east, to Exit One Ninety-three. I'm in my car now, I'm a little closer, so you'll see me when you come off. I'm calling another car, he'll be a couple minutes behind you. He's just leaving town."

"The Martins . . . they're trouble?"

"No, I couldn't say that," Youngie said. "They stay to themselves, they don't like having people on their land. They've run some hunters off, and we've had to warn them about carrying guns when they do it. And they got dogs. I think it's best if a couple of us came along."

"The sheriff told you what we're doing?" Lucas asked.

"Yup. That's another reason."

"Glad to have you," Lucas said.

YOUNGIE WAS AS TALL as Lucas, maybe sixty, gray haired with a Marlboro-man mustache. He was leaning on the front fender of his car, smoking a cigarette, when Lucas came off the interstate and pulled in behind him.

"Nice truck," he said, when Lucas got out. Youngie had cool blue eyes like Lucas's own, and they seemed slightly amused.

"I got it for the Magic Fingers seats," Lucas said, looking back at the blue Lexus. "Keeps you company on the long hauls."

Youngie glanced at the truck, biting just for a second, then back at Lucas, amused again. "You gonna catch Charlie?"

"Yeah. Or else kill him."

"I heard that about you," Youngie said. "The or-else part."

"Just the job I had," Lucas said.

"I hear you." Youngie put out his hand and Lucas shook. Youngie's hand was like a wood file. "Here come the kids . . ."

Another sheriff's car was coming off the interstate. Lucas could see two cops inside. "The kids?"

"They got three, four years between them," Youngie said. "I'll have them come in last."

"You really think . . . ?"

"If we ain't ready, why're we going out there at all?"

"That's a point," Lucas said.

. . .

YOUNGIE BRIEFED THE TWO young cops on the visit to the Martin farm. He would lead the way in, Lucas would follow, and the kids would come in and block and watch. "If there's trouble, you call in first, help us later," Youngie told them.

One of the kids, who was trying to hide premature baldness by shaving his head, hitched up his pistol: "We're cool," he said.

THE MARTIN PLACE was an aging farmhouse that sat foursquare at the top of a hill. A gravel driveway, badly humped in the middle, led up the hill to the side of the house and then behind it. Halfway up the driveway, a barn emerged from the umbra of the house.

The house was a turn-of-the-twentieth-century structure of two stories, gray shingles on the top, with twin dormers over a front porch. The porch had space for a swing, but no swing. The house, barn, and lawn were on a quarter section, a hundred and sixty acres, a square a half mile on a side.

To the left of the house was a cornfield; to the right, at the bottom of the hill, was an untended apple orchard, with knee-deep weeds growing up around a few dozen old apple trees, all crabbed over like aging crones. Farther up the hill, beyond the apple orchard and to the right of the drive, was a fallow field, deep in weeds. It had, in the not-too-distant past, been cultivated; Lucas could see the tangled yellow dead vines in what was once a squash or pumpkin patch.

Lucas pushed the Lexus up through the cloud of dust thrown up by Youngie's car. As they topped the hill, coming up to the space between the house and the barn, Youngie suddenly juked left.

Lucas went right and hit the brake and saw what Youngie had seen a half second sooner: three men had burst from the barn and were running toward the cornfield. A second later, a fourth man ran out of the farmhouse, headed down the hill, then slanted toward the cornfield like the others. One of the first three was oversized, and not fast.

Pope, Lucas thought, and then he was out of the car and running.

"WAS THAT POPE?" Youngie shouted. He had his hand on his pistol.

"I think so," Lucas yelled back. "Get some help in here."

He was fifty yards from the cornfield and could see cornstalks rippling in front of the running men. Youngie was shouting something at him, but he kept going, trying to sort it out as he ran. The big guy had gone right, and Lucas plunged into the field after him.

And was blinded.

Though the tops of the cornstalks were only a few inches higher than his eyes, the field might as well have been a rain forest. He stopped, listened, ran after the thrashing sound to his right. The other two men, he thought, had gone straight in, but Pope had been curling away, as though he had a destination in mind, as though he weren't simply trying to hide.

Lucas had his gun out now, jacked a shell into the chamber, locked the safety down: cocked and locked and a quick click from action. Farmhouses had guns, so Pope might have one. He couldn't see, the corn leaves were whipping him in the face; and it was hot in the field, stifling, and the leaves were sharp edged, cutting at him. What the hell had Youngie yelled? He knew what it was, but . . .

Meth lab.

That's what he'd said; and Lucas remembered the smell now, the sharp tang that might have been hog urine but wasn't. The Martins were making methamphetamine, which would probably explain their preference for privacy . . .

Stopped: listened. Heard nothing. Pope might also have stopped, trying to pick out Lucas running after him. Lucas squatted, listening for footfalls, peering down the rows at knee-high level. He'd been in corn-field chases a couple of times, once as a uniformed cop, doing just what Youngie had the kids doing now, blocking, and once as a detective. You couldn't see anything at eye level; too many leaves, but there was a cleared space from waist level on down, especially when the farmer used a weed suppressant.

Lucas crawled across rows, looking down them; and then heard the sound of a man running away, still farther to the right. Lucas ran in that direction, then jumped, got above the level of the corn for just a half second, jumped again, saw what he thought was movement, and went that way . . .

AND WAS HIT IN THE FACE.

The blow came without any warning and pitched him across two rows of corn and down on his stomach. He didn't know exactly what had happened, but the other guy was right there, and Lucas got the im-pression of size and red socks and heavy boots and thought one thing: *hold on to the gun, hold on to the gun.*

He rolled, unsure of whether he'd been shot or punched, his face on fire, blood on his hands, and he saw legs and felt another blow on his thigh. He was losing it, he thought, and he dropped the safety on the .45 and pulled the trigger, blindly, hoping to freeze the other man just for a second, just long enough to get a break.

And it worked; the other man lurched away with the explosion and Lucas caught sight of his lower body ten feet away, turned, and screamed, "I'll fuckin' kill you, stop . . ."

The other man ran and Lucas rolled and fired a second shot, at knee level, missed, but the other man suddenly stopped and shouted, "I quit. I quit. Don't shoot."

Lucas was on his feet now, blood streaming out of his nose and onto his shirt and suit; pain surged through his face and down his neck.

"Get the fuck over here," he told the big man. "Get the fuck over here and get down on your fuckin' knees, get down on your fuckin' knees . . ."

And he heard Youngie, some distance away. "Davenport, Davenport . . ."

"Over here, over here . . ."

The other man was down on his knees, his back toward Lucas, his hands webbed behind his head. He'd done this before.

"Look at me, Charlie," Lucas said.

"Look at you, who?" the other man said. He was overweight and block-headed and going bald and thick through the shoulders and arms, like a bench-press freak. He turned just his head. "Who the fuck is Charlie?"

LUCAS, STILL BLEEDING, held the man as he heard Youngie thrashing up through the field. "This way," he shouted.

Youngie pushed through the corn, pistol pointed at the sky, looked wide-eyed at Lucas and the kneeling man. "What happened? You shot?"

"Naw, he hit me in the nose. Goddamn it, it hurts. It's busted. Could you put some cuffs on this asshole? I'm leaking all over my suit."

They got the big guy on his feet and his hands cuffed, and Lucas put the .45 away, the stock all sticky with his blood. The guy's wallet was chained to his belt, and Youngie jerked it off the chain, flipped it open, looked at the driver's license. "Bobby Clanton, Albert Lea."

"I want a lawyer," Clanton said.

"Fuck you," said Lucas. He shoved Clanton in the direction of the barn. "Walk." To emphasize the order, he kicked Clanton in the ass, and Clanton stumbled and almost went down.

"You need a doctor," Youngie said to Lucas.

"Yeah, yeah. They're gonna push a goddamn stick up my nose and that's gonna hurt worse than it does now . . ." He kicked Clanton in the ass again.

. . .

YOUNGIE HAD SENT THE TWO young cops after the fourth man, and had called in a half dozen more on-duty deputies. "We'll get more in here as soon as I can find the people," he said. 'I'm hoping the other two will hunker down in that field long enough that we can get some guys spotting the roads. If they get out of the field, they'll be hard to track. They can be five miles away in an hour, if they can run."

"Where's the lab? You said meth lab?" Lucas asked.

"Yeah, I could smell it, but I didn't look. The barn, I think. We've had a rash of them."

"Manufacture of a controlled substance, resisting arrest, assault on a cop. I bet we can get Bobby fifteen years in Stillwater, if he doesn't have any priors. If he's got priors, then, whoops, I guess it's gonna be bye-bye," Lucas said. He kicked Clanton in the ass a third time.

Clanton staggered, caught himself, looked at Youngie, "You always torture your suspects?"

"Fuck you," Youngie said, but when Clanton was turned back toward the barn, he looked at Lucas and shook his head: no more ass kicking. Lucas nodded, touched the side of his nose. Everything felt solid, but there was an arcing pain when he pushed left to right, familiar from his hockey and uniform days. Maybe not busted, but cracked. He was still bleeding, bubbling blood, spitting, wiping his chin.

WHEN THEY GOT BACK to the farmyard, they put Clanton facedown on a patch of grass and then Youngie said, "Got another one." Down the hill, the two young cops were marching the fourth man out of the cornfield. Then another sheriff's car, leaving a plume of gravel dust behind it, turned in at the drive and Youngie said, "Keep an eye on Bobby; I'll put these guys on the road."

. . .

LUCAS SAT ON THE GRASS next to Clanton and tipped his head back, sniffing against the leaking blood. "You better talk to us, Bobby," he said. Blood trickled into his mouth and he spit again. Clanton didn't reply.

Lucas dabbed at his face with his knuckles, trying to keep the blood off his suit. "You better talk, Bobby, because you are in some serious shit. Look at me. You're gonna be as old as I am when you get out of Stillwater. You're gonna spend your young life in a cell the size of a fucking Volkswagen. You need me to go to court and tell them you cooperated."

Nothing.

Lucas: "You think you're tough. Maybe you are. I give you that. But you're stupid, too. Think how long it's been since last summer, everything you've done since then. Think about being locked up for fifteen times that long. Think about being locked up forever, if we put you with Charlie Pope."

Clanton twitched. Lucas turned his head down just for a second, snorted blood, but saw that Clanton had started to cry. "Better talk, Bobby."

YOUNGIE CAME BACK with a big gauze first-aid pad and said, "Here. You're still bleeding." Lucas took it as another cop car pulled into the yard. "We'll start pushing the field as soon as we have enough people."

Lucas said, "Ah," through the pad.

The two young cops arrived with the fourth man and put him on the grass a few yards from Clanton. "You shot?" one of them asked Lucas.

"Nuh-uh," Lucas said. The fire in his face was transforming itself into a first-class headache.

"Got punched in the face by the fat guy," Youngie said. He looked down at the fourth man. "Who's this asshole?"

"Sandy Martin, cousin to one of the Martin brothers. Says he doesn't know anything about a meth lab, he just came up to check the farmhouse."

"Must be why he ran when he saw us coming," Youngie said.

"Goddamn this hurts," Lucas said.

The two cops from the new car came over and one asked Lucas, "You shot?"

YOUNGIE AND THREE of the other cops cleared the barn. Lucas and the youngest of the deputies sat on the lawn next to the captives. "Take it easy in there," Lucas said, as the cops went in with drawn guns.

THEY WERE BACK OUT in ten minutes. Youngie, positively cheerful, said, so Clanton and Martin could hear him, "My, my, my. That's the biggest and best meth lab I've ever seen. And I've seen a few. Bobby, Sandy, if I were you guys, I would do *anything* I could to cut down the time, because right now, you're gonna do a stretch in Stillwater and then the *feds* are gonna want to talk to you."

"I want a fuckin' lawyer," Clanton said.

"I didn't do anything, I was just here to check the property," Martin wailed.

"Not giving us any help at all, are they?" Youngie said to Lucas. "I mean, we put them with Charlie Pope, that'd be a murder charge to go with the drugs."

Silence, then "Who the fuck is Charlie Pope?" Clanton asked. His face was still wet with tears. "This asshole"—he jerked his head at Lucas—"called me Charlie. Who the fuck is he?"

"You don't read the newspaper or watch TV?" Lucas said. "The guy who raped and killed a girl and then raped and killed a guy and killed the guy's little boy? That guy?"

Clanton was baffled. "That guy? What does that guy got to do with us?"

"We know Charlie hung out here," Lucas said. His whole face hurt when he talked. "His mom says so."

Clanton arched his back to get his head up out of the dirt. "Not since we been here. Maybe he worked with the Martins, but I don't know no Charlie Pope."

Lucas turned his head to Sandy Martin. "Is that right? He hung with you guys?"

"I can't believe this," Martin said. "I was just stopping off before I went fishing."

"The guys who ran . . . we believe one of them was Charlie Pope," Youngie said. "Look, we're gonna get them. All that plastic in the barn, all that is perfect for fingerprints. We got clothes and a couple of trucks. So tell us . . . what's their names? If one of them isn't Charlie Pope . . ."

"Ah, fuck you," Clanton said. He snorted once, then said something else.

"What?"

"Sean McCollum and Mike Benton, that's who that is," he said. "You'll get all their stuff anyway. Isn't no Charlie Pope."

"Where are the Martins?" Lucas asked.

"Alaska, I guess," Clanton said. "They rented us this place, and they went to Alaska. They aren't coming back until November."

"How long you been here?" Youngie asked.

"Since March," Clanton said. Then, "I want a fuckin' lawyer. I ain't sayin' no more, but there wasn't no fuckin' Charlie here."

Lucas turned back to Sandy Martin: "Is that right? The brothers are up in Alaska?"

"I can't prove it, but they said they were going there," Martin said. "They bought a new truck for the trip."

"And you never met Charlie Pope."

After a moment of silence, Martin said, "Look, I'm just watching the house, okay?"

Not a denial. Lucas looked at Youngie, who raised his eyebrows. "Sandy, this is a murder charge we're talking about here," Lucas said. "You give Charlie Pope one ounce of cover, man, you're right in it with him."

Another moment of silence, then, "He was up here. A month ago."

"A month ago. With Bobby here?"

"Yeah." Martin looked uncomfortable.

"You're fuckin' lyin'," Clanton said. He was angry, turning to face down Martin.

"You were talking," Martin said to him.

"You're full of shit, you little asshole," Clanton shouted. "They're gonna find out . . ."

"He was here," Martin insisted. "He was that guy who walked up the hill, he had that bag of doughnuts . . ."

LUCAS WAS LOOKING at Clanton's face as he absorbed what Martin had said. His expression shifted from anger to confusion and then to disbelief. He said, "That retard? The retard with the smiley T-shirt?"

"That's him," Martin said.

"I didn't know who he was," Clanton said, lifting his head to look at Lucas. And, "We ran that asshole off. He wanted to pick beans or some shit. We told him we didn't have no fuckin' beans, and to go the fuck away."

Clanton told the story, and it was short: Pope had been at the farm-house for ten minutes, having hitchhiked out from Austin. When he found out there weren't any beans, he walked back down the hill with his bag of doughnuts.

"What's this about the doughnuts?" Youngie asked.

"It was like he thought he might be camping out, and he needed food, so he bought doughnuts," Martin said.

Clanton said, "He's a fuckin' retard. He can't be the guy who did all that shit. He walks around in a smiley shirt with a bag of doughnuts, for Christ's sake."

Lucas pressed the pad to his face and said, "Jesus."

THE DEPUTIES CLEARED the farmhouse and found a hundred and fifty gallons of agricultural precursor in the kitchen—so much for Sandy Martin's tale of checking the house. With cops all over the place, and no real information about Pope, Lucas decided to head back home. He washed his face in the farmhouse kitchen sink, got a new first-aid pad from Youngie, and climbed into his truck.

"You oughta stop at the hospital," Youngie said.

"I'm only an hour and a half from home."

"There's gonna be a report, the gunshots . . ."

"You can do most of it. I'll either send you an affidavit or come down and talk to your county attorney, whatever you want . . . Now I just want to go home," Lucas said.

Youngie grinned: "Man, you look like shit."

"One of your guys already told me," Lucas said. He started the truck. "Thanks for the reminder."

THE DAY WASN'T QUITE DONE. He could feel his nose swelling, and blood still dribbled from one nostril. He stopped at a convenience store, paid five dollars for a bag of ice and some Ziploc bags to hold it, showed his ID to a gawking counter girl so she wouldn't call the cops, put a Ziploc bag on his face, and wheeled onto I-35.

Clanton, Lucas thought, had called Pope a *retard*. That was after a ten-minute acquaintance, if Clanton was to be believed. And Lucas believed him, on that much, anyway. Then he thought, *What if Pope was really this sophisticated Cary Grant kind of guy who for years . . .* He almost smiled to himself, but when he started to smile, pain arced down through his face.

That was Charlie Pope's fault, too.

HE SAW THE HIGHWAY PATROL car when he topped a hill. He went for the brake but knew it was too late: he could feel the radar waves passing through his nose. He was doing eighty-eight, and when the lights came up behind him, he pulled over. The patrol car idled in behind him, the patrolman calling in the Lexus's tag number. When the patrolman got out of his car, Lucas hung his ID out the window.

"Lucas Davenport, BCA," Lucas called back to him.

The cop stepped closer, looked at Lucas's shirt, soaked with blood: "What the hell happened to you?"

"I busted a meth lab with the Mower County sheriff's guys about an hour ago. One of the dopers knocked me on my ass and broke my nose. You can call the Sheriff's Department, if you want to check."

The cop took Lucas's ID, looked at it, handed it back. "You know how fast you were going back there?"

"Yeah, yeah. Man, I'm just trying to get home," Lucas said. "I'm really messed up."

"Jeez, you're gonna have a shiner, Davenport," the patrolman said with great sincerity. "You look terrible."

"Thank you," Lucas said. "That makes it fuckin' unanimous."

13

LUCAS WENT TO the Regions Hospital emergency room, where a doctor with warm soft fingers pushed his nose around, said the bleeding seemed to have stopped, and asked how Weather was doing in England.

"You know her?"

"I used to talk with her when I was doing my surgical rotation over at the university," the doc said. "She's got some amazing skills."

"I've seen her work," Lucas said.

The doc smiled at him and said, "I know. The famous tracheotomy. She used to tell us that if we really wanted to impress our boyfriends, we'd cut their throats."

She smiled; but Lucas thought of Angela Larson and Adam Rice, and grimaced. The doc, whose hands had been on his face, said, "*Ooo*—did that hurt?"

"No—so what's the diagnosis?"

She crossed her arms and looked at him with what might have been skepticism. "You got punched in the nose. It looks likes your poor nose has been through the routine before, I could feel some scar tissue on the bone . . ."

"Yeah, playing hockey . . . and one time . . . never mind."

"This time, it's only a crack, not a clean fracture. Best thing to do is to leave it. I'll put a plastic protective cup on it and give you a prescription for some pain medication. You may need it to get to sleep."

EVEN WITH THE PAIN MEDICATION, he couldn't sleep; but because of the pain medication, his brain got foggy and he couldn't think about the case, either. The protective cup drove him crazy, and at two A.M., he got up, pulled it off, and threw it away. He spent the rest of the night sitting in a leather club chair, semiupright, vacillating between slumber and stupor.

He did get a few hours: he last looked at the clock at five A.M. When Weather called at eight, he was asleep. The phone rang a second and a third time before he got to it; his back hurt from the unaccustomed position in the chair, and his face and neck hurt from Clanton's punch.

He picked up the phone: "How are you?" she asked.

WHEN HE GOT OFF THE PHONE, he went into the bathroom and looked at his face. He had a bruise the size of a saucer, a stupendous black eye; rather, a purple eye, with stripes of crimson and yellow-gray.

"Jesus H. Christ," he muttered.

He went back to his chair, closed his eyes. Another hour of unconsciousness, and the phone rang again. Sloan said, "I heard you got your nose busted."

Lucas groaned and looked at the clock. Time to go. "Yeah. My whole goddamn head hurts. I gotta sleep sitting up."

Sloan might have choked back a chuckle. "They splint it? Your nose?"

"Naw. They pushed it around a little and gave me some pills."

"Got a shiner, huh?"

"You're a ray of sunshine," Lucas said. "How's the disease?"

"I'm dying. Every hole in my body's got junk running out of it."

"I'd rather have the busted nose."

"I'd have to think about it for a while . . ."

LUCAS FILLED HIM IN on the meth-lab bust. Sloan summed it up: "You got nothing but hit in the face."

"No. I got something," Lucas said seriously.

"Yeah?"

"This Clanton guy, the guy who knocked me on my ass. We were on the lawn after we busted him, and I was pushing him on Pope. He didn't know who I was talking about. I was looking at his face when he figured it out—and, man, he couldn't *believe* it. He called Pope a *retard*."

"Mr. Politically Correct."

"Hey—we've been fighting the same thing. We've got all these really smart professionals at St. John's talking about Pope in a professional way. They'd *never* call him a retard. What they know about Pope is too complicated. But Clanton made it simple: he knew a retard when he saw one. And he's right."

"Huh." Sloan knew what Lucas was saying. "You think we're chasing the wrong guy."

"We could be," Lucas said.

"What about the DNA?"

"Oh, Pope was there, all right," Lucas said. "He did it, some of it.

But he's not setting it up. Maybe he does the act, but somebody else does the directing. Somebody else has a car, somebody else has the money, somebody else does his shopping for him—Christ, the guy can barely feed himself. There's gotta be somebody else."

"We need to find this Mike West guy."

"We need to find everybody who might ever have talked to Charlie Pope," Lucas said. "We need to get back to St. John's, talk to people."

"Not me," Sloan said. "I'm out of it for a while. I can barely fuckin' walk. I walk across the house, I get so dizzy I wanna puke."

"Hey—I'm not saying you gotta do it yourself, but that's what's gotta be done. I've got to talk to Elle some more. She was right from the beginning—it's not Charlie Pope."

WHEN HE GOT OFF THE PHONE, Lucas went into the bathroom to look in the mirror again. His face hadn't changed: it was still the color of an eggplant. The pain had changed: though it was duller than it had been, it had spread all through his skull, and he felt as though his front teeth might come out.

He couldn't use the pain pills. They kicked his ass. Instead, he took two Aleves, got a drawing pad from the study, along with the all the paper and reports generated so far, and headed back to the chair.

He was trying to get comfortable when the phone rang again.

Sloan said, "Me again. You got me thinking."

"Okay . . ."

"You say there's gotta be another guy."

"Yup."

"Then where do the Big Three come in? We know they're involved. Somehow. Who did they influence, Charlie Pope or this other guy?"

Lucas thought about it for a moment. A puzzle. "I dunno. We come back to Mike West again."

"Or somebody like Mike West," Sloan said. "I can't believe that they made a robot out of Charlie Pope, and then he just went out and *found* some brains for himself. You know, a smart crazy guy to *manage* him."

"Maybe . . . maybe it was somebody one of the Big Three knew before he went inside. Did any of those guys have accomplices? Did they work with anyone?"

"I don't know. I can get Anderson to pull all those old records, if you think it's worth doing."

"It is. We don't want to miss anything."

"I'll call him. Like, in ten minutes. Right now, I gotta get back to my toilet."

LUCAS PUT HIS KNEES up and propped the drawing pad against it, stared at the blank page. Got on the phone again, called Shrake, the BCA muscle who'd gone after Mike West. Shrake picked up on the first ring.

"You get even a sniff of him?" Lucas asked.

"Not even a sniff."

"What's his history? Does he wander all over the country, or does he stay close?"

"He's got family here, and they say he's generally around somewhere," Shrake said. "They do know he goes out west from time to time. Washington, Oregon, California."

"Look, call Minneapolis and St. Paul, and all the burbs. Tell them we need to drag the streets—this is a big priority now. This is right there with finding Charlie Pope."

IN THE SKETCHBOOK he wrote,

1. DNA
2. Kills in Minneapolis, Mankato

   3. Prison in St. John's
   4. Positive visual ID in Rochester, positive phone ID
   5. Mother in Austin, worked in area, seen in July
   6. Worked Owatonna; meet somebody there?
   7. Rice goes to Faribault bar
   8. Pope told Ignace that he'll kill somebody in the Boundary
      Waters . . .

How in the hell would somebody like Charlie Pope know anything about the Boundary Waters? Pope was a pickup guy, not a canoe guy. The second man again? He had to force himself to think *or woman*.

THE ALEVE WERE TAKING HOLD. He pushed himself out of the chair, found a Minnesota road map, and unfolded it. If you drew a cross made up of major highways south of the Twin Cities, he realized, you would encompass Charlie Pope's world.

Pope had killed Angela Larson at the northern point of the cross, a couple of miles from I-35 in Minneapolis. He'd been living in Owatonna, which was right on I-35, halfway between Minneapolis and the Iowa border. That was the center point. And he'd grown up in Austin, Minnesota, just a few miles from the Iowa border and not far east of I-35. That was the southern point.

The east-west arm of the cross ran through Owatonna, with Rochester on the east, where he was seen making a phone call, and Mankato to the west, where he'd killed the Rices. All three towns were linked by Highway 14.

As a matter of fact, it was almost perfect. He drew a circle connecting the four outlying cities, with Owatonna in the middle. The circle together with the highways looked like the crosshairs on a rifle scope.

HE CARRIED THE MAP back upstairs to the sketchbook:

    9. Must limit exposure; short drives?
   10. Too dumb to act alone; must be second guy . . .

Lucas thought about (10) for a moment, then added,
. . . who knows the Big Three.

HE WENT INTO the bathroom and shaved; the warm water felt good, but his nose was still clogged with blood, and he could only breathe through one side. That fuckin' Clanton . . .

In the shower, he decided that Pope was in his circle. Not for sure, but 80 percent. Somewhere, in a rough circle maybe a hundred miles across. He tried to do the math with the water pounding on his back. Something like 7,800 square miles, he thought. Lots of rabbit holes in 7,800 square miles of corn and beans.

With the water pouring on his head, he thought, *forlorn hope?* And then he thought, *beans?*

HE GOT OUT OF the shower, toweled off, went back to the bedroom, and sorted through the case reports. When they'd talked to Ruffe Ignace after the call from Pope, Ignace said a couple of times that he'd taken down everything Pope said "verbatim." He'd emphasized his own precision.

Lucas found the Ignace/Pope transcript in the report, and thumbed through it. According to the transcript, Pope had used the words *forlorn hope.* The words rattled around in Lucas's brain because he'd seen them in a Richard Sharpe novel by Bernard Cornwell. In the novel, the words had referred to a group of men who volunteered to be the first to attack a breach in a city wall during a siege. The survivors got otherwise impossible promotions . . . but they were also unlikely to survive.

Lucas put on shorts and a T-shirt and went down to the study, opened his *Oxford Encyclopedic English Dictionary. Forlorn hope* meant, exactly, a "faint remaining hope" or a "desperate enterprise."

He snapped the dictionary closed: Charlie Pope, the retard, had used the phrase precisely. And something else . . . He ran back up the stairs, still carrying the dictionary, and picked up Ignace's transcript. Didn't Pope say he'd thrown the baseball bat into a field of "whatever-it-is?"

Lucas found the line. Yes, he had. The whatever-it-is was *beans.*

Charlie Pope spent his entire life in a sea of soybeans, and he didn't know what a soybean field looked like when he was standing next to it? Now *that* was stupid, something you might expect from Charlie Pope.

He went back over the transcript. The language was what he'd expect from Charlie Pope, except for the "forlorn hope." And, come to think of it, Ruffe had him referring to a razor *strop.* Maybe he'd said strap and Ruffe had misspelled it.

Back to the dictionary: *strop* meant "a strip of leather for sharpening razors." Huh. Again, the precision. He'd have to talk to Ruffe . . .

HE FINISHED DRESSING, picking out a good-looking Versace blue suit and tie, a subtle Hermès necktie, blue over-the-calf socks with small coffee-colored comets woven into them, and soft black Italian loafers. He looked at himself in a mirror, took a pair of sunglasses out of his pocket, and tried a smile.

Fuckin' Jack Nicholson, he thought. Except taller and better-looking. He tried to whistle going out the door, but his face hurt when he pursed his lips.

. . .

RUFFE IGNACE TOOK two big phone calls.

The first was from Davenport. Ignace was sitting in the basement of Minneapolis's scrofulous City Hall, reading about the New York Yankees—his team—when his phone rang.

Davenport: "You sure he said 'forlorn hope' and 'razor strop'?"

"Hey. How many times do I explain the word *verbatim* to you?" Ignace asked. "That's what he said."

"But maybe he said strap, instead of strop."

"Sounded like strop to me. I don't even know what a strop is. It's like a sharpening stone, right?"

"No, it's more like a strap."

"Strop, strap, what the fuck are you talking about?"

THEN LATER, the second call.

Ignace was walking along Sixth Street, heading back toward the paper, playing Ruffe's Radio: *Thought I was a bum, shit, this jacket cost four hundred bucks. Wonder why they put the street cars right down the middle of the main street so they screw up traffic for the whole town? Look at that skinny chick, wonder if she's bulimic? She looks bulimic, looks sour . . . wonder how much Macallister makes, can't be two grand, can it? Maybe I oughta ask for another hundred, my review's when, when was the last one? March? Got a way to go . . .*

Like that. He was mumbling to himself, standing on a street corner, watching the WALK light when his cell phone rang. He fished it out of his pocket and slipped it open:

"Ignace."

"Roo-Fay . . . it's me." The coarse whisper. No question.

"Mr. Pope? Is that you?" Ignace had a reporter's notebook stuffed in his back pocket. He fished it out, walked sideways to the wall of the nearest building, and sat down on the sidewalk, the cell phone trapped between his right shoulder and ear. "How'd you get my number?"

"I called at the newspaper and told them I was a cop and it was an emergency and they gave me your cell phone. And I was telling the truth: it's an emergency, all right."

"What?"

Pope laughed. "I got her."

Ignace didn't make the connection for a second, and again said, "What?"

"I got her. The next one."

Ignace started taking notes. "Who?"

"Carlita Peterson. I been watching her for three weeks. Got her in my car and I'm leaving right now, taking her up the thirty-five right into the deep woods. Know where's this old empty cabin up there, you can camp out."

"Ah, Jesus, man, you gotta stop. You gotta stop . . ."

"I ain't gonna stop, Roo-Fay," the whisperer said. "Tell you what I'm gonna do. I'm gonna spend a little time with her tonight, take the starch out of her. Then I'm gonna kick her out in the woods tomorrow, give her a one-minute head start—I won't look, either, I won't look which way she runs. Then I'm going out with my razor. Maybe she'll get away."

"Ah, Jesus . . ."

"My other woman drove me to it; I been walking around with a hard-on for three days, the way she talks, she just drives me to distraction. But this'll fix it for a while. You know how, after you fuck, you don't have to fuck again for a while? Well, after I take this next one, I won't have to worry about taking my woman."

"Ah, jeez . . ."

"Hey, don't tell me it don't give you a little tingle in the back of your balls, thinking about it."

"Listen, Mr. Pope. Please. Let her go. C'mon, you gotta get help, please let her go. I'll write whatever you want, I'll write your whole story, whatever you want to say, if you just let her go . . ."

"Hey, fuck you, Roo-Fay. Too late for all of that shit. But I'll tell you what—you got the rest of today and all of tonight to find us. I won't do her until tomorrow morning; but that's as long as I'm gonna go. You tell that to the cops."

Click.

IGNACE STARED DUMBFOUNDED at the phone for a moment, then pushed himself up, unconsciously brushed the seat of his pants, took a couple of walking steps, then broke into a run, running as hard as he could, arms pumping, notebook in one hand, cell phone in the other, down to the paper, buzzing all the way: *Man, man-oh-man, Jesus, man.*

CAROL STUCK HER HEAD in Lucas's office and said, "If your nose doesn't hurt too bad to talk, a guy named Rufus is on the telephone. He says he's a reporter from the *Star-Tribune* and it's urgent."

Lucas picked up the phone: "Davenport."

"He just called me," Ignace blurted. "One minute ago. On my cell phone."

"Ah, shit . . . ," Lucas said.

"He said he took a woman whose name is Carlita Peterson, wait a minute, wait a minute, I got the number he was calling from . . ."

Lucas sat up and shouted at Carol, "We're gonna need a phone number run . . . Get Dave, get Dave on the line . . ."

Ignace said, "You ready? Here it is . . ."

He recited the number and Lucas shouted it to Carol, who shouted back, "Dave's running it . . ."

Lucas went back to the phone: "He said he's already got this woman?"

"That's what he said. He said he's going to take her up north and fuck with her for a while and then tomorrow morning he's going to turn her loose and hunt her down with his razor."

"You're sure it was him?"

"Same guy as last time."

Carol shouted, "Carlita Diaz Peterson, Northfield. It's a cell phone. The address is coming up."

Lucas yelled back, "Get the sheriff on the line. I think it's Rice County, but it might be Dakota. Get somebody over to her house. Tell the phone guys I want to know the location of the cell phone when he called . . ."

BACK TO IGNACE, the phone: "Are you at your office?"

"Yes."

"Stay there. I'll be there soon as I can. I'll need a typescript."

"I'll have it by the time you get here," Ignace said. He suddenly left his asshole persona and sounded like a worried human being: "Jesus, Davenport, he said he had her in his car, that he was already heading north."

LUCAS BANGED OUT the number for the co-op office, talked to Ray Reese: "Pull your socks up. The *Star-Trib* reporter got another call from Charlie Pope; he says he's taken a woman from Northfield and he's in his car heading for the Boundary Waters. Pull the trigger on the network. Now."

"Hang on."

Ten seconds later, Reese was back: "We're doing it. Anything else? You know where he's starting from?"

"Gonna get that in a minute. Tell everybody that Pope says he already picked up the woman. Tell them that: that he says he's got her, that if we miss him, she's gonna die. Tell them to be careful."

HE THREW THE PHONE back at the receiver and realized his hands were slippery with sweat: that didn't happen often. Up and out of the office: Carol was on the phone. "Where'd it come from? Where'd it come from?"

She waved him off.

He walked out of the office, ten feet down the hall, and then back, anxious to move, grating, "Where's it coming from?"

She was taking a note, then pulled the phone away from her ear: "It came from a cell in Burnsville." Burnsville was a big suburb right on the south side of the metro area: Pope was less than fifteen miles from where Lucas was sitting.

"Damnit. If he's heading north . . . He could be on either Thirty-five E or Thirty-five W . . ."

"Or city streets," Carol offered.

"Yeah. Call Burnsville. Tell them that. Pull out everything."

He went back to the map. If Pope was on either branch of I-35, he would just about be going through the downtown area of either Minneapolis or St. Paul. But the two areas were ten minutes apart, and he might also have gone either east or west on the I-494 loop.

Pope had called from precisely the place where they could get the least information on direction. But if he were going north, the possibilities narrowed down again once he got north of the Twin Cities. The most obvious route would be on I-35 north, but there were other major links going north.

If he was going north. He'd never gone north before.

Lucas thought of the bull's-eye he'd drawn on the Minnesota map that morning. He went back to the phone, called Reese at the co-op office: "Ray, listen. He called from Burnsville. That means if he's going north, he's in the metro area, so move the search area north about as fast as he could be traveling. Then, when the network is set, I want you to call all of the major nodes in the south end. He may be jerking us around when he keeps saying that he's going north. He didn't leave his home ground with the others, and from what I've been able to tell, Pope doesn't know anything about the Boundary Waters. So tell the people down south that he may be down there. Tell them that it's really critical that they don't ease off because they think he's going north . . ."

"I can get that out in five minutes."

"Do that."

Carol stuck her head in the office: "Two calls—Northfield police and Ruffe Ignace, that reporter . . ."

"I want both of them. Give me Northfield first."

HE PICKED UP his phone and a voice said, "Agent Davenport, this is Jim Goode down in Northfield. We've got a car at the Peterson house, and it doesn't look good. She didn't show up at work this morning. She's a ceramics teacher at St. Olaf, and the guys looked in the window of her house and they saw some cut rope on the kitchen floor. They called that probable cause, went in, they say the house is empty, but there's a smear of what looks like dried blood on the kitchen floor, not much, but a smear, and that cut rope."

"Seal the place off," Lucas said. "I'll send down our crime-scene crew . . ."

"It's sealed off now. I'm calling in all our guys, we're gonna do the streets, and the sheriff is running the county."

"Don't quit on it—there's a possibility that he's still down there."

"That cocksucker, if he's killed Carlita Peterson, he's a dead man," Goode said.

"You know her?"

"Yes, a little bit. She seemed like a nice lady."

"I'm coming down," Lucas said. "I've got a guy to talk to first, I might be a couple of hours."

IGNACE CAME UP: "Listen, instead of running over here, I got a transcript that I can cut and paste to Microsoft Word and ship it to you. You could have it in one minute."

"Do that," Lucas said. "I should have thought of it myself. Here's the address . . ."

HE CHECKED THREE TIMES, five seconds apart, and then the document came rolling in. At the top: "This is verbatim."

Lucas read down through the conversation between Pope and Ignace. Pope said they had until tomorrow morning. Some time, then. Not much, and he might be lying. Still, there was a chance.

He sent the document to the printer, then looked again at the language, searching for the kind of things he'd pulled out of the first call. Nothing struck him that seemed particularly important. Pope said he had the woman in his car, which implied a sedan or coupe, but not a pickup or an SUV. That eliminated about half the vehicles heading north . . . unless he was lying. Pope said he was "leaving."

Leaving from Burnsville? Was that where he was hiding? A big town, a major suburb. Lots of people around.

Most likely, Lucas thought, Pope meant that he was leaving the area, not that he was leaving that very minute. Lucas was still mulling over the conversation when Carol came in: "Channel Three just called. They've heard about the network alert from their cops reporter. Everybody else will hear about it in the next ten minutes. What do you want me to do?"

"Tell them that we've got no comment at this time . . . Do they have Peterson's name yet?"

"They didn't say anything."

Lucas stood up, picked up his sport coat. "Put them off. Tell them you can't talk without an okay from me, and I'm somewhere in my car. You don't know where."

"So where will you be?"

"Northfield. I'll be on the cell," Lucas said.

"And you're okay to drive?"

"Huh?"

"Your nose—your face. You don't look so good."

"Nah. I'm fine. Couple more Aleves, I'm good for the day." He touched his nose, gave it a tentative push, and winced. For ten minutes there, he'd forgotten about it.

He stopped at the co-op center, three guys, three computers, and three telephones in a room the size of a closet. Lucas said, "Probably a sedan or coupe. White, maybe an Olds."

They all nodded, and he was out the door.

EVERY ONCE IN A WHILE, Carlita Peterson would get together both the energy and the angle to give the backseat a good thump. She was lying on her face, or had been, and it gave him a hard-on thinking about her back there, desperate, trying to kick, feeling the rope cut into her.

Knowing the power.

The Gods Down the Hall always said that was the best part. The killing and the pain were fine, but when you could look into their eyes, and know they were feeling the power . . .

He'd stash her for the rest of the day, take her out tonight, just like he'd told Ruffe that he would. And tomorrow morning . . . He could feel the need coming on him, stronger than ever. The Gods Down the

Hall had talked to him about this, about the power and the need, so closely tied together, about the ecstasy that was coming . . .

ONE NIGHT WALKING BACK to Millie Lincoln's town house, Mihovil said, "Is Sherrie a very close friend with you?"

"Well . . . yeah. I guess," she said. "I mean, we don't hang out so much now that you're around, but we used to, you know. Hang out."

"I think she watches us make love."

"What?"

"The other night when I came over and we go back to the playroom and do it, and then we are resting, and I see a spot of light on the door. A minute later, I look back and it's gone. No light. Then a couple of minutes later, I see the light again. Just a little spot. So then we are doing it again, and I see no light."

"What was it?" Millie was intrigued.

"There is a very small hole in the door, like a nail hole, right under the bar that runs across the middle of it. When we are done, and you and Sherrie are in the kitchen, I look through the hole. All you can see is the bed, but you can see all of the bed. I think . . . when there is no light, she is watching. When you can see light, then her eye is not at the hole."

Millie could feel herself going a flame pink. The witch. What did she see? What had they been doing the last time . . . ? Millie thought about it and, if anything, got a little pinker.

"Why didn't you *say* anything?"

"Well, I am not sure. And you are friends. And I'm not sure she was watching. But I think she was."

Now a surge of anger. "Goddamnit. We're gonna have it out right now . . ." She stepped out a little faster.

"Wait, wait wait . . . ," Mihovil said. "Maybe, let it go this night."

"What?"

"What can it hurt? She watches, she doesn't do anything. You can't take pictures through the hole. She has no boyfriend, she just enjoys herself."

"You sound like you *liked* it."

"Well . . ." He shrugged and grinned. "Maybe I did like it . . ."

"*God*, Mihovil . . ." But, in fact, his comment produced a little thrill.

That night, when they were doing it, Millie kept an eye on the door—and that meant she had to keep her glasses on, because she couldn't see the little spot without them. Would Sherrie be suspicious? Millie didn't know, but she wanted to see if the little spot was there—and before they went in the bedroom, Mihovil had carefully turned on a living-room desk lamp that they'd calculated would provide the light.

And Millie saw the tiny light blink at her. This time, she got more than a little thrill: Mihovil had his head down between her thighs, and her head was propped on the pillow, her eyes cracked just enough to watch the light, and when the light blinked out—when Sherrie started watching—Millie felt a rush so intense that she wasn't sure she could stand it.

She cried out once, and again, and felt her heels drumming on the mattress as Mihovil had said they would, when she *really* got into it, and then an orgasm rolled over her brain like a tsunami. She could remember yipping, a noise she'd never heard herself make before, and then nothing was anything except the feeling of Mihovil's tongue in the middle of her existence, and her own self, going off . . .

14

LUCAS HAD TAKEN the truck to work, because the softer ride was easier on his broken nose. Now he stuck the flasher on the roof, punched the address of Carlita Peterson's house into his dashboard navigation system, cut too fast through the traffic on I-35, and got clear of St. Paul.

When the traffic had thinned, he reached into the passenger foot well and fumbled through his briefcase, looking for Ignace's transcript of the talk with Pope. Someplace, something in the document was not quite right. He wasn't sure what it was: just a vibration.

He found the transcript, pinned the paper into the center of the steering wheel with his thumb, and read it again. No vibration this time. But he'd picked something up the first time he'd read it . . .

He got on the cell phone and called Sloan at home: "Pope called and said he's picked up a woman named Carlita Peterson from Northfield. He says he's taking her north."

"Ah, no." Cough. "What'd he say exactly?"

Lucas read the transcript, flicking his eyes between the paper and the traffic he was knifing through. Sloan said, "Find out . . . never mind. If the house listing was to a Carlita Peterson, that probably means she's single or divorced and lives alone. That's three single people. We know Rice went to bars looking for women, and Larson used to go into Chaps when she got off work. I bet he's picking them up in bars or some kind of social activity . . ."

LUCAS THOUGHT ABOUT IT: Northfield was a college town just off I-35 and not far from Faribault, where Adam Rice had spent time at the Rockyard. If Lucas had been told that a sexual predator had been hanging out in Faribault and asked to guess where he would next attack, he might have guessed Northfield. A couple of thousand college girls would provide easy prey, and the college town's mix of student and farm bars, cafés, and stores would provide plenty of camouflage through which to prowl.

"I'll buy that," Lucas said to Sloan. "Listen: Any chance that Larson was gay, or had gay contacts?"

"Nobody said anything. She had a boyfriend . . . What are you thinking?"

"I'm thinking about the second man—or the second woman," Lucas said. "What if she's picking them up and Pope just does the killing? Nobody would ever see him in a bar. If she drives, nobody would ever see him in a car."

"Yeah, but you could make the same argument if it's a guy—he picks up women as a straight guy, or men as a gay."

"But: nobody ever saw Larson hanging out with guys in Chaps," Lucas said. "That paper you gave me said she mostly went in to chat with the bartender. And a woman would be more inclined to walk outside, or get in a car, with another woman, than with a man."

"Let me call around," Sloan said. "I'll get some guys asking questions."

"We've now got two people connected to colleges. Both the women. One a student, one a teacher."

After a moment of thought, Sloan said, "I don't see much in that."

"Neither do I, but think about it," Lucas said. And, almost as an afterthought, "How're you feeling?"

"Better. I get these coughing jags that make me think I'm gonna bust a rib, but I don't feel too bad. Maybe get out tomorrow . . ."

WHEN LUCAS RANG OFF, he realized that he'd become distracted, trying to read, talk on the phone, and drive all at once. He was speeding down a white line between two lanes, still running over a hundred. He guiltily moved back into the left lane; he hated to see other drivers on cell phones . . .

And goddamnit! What had he picked up in the transcript? Something had stuck in his mind like a gooey old song, and he couldn't stop thinking about it. Nothing obvious, something subtle . . .

He held the Lexus at a hundred; any faster and the truck felt unstable. As it was, he made it into Northfield in a little more than half an hour from his office. Following the GPS map off I-35 down Highway 19, he buzzed past the Malt-O-Meal plant, across the bridge and a long block up to Division, right on Division and left on Seventh, and up a long rising hill until he saw, on the left, two cop cars outside a small blue-gray clapboard house that stood in a copse of maples.

A couple of cops were leaning against a car and turned to look at his truck as he pulled to the curb. He killed the engine, pulled the flasher and tossed it on the passenger seat, and walked up the drive. A dilapidated detached garage sat just behind the house, and a stack of decorative birch firewood was piled next to a side door.

"Davenport?" one of the cops asked.

"Yeah—nothing?"

The cop shook his head. "Nothing you don't know about. A dab of blood, a piece of rope. It don't look good."

"Who all's inside?"

"Only our lead investigator, Jim Goode. The chief's down at the office, coordinating. If you're going in, you should go in the back."

LUCAS WALKED AROUND to the back of the house, climbed a short wooden stoop, and looked in through the screen door. Inside, a thin man in a plaid shirt and gray slacks was talking on a cell phone. He saw Lucas and said into the phone, "Just a minute," and then, to Lucas, "Lucas Davenport?"

"Yeah."

"I'm Jim Goode. If you hook the edge of the screen with your fingernails, you can pull the door open. The house is contaminated up to where I am."

Lucas hooked the door open, carefully avoiding the door handle. He was in the kitchen, a small room with laminate cupboards and a narrow, U-shaped counter covered with plastic; a double porcelain sink, chipped and yellowed with age; and a floor of curling vinyl.

The walls were real plaster, and there were pots everywhere, several with flowers, geraniums and cut yellow roses. A small breakfast table, covered with an embroidered tablecloth, sat under a bright window, with two brilliant blue chairs, one on each side. The arrangement looked both tidy and lonely. The house probably dated to World War II, he thought, and had last been updated in the seventies.

THERE WAS A FOOT-LONG smear on the floor, the purple-black color of blood. Somebody had stepped in it and smeared it. Not too much blood, Lucas thought: less than he'd lost when he was hit in the nose. On the other side of the kitchen was a curl of yellow plastic rope, the kind used to tie down tarpaulins. Goode was saying into the cell phone, "I do think we have to get them farther out now. Uh-huh. At least that far. And Dakota has to push down this way . . . Okay. Maybe we could try the Highway Patrol . . . Uh-huh. Okay. Davenport's here now, I'll be back pretty quick."

He rang off, put his hand out, and as Lucas shook it, he said, "We've got everybody we can find out on country roads. If he's really going to hunt her down, and do it around here, he's got to be moving around. We downloaded pictures of Pope and Peterson, Xeroxed off a few hundred of them, and we've got students from St. Olaf and Carleton going out in their cars, leafleting everything inside of twenty miles."

"Hope nobody stumbles on Pope."

"They're out in groups of three, except where they're putting up public posters in stores and phone poles, and then they're in twos," Goode said. "Everybody's got cell phones."

"Great," Lucas said. And it was—somebody had been moving fast. "What about this place?"

Goode pointed: "The blood and the rope. That's all we've got—but it really is blood, it isn't chocolate syrup or anything. It's pretty dry, but not completely, so he probably got her this morning." He was talking quickly, nervously, the words tumbling out. "We checked the house to make sure there was nobody here. Other than the check, we've stayed out. We're hoping your crime-scene crew . . ."

"They might find signs of Pope or a second person with him, but they won't help us find Peterson," Lucas said. "We gotta be careful in here, but I want to go through her personal records. Credit-card bills, that sort of thing. Did you see anything like that?"

"There's a little office in the second bedroom." Goode pointed down a hallway.

"Then that's where I'll be," Lucas said. "What about Peterson? Single or divorced? Kids?"

"Divorced two years. No kids. Ex-husband's a teacher at the high school."

"Check him?"

"At the exact time that call got to your reporter up in Minneapolis, he was halfway through a physics class. It's not a copycat."

"How about Peterson? She good looking? Has she been out on the town?"

"Pretty average-looking, forty, a little heavy . . . Hang on. There's a photograph." He stepped over to a kitchen counter, pushed a piece of paper, and pointed at a snapshot. "We're not touching it, because we thought maybe Pope shot it. Brought it with him. But that's her."

A woman with brown hair, a squarish chin held up a bit, direct dark eyes.

Goode continued as Lucas looked at the photo: "We don't know if she's been on the town. She's been divorced two years, so she might have been looking around."

"Okay. This is critical, because everybody that Pope's killed has been single, and out on the town at least a little bit," Lucas said. "It's about the only thing we can find that all three had in common. Get some guys, talk to the neighbors, talk to the people at Carleton. I want to know who she hung out with, who her friends were. I want to talk to her ex. I want to do this as quick as you can get them here . . . Or not here, but someplace close by."

"I'll set something up," Goode said. He took a calendar out of his pocket, took out a card, and scribbled on it. "My cell phone. You think of a single thing, call me, I'll be right outside on the street, talking to neighbors."

"Okay."

Lucas turned away and took a step, and then Goode asked, "What are her chances?"

"Man . . . ," Lucas shook his head. "If he's telling the truth, and she's still alive? About one in hundred, I'd say. We're gonna have to take him while he's moving her."

GOODE LEFT, and Lucas went back to Peterson's home office. Her desk was made of four file cabinets, two each on either side of a knee space, with a red-lacquered door spanning the knee space. A Macintosh laptop sat in the middle of the desk, with a cable leading to a small HP ink-jet printer on the left. A telephone sat next to the printer, along with a radio-CD player; a CD, showing a slender woman standing in the rain with an umbrella overhead—*Jazz for a Rainy Afternoon*—sat on top of the player. And there were pencils and ballpoints in an earthenware jar, a bottle of generic ibuprofen, a Rolodex, a box of Kleenex, a scratchpad, and a bunch of yellow legal pads.

The walls around the desk were crowded with cheap oak-look bookcases, six feet tall, the shelves jammed with books. More books and papers sat on top of the bookcases, and more paper was stacked on the floor.

And he could smell her. She had been in the room not too many hours earlier, wearing perfume, a subtle scent, just a hint of lilacs or violets or lilies of the valley—something woodland, wild, and light.

THE SCENT CAUGHT HIM by surprise. For a moment, he lay his forehead on the front edge of her desk, closed his eyes. A few seconds passed, and he sat up, pushed the "on" button on the Mac, and began going through the desk litter, starting with the scratchpad, the notebooks, and the Rolodex. Anything that might show a place, or a date, or an appointment.

He found phone numbers with a couple of first names, some appointment times noted with places that seemed to refer to student meetings. Could the second guy be a student? Seemed unlikely—what student would want to hang with Pope? But everything he found, he set aside.

When the computer was up, he went into the mail program and started reading down through the "in box," the "deleted" and the "sent" listings. More names, with e-mail addresses; most of the e-mail was from students, a few from fellow faculty, one from a woman who was apparently a personal friend who wanted to know if she was going up to MOA Saturday. Mall of America? Two e-mails came from a guy with the initial Z who Lucas thought was probably Peterson's ex-husband, concerning cuts from a jade tree. Most of the rest came from ceramics people scattered around the country. Receipts from Amazon, old travel reservations with Northwest, Hertz, and Holiday Inn, and miscellaneous life detritus made up the rest.

Nothing leaped out at him.

He pulled open the file cabinets: she was meticulous about finances, and one cabinet contained file folders of her American Express and Visa bills. Lucas went through them line by line, noting the few times she'd used her credit cards in what appeared to be restaurants. There weren't many, and most were out of state.

He made notes on all of it and was still working when Goode called back.

"Marilyn Derech is a friend of hers," Goode said. "She lives down the street, three houses down. We can use her family room to talk to people. I've got them coming here, we've got a half dozen coming so far. There are a couple here now . . ."

"I'll come down. I've got some more names," Lucas said. "Did you ever find her purse?"

"Uh . . . we tried not to track through the place much, but it seems like I saw a bag by the couch facing the TV in the front room."

"Okay. Give me five minutes."

He found the bag, pawed through it. Again, her scent hit him in the face. And Jesus, the old cliché about women's handbags had never been wrong, he thought. She had everything in there but a fishing pole. Lots of paper: receipts from the gas station, notes from students, a withdrawal slip—forty dollars—from an ATM, bundled Kleenex, loose change, glasses, a glasses-cleaning cloth, a billfold with thirty-five dollars in the cash slot and some change in the clip section.

Car keys in the bottom of the bag. A rock; an ordinary black smooth basaltic stone, and he wasn't the least bit mystified: Weather picked up that kind of stuff all the time. Lipstick. A ChapStick. Another ChapStick. More ibuprofen.

Nothing: he felt like throwing the bag through the fuckin' front window.

Turned around in the room. She'd just been here, and now, she was God knows where. His eye caught the clock on the stove in the kitchen, through the archway from the living room: as he glanced at it, the display changed, clicking off a minute.

He could feel the time trickling away.

HE GOT HIS NOTES and hurried outside; a cop was still leaning against the car, designated, he guessed, to keep an eye on the house. "If the phone rings in there . . ."

"It won't—they're being routed downtown."

"Good. Where's this place . . . ?"

The cop pointed farther up the street and across. "That white house. The one . . . There's Jim."

Lucas saw Goode step out on a porch and look down toward him. He went that way, fast.

"GODDAMN TIME," he said to Goode as he hurried up. "We've got no time."

"I know, I know . . . I got six people here." Goode looked at his watch. "We sent a guy downtown to get her ex-husband, he's been down at the station . . ."

"What's his name?"

"Uh, shit—Zack? Zeke?"

Lucas nodded: "Okay."

MARILYN DERECH WAS a plump blond woman who looked scared: wide-eyed and scared. Four other women and a plump man, who all looked scared, sat on the living-room couch and chairs, and two more kitchen chairs Derech had brought into the living room.

Lucas introduced himself, got their names: "We're really in trouble here," he said. "Does anybody know anything about her social life? Who she was seeing, where she went at night? Was she dating, did she go to bars?"

After a moment of silence, one of the women flipped up a hand. "We went to a restaurant up in the Cities, they have wine and music." The woman had introduced herself as Carol Olson. She looked about forty, with medium-brown hair, a thin nose. "On Grand Avenue in St. Paul, it's called BluesBerries."

"BluesBerries—I know where that is," Lucas said. "Did you talk to guys, did you . . ."

"We just went up and had some wine and listened to music, and then we had dinner . . . we didn't really talk to anybody."

"Only the one time."

"I only went the one time, but I think she'd gone up a couple of times." Then she stopped and put a hand to her lips. "Listen to me. I'm trying to protect her reputation. I don't *think* she went up, I *know* she did. She knew the place pretty well, where the best parking was and everything. She liked it because she thought . . . it was interesting and safe and she wouldn't see anybody from Northfield up there."

"Why wouldn't she want to see anybody from Northfield? She was divorced."

"Yes, but Zach is around. He's not dating anyone," Olson said. "When they broke up, it was sort of her that did it. She wanted a little . . . more."

"Adventure?" Lucas asked.

"More of something," Olson said.

"I'm not being cute," Lucas said. "Was she looking around? Was she hanging out? Was BluesBerries it, or was she hitting the bars? Did anybody ever hear of a place down in Faribault called the Rockyard?"

The guy, who had introduced himself as Tom Wells, knew about the Rockyard. "I live up the street, my business sells commercial sanitary supplies—toilet paper and paper towels and cleaning stuff . . . the Rockyard is one of our accounts. If you were going to pick one place where Carlita Peterson would never go, that's it."

"But would she *know* not to go there?"

"She'd know," he said. "She wouldn't go there."

"If you took Carlita to a strange city and told her to find a place to eat, the first door she walked through would be the best restaurant in town," said a woman named Ann Lasker.

"But maybe she'd go there for an adventure? To the Rockyard?'"

"Her adventures wouldn't come in the form of a biker," Wells said. "If she was looking for action, it'd maybe be a"—he looked around at the women—"what? A history professor who sailed?"

A couple of them nodded.

LUCAS WORKED THEM THROUGH: Where did she go, whom did she see? The answers were "not far, and not many, outside the school."

Fifteen minutes in, Zachery Peterson arrived. He was a tall man, too thin, in a pale blue short-sleeved dress shirt, dark blue slacks, and brown thick-soled shoes. He wore tiny rimless spectacles and had a sparse, two-inch ponytail tied with a rubber band. He stood with his hands knotted in his pockets.

He hadn't heard from his ex-wife in two weeks: "We talked about once a month," he told Lucas, looking uncomfortable. "We hadn't really settled everything from the divorce yet. It was going slow."

"Did she mention any kind of relationship with anyone, *any* kind of relationship?" Lucas asked. "Did she have any new girlfriends? Anybody?"

They all shook their heads; and they went down his list of questions. Lucas was watching Peterson, caught him once wiping an eye, and wrote him off as a suspect.

"If he took her, he took her from the house, early. Did anyone see a car? Could you call all your neighbors and ask if anybody saw a strange car . . . ?"

GOING OUT OF THE HOUSE, he looked back and caught the kitchen clock in the Derech house: an hour had gone by. Another one. He was nowhere.

Sloan called: "I can't find anyone who'll tell me that Larson was gay, or ever had any gay contacts, or even knew a lesbian, for that matter."

"Everybody knows a lesbian," Lucas said. He was outside on Derech's lawn, looking at the sun.

"Everybody but Larson."

LUCAS WENT BACK to Peterson's house, into the detached garage, pulled her car apart. Nothing to work with. Nothing. Back into the house, into the paper. Desperation pulling at his shirttails. Somebody called, "Agent Davenport?"

"Yeah . . ."

Back past the stove clock to the back door. A cop was there, in uniform. Another man stood in the backyard, an elderly man, cork shaped, with white-straw hair, wearing a cap that said TOP GUN. He had a small black, brown, and white dog on the end of a thin leash. The dog kept jumping straight up in the air. Lucas thought it might have been a Jack Russell terrier.

The cop said, "Mr. Grass lives around the block . . . well, around two blocks. He was walking Louie this morning and thinks he may have seen a guy around here that he'd never seen before."

A pulse of hope.

Lucas stepped outside, trying to relax his face. "Mr. Grass? Your first name is . . ."

"Louie . . . just like the dog." He frowned at Lucas: "What the hell happened to your face, son? You look like you went three rounds with a better boxer."

"That's about right," Lucas said, touching the loop of bruised skin under his eye, wincing. "A guy plugged me right in the nose . . . Listen, tell me about this car."

"Silver car . . ."

"Not white?"

"Mmm, looked silver. Could have been white, I guess. I saw him down at the bottom of the block going around the corner. I thought he might be lost because he was going slow."

"No way you would have seen the plates . . ."

"I did see the plates, but I don't know what the number was. It was Minnesota, though."

"Could it have been an Oldsmobile?"

"I don't know . . . Do they have an SUV?"

Lucas grimaced. "An SUV? It wasn't a sedan?"

"Naw, it was an SUV," Grass said. "I couldn't tell you what make, they all look alike." He picked up Lucas's look of frustration and said, "I'm sorry."

"The driver . . ."

Now Grass shook his head. "Didn't see his face. I was going this way, he was going the other way, and he was looking away from me . . . but he came down this street, all right. Early. Before six o'clock. This goddamn dog has a bigger prostate than I do, I think. He starts jumping up and down, yapping, wants to get out and pee first thing."

"Mr. Grass, if you can remember *anything* else . . . this is really critical . . ."

Grass looked sad; thought and shook his head. "I'm sorry, son. I saw this car go by, all by itself, early, slow, and it just stuck in my mind. But I didn't pay it any real attention."

"Think about it, will you?" Lucas asked. "Any little thing."

They talked for another minute, then Lucas got on his phone and called the co-op: "Listen: we've got a second guy who says the car may be light, silver or possibly white. But he says it's an SUV. Put that out: tell everybody not to rely on it, we're still looking for a white Olds, but if anyone spots a silver or white SUV in a sensitive area, stop it."

THE AFTERNOON SLOPED into evening. Lucas felt like he wanted to prop a couple of two-by-fours under the sun to keep it from going down. The crime-scene people arrived, confirmed most of what they already knew: there was blood on the kitchen floor. They also pointed out two small round black marks the size of dimes, on the vinyl floor. Since there were only two marks, there was a good chance they'd been made by the killer.

"Black-soled athletic shoes," the crime-scene tech said. "Soft rubber. It rubs off easy, on vinyl. If she'd been wearing them, we'd probably see more of them. It's almost impossible to keep from rubbing them off . . ."

"How many people in Minnesota wear black-soled athletic shoes?" Lucas asked.

"Lots," the tech said. "Maybe hundreds of thousands."

LUCAS WORKED THROUGH the rest of the files in Peterson's office and learned a lot about Peterson, but nothing helpful. He went so far as to dump her entire e-mail list to the co-op, to have them run against car registrations, looking for a white GM car or a silver SUV.

Nothing.

Minnesota is a tall state, Lucas thought, going out into the yard, looking at the half dome of the sun as it sank behind the house next door, but even if he was going all the way north, he'd be there.

A great summer evening; there'd be a few car deaths and a few more cripplings, a couple of shootings—maybe—and somewhere a woman was waiting to be butchered.

He couldn't stand it.

STANDING IN THE YARD, he talked to Sloan again—Sloan had gone downtown so he'd have access to a police computer—and to Elle, and even to Weather, whom he reached before she went to bed.

"You say *Sloan* is going psycho . . . you sound like *you're* going psycho," she said. "I don't think it's healthy for both of you to be crazy at the same time."

"Sloan says he's gonna quit. He sounds serious." Silence, two seconds, five seconds. "You still there?"

"I was wondering what took him so long," Weather said.

"Ah, Jesus, I'm trying to talk him out of it."

"Don't do that. Let him get out."

"Gotta find this goddamn woman," Lucas said.

"Yes. Do it."

HE WENT DOWN to the Northfield police station, a red-brick riverside building shared by the cops and the fire department. Three cops were sitting in a conference room, two city guys and a sheriff's deputy, Styrofoam cups scattered around, the smell of coffee and old pastry; a police radio burped in the background, a harsh underline to the hunt. The main dispatch center for the region was in Owatonna, well to the south, and the cops inside the station were just waiting for any call that needed a quick reaction. Not what you'd expect, Lucas thought, for a major search operation—but the fact that there was nobody in the office meant that everybody was on the road.

Stopping white cars. Stopping light-colored SUVs.

Stopping cars with single men in them. Stopping cars that looked funny; acted funny; might be out of place.

Glassing hillsides in the woods, as though they were hunting for deer, or elk.

Fighting the sundown.

AFTER DARK, the action slowed. Reports came in from the Boundary Waters. Nothing there.

Lots of cars stopped.

Lucas watched, waited, and talked. At eleven o'clock, tense but bored, tired of jumping every time one of the radios burped, he borrowed a yellow legal pad and began to copy the names of rock songs onto a piece of paper. One hundred and twenty songs, when he finished. He looked at the list, crossed off two songs, added one that Carol had suggested that morning —Robert Palmer's "Bad Case of Loving You," which Lucas thought was on pretty shaky grounds to make the top 100, if not in outright quicksand. Still, a good tune . . .

He stood up and said, "Jesus Christ, where is she?"

A half an hour later, he'd rolled and rerolled the paper with the rock list until it looked like a cheap yellow cigar. He finally stuffed it in his pants pocket and was about to go out for a Coke when a Goodhue County deputy was routed through to the dispatcher in Owatonna, and then back out to the countryside. He was breathing hard: "Guy . . . white truck I think, SUV, turned off when he saw my lights, running fast, dumped his lights, I think he cut across a field because I lost him, I don't know which way he's heading now, but he was heading west when I first saw him, I'm gonna go another mile or two south, see what I can see, cut my lights and creep back up the road, I think maybe he's just pulled off, you got somebody west of here on Nineteen?"

"Yeah, we got a couple guys, I'll get them headed that way."

"Tell them to shut down the flashers, he saw mine and dodged . . . I'm not seeing anything . . ."

"Jesus Christ," Lucas said, as the dispatcher talked to cops farther out. "Where is this, where is this . . . ?"

One of the cops poked a map; his finger touched a spot where Goodhue, Rice, and Dakota counties came together.

Then another guy came up and shouted, "Whoa, whoa, whoa, guy ran by me moving fast . . . high lights. He was doing eighty-eight, I think it's the SUV, I'm turning. I'm on Nineteen, Jenny, get me some help up here . . ."

"C'mon," Lucas shouted at the radio.

The deputy shouted, "Ah, shit, he's gone, he's killed his lights, I don't know, shit, don't know whether he went north, south, or straight ahead. Goddamn . . . I'm going north on Boyd, that was the first turn, but he maybe ditched somewhere, do we have anybody west on Nineteen? Or south, we need somebody south . . . Man, he was moving. Andy, if you're still around Waterford, get over to Nineteen and head east. He may be coming at you, I don't know what color the car was, his high lights were on, but I think it was an SUV . . . I clocked him at eighty-eight . . . He could be going south, do we have anybody south . . . ?"

Lucas listened for another few seconds, then asked, "Where is that?"

One of the cops jabbed a finger at a wall map. "Tommy was coming west on Highway Nineteen when he saw the guy, and the guy disappeared here. Tommy went north, Andy is coming in this way . . ."

Lucas looked at it, said, "Maybe he should have gone south *here* instead of north . . ." He was second-guessing the guy on the scene, and he had absolutely nothing to base it on, except his own case of nerves.

"Flip of the coin," the cop said. "It's all cut up over there, hills and farm plains. We—"

He shut up for a moment as the dispatcher said, "Manny, are you up?"

"Yeah, I'm moving, but I'm way over northwest of town."

Lucas looked at the map for another minute, then said, "I'm going out there. South. I can be there in five minutes."

"Big chunk of territory."

"I'm doing nothing here," he said. "And there's nobody out there right now."

HE FELT BETTER as soon as he got in the truck. He put the light on the roof and ripped south out of town, working with the navigation system on his truck. If the guy had been going west on 19 and turned south, and was trying to dodge cops by taking a twisty route out of trouble . . . Lucas manipulated the scale of the map up and down, running out to One Hundredth Street at high speed. There were few cars around—more pickups than anything—and few of them were moving fast, as far as Lucas could tell without radar. He punched the number of the Northfield center into his cell phone: "This is Davenport—any action?"

"Tommy's coming south again. Andy hasn't hit anything on Nineteen, he's going to turn south on Kellogg, but the guy's gotta be way south of that, if he went south. Most likely, he's ditched in some woods off Nineteen."

"I'm running with a single flasher on One Hundredth Street, I haven't seen anything yet."

"Have you crossed Kane?"

"About a minute ago."

"Then you're coming up on Goodhue. It's gravel down there, I'd suggest you head south, then come back west on One Hundred Tenth. There are a bunch of little streets south of there on Kane."

Lucas traced the suggested route on his nav system, thought it sounded reasonable. He cut south on Goodhue, spraying gravel.

The night was hazy, the lights of the surrounding small towns showing up as ghosts on the sky. He took Goodhue across some railroad tracks to One Hundred Tenth, cut west, hesitated at the next crossroad, and turned south again. He zigged back and forth, following the dusty gravel roads, narrow, no shoulders, houses flicking by in the night; some of the houses were old farmsteads, some looked like they'd been airlifted out of a St. Paul suburb. Most showed a yard light; and though the night was deadly dark, it was pierced all around by yard lights, mercury-vapor blue and sodium-vapor orange, and far away, the red-blinking lights of radio towers.

Hard-surface road now.

He flicked through the tiny town of Dennison, decided he was getting too far east—the vehicle they were hunting had been heading west—did a quick U-turn and whipped through Dennison again, past the Lutheran church, down a hill, a bank, a Conoco station, a car dealer, all with small lights alone in the night, empty . . .

His nav system said he was on Dennison Boulevard and then Rice County 31, as though it couldn't make up its mind. The town lights were fading in his rearview mirror when he saw a car's taillights flare ahead of him.

No headlights; just the taillights. He felt a pulse: somebody running?

"Get the motherfucker," he muttered to himself.

He was doing seventy. He shoved the accelerator to the floor, looked at his navigation system. Nothing going south; just a Lamb Avenue going north. He stabbed at the nav system's scale button, moving it to the largest scale. A thin line came up, heading south, also identified as Lamb Avenue. Had to be a small road, a track. The car without lights, if it *was* a car without lights, had just turned into the hard countryside. Had he done it because he'd seen the roof light on Lucas's truck?

Lucas grabbed the phone, just had time to punch up the Northfield center before he slid into the mouth of Lamb Avenue. "I got a guy running without lights. I still don't see him. He's heading south on Lamb off, shit, I think it's Thirty-One or Dennison . . ."

"Got you, Lucas. We'll call dispatch, get some guys down there. Right now they're all up around Nineteen . . ."

Lucas punched off and tossed the phone on the passenger seat. He flashed past a bunch of derelict semitrailers, sitting in a farm field, and what looked like an impromptu junkyard. Two green spots came up on the right shoulder, and Lucas had time to pick up the red-striped cat in the weeds, hunting; up a hill, down another, the road narrow, the gravel pounding up under his wheel wells, rattling like hail.

Came up to the top of a hill and, in his high lights, saw the truck dust. He'd been going through it, but now he realized he could use it to track the man ahead of him. As long as the runner stayed on gravel, Lucas could follow the dust hanging in the still night air.

A culvert crossing flashed by . . . then a crossroads: which way, left, right, straight? He swung the truck in a circle, realizing that he was losing time, saw the dust hanging over the road to the right, went that way: the nav system said Karow Trail.

He was pushing the truck as hard as he dared, sliding through curves, flashing past farmhouses and mailboxes; caught in his lights a driveway with four cars parked in front of a metal shed. What if the guy in front of him pulled into a farmyard and just let him roll by? He'd never know . . .

The nav system was saving him. Without it, he might never have seen the turnoff to the even smaller James Trail. He slowed, went past the intersection, still on Karow, and suddenly was in clear air. He stopped, jammed the truck in reverse, backed up to James, and headed west. More dust, but losing great gouts of time. He needed to call in his location, but the road was so twisty, dark, narrow, that he couldn't take his hands off the steering wheel.

Around a bend, around another bend, almost losing it . . . then there, the taillights flickered up ahead, once, twice, then a one-second shot of headlights . . .

Nothing on the nav system. A driveway? He was coming through a turn, going into another one, and off to the right, he could see vehicle lights of a bigger highway. He didn't know which one, because the nav-system scale was too large.

Another flash of taillights, directly north of him, headed toward the bigger highway. He slowed, looking for a side road: and found what looked like a tractor turnoff into an oat field. He pulled into it and saw the tracks cutting across the oats. As his headlights swept the field, he saw another flicker of taillights, and then another . . .

Somebody out there, running across the open field, heading toward the highway.

Lucas went after him, bumping now, the truck almost uncontrollable, his speed dropping to twenty-five, to twenty, to fifteen . . .

BUT THERE!

Headlights flared ahead of him, then disappeared over the rim of a hill. The guy could no longer run without lights. And whoever it was

was only two or three hundred yards ahead of him. Lucas flashed on the chase back at the Martin farmhouse. He didn't dare to hope that it was Pope. The hope itself would jinx him. A meth distributor? There were dozens of labs south of the metro . . .

The truck bounced and jounced and struggled along the track, pain banging through his face, spreading from his broken nose: he ignored it, clenched his teeth. He saw movement to his left, quick, jerked his head that way. Gone: a cow?

"Fence," he said aloud. He was running parallel to a fence and slightly downhill. Up ahead, his headlights were showing nothing but darkness. Hill coming up, he thought, and a few seconds later, he was over the lip of it.

Closer now, maybe two hundred yards ahead, he could again see the other vehicle's headlights bouncing wildly over the countryside, heading down, down toward what looked like a crack in the earth. Still couldn't make out anything of the car: just the light on the fields it was crossing.

Moving faster and faster: closing in. Moving faster.

"Fuckin' hold on . . . ," he said.

Another hill, another lip, even steeper, and the car disappeared again, only to suddenly reappear, bucking wildly, then suddenly heading uphill. The guy had made it to the far side of the valley but was only a hundred yards ahead, his taillights clear ovals now. Lucas groped for the cell phone with one hand, couldn't find it on the passenger seat.

"Goddamnit." The ride had thrown the phone on the floor, and he couldn't see it.

Ahead, the other car slowed, made a sharp wiggle, then moved forward again, away from him, only seventy-five yards, less than the length of a football field.

Just a moment too late, Lucas saw the black line in his headlights. The crack in the earth, and he remembered how the other car had suddenly bucked so wildly. A creek?

He jabbed at the brake, dropped over a short, steep bank, and hit hard, water splashing on the windshield. He floored the accelerator, and the car bucked and hit something hard, got sideways. He wrenched the steering wheel back to the left, and hit the far bank of the creek with a heavy whack that stopped him dead. He tried to push up it, but he could feel wheels spinning in sand. He reversed, tried to get straight, hit the bank again, stopped. Backed up again, tried again, near panic now: he was losing him. How'd the other guy gotten out?

Stymied, he groped in the glove compartment, found a flashlight, got out of the truck into ankle-deep water, and looked at the situation. He was stopped dead in the middle of a small creek, a six-foot-wide trickle of water in a bed maybe thirty feet wide. Nothing but sand under his feet.

When he shined the light on the opposite bank, he picked out two narrow tracks, tractor tracks, going up the far side. He'd simply missed them, missed the alignment when he went into the creek.

He jumped back in the truck, backed it down, found the two small tracks in his headlights, and pushed up them. As the other car had, the truck bucked up and then he was on dry ground again: but he'd lost three or four minutes.

He continued up the hill, fast as he could. He saw the track disappear in front of him, remembered that the other car had wiggled up the hill, slowed, spotted the wiggle, and followed it up. A moment later, the track intersected with another highway, the highway where he'd seen headlights.

There were taillights in sight, both east and west: the nav system told him he was back on Dennison Boulevard.

Decide.

He looked both ways, remembered the cell phone. He found it under the front passenger seat, punched up the Northfield center.

Decide. He said, "Shit," and turned west, accelerated.

"The guy took me across a field," he told the Northfield cops. "I'm

on Dennison, but I don't know exactly where. Near James. I'm heading west . . ."

"We got guys on the way, but they're east of you, we'll vector them
in there."

He gave it everything the truck had, blowing by two pickups and a
Toytota Corolla before coming back into the lights of Northfield.

"Shit. Shit." Lucas pounded the steering wheel with the heels of his
hands. Northfield was a big town, crowded with every kind of car. The
guy was gone.

THEY DID HEAR from the driver, though.

At two-thirty, Lucas had just gotten back to the Northfield center
when Ruffe Ignace called, freaked: "Pope just called again. He wouldn't
talk to me. He wants your cell-phone number. He didn't say why. I lied
and told him I didn't have it but I might be able to get it. He said he
would wait five minutes and then he was going to throw the phone in
a ditch. You've got four minutes to decide."

"Give him the number," Lucas said.

LUCAS CALLED THE co-op center on one of the Northfield center's
phones and told them about the cell-phone call. "Find the cell," he said.
"He's gonna call me. You got my number. He's probably using Peterson's phone again. Find the fuckin' cell. Find the fuckin' cell."

AND THEN POPE CALLED.

"Agent Davenport," he drawled. He spoke slowly, with the same
whispery voice that Ignace had described. Lucas tried to penetrate it:
husky, a middle tenor. Could it be a woman? "That was you that chased
me through that crick, wasn't it?"

Lucas was astonished. The question froze him, and he asked, inanely, "Where are you?"

"Out here in the woods where I always am. Miz Peterson is still okay. Well, she wouldn't say that, I guess. I had me a little pussy before dinner. And after dinner. And for dessert. She's right here. You want to talk to her?"

Not a woman. A woman wouldn't talk like that—unless she were very, very manipulative. "Listen, man, you really need our help . . ." Lucas felt absolutely stupid as he said it.

"Nah. I'm doing okay. I thought you had me there for a minute, those first two cops, and then you. When I got loose I heard them talking about you on my scanner, said you almost wrecked your truck in that crick. I wondered what happened to you. I hit that sonbitch just right, I guess. Never saw it—nothing but luck."

"Listen, Mr. Pope . . ."

"Didn't call me no Mr. Pope when you had my ass in St. John's. But listen, don't you want to talk to Miz Peterson? She was in the back the whole time. Here . . . Miz Peterson. This is the law. Talk to him . . ."

There was the sound of flesh against flesh, as though somebody had been slapped, the tenor, "Talk to him, bitch," and then a dry, ragged woman's voice, *"Help me . . ."*

"That's good enough," Pope said in his whisper. "We gotta go." And then: "Well, it's been fun, but I gotta say good-bye, Agent Davenport."

"You gotta . . ."

Click.

LUCAS WAS SCREAMING at the co-op center, and they came back: "The cell's in Owatonna. It's Peterson's. He got around you and went straight south."

"Get the goddamned people moving around there, get them moving . . ."

"They're moving now, everything we've got."

Five hours later, Lucas was on a dirt road west of Owatonna when he got a call from the Blue Earth County Sheriff's Department. There were a couple of clicks and he was patched through: "Lucas, this is Gene Nordwall, I'm down south of Mankato, little west of Good Thunder."

"Gene, you heard?"

"Yeah. We found her," he said.

"You found her?" Lucas asked. "She's alive?"

15

WAYNE'S FOUR CORNERS INN was a rambling white structure that sat on top of a ridge where Blue Earth County 122 and County 131 crossed each other. There were two nonfunctional gas pumps out front, with crown-shaped glass globes on top, left over from the 1950s, and left in the parking area as a statement of the inn's antiquity. To the left side of the inn, just outside the gravel parking area, was a pi-shaped structure that might have been a medieval gallows, built of rough four-by-four lumber.

Lucas recognized the structure as soon as he pulled into the parking lot, outside the collection of cop cars. They were rare, in recent times, but as recently as the 1960s and 1970s they had been ubiquitous in the countryside. They were hanging bars, meant to display the carcasses of the biggest local bucks taken during deer season.

Carlita Peterson's body hung by the neck from the crossbar.

Not so much a body, as a carcass; Lucas had already been told, and walked toward the hanging bar with his eyes averted, not wanting to look.

A cop was there, and said to Lucas, "This is awful."

Lucas looked now: no way to avoid it.

Peterson's throat had been slashed; that had been the killing stroke. But after she'd been killed, she'd been gutted, and her empty body, slashed from throat to anus with a cutting tool, hung in the cool still morning air.

LUCAS LOOKED AWAY, then stepped away, shaking his head, his hands trembling. He'd thought that they might get her back.

NORDWALL SCUFFED UP in his cowboy boots, not looking: "He fuckin' gutted her."

"You gotta get some people out in the woods, looking for the . . ." Lucas stopped. He knew the phrase, but he didn't want to say it.

The sheriff said it for him. "The gut dump."

"Yeah. I would think it would be close by," Lucas said. "He chose this place for display. Look for crows. You should see crows flocking around."

"I'll put it out right now."

"Tell everybody to walk easy. When we find it, we'll backtrack to where he held her, we gotta see if any of the neighbors saw cars in the night, anybody coming or going . . ." The sheriff nodded, and Lucas finished: "Shit, Gene, you know the routine. We know Pope is involved, somehow, so processing isn't so important . . . unless we can come up with a second name. What's important is the car—what are they driving, where were they headed?"

"I'll put it out. You gonna be here?"

"No. I'm going home for a while."

. . .

LUCAS WAS WALKING back down the hill to the parking lot when he saw a brown Chevy slowing at the turnoff; the man inside showed an ID to the cop at the corner, and then the car continued into the parking lot and pulled in a slot down from Lucas. Sloan got out.

"How're you feeling?" Lucas asked, automatically.

"Tell you in a minute," Sloan said. He looked pale, and drawn, but he often did, especially in the morning. He headed up the hill toward the hanging bar. Lucas leaned against the truck, watching him go, waited.

AS HE WAITED, another familiar face came up. Lucas searched for a name, and the man helped him out: "Lucas—Barry Anderson, Goodhue." He was the sheriff of Goodhue County, wearing tired civilian clothes, tan slacks, and a red plaid shirt. Like Lucas, he'd been up all night; the chase the night before had started just inside Goodhue County.

"I know where he was going last night," he said grimly, looking up the hill. "We got a bar at a place called Old Church—there's no church anymore, burned down twenty years ago, but there's a bar and they've got a deer rack. Wasn't five miles from where that first deputy jumped him."

"Ah, jeez . . ."

"Wonder what made him pick the one up there?"

Lucas thought about it for a moment, as he watched Sloan sloping back down the hill. "He was going for a deer rack, like you say. He went for the one that was closest to Northfield. Try to increase the shock. Hang her right up in front of her neighbors. When we closed him out of there, he came down here."

Anderson's head bobbed. He said, "You know, I'm a good Christian, born again. I accept Jesus Christ in my life and know I will face him at judgment time. But if I caught this . . . this *cocksucker* . . . I would cut his head off."

SLOAN WAS BACK: "Not something I'd want to see a second time," he said softly.

"Shouldn't have come out," Lucas said. He introduced Sloan and Anderson, and Anderson said, "I better go up."

Lucas and Sloan stood there for a few seconds, for ten seconds, and then Sloan said, "Now what?"

"Same thing we're doing. Full-court press. He's working fast now," Lucas said. "I called Elle on the way over here, she said he's breaking, he's losing control of his own actions. We're gonna see another dead one in the next few days."

"If it's like we think . . . if it's two people . . . she thinks they're both breaking?"

"She doesn't think it's two people. Or if it is, they've somehow meshed their personalities. One of them has taken over the other."

ANOTHER LONG SILENCE, cops trudging by, up the hill or down. Lucas said, "I can't figure out how he's avoiding us."

"He's not. We almost caught him last night," Sloan said.

"We didn't," Lucas grunted.

Sloan said, "Here's a possibility: suppose he's in some kind of closed van. The driver is a woman. They come up to a checkpoint, he hides— under a rug, or somehow, so nobody sees him just looking in the window. In the meantime, the woman shows the cop her ID, and they wave her through. We were moving so fast that we don't know who we stopped; we must've stopped ten thousand people last night, all over the state."

"Wasn't a van. It was a small SUV. A Subaru, like that. Had vertical taillights."

After another pause, Sloan said, "I don't know what to tell you," and a moment later he added, "I'm talking bullshit. I'm babbling."

"The next time, we not only stop people, we jot down every single license plate, and run them to see who we get," Lucas said.

Sloan shook his head: "Man . . ."

"What the fuck else are we gonna do?" Lucas demanded, the anger riding on top of his voice. "Look at that fuckin' woman hangin' up there. What the fuck are we gonna do?"

Sloan said, "I hate to think that we're waiting for the next one, to start writing down numbers. There's *gotta* be something better than that."

ON THE WAY HOME, Lucas's cell phone rang. The incoming call was from a BCA number, and he flipped it open: "Yeah?"

"John Hopping Crow says he's got to see you, *right now*," Carol said, emphasizing the *right now*. "I told him that you were under a lot of stress, and didn't sleep last night, and were heading home. He said, quote, 'I don't give a fuck if he's been shot in the balls, tell him to come here before he goes anywhere.' Unquote. He wouldn't tell me what about."

"They got DNA on a second guy?" It was the only thing Lucas could think of that might be important enough. None of the other catalog of current cases amounted to much.

"I don't know," Carol said. "He says he'll be waiting in his office. He sounded scared."

"Scared?"

"That's what he sounded like," Carol said. "And you know how polite he is. He's never said 'darn' around me before, and now I'm getting 'shot in the balls.'"

"Tell him twenty minutes," Lucas said. "I do feel like shit."

"With your poor nose, and this poor woman . . ."

"Let's talk about it some other time," Lucas said. "Like next year."

WEATHER CALLED: he told her about Peterson. "Oh, my God. I wish I was there to help you. Do you want me to come . . ."

"No. Won't help. Right now, I just gotta get some sleep."

LUCAS FELT LIKE his ass was almost literally dragging up to Hopping Crow's small office: getting too old for this all-night shit, living on coffee and vending-machine cookies.

Hopping Crow's office door was closed, and Lucas knocked. He heard a chair scuff back, and the door opened a bit. Hopping Crow's dark eyes peered out. When he recognized Lucas, he pulled the door open, his eyes flicking up and down the hall.

"Come on in."

"Jesus, man, you're in a sweat," Lucas said.

Hopping Crow pointed at a chair and moved around behind his desk and sat down.

"We've got a big, big problem." He said it with a dark urgency.

Lucas shrugged. Whatever the problem was, it wasn't as big as Carlita Peterson's had been. "Well?"

Hopping Crow pushed his chair back to the wall, then sat on the front edge of it. "Three days ago, a couple of guys were fishing for mud cat down in the Minnesota River by Mankato. North of Mankato. Downstream, by the County Eighteen Bridge, wherever that is. Anyway, they hooked onto something. They were using these big hooks and heavy line, and they yanked it up, and they came up with part of a man's decomposing hand."

"Surprised that there was anything left, if there're mud cat in there," Lucas said.

"Shut up. Just listen," Hopping Crow snapped. "Anyway, they

brought in a dive team, and they looked around, and they found a de-composed body wrapped in a logging chain. They fished it out and sent us some samples for DNA and the medical examiner did some dental X rays, I understand. They'll be looking for a match. The medical examiner says the body was in there for maybe a month."

He dropped his head and, with both hands, slicked back his long black hair.

"And?" Lucas was leaning forward now, truly curious.

"We got a match on the DNA. Nobody knows but me and Anita Winter. I shut her up, told her if it gets out, I'd fire her ass. I just . . ." He stopped, as though unable to continue.

"Who the fuck was it?" Lucas asked.

Hopping Crow looked up. "Charlie Pope."

LUCAS DIDN'T REGISTER the name for a half second: the words were something like another punch in the nose, leaving him stunned and disoriented. He opened his mouth, realized what he was about to say was stupid, and closed it.

"Say something," Hopping Crow said.

"What the *fuck* are you talking about?" Lucas shouted.

"Don't yell—it's not us. We didn't fuck up. The DNA matches both our bank and the blood we took off Rice's fingernails. We're going back right now . . ." Hopping Crow snatched the phone off his desk and hammered in a few numbers, listened, and then said, "It's me. You see anything yet? Well, what do you think you see? Well, when can you confirm that? How much? Call me back."

He slammed the receiver back in the cradle: "Okay. When we do DNA, we don't examine the blood cells. That's not part of the deal. You just don't do that."

"So?"

"So I had Anita take some of the back sample from Rice's fingernails and put it under the 'scope. She says she can see blood cells that have burst."

"I don't know what that means. Burst?"

"That means that they could have been frozen. That means that the guy killed Pope, took blood from him, and planted it on the body."

LUCAS LOOKED AT Hopping Crow for a long three seconds: "You gotta be shitting me."

"I shit you not."

"Charlie Pope was never out there to find," Lucas said.

"That's right. The medical examiner says he's been dead for at least a month," Hopping Crow said. "How long ago did he disappear?"

"Little more than a month, now."

"There you are."

LUCAS CONSIDERED THE PROBLEM for another long minute, then he leaned forward and tapped Hopping Crow's desk with his index finger: "If this gets out, there's going to be hell to pay. The media will look for somebody to drop a brick on. Me, or, maybe, you. Or both of us, or all of us."

"I know that."

"So you tell Anita that her job's on the line," Lucas said. "Sooner or later, somebody will find out that we didn't look at the blood cells under a microscope."

"We *never* look at them. *Nobody* does. DNA's a whole different *thing*."

"Think that'll make any difference to the TV stations?" Lucas asked.

Hopping Crow thought about it for a moment, then said, "If it was presented exactly right . . ."

"Bullshit. There's no way to present it. There's a kind of Occam's razor that applies to TV: the simplest answer is the best," Lucas said. "The simplest answer is we fucked up. People can understand that. All this science shit, they don't understand. It might as well be magic."

"So what are we gonna do?" Hopping Crow sounded a little desperate.

"Gotta find this cocksucker."

"Yeah, right. I can see us holding off on mentioning this for a day or two, but what if he grabs somebody else like this Peterson woman?" Hopping Crow asked. "What do we do then, tell a million cops to look for Charlie Pope? And what do I tell the medical examiner?"

"Tell him you came up negative. That's what he expects, anyway."

"Ah, man." Then: "What are you going to do?"

"I gotta talk to Rose Marie and maybe the governor. Figure something out. In the meantime, you get Anita and you tell her that I personally will run her out of the state if she says a fuckin' thing to any-fuckin'-body."

LUCAS STOPPED AT his office and made a call to Del Capslock, his lead investigator. Del was working dope with a task force from the suburban town of Woodbury, trying to figure out who was putting methamphetamine into the high school. Lucas called him: "What are you doing?"

"Reading a magazine and watching a house."

"Could you break off?"

"If I had to."

"Get in here, quick as you can. I've gotta go talk to Rose Marie, just wait in my office. Get Jenkins and Shrake, too."

ON THE WAY TO Rose Marie's office, Lucas thought: *What about Mrs. Bird, the old lady from Rochester?* She'd identified Pope as making the call to Ruffe Ignace. She'd *seen* him, on the phone, she said. She'd picked him out of a photo lineup . . .

ROSE MARIE ROUX had once been a state senator from Minneapolis and knew how the legislature worked, which didn't always help. The financial crisis had escalated to the point that a special session had to be called if the state wanted to keep the parks open and continue to pay for cops, snow removal, and highway repair.

Rose Marie was in charge of cops, and she was pulling her hair out: when Lucas showed up at her door, she looked like somebody had tried to electrocute her, her parlor-blond hair standing out from her ears like fighter-jet wings.

"Tell me you got good news," she said.

Lucas groped for words for a minute, then said, "We found Charlie Pope."

Her eyes lit up.

A FEW MINUTES LATER, she said, "I'll get even with you, someday, for that 'We found Charlie Pope' line."

"Yeah, yeah," Lucas said. "The question is, What do we do?"

"I'll talk to the governor," she said. "Usually, it's a bad idea to keep this sort of thing from the media. They'll eventually find out, then they'll start screaming 'cover-up' . . ."

"Which it is . . ."

". . . and nobody in public office wants to hear that," she said. "The media's their own judge and jury on cover-ups, and we've got no say."

"So you think we should make an announcement?" Lucas asked. He was skeptical, and showed it.

She turned in her chair so she could look out her window, rocked back and forth a couple of times; her face took on the blank expression she assumed when she was plotting. After a moment, she said, "No . . .

We start talking secretly to a few sheriffs about the white car and the silver car and about a probable second man. You've been kicking that idea around for a few days anyway. Sloan will back us up on that. The media already has the white car, and sooner or later they'll hear about the second man and the silver car. They'll know that something is going on, and they'll write about it . . ."

"And?"

"And then we tell them that we knew that Charlie Pope wasn't the guy, and that we were trying to outwit the real killer by not letting him know that we were on to the frozen-blood thing," she said. "That they—the media—ruined it all by releasing the second-man theory. It's all their fault."

"Jesus." Lucas was impressed.

"I have to run this by the governor." She poked a finger at Lucas: "In the meantime, you gotta find this guy. Start filtering out the word on the second man, for the media. Then find this motherfucker. If you find him soon enough, all this becomes moot."

SLOAN AND ELLE had to know.

Lucas didn't want to tell them on the phone. Sloan hadn't been officially working that day and had come down to the Blue Earth murder scene on his own hook. Lucas called his office, was told that he was probably at home. Called Sloan's home and got his wife.

"He's out walking, Lucas. He's pretty shook up about Peterson."

"I need to talk to him about the case. We've got a thing going on . . . Could you ask him to call me?"

"I will, but listen, Lucas: don't try to talk him out of quitting," she said. "Don't do that."

"Ah, jeez . . ."

"Lucas, he needs to do something else. I remember when you had your little problem, and Sloan's working on something like that. I don't know if he'll go into a full-blown clinical depression, but he's walking around the edges of it. Work's making it worse."

"Is he sleeping at night?"

"No. That's why this cold got on top of him," she said. "He's completely exhausted. He hasn't slept since he found Angela Larson, and then couldn't find who'd killed her."

"All right. I'll keep my mouth shut."

"I'll have him call you, as soon as he gets back."

ELLE.

Lucas decided that he needed to talk to her in person. He stopped at his office, saw Del, Jenkins, and Shrake gathered around his desk. Carol stopped him in the outer office and said, "You need to fill in some paper on the guys in the co-op center. It can't wait, and I don't know the answers; payroll needs it an hour ago."

As he filled in, signed, and initialed the papers, he could hear the three cops talking through the open door of his office; they were talking about Sloan:

"He's got the angst," Jenkins said in his gravelly voice.

"I thought it was the zeitgeist," Shrake drawled.

Del said, "I thought angst *was* the zeitgeist."

After a pause, somebody said, in a midwestern male version of valley-girl-speak, "Well, *duh*."

LUCAS, A LITTLE PISSED, signed the last of the documents, stepped into his office, and said with a little heat, "Off Sloan's back, for Christ's sake. He's fucked up."

"Hey," Del said. "He's our friend, too."

"All right." Lucas bobbed his head and backed off: "Sorry: I got a problem. It's biting me. You three gotta find Mike West. Del: Jenkins and Shrake will fill you in. They've looked, came up empty, but now: this is critical."

"What about Pope?" Shrake asked.

"We're working on a two-man theory," Lucas lied. "We need West."

"There wasn't much . . . ," Jenkins began.

"Fuck that. Roust people. Everybody. Take your saps with you," Lucas said.

Jenkins's eyebrows were up. "You're serious."

Lucas was cold as ice: "Find that fucker. I want you to find him today. You want to know why, ask Crime Scene for some photos of Carlita Peterson."

"We heard about that," Del said.

"Look at the pictures. Then get out there. And fuck that take-it-easy shit," Lucas said.

TEN MINUTES TO ST. ANNE'S. Lucas parked in an illegal spot, threw a "Police" card on his dashboard, and hustled across campus. The Psychology Department secretary told him that Elle was having office hours and invited him to wait. He sat outside Elle's door, in a wooden chair of solid brown oak, watching the college girls coming and going in their summer clothes, big and blond and athletic, Minnesota Catholics.

He waited for ten minutes before Elle's door opened, and another blond Catholic girl popped out, carrying a stack of books. Elle was a couple of steps beside her, saw Lucas, and said, "Oh, no—what happened?"

"We gotta talk," Lucas said.

HE TOLD HER about the discovery of Pope's body, and about Peterson, about the chase the night before, about the phone call, about the hanging stand. She sat silently, intent, nodding, leaning toward him, her rimless glasses glittering in the overhead fluorescents.

When he finished, she said, "Yes. He is intelligent. He is a planner. He is daring. *This* is the man I told you about."

"And that's all you've got to say."

"I can't give you his fingerprints, Lucas. I can tell you that he is probably physically attractive, in some way, enough to attract the interest of single women. He won't stop . . . and I'd say that something happened to him, to trigger him . . . To get him started on this."

"Like what? You mean, like he was in a car wreck and smacked his head and came out crazy?"

She smiled at him: "No. But something made him start. Something exposed him to a trigger. Oh, one other thing: I think, because the two women were markedly different in age, that he most likely is between them in age—young enough to attract the younger women, old enough to interest the older woman."

They talked for a few more minutes about the killer, and then Lucas switched the topic to Sloan: "His old lady says he's depressed. Maybe cycling down."

"Your job will do that. You should know that, of all people."

Lucas had suffered through a clinical depression a few years earlier; it hadn't recurred, though on bad days, he could still feel the beast out there.

"He's thinking about retiring," Lucas said.

"Might not be a bad idea. Retirement can sometimes *trigger* depression, but in Sloan's case . . . Your job is too much. Not many people can take it, and those who can, if they do it long enough, can start to lose it," she said. "They self-medicate with alcohol or drugs. Or they turn into monsters. This is all very complicated, Lucas. Sloan's wife should get him to a doctor if he really gets down."

"I'll get him to go, if he seems like he's falling off the edge," Lucas said. "He knows what happened to me—and I've told him that if I ever go back down, I'm going on the pills. I'm not gonna try to sweat it out again."

"That was so foolish . . . ," she said.

"I don't like the idea of chemicals messing with my brain."

"When you're depressed, chemicals *are* messing with your brain," she said. "You're just using other chemicals to fight back."

"Yeah, yeah . . ." Lucas's cell phone rang. "That's probably Sloan now."

HE MET SLOAN at the Odyssey, a Greek beer joint and pool hall near the Lake Street Bridge on the Minneapolis side of the Mississippi. Sloan did look tired; Lucas suggested a round of nine ball might wake him up, but Sloan shook his head. "Don't have the edge," he said. "I could use a beer."

They got a couple of Leinies long necks and carried them to a booth. A couple of hard-looking guys were shooting pool in the back, leather vests, oily jeans, fat leather wallets sticking out of their back pockets, tied to their belts with brass chains. They looked dirty, as they should: they were Minneapolis intelligence cops, and they ignored Lucas and Sloan.

Sloan said, "Okay, so something's up. What is it?"

Lucas said, "Some fishermen down in Le Sueur County snagged a body in the Minnesota River. Actually, all they got was a piece of a hand. Scuba divers brought up the rest of the body, big chain wrapped around it. Medical examiner said the guy'd been in the river for a month."

Sloan jumped to a conclusion: "Another Rice thing? He did a guy first?"

"No. It was, uh, Charlie Pope."

SLOAN LOOKED AT HIM for a long time over the beer; he seemed almost amused. And smiling, he said, "You gotta be shitting me."

"I said that exact same thing to another guy about an hour ago."

Sloan took a pull on the long neck, smacked his lips, sighed, and said, "I'm gonna fuckin' quit."

"I talked to Elle when I couldn't get you. She says this clears up the confusion. The guy we're looking for is smart, organized, probably good-looking. Probably in his thirties . . ."

He ran down the rest of it for Sloan, who then asked, "But what about Mrs. Bird? She saw Pope standing by that wall phone."

"I thought about that," Lucas said. Then, "*We* did it."

"Huh?"

"We contaminated her. That's the only thing I can think of."

Sloan pulled his feet into the booth, onto the seat, closed his eyes, thinking, and finally, reluctantly, nodded. "All she did all day was watch TV. Nobody ever came to visit her. Pope's picture was on TV every fifteen minutes. So then we came with my photo book, and we treated her like she was important, and she looked in the book and sure enough . . ."

"She sees a familiar face, and picks it out," Lucas said. "That doesn't mean she didn't see somebody on the street. She probably did."

"But not Pope. And now she's got Pope's face in her head, and she'll never think different."

"We were too fast with the book," Lucas said. "We should have tried to get a description. We fucked up."

"So who knows about the white Olds," Sloan said. "That always seemed a little weird . . . she could have pulled that right out of an old movie."

"So. Pope's dead. Where does that leave us?"

"First, but *not* most important, we start covering our asses," Lucas said. He told Sloan about the second-man theory. "Do you know who's leaking to Ignace?"

"I've got an idea."

"Get your group together, leak the second-man thing to him. It'd be nice to have it in the paper tomorrow. Then, the most important thing . . . we gotta find the guy. We've gotta think about it. We've got quite a bit of information, we need more."

"How about another trip down to St. John's? See if we can scare anything more out of those assholes?"

"I thought of that, too. That's where it all starts. Let's do it tomorrow morning. I've got to get some sleep, and I've got three guys out looking for Mike West: I'd really like to get that guy."

"I'll get my guys working on it, too. Have Del call me."

"Good. I'll be at home. Call when anything happens. I'll call St. John's right away, set up the trip. Why don't you come over to my place at, like, seven o'clock tomorrow morning."

"See you then."

16

LUCAS TRIED TO SLEEP but was too wired; he watched CNN for a while, went out for a walk, trying to smooth himself out. Got a sandwich, walked back home. Read the murder file again, the latest information from the co-op center.

Called around: nothing moving but the news.

"We're starting to attract some serious attention now," Rose Marie said, in a late-afternoon call. "We'll make the networks tonight. We'll start getting some out-of-towners."

"That always helps," Lucas said.

He finally got to sleep at seven o'clock, only to wake up in the middle of the night, sweating, disoriented, worried about the sudden silence around him, and the beeping sound, like a truck backing up. His face hurt, but a dull pain: the worry came from something else.

Then *boom/crackle/flash*: a thunderstorm rolling in. What else? There was more. He sat up, glanced at the clock. No clock. He got out of bed, listened, flipped on the lights. No lights. He looked out the window, the hair rising on the back of his neck, the killer's phone call in his mind. The guy knew who he was . . .

No lights on the street. He got his pistol, padded out through the living room, moving confidently through the house in the dark. He'd designed the place; he knew every inch of it. In the kitchen, he looked out the back windows: no lights.

Power outage. The beeping sound continued. He went into the study, crawled under the desk, turned off the computer's battery backup system, and the beeping stopped. He flipped on the lights in the kitchen; nothing happened, but they would tell him when the power came back on. He moved into the living room, awake now, feeling the impulse from a spurt of adrenaline, dropped into a chair, the .45 in his lap.

Thought about it. He was still thinking about it, getting nowhere, when the lights came back twenty minutes later.

IN THE MORNING, before he shaved or showered, he called Del. The phone rang for a moment, then Del came up; he sounded as wired as Lucas had been.

"You up?" Lucas asked.

"I haven't been to bed yet. We got a line on West, but it's thin." Tires squealed and a horn honked in the background. "We're looking for a guy named Gary who begs for money at the McDonald's stoplight in Dinky Town," Del said. "Problem is, Gary is drunk somewhere and probably won't show up before his shift starts at eleven o'clock. He supposedly has been hanging out with West."

"Where does he work? Gary?"

A moment of silence. Then, "I just told you. At the McDonald's stoplight in Dinky Town. That's where I am now." In his mind's eye,

Lucas could see exactly where Del was standing—a pay phone famous for dope deals.

"He has a shift?"

"It's a good spot. He works it from eleven to three. These two other guys have it from seven to eleven, and three to six or seven. They share the sign: HOMELESS IRAQ VETERAN, STRUGGLING WITH AIDS. The night guy might be West, but we're not sure."

"You don't know where this Gary guy sleeps?"

"One of the tunnels, I guess," Del said. "We're trying to figure that out now."

"Shrake and Jenkins still with you?"

"Yeah. Shrake had some leftover amps, and we're feeling pretty good," Del said.

"Shhh . . ."

Del said, "Well, we took you serious when you told us to take our saps."

"That's right. I'm heading down to St. John's. You find this guy, call me."

SLOAN WAS RIGHT on time. They took the truck, headed south. Sloan wanted to talk about the security hospital, and rock 'n' roll.

"If the Big Three trained somebody, they had to have access to him. We know that Charlie Pope had access," he said. "The question is, Who else had that kind of access? The training couldn't have been quick, it would have taken awhile."

Lucas wasn't sure about that. "Why would it take awhile? Assume that the guy is already nuts, and just needed to be pointed."

"Ah. But he's not just nuts, he's *smart*," Sloan said. "Smart people have their own ways of doing things, even if they're crazy. They *really* got to this guy. They remodeled his brain. They had to *convert* him."

"I'VE GOT A bad feeling that nobody'll really know about who-all had access," Lucas said. "The place is only halfway a prison—all kinds of people go in and out of the secure wing. Half the menial work in the hospital is done by inmates."

"But this guy—the killer guy is major nuts. How many people who were major nuts have been recently released, *and* had extensive access?"

"Other than Mike West."

"Ah, he's not major nuts," Sloan said. "He's just one of those poor-fuck schizophrenics who can't deal."

THEY RODE ALONG for a minute, and Lucas said, "We would have asked all these questions one day after the Rice killings, if we hadn't found Pope's DNA. Absolutely sidetracked us."

"No it didn't," Sloan said. "We would have had no idea about the hospital if it hadn't been for the DNA. He actually put us *on* track."

"Not if he was going to kill them like the Big Three wanted them killed," Lucas said. "Angela Larson might have been a coincidence, being killed like Taylor would kill her. But when Rice was killed like Biggie Lighter would have . . . cut off Rice's dick . . . we would have noticed. Somebody would have."

Sloan scratched an ear. "Huh. I didn't think of that."

"Because we were sidetracked," Lucas said. "The guy's been running us like a railroad."

FARTHER DOWN THE ROAD, Sloan said, "I got two words for you. About the rock 'n' roll list."

"Rock 'n' roll? That's three words."

"Two words: Lou Reed."

"Lou Reed . . . 'Walk on the Wild Side.'"

"It's not on your list. I heard it the other day when I was lyin' on my ass, and I thought, 'Jesus, that's gotta go on the list.'"

"You're right, but the list is too long," Lucas said. "I have to start cutting songs. I was thinking, maybe I should limit it to one song per group—but I can't figure out how to do that, either. I'd leave out some of the best ones."

"You know what else you don't got?"

"What?"

"'Mustang Sally.'"

"Ah, shit."

"You've got a choice between Wilson Pickett and Buddy Guy," Sloan said.

"I can't make that choice."

"Life sucks and then you die."

SLOAN HAD STARTED calling the security hospital the "bat cave" and as they were driving up the kill, the phrase kept going through Lucas's head. The place didn't look anything like a bat cave, but it *felt* that way—felt like a haunted English country house, except bigger.

"We don't tell them about Pope," Lucas said, as they got out of the truck.

"Of course not. We talk about the second man."

INSIDE, they were taken to the director's office; Lawrence Cale had been fishing the first time they visited, and they hadn't met him. He was a tall, slender, balding man, in his middle fifties, wearing too-large glasses that magnified his eyes. He reminded Lucas of the farmer in Grant Wood's *American Gothic* painting. He was chewing on a toothpick.

"My deputy says the last time you two were here, you, *mmm*, seriously disturbed some of the patients," he said, after pointing them into visitor chairs.

"That's right," Lucas nodded. "They were pretty much having screaming fits when we left."

"That's not funny," Cale said. "It can take days, weeks, sometimes, to calm them down."

"I see that as your problem," Lucas said. He was tired of this *patient* shit. "Those three guys are responsible for three ordinary nice people being tortured to death."

Sloan was digging in his briefcase, pulled out an eight-by-ten print, slipped it across the desk. "This used to be Carlita Peterson. She was a college professor. They haven't found the gut dump yet."

Cale took in the picture, flipped it over, and passed it back to Sloan without comment. "I had Chase, Lighter, and Taylor transferred to isolation. They don't see anybody but staff. No radio or television. Everything that is said to them is taped, and we review the tapes daily. They are allowed two books a day. They specify the genre, and we choose the books, so nobody can plant a message in a book. And we check the books before they go into the cells."

"How about coming out? What happens with the books?" Lucas asked.

"We check them again, for codes. We know most of the ways—pin holes over letters, that sort of thing. We make damn sure that nothing's coming out, either."

"All right. Are you taking us in?"

"No, Sam O'Donnell and Dick Hart will take you down. They know those guys. And it's best if they don't see me. I make the decisions on their disposition, and if I went down there, they'd be talking to me, not you."

"We'll try not to disturb them any more than we have to," Lucas said.

Cale said, "*Mmm*, that picture you showed me . . ."

"What?" Sloan asked.

"Fuck 'em. Do what you need to."

O'DONNELL AND HART were waiting on the other side of the security wall. When Lucas came through, Sloan a few seconds behind, Hart said, "We heard about the professor. That goddamn Pope; I never saw this in him."

"The killer?"

"I saw the killer, I never saw . . . this."

O'Donnell said, "Charlie was one of those guys that nobody liked, but you could see, sometimes, that he was trying to be likeable. He wanted people to like him. But Lighter and Taylor and Chase turned him into a . . . I don't know. He's like one of those movie psychos, Freddie or the hockey-mask guy, or somebody."

"Might not be Pope," Lucas said.

The two docs stopped in their tracks. "What?"

"You guys suggested it the last time we were here—Dr. Beloit, maybe. Our own psychologist up in the Cities came up with the idea independently. We think Charlie Pope is being handled by a second man, or a second woman. Somebody who does the planning, does the driving . . ."

Lucas explained, and they started walking again, the two docs taking it in. When Lucas finished, he asked, "Anything more from any of them? The Big Three?"

"Not really," O'Donnell said. He flipped his long hair, unconsciously touched a silver earring. "They just bitch and moan about being down in the hole."

THEY TOOK AN ELEVATOR DOWN, a camera looking at them through a recessed glass plate. Two floors below the entrance, they got out, into a tiled corridor that felt like a basement—sound was muffled, and though the air was cool, it felt damp. They passed a couple of staff members, who nodded and went on their way, and stopped at an electronically controlled door with another camera. Hart pushed another button, a woman's voice said, "Hey, Dick," and Hart said, "Hey, Pauline. It's me, Sam and Davenport and Sloan. They should be on your list."

"Yes, they are. Opening up."

The electronic lock clicked, and O'Donnell pulled the door open. "What would they do if we were imposters and had a gun in your back?" Sloan wondered.

"They'd know," O'Donnell said, smiling. Dropping his voice, he said, "Her name ain't Pauline."

The corridor was dim. They could see a dozen rectangles set into the walls, eight of them dark, four lit. All one-way glass. "The Big Three and a guy who tried to cut his buddy with a broken plastic spoon," Hart said. "Where do you want to start?"

"How does it work?" Sloan asked.

"There's a release button next to each window panel. You push it once and the one-way glass slides back and you're looking through a glass security panel. That's if you want him to see you. The talk goes through a microphone with a speaker. The guys in the other cells can't hear what you're talking about, unless you want them to. Then you can turn on their mikes."

THE ISOLATION CELLS were simple: a bed, a toilet, a sink to wash in. The walls were beige, the blanket on the bed was green, the fixtures were white, the uniforms were a washed-out French blue, like the medical scrubs that Weather sometimes wore around the house.

Taylor was sitting on his bunk, staring at the one-way glass. "Can he see us?" Sloan asked.

O'Donnell shook his head. "No, I've checked it a hundred times.

But I think, sometimes, that things are so quiet down here that they pick up vibrations of people walking by. Half the time we come down here, they're staring at the glass. When you look at them on the video, they're hardly ever looking at the glass. There's nothing to see."

"Open it," Lucas said.

Hart pushed a button, and the glass slid slowly back. As soon as it started moving, Taylor stood up and walked toward it. "You guys," he said, when he saw Lucas and Sloan.

"Yeah, we need to talk to you," Lucas said. "We need to get a name from you. The name of the guy you sent out there."

Taylor wagged his head and showed a short, yellow-toothed smile. "I don't think you got enough for that." His voice, coming from a lowest-bid speaker, sounded like a robot's.

"Let me tell you what we got," Lucas said. Taylor crossed his arms and leaned against the windowsill. "The federal district attorney has decided that your victims . . . the victims of the guy you sent out . . . were kidnapped. That's a federal offense, and the victims were killed. They're going for the death penalty. If we put you with the killer . . . well, you won't have to worry about being penned up anymore."

"Don't have the death penalty in Minnesota."

"The state doesn't—but we're talking about the feds. They definitely do."

Taylor's gaze seemed to turn inward for a moment, and then he shrugged. "Gotta go sometime. Tell me—did our boy get another one? Did he hunt her down?"

"Hey, you're not gonna shock us," Sloan said. "We've been dealing with dildoes like you for our whole lives. Let us tell you the rest of it."

"So?"

"So we're making this offer to all three of you. Whoever gives us the name, that guy gets a pass," Sloan said. "The other two get transferred over to Illinois, where they get the shot. One of you will think it over and talk. He'll get to wave good-bye to the other two."

"You're really fuckin' me up," Taylor said, his voice flat, and with no change of expression. He ostentatiously looked at his fingernails, "I can hardly stand it."

"All right," Lucas said. He reached for the button that opened and closed the panel. "Enjoy the next few months, or however long it turns out to be . . ."

Now an expression flicked over Taylor's face. "What's that supposed to mean?" he snapped. "Rules say we can't be kept here for more than two weeks without relief."

Hart shook his head. "That's not quite right. Two weeks if you've shown recognition and contrition. Every day that you don't is a new offense. You won't be out of here until your boy is caught."

"Or until you get transferred to the federal pen," Lucas said. He pushed the button to close the glass panel, waited for an objection from Taylor, and got nothing but ten seconds of silence. Then, in a teasing baby voice, Taylor said, "I know you're still standing there."

O'Donnell sighed and pushed the microphone button, turning it off. "Next?"

THEY DID BIGGIE NEXT. Biggie was naked and masturbating. "Go away. I need my privacy to jerk off." He twiddled his fingers at the surveillance camera.

"I need to tell you about the special offer," Lucas said. Biggie never stopped while Lucas recited the death-penalty threat.

Biggie said, "Hey, you know what? Having you watch is gettin' me harder. This is really good."

"I'll come and watch you take the needle," Lucas said, turning away. To Hart: "Shut the window."

"I'm gonna come. Don't you wanna watch?" Biggie shouted as the window slid shut, "Maybe you can get our boy for not having a hunting license . . ."

O'Donnell punched the microphone button and said, "Hard to threaten a guy when he's in isolation. Maybe we should have moved them back to their regular cells. Might as well be dead as down here."

"Almost pointless to talk to Chase," Hart said. "He's going downhill fast. The catatonic and manic periods are getting longer, the transitions are getting shorter. He was down for almost thirty-six hours, ending last night, then he went through transition and now he's going manic. When he's manic, there's nothing left but the instinct to kill."

"Let's try him," Lucas said. "Might as well, since we're here."

THE GLASS SLID BACK, and Chase hurled himself at it, his fingers like claws, his mouth open, his eyes sparking with hate. Like Biggie, he was naked: he hit the glass like a bug hitting a windshield, bounced off, came back at it, scratching at the glass, prying at its corners, his fingernails breaking, blood slipping across the glass. He was wailing, like an injured big cat, like a jaguar. Hart was shouting, "Easy, easy, easy . . . You wanna get out, wanna get out . . ."

Chase seemed not to hear him. He hurled himself at the glass again, hitting it with his face, beating it with his fists; behind him, the cell was torn up as much as it could be, as most of it was concrete. He hadn't simply taken off his clothing, he'd taken it off and shredded it; he'd done the same thing to the blanket, and the mattress, which was covered with nylon and bolted to the bed, was streaked with blood, where Chase had been tearing at it.

"Close it, close it," Lucas shouted at O'Donnell, and the window slipped shut. The microphone was still on, and they could hear the continuing animal wail until Hart reached out and cut it off.

"Goddamnit," Sloan said. "Maybe you ought to do something. Like sedate him."

Hart nodded: "We try, but chemicals don't have much effect on him anymore. If we give him enough to really calm him down, we might kill him."

"Well, that'd calm him down," Lucas said. "He's like a fuckin' were-wolf, or something." Then, to Sloan: "We're wasting our time."

"Listen, we can work on Taylor and Biggie for you, keep talking up the death-penalty thing," O'Donnell said. "Is that for real?"

"It will be," Lucas said.

"We sorta . . . oppose the death penalty around here," O'Donnell said. "By and large."

"So do we," Sloan said. "By and large."

THEY STOPPED FOR LUNCH on the way back, cheeseburgers at a McDonald's.

"I don't care what anybody says about the shit McDonald's feeds you," Sloan said. "They *do* know how to make a French fry. You gonna eat those?"

They were finishing the French fries when Del called: he was even more wired than he'd been in the morning.

"Man, you gotta find a place to lie down," Lucas said. "You're yelling at me."

"We're getting a little frazzled," Del shouted. "Listen, where are you? How fast can you get up here?"

"Forty-five minutes, depending on where you are. You find West?"

"We know where he is. We talked to a chick who just saw him. He's walking around with his bag along the riverbank. We've got some Min-neapolis cops coming over to help. He might be in one of the caves."

"All right. We're coming. Be careful in those fuckin' caves, man."

17

A MINNEAPOLIS PATROLMAN spotted Mike West walking along the riverbank more than a mile downstream from where the woman had seen him—"When she said she saw him five minutes ago, what she meant was, she saw him half an hour ago," Del told Lucas and Sloan.

Del was wearing jeans, a T-shirt, and for some reason—odd on a hot day in the middle of the summer, though nobody mentioned it—a navy-blue watch cap. With his weathered face, he looked like the Ancient Mariner, except in a Metallica T-shirt. "We spent another half hour crawling all over the riverbank by the university, and he was already down by St. Thomas."

"So where is he?" Lucas asked. They were parked with a half dozen cop cars on Mississippi River Boulevard, looking down into the river gorge that separated St. Paul from Minneapolis. The sides of the gorge were steep, but not sheer, and covered with trees and brush. Outcrops of sandstone were showing through the greenery; the Mississippi snaked through the bottom of it, in its usual summer dress, mud and beached carp.

Del shrugged: "He must've seen us coming, because he fuckin' vanished. Dick Douglas spotted him, called it in, then went down after him. Never saw him again."

"Caves," Sloan said.

"Douglas was sure it was him?" Lucas asked.

"It's the guy we were told about. We found Gary, the panhandler. He said this was our guy, this Mike West. Calls him Mikey. He pointed us at Sandy, this woman, who knows West pretty good. She's a graduate student up at the U, she works in a cafeteria and gives him leftover food."

"We ought to get Sandy down here," Sloan said.

Del nodded: "She's on the way. Jenkins and Shrake went to get her."

"Jesus, I hope you told them to go easy," Lucas said. Shrake bragged that when it came to pickups, they had a .740 slugging percentage. He wasn't sure Shrake was joking.

"Ah, they're all right," Del said. "They get a little antsy sometimes."

They found West before the woman arrived. A couple of cops halfway down the hill, and two hundred yards south, started yelling and humping around one spot on the hill. A group of college students, who had gathered on the sidewalk, cheered, then booed. Lucas could see the cops bending into the hillside and then yelling some more. "What the hell's going on down there?" Del wondered. They all started down the hillside, holding on to tree limbs and brush, skidding along in their slick-soled city-cop shoes.

"What?" Lucas asked when they got to the cops. More cops were crossing the hillside to where they were standing.

"There he is," said one of the cops. He was hot and pissed off. He pointed at the hillside, and Lucas took a moment to see what he was pointing at—the worn white soles of two gym shoes, six or eight inches into a hole so small that it seemed impossible that a man could be on the other side of them. The hole, worn by water out of the rotten rock, apparently extended straight back into the hillside.

Lucas stooped to look, and Sloan and Del scrambled around behind him "Come out of there," Lucas said. He heard what might have been a muffled reply.

"He's holding on to something, inside there," one of the cops said. "We tried to pull him out, but we couldn't budge him."

"How about some shovels?" Del asked.

"It's mostly rock; we'd need jackhammers."

"We could try dynamite," somebody suggested, with a snigger. Most of the cops were now enjoying themselves: watching the heavyweight detectives looking at those two fuckin' feet. "Or maybe we oughta send for a proctologist," somebody else said. "I bet *he* could hook him out."

"He's not going to smother in there, is he?" Lucas asked, looking at the shoe soles.

"Fuck if we know," said the cop.

Del started to laugh, and Sloan shook his head and turned away.

"Stop laughing and give me a hand," Lucas said, irritated. Del came over and they managed to wedge their hands into the hole and grab hold of the man's ankles. There were more muffled comments from inside the hole. "Pull."

They pulled, pulled some more, and nothing moved. "We're gonna hurt him if we pull too hard," Del said. "We're gonna pop his knees."

"Why can't anything be easy?" Lucas asked, giving up, dusting his hands together.

Sloan said, "Anyway, here're Shrake and the woman."

THEY SAW SHRAKE coming down the hill, one hand on the woman's arm. Jenkins, who had apparently stopped to light a cigarette, trailed unhappily behind.

The woman, Sandy, was young and round faced, and dishwater

blond. She looked concerned in the way that nurses looked concerned when told of pain and illness—a kind of reflexive sympathy.

"Can you help us?" Lucas asked. "He's wedged himself inside."

"I can try," she said, looking doubtfully at the soles of the gym shoes. "He gets scared sometimes." She knelt: "Mike? This is Sandy," she shouted. "This is Sandy from the cafeteria. The police don't want to arrest you, they want you to help them. They need you to help them catch somebody else."

Nothing.

"Mike, you're going to hurt yourself if you stay in there. You'll run out of air . . ."

SHE CONTINUED TO TALK, reassuring sometimes, pleading other times. There were muffled replies, but no movement, and nobody could decipher what West was saying. West twisted and retwisted his feet, but gave no sign of giving up. Lucas finally stepped away and asked Shrake, "How're you guys doing?"

"Gettin' tired. I'm too old for this all-night and all-day shit."

Jenkins blew some smoke and nodded: "Me too."

Shrake said, "Butt me," and Jenkins held out a pack of Marlboros. Shrake took one and lit it with an antique brass Zippo; the smell of lighter fluid hung in the air for a moment.

"I really appreciate all this," Lucas said, gesturing down the hillside. "Put in for every minute of overtime. I'll sign anything reasonable. And you don't have to stay here—you can take off if you want."

"I'd like to see the little asshole's face before we go," Shrake said. "That's all I've seen of him." He nodded at the hole. "The bottom of his feet."

Sandy shouted, "We're having pumpkin pie tonight, that's your favorite."

"You want me to get him out of there?" Jenkins asked.

"With whipped cream," Sandy yelled.

"He's really wedged in," Lucas said.

"Fuck a bunch of wedges. Let me talk to him for a minute. And get that broad out of there, she ain't helping the situation."

"I don't want him gassed . . . ," Lucas warned.

"I ain't gonna gas him, for Christ's sake," Jenkins said. "Just let me talk to him."

"Whatever," Lucas said. "No saps."

"Get the broad out of there."

THEY TOLD SANDY that they might have to work on another concept and eased her away from the hole. She went up the hill white-faced, looking back, afraid the cops were going to do something weird, like shoot West in the feet.

Jenkins did do something weird. He leaned into the hillside, fumbled around West's shoes for a moment, then started untying one. He took his time getting it loose: West twisted his feet around, trying to get away from the hands, but apparently couldn't get any deeper into the hole.

"You know what I'm doing, Mikey?" Jenkins shouted into the hole. "I've been looking for you for two days. I'm really tired, and now you're fuckin' with me. So I'm gonna take your fuckin' shoes off, and if you don't come out of there, I'm gonna throw them in the fuckin' river. 'Cause I'm pissed off."

There was more muffled noise from inside the hole, more foot twisting, and then Jenkins, still taking his time, pulled the first shoe off. There was a sock under it, black and shriveled and wet with sweat or river water. The ankle above it was almost as black as the sock. Jenkins touched neither.

"That's one shoe," he yelled into the hole. "I'm gonna put it right here, until I get the second one. Then I'm going to throw them into the fuckin' river, I swear to God."

He started working on the second shoe, taking time to untie it, and suddenly one of West's legs extended a few inches, and then the other, and then the first one a few more. Somebody said, "He's coming," and with some muffled shouting, Mike West squirmed out of the hole, tears in his eyes, dragging a plastic garbage bag behind him. "Don't take my shoes, man," he said to Jenkins. "Don't take my shoes."

"I ain't gonna take your shoes," Jenkins said. He sat back and took the Marlboros out of his pocket. "You want a smoke?"

WEST WAS A PHYSICAL WRECK. He was short, skinny to the point of emaciation. His face was grimed with dirt, both old and new, and his cheekbones stood out like axe edges in a field of blemishes. His hair, a uniform four inches long, looked as though it had been cut with hedge clippers and stuck out from his head in dirty brown clumps. His eyes were wide, blue, and frightened. He was wearing a open long-sleeved flannel shirt, North Face nylon drawstring pants, and a theme T-shirt. The theme was outer space—a small black circle on top, labeled URANUS, with a much larger black circle below it, with the caption, URANUS IN PRISON.

"I didn't do anything," he said to Jenkins.

"Tell this guy here," Jenkins said, turning a thumb at Lucas.

"We don't think you did anything," Lucas said. "We just want to get you a shower, maybe get a McDonald's or something, maybe get your clothes washed, and talk."

West wrapped his arms around his garbage bag: "Talk about what?"

WEST WAS WILLING enough to talk, when he remembered to. He was one of the legion of the lost, a schizophrenic who could tolerate neither his condition nor the drugs that treated it. As Lucas and Sloan talked him along, he'd break off to stare, to mumble, to twitch. He had an uncle, he said, who pinched him. Hard. "I know he's not really there," he said to Lucas, "but I can feel him. He hurts. What an ass wipe he is."

WEST HAD OCCASIONALLY stayed at the St. Paul Mission. They took him there in the back of a Minneapolis squad, got him a shower. Sandy, his friend, had voluntarily stopped at a Goodwill store and picked up clean clothes. She waited outside while West dressed, and he looked at himself in the mirror—jockey shorts, white T-shirt, plaid shirt, stone-washed jeans. "I look really square, dude," he said, with an unhappy grimace.

"Ah, you look okay," Lucas said. West went away for a minute, mumbled to an unseen presence, flinched, said, "*Ow.*" Lucas touched him on the shoulder: "You really look good."

West came back. "What?"

"You sure as shit smell better," Del added.

"I'm gonna miss my turn at the stoplight," West said. "And I'm not gonna make a dime dressed like this."

"I'll give you a couple bucks," Lucas said. "If you're reasonable."

"A couple bucks? Man, I need thirty bucks a day just to make my nut," West said. He tended to slip into a whine when things weren't going well.

Lucas: "You want to eat or what?"

THEY ATE IN A BAR, Coney Islands and sauerkraut and beer. Sandy wanted to come along, but they thanked her for her trouble and sent her on her way. "He'll be okay?"

"He'll be back on the job tomorrow," Del said.

As they were walking over to the bar, Del chatted with West. When they got there, Del hooked Lucas by the arm before they went inside, and he said, "West didn't kill anybody."

"Seems pretty unlikely," Lucas agreed.

"It'd be the most unlikely thing I've ever run into—he's scared all the time, he's got dead relatives plucking at his shirt and his hair, some days the sidewalks melt and get weird and his feet stick in the concrete."

"Ah, man."

"With some people I'd say it might be an act; but with him, it's not."

WHEN THEY TOLD WEST what they wanted—explained the situation—he said, "You shoulda come to me first."

"Well, Mike, we tried," Sloan said. "We've been looking all over for you."

"I've been workin' the same spot every day, six days a week, for a month, dude. Really fuckin' first-class police work, huh?"

"So . . . what do you think?" Lucas asked.

"I woulda told you that it wasn't Charlie. Charlie might have killed one or two of them, but then he would have hid them and run," West said, adding more raw onions to the Coney Island. "He would have got scared. He wouldn't have done anything to them. I mean, except fuck 'em and kill 'em. He wouldn't torture anybody."

"That's what we're figuring out," Lucas said. "We've talked to all those guys, you know, the shrinks and the security guards, and they can't give us a name. I mean, we thought we had a name—Charlie. It turned out it wasn't him. Then we got another name. Yours. Everybody said you were Charlie's friend, and you worked down there around the Big Three. So, one way or another, we figured you might know who *else* was talking to the Big Three."

West shuddered. "Those guys. Those guys are really *nuts*. I mean, all of us were nuts, except maybe Alison. But they were *really* nuts."

Lucas bit: "Alison?"

West had a mouthful of Coney Island, chewed it, swallowed carefully, and for a moment went someplace else, his mouth half open, three inches from taking a new bite. After a long moment, he suddenly came back, his eyes shifting, and he said, "Yeah. Alison. She wasn't nuts, she was just in there for the money. She didn't make any secret of it."

Del looked at Lucas, and Lucas rubbed his forehead with both hands: "I don't want to know."

Del said, "I gotta know." To West. "Okay, what about Alison? What do you mean, she was in it for the money?"

West looked a little surprised: everybody knew about Alison. He put on a patient voice, as if talking to a village idiot, and said, "Where else are you going to meet rich guys that no other women want? I mean, there are always a bunch of guys in there for evaluation. Some got the big bucks. Especially the obsessive-compulsives; but the paranoids do pretty good, too."

"She's in there . . . to date?" Del asked. This was the kind of informational nugget he treasured.

"Yeah. What have I been telling you?" West finished the last of the Coney Island, held up a finger to the waitress, pointed at his plate, and mimed, "Another one."

LUCAS WRENCHED THE CONVERSATION back on course: "So give me two names," he said. "Who are two people most likely to have been taken over by the Big Three? Include women—do women work around them?"

"When they're not in isolation," West said. He twitched, said, "*Don't*," and pulled away from his invisible uncle, tears coming to his eyes. Lucas looked away, but then West went on, as if there'd been no interruption. "Okay: Danny Anderson. He got out a couple of months before I did, and he was pretty . . . dim. Like you could take him over."

Sloan stirred, and asked, "Who else?"

West scratched his head with a fork and finally said, "You know what you're asking is, who knows those guys? The answer is, lots of people. But I don't know anybody who was likely to get taken over. I tried to stay away from them, and so did everybody else. I mean, those guys weren't just nuts, they were *nasty*. They'd yell shit like 'Hey, ugly boy, hey pimple boy, your dick as big as that pimple on your nose?' And Biggie was aways yelling at guys to show their asses. Or Taylor would yell at some woman that he had some grease for her pussy, and he'd have like a handful of come. I mean, who is gonna get taken over by somebody like that? When you're trying to stay away from them?"

Sloan said to Lucas, "Dan Anderson's been in California since two days after he got out, living with an aunt. He had to check in with the authorities out there because it was a sex crime, and they've tagged him ever since. He's not the guy."

West was disappointed: "Never liked him. He was an ass wipe."

"So you got no names," Lucas said to West. "You're not helping us much."

West was drinking a Budweiser through a straw. "No. That's not right. I got about a million names. I knew everybody in the place. But I don't know which one it is. Like I said, it all seems wrong to me. Hardly anybody hung around those ass wipes."

They all sat there for a minute, then West said, "What time is it?"

"Two o'clock," Lucas said.

"If somebody gives me a ride, I could still make it over to my light."

OUT ON THE SIDEWALK, squinting in the bright sunlight, West burped beer fumes and said, "Sorry I couldn't help. This guy sounds like a serious ass wipe."

"Ah," Lucas said and stepped away.

"You know, I do got an idea, when I think about it. Ones who might have got their brains changed," West said. He said it with the self-conscious smile of a bad comedian about to deliver a worse joke.

"Who?" Sloan said.

"Like O'Donnell and Jimenez and Grant and Hart and Sennet and Halburton and Grosz and Steinhammer . . . those are the guys who hung around with the Big Three all the time, talking to them. Docs and guards."

LUCAS STARED AT HIM for a long beat, then looked at Sloan and said, quietly, "Oh, shit."

Sloan said. "No way."

Lucas nodded: "Way. Ah, Jesus, Biggie told us, and I missed it."

"What?" Del asked.

"What?" West said after him. His eyes were sharp and blue: no sign of vagueness now.

Lucas said to Del, "Take Mike over to Dinky Town or get him a cab or something. Sloan and I gotta talk. Here." He dug into his pocket, took out two twenties and a ten, handed them to West. "Catch a cab, take a bus, I don't care, that makes your nut for the day. We gotta go."

LUCAS HEADED OFF, hurrying, Sloan jogging after him to catch up. They'd left Lucas's truck at the mission. Sloan caught up with him and said, "Wait, wait, wait—you think a staff member?"

"I think it's possible," Lucas said. "It's one thing we haven't looked at. Goddamnit. When we were talking to O'Donnell and Hart, they made a big deal out of how nothing goes into the cells and nothing comes out. Those guys are supposed to be super-isolated. Total information blackout."

"Yeah. So?"

"So Biggie yelled something about arresting the killer for not having a hunting license. Taylor knew it, too, that there'd been a hunter-oriented killing. And they didn't try to get any details out of us. You know why? Because they had the details. And the staff was specifically *forbidden* to talk to them about any of the crimes, right?"

"Yeah, but . . ." Sloan frowned.

"And down in the isolation wing, nobody goes in but staff."

Sloan thought about it, then said, "You know lockups, Lucas. People tip other people off, even when they don't mean to. Supper comes, Taylor asks the guy if the hunter has killed a woman yet. The guy looks away, and Taylor *knows* . . ."

"That's a possibility," Lucas admitted. "But the way they were behaving . . . C'mon, Sloan. Think about it. *They knew all about it.* This wasn't a tip."

Sloan rubbed his head, looked back toward the disappearing figures of Del and West. "Jesus. I hate to think . . . they're doctors."

"Maybe a guard. Maybe a food guy. But we've hit a blank wall trying to find another candidate among the inmates . . ."

"Yeah . . ."

"We gotta go back there. We've got to look at tapes for the last two days."

"Goddamn," Sloan said, more to himself than to Lucas. "Is this *possible?*"

18

DR. CALE WAS WAITING in his office. Their escort dropped them, and Cale shut the door. "All right: What's going on?"

"We need to see the tapes for the isolation cells for the past two days," Sloan said.

Cale rocked on his feet, his hands in his jacket pocket: "Why?"

"We want to see who's been talking to the Big Three," Lucas said.

Cale drifted down his wall of books and papers, looked at a plaque, then said, sadly, "Nobody talks to them but staff."

Lucas said, "That's why we need to see them."

Cale continued drifting along the books, turned the corner at his desk, sat in his swivel chair, and turned until his back was toward them, and he was looking out the window at the Minnesota woods and the river valley beyond. "You think a member of the staff might be passing them information?"

"Something like that," Lucas said, his voice cool, neutral.

Cale hadn't become head of the hospital by being stupid: he swiveled to face them, took off his glasses, rubbed one eye with the heel of a hand, and said, "Oh, boy. Who are you looking at? Grant?"

"Why do you say Grant?" Lucas asked.

"He's the new guy. Been here less than a year. The other guys have been here longer."

"Grant would be interesting," Lucas said. "Any reason to think . . . ?"

"He sometimes seems a little naïve . . . uncertain of what he's doing. He seems to struggle," Cale said. "But that's often the sign of a good therapist—a guy who doesn't fall into routine and cliché."

"Is he good?"

"He *is* good," Cale said. "He has a fine touch with patients, especially the lost souls. You know, the quiet ones, the helpless ones—well, like Mike West. And I have to say, he came highly recommended."

"Doesn't have to be a therapist," Lucas said. "Could be anybody who's had intimate contact with the Big Three."

"That's a lot of people. Until they went into isolation, at least. Dozens of people, including staff members, in here," Cale said. "Then there are outsiders. We contract for some medical services, for example, and Biggie, in particular, has been having problems. He's a borderline diabetic, he's got circulatory problems, and his PSAs are out of sight. He's gonna lose his prostate in the next few years."

"We need a list of the outside docs," Lucas said. "We still want to see the tapes."

"Okay. Let me call Security. They can put you in the monitoring room and run them right there."

"We could use a little privacy," Lucas said. "But we'd also like somebody who can identify the people going in and out."

"I'll get you Leon Jansen. He's one of our security people, knows everybody, and he can keep his mouth shut."

"And he doesn't have access to Biggie."

"No. Not since they went into isolation, anyway."

CALE CALLED JANSEN on a voice pager; he showed up a couple of minutes later, a tall black man with a hard face and close-cropped hair. He wore a small green crescent moon on a chain around his neck, which Lucas recognized as some kind of Muslim symbol. Cale introduced Lucas and Sloan and explained the problem. Jansen said, "Most unusual. Well. Come this way."

"Wish I could wish you good luck," Cale said as they went out the door.

Lucas and Sloan followed Jansen back out through the hospital, toward the security wall. "Are you conversant with our security structure?" Jansen asked. His language was formal, almost academic.

"We've been through the wall a few times . . ."

"The cage is essentially a booth with armored glass on all sides. From the outside, you have to go through the barred door to get to the security booth. The door closes, and then you go through the scanner process . . ."

"We did all that," Sloan began.

Jansen ignored him and continued. "When you're cleared through the scanner, the person manning the booth opens the interior barred door, and you can proceed. The point here is, you can't open both doors at once. There's an electronic interlock that won't allow it. The people in the booth are completely isolated from the outside. While they're in there, it would take military munitions to get them out. Gas won't work, guns won't work."

"And that's where you monitor the cells from," Lucas said.

"Yes."

"Could the guys inside the booth talk to the inmates through the intercom system?"

"Of course. And they do," Jansen said. "They're on the tape."

"Could somebody turn off the tape?"

"Could . . . but it'd be apparent in the time code, and the recorder notes when the tape is taken down. Also, the cage is about the size of two bedrooms, and there are always at least three people in there. You couldn't have a conversation that's not overheard." He put a finger along the side of his nose, like Santa Claus, thinking, then said, "But you know, given human nature . . . the monitoring room is at the far end, and there's a door that closes between the monitoring area and the main booth. You might find some excuse to close the door, and then talk to an inmate . . . but I would find that odd."

"Huh."

THE EXTERIOR DOOR slid open as they came up to it. They stepped through it, into the middle space where the cage was, and the door closed behind them. Cale had called ahead, and when both the interior and exterior barred doors were closed and locked, one of the people inside the cage popped a door and Jansen led them inside.

"We need to look at some tapes, people," Jansen said to the three people in the booth, two women and a man. "Dr. Cale has probably talked to you, so you know that we're required to view them privately."

"What're you looking for?" the male guard asked.

"Don't know," Sloan said genially. "We're looking at the Big Three, and anything would help."

"This way," Jansen said. He took them into a second small room, where one wall held three dozen small monitoring screens and a couple of larger ones. Only half of them were turned on.

"We monitor the isolation rooms constantly, and tape them. We also monitor what we call 'watch rooms,' where we put people who might be at some risk of attempting suicide, and also the high-risk individuals, like the Big Three," Jansen said. "The rest of the cameras are scanners and are meant to pick up disturbances in the hallways and recreational areas and so on."

"We're interested in the Big Three, going back three days," Lucas said.

BY FAST-FORWARDING, they got through the tapes for the Big Three in two hours. The three had no privacy at all: they used the toilet, masturbated, exercised, slept, screamed, ate before the unblinking camera eye. At first, it carried a voyeuristic fascination; two days in, they just wanted it to end. The boredom was grinding, and Lucas began to empathize with Chase's wish to die. Lucas looked for seams in the tape, where it might have shut down; but it was seamless. Nobody, as far as they could tell, had said anything about the Peterson killing.

"Could it be a code word, telling them that the killing was done?" Sloan asked. Jansen glanced sideways at him, an idiot glance, and Sloan said, defensively, "All right, it's not a code word."

"There's gotta be something," Lucas said. He'd written down a list of names of the people who'd gone through the security area; there were thirty of them.

"Every single person you've seen in there—half the staff, I didn't know that many people went in and out, to tell you the truth—but every single person knows he's on tape," Jansen said.

"You can't see them very well, unless they're right up against the viewing panel," Lucas said. "Is there another angle?"

"Yeah, we have one of the scanning cameras at the end of the hall."

"Let's see that."

They spent ten minutes fast-forwarding through three days of the staff coming and going. "I keep thinking, the *food*," Sloan said. "It's the only thing that consistently goes into the cells."

They thought about that for a moment, and then Jansen said, "Suppose one of the guys delivering the food wrote down what happened, like a little strip of paper, and put it in the mashed potatoes . . ."

"Let's look at the guys bring in the food."

Seven different staff members delivered food over the three days. The food went into the cell on a kind of metallic lazy Susan device. "Wouldn't even have to put it in the food—you could just drop it on the tray when you put the food in the slot," Sloan said. "The cameras aren't so good that you could pick that up."

They watched the three men eating, saw nothing out of the ordinary, except that Biggie had bad manners, eating with his hands as much as with his spoon.

"Okay," Lucas said, when they were done. He was discouraged. "Maybe this isn't it. Goddamnit, I thought I was on to something."

"Want me to go down and drop Peterson's name on Biggie? Or on all three of them?" Jansen asked. "I could mention 'a Peterson thing' in passing, see if we get any reaction."

"It's an idea," Lucas said, considering him. "You're not going to get anything from Chase, though. He was hypermanic this morning."

"He's gone over the top and is on the way back down," Jansen said. "If I go now, I might catch him before he crashes. You could watch from here, in real time."

Lucas nodded. "Let's do it."

CHASE GAVE IT AWAY. Jansen rolled the observation window back and said, "How're you doing? Sleepy?"

"Man, I'm dying," Chase whimpered. "I'm going out. I'm like a light, I'm going out." He put his hands on both sides of his head and squeezed: "Why am I like this, Mr. Jansen?"

"We don't know, man." There was a note of sympathy in Jansen's voice, and it resonated.

Chase said, still holding his face, "If I could just, if I could just . . . If I could get out of here just for a couple of hours . . ." He sounded desperate, like a man who needed water.

"That's gonna be tough, since the Peterson thing. The director is adamant about keeping the three of you under wraps. That might not seem fair . . ."

Lucas liked the way he did it: in passing, as part of another idea, the raisin in the rice pudding. Chase's hands came down; his face was brighter, and his thin lips turned up in a joker's smile. "You know about that? How he got her . . ."

"I've heard the usual stories," Jansen said, noncommittally. He looked over his shoulder, as though he shouldn't be talking about it.

"So cool. He fucked her all night. He had her tied up, he had this rope around her neck like a fuckin' bridle, he fucked her all night. Six, seven, eight times. The bitch could hardly walk in the morning. He took her up there, rolled her out of the car, naked as the day. Then he says, 'You got a hundred yards and then I'm coming.'"

"She ran, but there was no place to go, so she ran into the woods." Chase was leaning on the viewing glass now, face only inches from Jansen's.

"She was screaming: but there was nobody out there. He caught her by this big tree, and she tried to run around it, keep the tree between them. Then he caught her and there was a creek and she fell into it, and that's when he got her; right on her shoulder blades. She had this long black hair and he pulled it up and zip with the razor. Then you know what he did? He did like this victory scream, he screamed . . ."

And Chase screamed, his head thrown back, his mouth open, his eyes glazed . . . and then he staggered backwards onto his bed, as though he'd been struck by lightning, his tongue out now, his body vibrating, words bubbling out, all nonsense.

Jansen disappeared from the camera view, and they could hear his voice from down the hall. Calling for help?

Sloan said, "That's not something you see every day."

. . .

THEY WERE BACK in Cale's office: "They got the message some-how. In detail. There's nothing on the tape, so it wasn't oral. It must have been written and delivered with the food," Lucas said. "We've got a list of the people who were around when food was delivered. Seven orderlies, three therapists. There were also two doctors and two more therapists in and out of the hallway, who looked or spoke to the Big Three at one time or another."

"Goddamnit. I can hear them building the crucifix, up at the Capitol," Cale said. He spun his chair, looking out his window. "And it's so hard to believe. I've known Dr. Hart for ten years, and he's a fine man. So is O'Donnell, despite all the hair and the hip bull-shit. Dr. Sennet has been controversial sometimes, but he's a good therapist."

"I'm most interested in O'Donnell, Sennet, and Halburton," Lucas said. "They were both nearby when the food deliveries were made. I mean, right there."

Cale spun back to face them and shook his head. "I can make one suggestion: we could hope that whatever went into the cell stayed there. They could have flushed it, or eaten it, but sometimes . . . people like this will hold on to something as an artifact. A trophy. If we lock them down and shake down the cells, we might come up with one of the notes. That might give us something."

"Do that," Lucas said. "There's nothing we can do to help you—but I want the personnel files on those fourteen people. I'll need to copy them and take them back to St. Paul; and I'd like to get copies of the tapes, if I could. I don't know—maybe we missed something, because we were going through them too fast."

"I'll get it started," Cale said. He pushed himself heavily out of his chair and said, "God Almighty."

LUCAS CALLED THE Blue Earth County sheriff's office and gave them the information about the murder having been done in a creek, in a place remote enough that Peterson could scream and not be heard; but because of the search for a white car, Lucas couldn't believe that the killer would drive far with the body.

So: a creek close to the point where the body was found.

That done, he joined Sloan in Xeroxing the fourteen personnel files, while Cale organized the shakedown. They were halfway through with the paper when Cale came back to say that they were doing all three cells simultaneously, and included body-cavity searches.

"We're taking out every piece of cloth in there, including the mattresses, all the books, the clothing, everything. We'll shred all of it."

"How long?"

"Another hour. We've got six people working on it. Biggie was very unhappy. Taylor acted like he didn't care, and Chase is gone. I'm thinking of moving him to the medical ward."

THEY WAITED THE HOUR, browsing through the personnel files. Cale came back shaking his head. "Not a thing."

"You couldn't have missed it."

"No. You don't even want to know where we looked."

Lucas exhaled, slapped his knees, and stood up. "Dr. Cale, thank you. You've been a big help. We've made serious progress here. We're gonna tear up these files and maybe call you back tomorrow with some questions."

"You're gonna get the guy?" Cale asked.

"Yeah. Soon, now. A few days, at most."

Cale looked down the hall, where a woman was pushing another woman in a wheelchair, both of them laughing. "I wish we heard more of that around here. Not enough of that."

THEY DROVE BACK NORTH through one of the long, beautiful summer twilights, a few stars poking out like theater lamps, a moon coming up in the east, lopsided but nearly full. They didn't talk much; they were both running through the tapes in their heads. Sloan would occasionally turn on the reading light and look at one of the Xeroxed files.

After a while, Sloan said, "Besides Hart, O'Donnell, and Sennet, I think we should take a close look at Grant and Beloit. For reasons that are a little stupid."

"How stupid?"

"They both get great ratings from the patients. I figure, that's maybe because they identify with them."

"Ah, Beloit's out. The guy I talked to the other night—that was a *guy*. Regardless of the voice, he talked like a guy would. Like a shitkicker, like you'd expect from Charlie Pope. And didn't Taylor, when he was yelling at us about the license, say *him*, or *he*?"

Sloan thought for a moment. "I think it was, 'Our boy.'"

"'That's right,'" Lucas said. "'Our boy.' You think that might have been put on to steer us away from a woman?"

"It's possible, but . . . not likely."

"If he was, he was giving away the license thing at the same time. I don't think that was deliberate," Lucas said.

"Right. I knew that. So we scratch Beloit."

"About ninety percent," Lucas said.

A BIT LATER, Sloan said, "Cale was right about building a crucifix. He'd be a prime candidate for it."

"Or us, depending on where we are when the music stops," Lucas said.

LUCAS DROPPED SLOAN with a Minneapolis cop car on the south end of the city, went on to St. Paul, and picked up a tape machine that would work with his home television; took a long walk to a Baker's Square restaurant on Ford Parkway and ate dinner; stuck his head in a Half-Priced Books; window-shopped a jewelry store, thinking about a welcome-home gift for Weather; and ambled back home, hands in his pockets, a tattered, pirate copy of Ernest Hemingway's poems under his arm. Mulling, all the way, the assemblage of information.

They were like squirrels who kept coming up with nuts they couldn't crack, he decided.

They had a guy who'd deliberately faked DNA, knowing that it would point the finger in the wrong direction. Who'd know about that? When he thought about it, he decided that . . . just about everybody would know.

A medical doctor, for sure—and Beloit was a medical doctor, though, unfortunately, she was also female, and the voice wasn't female. And almost any of the professionals at St. John's would know, because the state DNA bank made a big deal out of getting samples from all convicted sex criminals. Besides, after the rash of crime-scene investigator shows on TV, half the TV watchers in the country knew about DNA. Hell, even George Bush would probably know about it.

So that went nowhere.

The killer used, or tried to use, Ruffe Ignace to point them in the wrong direction. Serial killers occasionally talked to the press or the cops, so that was nothing new, but usually they were looking for glory or turning themselves in. This guy pretended to be looking for glory, but he was actually trying to use Ignace in a manipulative way; or maybe he was doing both, but the manipulation was certainly there.

Lucas thought about the meth lab. Could the killer have met Charlie Pope there? It was one nexus of criminals . . . but he didn't really need that. He had a nexus of criminals in the security hospital, all that he required. The hospital was part of it . . .

And then the real nut of the thing.

How had the Big Three learned of Peterson?

If he could crack that . . .

But then, how'd they known of Rice and Larson?

BACK AT THE HOUSE, he read the personnel files with the tapes running behind them, at about four times actual. The staff members came and left in a herky-jerky speeded-up way reminiscent of old silent films; every once in a while, he would slow the tapes down to watch the action.

The only people to actually go into a cell were Beloit and another doctor named Rosen, and they were always escorted by two orderlies, and they never went into the cells of the Big Three, only into the cell of the fourth man, who was being disciplined for attacking another patient. They went in, gave him an insulin shot, and left. Routine.

O'Donnell and Sennet actually helped deliver food, keying back the security panels, chatting with the Big Three as their meals were delivered. Chase went from slow to manic to crazed to cooler to slow and finally to catatonic as he watched. O'Donnell moved in a way that blocked the hall camera from the food tray. Lucas picked it up on the second delivery. He made a note.

Sennet did nothing but chat, and sometimes not even that, standing beside the meal-delivery man as the food went into the cell. He would occasionally make a note on a clipboard.

Grant went only once, with Hart. He carried a notebook but never opened it; peeled off a good-looking sport coat, rolled up his sleeves, talked with Biggie; walked down toward the camera, following Hart to

Chase's cell, chatted with him for a moment; said nothing to Chase, only watched as the other man wandered helplessly around his cell.

When they closed the window to Chase's cell, Grant said to Hart, "His personality is coming apart. We've got to get him out of here."

"I don't think they'll let us do that, not until they catch Mr. Torture Guy."

Hart actually leaned against the security glass with one hand. Lucas ran the tape back: Hart had done that several times, at the different cells. Could he have written something on the palm of his hand? That seemed far-fetched; but Lucas made a note.

He didn't find much in the personnel files: he'd give them to the coordination center in the morning, have them run them.

That night, trying to sleep, he kept coming back to the tapes. Something went into the cells, right under his eyes. How had they done it?

Or maybe the killing had been planned in the smallest of details beforehand, and Sloan had been right in talking about a code. All it would take would be something like . . . he tried to think of something.

Like Grant taking off his sport coat.

Like Hart leaning against a window.

Like Sennet or O'Donnell using some kind of key word, or perhaps something as simple as eye contact, with a nod and a smile.

Something, and it was right there, and he couldn't see it.

19

THE MAN WITH THE whispery voice was worried now. He'd thought to easily take ten, or fifteen, or twenty . . . and then maybe drift away, and start again somewhere. He'd toyed with the idea of faking his own death in the style of himself, just for the implicit humor of the situation . . . Set it up by killing a couple of people and never revealing where he left them . . .

Now, that'd be tough. The cops were nipping at his heels—that god-damn Pope was the one who did it to him. He'd come back like the ghost of Christmas. If he hadn't . . .

Without that accident, without those fuckin' fishermen, they would have been looking for Pope for another year. He'd seen the activity down by the bridge, the divers, the cops, and as soon as he'd seen it, he'd known that Charlie had come back.

The Gods Down the Hall had said that this might happen; that some weird happenstance would trip him. They'd told him in detail how they'd been caught, how small slips led to bigger ones, until finally they stepped on the fatal banana peel. To prevent that, to prevent the cops from isolating one man, they had to be fed options until they choked on them, Biggie said. Feed them leads that point away, he said.

If all else failed, they said, it was better to go out in a blaze than in a cage.

Biggie Lighter had grinned at him and said softly, "They got a name for it, the good Christians do."

"Yes?"

"Armageddon. The final battle. If it comes to it, think how good that would feel . . ."

IF THE FINAL BATTLE was coming, the man with the whispery voice wouldn't leave Millie behind. Couldn't do that—he'd waited so long to take her . . .

THE NIGHT THAT the killer came to visit, Charlie Pope had been dozing on a broken-back couch in front of the TV. The killer, who'd scouted the trailer park the night before, nosed the state car past Charlie's back door, then reversed and snugged up to the trailer. He sat for a moment, watching and listening, then took the book-sized medical kit off the front seat, climbed out, and knocked on Charlie's back door.

The killer was a slender man, dead white and muscular in a knotty, workman's way, with a barbed-wire tattoo on his left biceps and a German art-deco eagle on his back, just above his buttocks. He had three black dots in a triangle on the web of skin between his right thumb and forefinger, and he told people—mysteriously reticent about the details—that he'd gotten them in the army. Everyone in the unit had one, he said. He couldn't say what unit that was. Always the wisecrack, delivered with the well-practiced, engaging grin: "I could tell you, but then I'd have to kill you."

Charlie took a minute to answer the knock. He was burly-gone-to-fat, hairy, still half asleep, dressed in jeans and a yellow smiley-face T-shirt, his gut pushing out in the gap between shirt and pants; he stood blinking in the porch light. "Hey, man. What are you doin' here?"

"Drop-in drug check, Charlie. Required by law," the killer said. "I need a blood sample."

"Ah, shit. This time of night?" But Charlie stepped back so the killer could step inside with him. "I didn't even know you could do that . . ."

"Required by law—and I've got some questions to ask," the killer said. There was steel in his voice now. Never let an inmate get on top of you, even after they stopped being inmates. "Take fifteen minutes. How've you been feeling?"

"Not too bad—I hate the fuckin' job, though. Get up at five o'clock, lift them fuckin' cans all fuckin' day. Hurts my fuckin' back. Better'n that fuckin' hospital, though."

The door opened into the tiny travel-trailer kitchen. The killer held up the kit and said, "Let's get the blood test out of the way. Give me your left arm."

The syringe was already loaded, lying there in the case, along with the Ziploc bag, vinyl gloves, the scalpel, and the six-foot coil of nylon rope. He had an alcohol wipe in a single-sized paper pack; unnecessary, but it added a subtle hint of innocence. If you were going to murder somebody, why would you swab his arm with alcohol?

So Charlie turned, and the killer ripped open the swab packet, wiped Charlie's triceps, picked up the needle, and gave him the injection.

"Feels more like it's going in than coming out," Charlie said over his shoulder.

"*Mmm.* You haven't been messing with any drugs, have you, Charlie? Cocaine, meth, even grass—that wouldn't be good."

"Honest to God, I don't got money for fuckin' cigarettes."

The killer pulled the needle out, dropped it in his kit, then pointed Charlie to the couch. "Why don't you sit down, we'll fill out this questionnaire, and then I can get out of your hair. Let you sleep," he said.

Charlie obediently plopped down on the couch. The killer took a slip of paper from his shirt pocket, looked at it, and then said, "Have you been dating?"

Charlie goggled at him. "Dating? You gotta be fuckin' kidding. Everybody in town knows what I was arrested for . . ." His eyes drooped, and he yawned, and he mumbled, "I couldn't get a fuckin' date . . . Jesus, I'm sleepy. Must've been the blood you took out."

Either that or the overload of phenobarbital that he'd just put in, the killer thought, amused. Enough to kill a horse. Charlie tried to get up, struggled, then fell back on the couch . . . "I don't . . . I don't . . ."

He was out. The killer's heart was beating a little faster now. He was insane, but not immune to fear; in fact, his whole life had been lived in fear. At this point, he could bullshit his way out, he thought. In five minutes, if he went ahead, he couldn't. He leaned forward from the kitchen chair, examining Charlie's slack face. Well . . .

He had vinyl gloves and a scalpel in his medical kit, and a Ziploc bag. He pulled on the vinyl gloves, knelt next to Charlie's body, turned his arm, and cut off Charlie's little finger. Charlie twitched once, then went still again. The killer wrapped the bag around the stump of Charlie's finger, watched until it contained an ounce or so of blood, dropped the finger inside, then got the rope.

He murdered Charlie with the rope. The drug would have done it, in time, but he didn't want to waste that time—didn't want to be inside Charlie's place any longer than he had to be. So he stood behind the other man, put the rope around Charlie's neck, and pulled hard. Held it; held it; held it. In a minute or a little more, Charlie began to shake. That went on for a short time, less than a minute, the killer thought, and still he pulled on the rope. Held it.

Sweaty work, killing somebody with a rope. Like hanging on to a rope tow up a ski slope. He was tough, but his arms were shaking by the time Charlie was dead. It took much longer than in the movies. As a psychotherapist, he thought, a medical professional, he should have known that; he giggled a little at the thought.

When he was sure that Charlie was dead, he looked at the hand with the amputated finger. The flow of blood had stopped. He pulled the bag off Charlie's hand and then stuck the mutilated hand down the front of Charlie's pants, right down by his crotch. He put the bag on the kitchen table.

As he worked around the body, he thought about what he'd just done. He'd killed four people before Charlie, all male, all street people, but never for the simple pleasure of it. The killings had delivered a rush, but the rush had been agonizing, like an overdose of ice. Three of the men had something the killer wanted: money, drugs, food, clothing, a radio. The other man, the fourth man, had been a predator himself, had come after the killer's cash. The attack had come at night, under the pier at Santa Monica; the attacker died with a five-inch blade in his throat.

Then, there'd been nothing but fear. The Gods Down the Hall said that was to be expected: but when you penetrated the fear, there came the most exquisite pleasure. When you took control, the fear dropped away, and you were at peace.

That hadn't quite been the case with Charlie: Charlie had been more in the manner of a business killing, setting up what was to come next. But there had been a tingle, a sketchy, uncertain pleasure in the process. Not enough. He was reaching for something much more complicated, and much deeper.

When he was ready, he turned off the lights, stepped outside, popped the trunk of the car, took out an old canvas duffel bag, then backed up, sat on the stoop for three minutes, and simply listened. Listened to the bugs, the buzzing of a mosquito trap somewhere, the seeping-in sounds of a TV from another trailer, the burr of air conditioners. When he was satisfied that there was nobody close, that he couldn't be seen, he stepped back into the trailer, grabbed Charlie by the belt, and dragged him through the door, down the steps, and loaded him into the car trunk.

The killer was strong, but the body was loose and floppy and heavy, and he had to struggle to get it inside. The body landed with a thud and a clank on top of the pile of logging chain. With the trunk lid down, he went back inside the trailer, carrying the duffel bag, and walked back to the bedroom.

He stuffed Charlie's few personal possessions in the bag: Charlie hadn't been out long, hadn't made any money, so there wasn't much: shaving gear and deodorant, a cheap Timex, jeans and shirts and underwear. On the way back through the kitchen, he noticed a thin brown streak on the kitchen floor. Dried blood? Where had that come from? He checked himself. Not bleeding anywhere. Maybe he'd squeezed some out through Charlie's jeans . . .

He got a handful of toilet tissue from the bathroom, soaked it in water, and wiped up the streak, looked at it: even dissolved in water, it was brown. Maybe steak sauce or something, he thought. He threw the wad of paper in the duffel bag, picked up the plastic bag with the amputated finger, turned off the light, and carried it all out to the car. The duffel bag went in the backseat, the plastic bag under the front seat.

He was done, but he sat a moment, reviewing it. He'd programmed this pause into the killing. He could not come back, so if he'd forgotten anything . . .

He thought, and thought for another minute, and he slipped his left thumb under the vinyl glove of his right hand, ready to peel it off, and then the word *bracelet* popped into his head.

Good God, he'd forgotten the bracelet. He got out, a thread of panic running through him. There was no way he could have forgotten the bracelet. He popped the trunk again, got the small bolt cutters from the spare tire well, fumbled in the dark until he found the bracelet on Charlie's ankle, cut it loose.

He carried the bracelet between his little finger and thumb up to the trailer and inside. He dropped it next to the couch, about where it might land if you sat on the couch to cut it off.

Anything else? The panic was still there, and he ran through his mental to-do list. He'd gone over it a hundred times in his mind, or even a thousand times, and here, at the critical moment, he'd forgotten the *bracelet*.

But there was nothing else. He got back in the car, turned the ignition key to the second stop, let the windows roll down. He sat and listened some more. When he was as sure as he could be that he wasn't watched, he headed out to Interstate 35.

On the highway, a sudden cold squirt of adrenaline made his hands shake on the steering wheel. Christ, he *couldn't* have forgotten the bracelet. The excitement of the killing had done something to him, had taken him to a level where the mundane realities of the process had slipped away from him. He *had* to check for blood, he *had* to clean up, he had to do all the little chores that the Gods Down the Hall had forgotten. He had to remember, the Gods Down the Hall were smart enough, but they were *Down the Hall* because they'd gotten careless.

He never thought it would happen to him, a mistake like that, an oversight, because he was too smart—but now he saw how it could happen. The motion, the push to move, could get on top of you. Next time, he would have a checklist with him, a written to-do list. If he were going to kill for pleasure, he'd mix hard science with the art of passion. No way he wanted to end up Down the Hall—far better to be dead.

THE NIGHT WAS WARM and hazy, with a low overcast, and as the killer drove across the prairie, the small towns would first come up as a glow in the sky, street and business lights reflected off the cloud base, then as points of light, then as a harsh blue-white and orange-white grid. He passed through them silently, slowly, safely, taking no risks with the speed limit.

Forty-five minutes after the killing, he pulled into a turnout at a historical marker. He drove by the place daily and had never seen a car in it. At the same time, the turnout road ran through a small alley of trees and brush, out of sight of the road.

He got out, lifted the trunk lid. Charlie was lying on a carefully arranged bed of logging chain. He pulled loops of the chain around the body and, with precut five-inch loops of aluminum wire, fastened together opposing links from the chain.

He worked quickly in the weak light of the trunk lid, listening for cars on the gravel road; nobody came down it in the hurried, heavy five minutes of work. He was alone with the dead man and felt a small curl of hair-raising superstitious dread. What if Charlie's eyes opened . . .

He giggled again. Hell, he'd have a heart attack is what would happen. But Charlie was as dead as a carp on a riverbank, and his eyes didn't open. The killer shut the lid on the car trunk, backed out of the historical site—he had no idea of what it marked—and on to the road.

The bridge was only a half mile away. He took the gravel out to the blacktop, turned left, idled over a low hill. A car was coming toward him. He saw it move to the middle of the road as it crossed the bridge, then back to the right as it cleared it. He idled along at forty miles an hour, checking the rearview mirror, looking for lights, and watching for lights out front . . .

When he was sure he was clear, he hurried on down the hill to the bridge; stopped in the middle of it, popped the trunk, and walked over to the railing and looked down. Sometimes fishermen parked beside the bridge: there was just enough space for two cars. Never, as far as he knew, at night: and there was nothing this night . . .

He went back to the car trunk, dragged Charlie out. With the extra weight of the chain, he struggled to get him to the railing. When he got him there, he had to lift Charlie's legs first, prop them on the railing, then walk around to pick up Charlie's head.

And when he did, the feet fell off the rail. He was breathing hard and felt a little panic rising in his throat: this was impossible. He couldn't get the body high enough to prop up the head end. He finally bent it upright, got Charlie's neck hooked over the sharp edge of the rail, took a breather for five seconds, then hoisted the dead man's chest over, balanced the body, then got the feet going. The chain caught on the edge, and he spent a moment wrestling back and forth, the chain making a loud ripping noise on the metal guardrail.

And then Charlie went, falling into the darkness. A moment later, the killer heard a satisfying splash from below: Charlie's last dive was a belly flop into thirty feet of water.

He brushed his hands together, felt the stickiness. As he walked around the front of the car, he looked at them in the headlights. Jesus: he was covered with blood. Hadn't thought about that, either, Didn't have any way to clean up. He knelt in the headlights, looking as his shirt. More blood . . .

Man, the complications were piling up. If he was going to do all this, if he was going to do what the Gods Down the Hall demanded that he do, he was going to have to get a hell of a lot better than this.

And quick: they were hungry for the first woman. Tired of descriptions, tired of what-we-might-do.

They wanted meat. They wanted it now.

He thought about Millie Lincoln. The woman did crazy things to him, and the thought of her blood drove him into a near frenzy.

Not now; if he took Millie Lincoln, the cops would be on him for sure.

But he would take her later. He licked his lips at the thought. Millie.

. . .

MILLIE LINCOLN HAD a decent body, she thought—not Hollywood quality, but decent. Maybe she could lose a few pounds. She looked at herself in the full-length mirror that she and her roommates had pinned to the back of the front door: Okay, maybe ten pounds . . .

"You think my ass looks fat?" she asked Mihovil, who was sitting on a couch, reading a Dilbert cartoon book.

"I would have to see it closer . . ."

"Hey: does it look fat, or doesn't it?"

"Every time I see it good, I get hard," he said. 'What more do you want?"

She went over and plopped on the couch next to him and said, "Pizza."

"I think so. I am starved to death."

But he kept his nose in the book, not quite ignoring her. She crossed her legs and put them across his. He said, "Pizza," and dropped the book on the floor, and brushed his hands up and down her legs. "*Mmm*. You're sticky."

"Haven't shaved my legs in a week," she said.

"Don't shave your legs until I come back," he said. "Tomorrow. Tomorrow I will shave your legs for you."

"*Really*." Sounded okay.

"I am very good with a razor. You will see."

"*Mmm*."

THE NEXT EVENING, the roommates were gone, and they moved into the shower.

Mihovil told her that the first great thing he'd experienced in the States was the shower in their apartment in New York. They hadn't had running water in the refugee camp, and when his family got to New York, got the small apartment in Brooklyn, it had been like heaven.

"Wasn't heaven—was the fucking Yugoslavian ghetto, but it seemed like heaven, and all this hot water from the shower. I could stand in the shower for an hour—I took a shower every morning before school and every day when I came home and every night before I went to bed. You cannot understand hot water coming from the wall until you haven't had it."

When he got his residency and moved into his own apartment in downtown Mankato, he'd unscrewed the showerhead and replaced it with one he bought from a local hardware store; a showerhead that produced a torrent of water.

"My mother always said the best thing about America was a kitchen with a real stove and a real sink and everything works; I always thought the shower. And the toilet, of course."

HE GOT HER IN the shower and said, "First we soap your legs. Huh? We need some nice shaving soap."

He'd brought it with him. He shaved from an old-fashioned mug, with a shaving brush; but the thing that really turned her crank was the razor.

He produced an ancient-looking leather-covered box and from it extracted a straight razor with a mother-of-pearl grip. "From my homeland," he said. "My father gave it to me when I came old enough to shave."

The hot water was pouring down over her belly and legs, and Mihovil lathered her legs with the brush—the brush felt amazing, the brush was something she decided she couldn't live without—and then began carefully shaving her legs, carving his way upward, kneeling on the dirty old tiles, his hands soft and the blade like a piece of light cutting through the prickly leg hair . . .

Like any number of college students with good bodies, Millie liked to lie in the summer sun in a bikini; and a bikini required the removal of patches of pubic hair, left and right. The problem was that when you shaved, you often got nasty red bumps from ingrown hair. The idea of shaving off all her public hair had never appealed to her, because she suspected that she'd turn into one gigantic infected red bump.

But Mihovil, shaving up her legs, simply didn't stop. He just kept going. And the brush felt so good . . .

Mihovil could feel her trembling as he played with the razor and then with the brush, with the razor and the brush, razor and brush . . .

Millie began to whimper, and she knotted her hands in his long Jesus hair, and she began to cry out . . .

20

WEATHER CALLED AT eight o'clock. Lucas fumbled the phone receiver and hit himself on the nose, which hurt.

"How are you?" he asked. He couldn't feel blood moving, but he could taste something in the back of his throat.

"A little tired," Weather said. It was two o'clock in the afternoon in London. "After I talked to you yesterday, we had a six-year-old girl come in. She was hurt in a car wreck. I assisted. There were only two of us on the plastic-surgery staff still around; I was about to leave when she came in. Wound up staying until midnight, and we were working again this morning at seven."

"Get her fixed?"

"Yup. Looked bad, but kids heal, if you get them fast enough."

"Her face?"

"Yes. She was in the front seat of one of those tiny cars they have here." The girl, belted in, had been playing with a toy laptop with a plastic screen. The car she was riding in was rear-ended and jammed into the car in front of them. The air bags went, and they punched the laptop into the girl's face, Weather said. "The plastic shattered, and she had ten or fifteen cuts, three bad, up and down the right cheek and temple."

"Ah, man." Lucas could imagine it: he'd seen similar stuff when he was in uniform with the Minneapolis cops.

"She'll show the cuts for a while," Weather said. "In a couple of years, you'll have to know her to see the scars."

"And you only assisted."

"Well, technically. I'm not licensed here, so Jerome was the lead surgeon—but on the tricky bits, he stepped back and let me do the work."

"Smart guy."

"Yes. He is. And really, really good-looking," Weather said. "Have I mentioned that? He's like a rock 'n' roll surgeon, you know? Big muscles, good shoulders, nice tan, except for the little white circles around his eyes. We women get really excited when he's around. Did I say excited? I meant *aroused*."

"Thank you. I needed that, I'm feeling so good anyway."

The light tone went way: "No luck, huh?"

"No."

"You're stuck?"

"Pretty stuck . . . maybe gaining a little ground."

"How long?"

"Soon—I'm not so worried about how long, as how many," Lucas said. "Elle says he's manic, that he's moving really fast, he's like a smart killing machine."

He told her about looking at the tapes, about Sloan's increasing gloom, about Mike West burying himself in the hillside, about Chase's descent into a rabid lunacy . . . He told her about not being able to see what was going on in the isolation cells.

"Something happened, but I couldn't see it. That's the second time I've had the problem, of knowing something was there but not being able to see it."

"What's the other thing?" she asked.

"There's something in the notes that this reporter took the last time he talked to the killer. I can feel it, but I can't figure out what it is. Sloan doesn't even feel it."

"Want to read it to me?"

So he got the papers, read through it, aloud. When he finished, she was quiet for so long that he said, "Weather? You still there?"

"Just thinking. You say there's something in there? You mean, his syntax, or the facts of what he's saying, or what?"

"I don't know," Lucas said.

"I could see only one thing, but it's probably just a mistake . . ."

"What?"

"He said he was taking this Peterson woman up I-35, but he said *the* 35. I've never heard anybody from the Midwest say that. *The* 35. I've only heard that in Los Angeles."

There was an almost audible *bing* in the back of Lucas's brain, and a little cloud lifted off his cerebral cortex. He laughed and said, "Hey. That was it. I could hear it, but I couldn't see it."

"You think it's important?" She sounded pleased with herself.

"Could be. The guy could come from California," Lucas said.

"Maybe he's just a fan of *Boob-Watch* reruns."

"Maybe. And maybe not. Maybe he's from California. If this pans out, I might have sex with you when you get back."

"That's so *good* of you."

"By the way—the rock 'n' roll surgeon. The reason the guy's got white circles around his eyes is he spends all of his spare time in a tanning booth . . ."

"I knew that . . ."

. . .

LUCAS SPENT THE DAY working with the co-op group. They didn't have much to coordinate, so he had them review records on the St. John's staff members picked as most-likelies. One of them, an orderly, had a felony record, but from thirteen years earlier. He'd done a year in Stillwater for a pharmacy break-in, had gotten Jesus while he was inside, and hadn't been arrested since.

Three more, also orderlies, had minor criminal records, misdemeanors, one apparently as a result of mental problems that had been treated with drugs. He had good performance reports; of the other two, one had been arrested for a gross violation of fishing laws—caught with 532 bluegills in an oil barrel, which was roughly 500 over the limit, Lucas thought—and the other had been arrested for shoplifting at Target.

None of the four had a record of violence.

Lucas looked for California and found it three times. An orderly named Lee Jones had gone to CalArts in Valencia, California, for two years. He looked in an atlas and found it at the north end of the San Fernando Valley, exactly the kind of place that they would say "*the 35.*"

Jones had no record; he had a citation for painting a mural-sized landscape in the cafeteria.

And two of the docs had connections with California: Sennet and O'Donnell had both worked at psychiatric clinics, O'Donnell in San Francisco and Sennet in San Diego. Lucas wasn't sure whether they would say "the 35" in San Francisco but thought they probably would in San Diego, since it was so close to LA.

Hart had been born, raised, and educated in Minnesota. No California connection at all. Grant was from a town called Holcomb in Colorado, had been educated at the University of Colorado, and worked at a private hospital in Denver before moving to Minnesota. Beloit was born in Chicago, did her undergraduate work at Illinois, got an M.D. at Iowa, and was married to a professor of anthropology at Mankato State.

Hmm, he thought. He'd known that Beloit was married, but he'd gotten a distinct not-very-married vibration from her. Then he thought: *So what?*

He combed the files, looking for something, anything . . . took a call from Sloan: "I've gone over these files until my eyes bleed," Sloan said. "I don't see much."

Lucas told him about *"the 35,"* and Sloan snorted: "You give me a hard time about my ideas. That's the weakest thing I ever heard of."

"Yeah? You ever heard '*the 35*' from a Minnesotan?"

"Jesus, Lucas, I wouldn't even notice . . ."

Lucas sighed. "It's a little light. Keep plowing: something will pop. We gotta get the files on the outsiders, too. The docs they bring in."

Sloan said, "How about this: Why don't we get search warrants for, say, the top five suspects? Everybody who's been to California? Or everybody who's smart enough, and we can't otherwise eliminate? We've got the group narrowed down."

"Ah, jeez, I don't know," Lucas said. "It'd be tough; I'm not sure you'd find a judge who'd go for it."

"Not up here, maybe. So we call around to all the sheriffs, find one with a district court judge who's a friend—there's gotta be something going on in all those small towns. We could get a bunch of warrants all at the same time and serve them all at once. Nobody would have time to appeal, to get the warrant thrown out. And the warrants would hold up in court if we found anything, even if they later decided the grounds weren't too good."

Lucas considered: "The judge would have to be either crooked or a moron . . ."

Sloan said, "Or a friend. If we used every little stick of information we've got that points toward the top five, say, along with the pictures of Peterson and Rice and Larson as convincers . . . I'd bet we could get it."

"One problem," Lucas said. "Who are the top five?"

"Or six or seven or eight . . . we keep going through these lists, we've gotta start eliminating some of them."

LUCAS WAS STILL RELUCTANT: "If we don't get the guy the first try, and we all get hit with a shit storm . . . what're we gonna do when we really need one, and the grounds are still pretty shaky?"

"All right. Let's do this—we keep working the files, we keep talking to people here and at St. John's. Tomorrow or the next day, if we're not making any progress, we go for it. See if we can get the warrants. We gotta do *something* before we have another horror show."

AT NOON, Lucas got a call from Nordwall.

"We found the gut dump, right in a dry creek bed, like he said it would be. The GPS says it's four miles from the hanging post. By road, maybe six."

"Anything?"

"One thing: we think we found a footprint. He's not a huge guy: he has smaller feet, maybe size ten."

"Okay. That's good."

"Crime Scene is coming, maybe they'll find more."

LATER THAT DAY, the co-op got another batch of files from Cale— all the contract people who had substantial contact with the Big Three.

Too much paper; too much. Too many little facts crawling around Lucas's head. At the end of the day, he was more confused than when he started.

HE HAD TWO CALLS the next morning. "Hey. Closing in?" Weather asked.

"Not exactly." He yawned, and rubbed the stubble on his cheek. He told her about the warrants idea.

"As long as you won't get in trouble . . ."

"Ah, I've *been* in trouble. They keep giving me better jobs."

"So I had another thought . . ."

"What?"

"Lynyrd Skynyrd, 'Gimme Three Steps.' The perfect cop song."

"How would you know about Lynyrd Skynyrd?" Lucas asked.

"They were playing it in the operating room this morning . . ." Weather operated a lot, sometimes two or three times a day, two hundred and fifty times a year. Most of the operations were small—scar revisions, excisions of various undesirable lumps and bumps—and some were enormously complicated, done only after weeks or months of study.

"I thought you guys listened to Mozart," Lucas said.

"Not when the rock 'n' roll surgeon's working . . . So everything's okay there? With you personally?"

"Sure. Why?"

"Things are a little tense here," Weather said. "We've just heard that France has raised its terror-alert level. They think something's going on."

"Really?" Something else to worry about.

"Yes. They've gone from *Run* to *Hide* . . ."

The joke was so unexpected that Lucas snorted, and hurt his nose again. He said, "Oh, Jesus, don't make me laugh . . ."

"The only two higher levels are *Surrender* and *Collaborate*," Weather said.

"You're killing my nose, goddamnit," Lucas said. "Davenport's a French name, by the way . . ."

THE SECOND CALL came a few minutes after nine o'clock as Lucas stood naked in front of his chest of drawers, digging around, certain that there was one more pair of clean shorts. He'd seen them the day before . . .

He ran the washer according to a severely logical schedule based on need: he had, he thought, perhaps twenty pairs of shorts. Why wash after only five or ten pairs have been used, as Weather would, thus putting all that extra water down the drain and through the sewage plant, when you could wait the whole twenty days and only have to wash once? Of course, if you miscalculated . . .

He had just found the pair of shorts when the phone rang; he stepped over to the table and took it.

Dr. Cale, from St. John's. "We've, uh, had what is sort of an anomalous situation out here. I really feel stupid for calling you, but I decided it was best not to put it off."

"What?" Lucas asked; he felt a tingle.

"Well, uh, after you left here, uh, the word that you were looking at staff members got around pretty quick. Not from Jansen. Apparently, somebody in the security booth overheard enough to understand what you were looking at, and the gossip got started . . ."

"What? What happened?"

"Sam O'Donnell didn't show up for work this morning," Cale said. "He's an hour and a half late. Nobody knows where he is—he's not at home, we checked. At least, he doesn't answer when we knock. Doesn't answer pages or his phone. Nobody's seen him."

"Okay, okay—this is something. I'm coming down there," Lucas said. "If he shows up, call me on my cell phone. I'll be there in an hour."

HE AND SLOAN did the running hookup, taking the Porsche back through the bean- and cornfields, past the truck gardens and river-bottom fields; there'd been a bug hatch of some kind, and they started picking up serious splatter every time they crossed a bridge. On the way down, they called Nordwall, the Blue Earth County sheriff, and arranged for a search warrant.

The sheriff called back: "Thought you'd want to know. He drives a gray Acura MDX."

"Excellent!" Lucas said.

SLOAN HAD A LAPTOP with him. He called Cale, got O'Donnell's address, plugged it into a Microsoft map program, and took them through St. John's into an exurban neighborhood between St. John's and Mankato. They cleared the top of a hill, where Lucas expected to find the house, but then twisted down a narrow blacktop road into a deep creek-cut valley, and along the creek for a half mile. They spotted a sheriff's car at the bottom of a gravel driveway, slowed, and turned in. A deputy came over and said, "Davenport? The sheriff's up at the house. They haven't gone in yet. They're waiting."

Lucas took the Porsche up the drive, found a modern redwood-and-stone house set to look down the valley; the slope behind the house was heavily wooded, burr oaks with fat dark leaves. A separate building, a workshop or second garage, was visible behind the residence. A blue Buick and a patrol car were parked in front of the attached garage. Nordwall was standing next to the Buick with a deputy, who was swinging a wrecking bar like a baseball bat. Lucas and Sloan got out of the Porsche and walked over.

"Get the warrant?" Lucas asked.

Nordwall nodded: "Yup. Hope he didn't go out for a loaf of bread . . . you think he's the second man?"

"Uh, we gotta talk about that," Lucas said. "Let's take a look inside."

The deputy said, "The sheriff wanted to wait for you, but I looked in the back window. This guy might be running. There's a whole pile of clothes on one bed, and a suitcase, like he left it behind."

Lucas said, "Let's open it."

The deputy had done it before: "The back door's the best. There's extra space around the jamb—I might be able to pop it without breaking it."

He broke it a bit but not badly: the door came open, and Lucas stepped up and pushed it fully open. The thin odor of marijuana was right there. "Doper," Lucas said.

Sloan, a step behind, sniffed. "Smells like Ontario Red, Two Thousand Two." The deputy looked at him oddly, and Sloan said, "Just kidding."

THE HOUSE WAS A bachelor's nest—wood and leather, a sixty-two-inch projection television, a spa on the back deck, a bar off the kitchen. It was neatly kept, but not too neatly kept; idiosyncratic in a way that Lucas recognized as single, everything done to a lone occupant's style.

They cruised the house quickly, looking for a body. There was no body. As the deputy said, there was a suggestion that O'Donnell had gone in a hurry—he'd hauled most of the clothing out of the main closet in the bedroom, had thrown it on the bed, and had apparently picked whatever he needed, not bothering to rehang what he hadn't taken.

An overnighter case sat next to the bed, empty. Not enough room?

Lucas went down to the unfinished basement, found a workshop and sports equipment—two kayaks hanging from the ceiling, a half dozen paddles on the wall, and an ammunition reloading setup on a workbench. When Lucas went down to the basement, the deputy went out back, looked in the outbuilding, returned as Lucas was coming back up the stairs, and said, "Car freak—he's got a five-liter Mustang and a Trans Am in there."

"What color are they? The cars?"

"Red Mustang and white Trans Am."

Huh. The Trans Am was not likely to be mistaken for an Olds, if the witness knew a lot about cars and had time to think about it. But white robbers, standing six feet from their victims, were often described by the victims as black, because the victims *expected* a robber to be black. Eyewitness testimony generally ranged from suspect to horseshit.

Sloan called from the kitchen: "In here."

They went that way and found him with the freezer door open on the refrigerator: "There's some blood in here. Can't see it very well. About the size of a dime."

Lucas looked in. A layer of frost covered the blood. "Probably had a steak."

"Probably," Sloan said.

Lucas turned to Nordwall. "Charlie Pope's blood . . . uh . . . We need to pull this blood out of here and get it up to our lab just as fast as we can. Could you get your crime-scene guy to take it out, and run it up there?"

"Yup. He's standing by, in case we needed him," Nordwall said. "How fast can you get DNA back? If it's human? I mean, it always takes us a week . . ."

"A couple-three days if you push," Lucas said. "But they can do a blood-type immediately. That might tell us something."

A ROOM THE SIZE of a large closet had been used as a home office. Lucas pulled file drawers until he found bank statements. "Do you know anybody at River National?" he asked Nordwall, after the sheriff had made the call to the crime-scene guy.

"Yeah, I know everybody."

"Call them. Find out how much he left in his account . . . looks like he's only got one account, checking. A month ago, he had . . . six thousand."

Nordwall went to make the call, and Lucas sat down at the desk and brought up the computer, a Dell tower. The computer wanted a password before it would work. Lucas shut it down.

Sloan came in with a handful of paper: "He cut out newspaper stories on the killings."

"All right, all right, that's good," Lucas said. He thumbed through the stories—they'd been cut from a half dozen papers. They were rolling downhill now. "He was collecting them. Better and better."

The deputy came in: "There's a gun safe in the back bedroom, in a closet. It was open. A rifle and two shotguns."

"There's a reloading machine down in the basement," Lucas said. "Run down and see what kinds of dies he has . . . see if there's any brass lying around."

The deputy disappeared, and Sloan asked, "Anything in the bills?"

"He buys all his gas in Mankato . . . he bought one tank in the Cities, in Bloomington, right down by the mall. So . . . that ain't anything."

The deputy came back: "There's brass for a .40 and a .45."

"So he's got two pistols," Sloan said.

AND NORDWALL CAME BACK: "O'Donnell cleaned out his account yesterday afternoon. He took out five thousand, and later in the day, he hit his ATM for another five hundred."

"Do they know . . . ?"

"It was him. Personally. They know him. Told the teller that he was buying a car, and he'd sell one next week and put it all back."

Sloan looked at Lucas and nodded.

"I put out a pickup on the Acura, but just locally," Nordwall said. "You want to go statewide?"

Lucas looked around the house: they had the trophy news stories, and a spot of blood. A missing man, missing money, and some missing clothes. "Yeah. Let's go everywhere," he said.

NORDWALL CALLED INTO his office, staying in touch. Lucas heard him say, "Well, Jesus Christ, just lie about it. Later we can say you hadn't been clued in. Yeah, lie. And if they ask you if I told you to lie, lie about that."

"What the hell was that?"

"A local reporter called and asked if we were looking at a staff member at St. John's."

"Ah, Jesus," Lucas said.

"Wasn't us," Nordwall said. "It's the goddamn hospital. That place leaks like a sieve."

Lucas thought about it for a minute, then said to Nordwall. "Let's go take a walk around the yard."

Nordwall said, "What?"

OUTSIDE, LUCAS SAID, "I didn't want your deputy hearing this. I just don't want to leave you hanging in the wind, you got that election coming up . . . So now you're gonna be one of about seven people in the state who know it. You gotta keep your mouth shut. I mean, don't tell your wife."

Nordwall looked at him with a bit of skepticism. "You know something *that* important?"

Lucas said, "A few days ago, some fishermen pulled a body out of the Minnesota River up in Le Sueur County, by Kasota. It had been in the water a month or so."

"I heard about it. It's right across the county line. You think O'Donnell did it?"

"I'm sure our killer did it, O'Donnell or whoever," Lucas said. He pivoted to face Nordwall. "The body was . . . Charlie Pope."

Nordwall's mouth dropped open. After a few seconds, he said, "You gotta be shittin' me," and Lucas had to smile.

LUCAS EXPLAINED. Going back in the door, Nordwall muttered, "You're playing a dangerous game, Lucas. It's the right thing, but if you don't get this guy . . . the media are gonna scalp you."

"We're gonna keep it quiet for just a couple more days," Lucas said. "Let's see if we can jump O'Donnell before he knows we're looking for him. We'll check and make sure we've got all his cars. We'll get the tags for the MDX and mugs out to all the highway-patrol troopers here, down in Iowa, Wisconsin, and Illinois, out in the Dakotas. Check the airport and see if the MDX is there, and if we can spot a plane ticket. What else . . . ?"

They worked out a program and started running it.

21

AN HOUR AFTER Lucas got back to BCA headquarters, the cops at Minneapolis–St. Paul International called and said they had the MDX. "We haven't opened it," the cop said. "I can see what looks like a parking ticket on the floor—that'd give us an exact time it came in."

"Don't touch it," Lucas said. "I'm sending my crime-scene guys over. Have somebody stand by the truck."

While the crime-scene truck rolled, Lucas got the co-op center calling the airlines, looking for the ride that O'Donnell took out of town. He watched them work it for a while, got bored when nothing happened, walked down to the canteen, and got a cup of coffee.

Hopping Crow called: "The blood in the refrigerator was frozen, of course. We don't have a DNA yet, maybe by tomorrow. I can tell you that it's human, and that it's Charlie Pope's blood type. Pope was an O positive, O'Donnell's records say he's an A positive. So."

"So Pope's blood was in O'Donnell's freezer."

"Probably his. Peterson's was also O, but we don't have any reason to think her blood was frozen."

HE WAS IN his office when the Crime Scene crew called. "The parking ticket on the floor was from seven o'clock last night."

"I'll pass it on to the coordination center. What else?"

"Nothing really, just the usual car junk. He was pretty neat. We'll be done in a half hour. You want us to take it to the impound?"

"Yeah. Seal it up. We may want to go over it with a microscope, depending on how things break."

The same guy called back twenty minutes later. "We found some blood. It was under the mat in the cargo compartment. It looks relatively fresh . . . it's dry, but not dusty. Thought you ought to know."

"We need a blood type and DNA," Lucas said. "Get it back here as quick as you can."

THEY WERE RUNNING NOW. He got another blood type: it was O again, could be Pope, could be Peterson. He made a mental bet on Peterson. He called Hopping Crow, to tell him to push the tests. "We'll know by tomorrow night," Hopping Crow said. "Who knows, maybe it's somebody else?"

"Don't even think that."

They picked up bits and pieces of information about O'Donnell and his lifestyle all through the day, but nothing that would point a finger. Cops were talking with a kayak club, a singles cycling club, the last woman O'Donnell was known to have dated. She said, "It came down to a choice between me and the Pontiac, and I had the feeling I wasn't going to win. So we sort of broke it off . . ."

Early in the day, Lucas felt that the logjam was breaking, that the ice was going out, that the peel was coming off the banana. And then everything slowed, and he began to see nothing but trivia . . . He wandered out of the office at nine o'clock, discouraged.

Where the fuck was he?

RUFFE IGNACE LAY AWAKE in bed, listening to Ruffe's Radio, cataloging the day's events and insults: *What the fuck is she doing, telling me that I have to watch my adverbs? She wouldn't know an adverb if one jumped up and bit her on the tit. Green is a bad color for me, it makes my skin look yellow; gotta get rid of the green golf shirt. I wonder if my dick reaches up to my bellybutton when I'm really hard? I don't think it does. Does anybody's? Maybe I oughta get dressed and go out for a slice . . .*

When the phone rang, he said, "Pope," and he scrambled through the dark to the phone charger, fumbled with the phone, punched the TALK button: "Ignace."

And it was: "Hey, Ruffe. Thought I'd call you and say good-bye."

"Good-bye? Where are you now?"

A rumbling, wheezing, whispery laugh, and then, "If this phone is tapped, you'll find out soon enough. Anyway, the police were getting too close: this Davenport guy is smarter than I expected."

"I don't know anything about that—as far as I know, they've got no idea where you are, Charlie."

Another whispery chuckle: "That's another thing. My name isn't Charlie. Charlie, unfortunately for him, but not for the rest of us, is in a black bag somewhere. That's what caused the trouble—I threw his dead ass into the river. Life was sweet until he came floatin' up. Anyway, the cops found him, and they know."

"They *know* they're not looking for Charlie Pope? Jesus Christ . . . who is this, anyway?"

"They don't know who I am yet, so I'm not going to tell you. In any case, I'm moving on. Maybe . . . New England. Manhattan. I've got to think, I've got to see what I'm becoming, the Gods Down the Hall . . ."

"They *know* you're not Charlie . . . ?" Ignace was outraged: *And they hadn't told me?*

"I'll tell you something else: they might figure out who I was, but they don't know who I'm becoming. And they don't know who I've been, or how long I've been doing this . . ."

"Jesus, how many . . ."

"More'n you know, Roo-fay. The Gods Down the Hall told me I was growing. But they say that at some point, your control begins to fade, the appetite takes over. It's dangerous, but it feels so good. I can feel that, now. I didn't know what they were talking about, but now I do, and it feels wonderful. When it's time to go, I'll go, but I think . . . maybe I don't want to go just yet. I want some more."

"What are you talking about?"

"Change, Ruffe. Appetite. Blood. Moving . . . well, because you're probably tapped, I'm going to go now. Got to keep moving. Keep moving . . ."

He was gone.

Ignace stared at the phone for a few seconds, then jumped up, turned on a light, found his Palm Pilot, and brought up Davenport's home number. Dialed.

LUCAS WAS STARTLED awake by the phone. His hardwired phone, not the cell phone. He glanced at the bedside clock, thought "Ignace," and picked up the phone.

"He just called to say good-bye," Ignace said without preamble. "He says he's running. He also says he's not Charlie Pope, that Charlie Pope is dead, and that you've known about that. That you've misled everyone . . ."

"Slow down, slow down . . . ," Lucas said. He swung his feet to the floor, hunched over the phone. "We just found out about Pope. What'd he say? You say he's running?"

"Who is he?"

"We're not sure . . . this was on your cell phone?"

"Yeah. You should have it."

"Listen, Ruffe, everybody I've talked to said you're an asshole, but you seem to do the work. Okay? That's what I think. Just don't give me any shit about misleading the press. We're trying to save some poor innocent fucker's life, and we don't even know who he or she is, yet. We've already failed to save three other innocent fuckers. Okay? So don't give me any shit, and when this is all done, I'll sit down and talk to you. I'll give you the whole thing. Not to TV, not to the *Pioneer Press*, not to anybody else there at the *Strib*. Just you."

"You mean everything?" Ignace demanded. "When you get him, I get it first? If you get him?"

"No, not that. That's going to be a breaking news story that we can't contain," Lucas said. "I mean an inside feature, a blow-by-blow of who said what and how we pushed this to where we are . . ."

A moment of silence, then: "Deal. I think. I'm gonna have to talk to the boss about Pope."

"Tell her to call me. Tell her to call. In the morning. I gotta hang up now and listen to the tape. I gotta find out where the call came from. I'll be in touch."

O'DONNELL HAD CALLED from Chicago. Lucas called the Chicago cops, asked for help: a detective called back half an hour later and said, "Not much we can do for you, pal. That number's a pay phone out at O'Hare. This guy going somewhere?"

"The phone's in the airport?" Lucas asked.

"No. A hotel just outside. A Hilton, with a phone in the lobby."

"Could you check the register?"

"Nobody by that name," the cop said. "What is it with this guy?"

"I kinda hate to tell you this . . ."

The Chicago cops were not happy with the news. "We got enough of this shit without importing yours."

HE CALLED THE Minneapolis–St. Paul airport cops again, asked them to recheck airline tickets.

"We already did that," an airport cop said.

"Yeah, but you did it in the afternoon. Now the guy shows up out by O'Hare at midnight. Maybe he was in the airport when you were looking for tickets. Maybe he didn't fly until ten o'clock."

"Listen, I don't mean to sound disrespectful, but we've got limited resources."

"How about if the governor called you?"

WHEN HE WASN'T talking with cops, he listened to the recording of Ignace's phone call. In terms of factual information, there wasn't much, but there *was* that voice. He got Cale out of bed: "Who socialized with O'Donnell?"

"The junior staff . . . Probably the most active social person is Dr. Beloit."

"Got her number?"

Beloit's husband answered, got irate when Lucas asked for his wife, was skeptical when told it was a police emergency, and finally Lucas shouted at him: "I'm a state BCA agent, and I need to talk to your wife. Now. Or should I have a cop come over there and take her downtown?"

Beloit was dazed, being awakened at two in the morning. When she finally understood who was calling, he said, "I want you to call our headquarters in St. Paul. There's a guy there, his name is Ted. He'll play a tape of a call to a newspaper reporter earlier this evening. None of this is public: if you let this out, I'll come down and run over you with my truck, okay?"

"Okay, but what do you want me to hear?"

"I want to know if it might be Sam O'Donnell calling. It doesn't sound like him, but it does sound like somebody disguising his voice."

"I heard people were looking for Sam . . . we were a little worried."

"Who's we?"

"Everybody."

Lucas thought: *Ah, shit. Everybody in the state would know in a couple of days* . . . He said, "Just call Ted, okay? Here's the number . . ."

SHE CALLED BACK five minutes later. "I hate to say this, but that could be Sam."

"You think?"

"We have a Christmas play every year, and Bob Turner, I don't think you've met Bob . . ."

"No."

". . . Bob plays Santa, and Sam plays one of Santa's elves. Some of the patients have parts. You know. Anyway, Sam always plays the elf as a, *mmm*, pervert, for lack of a better word. He talks about going down chimneys and catching people making love. I mean, that's sort of the running gag. Every chimney he goes down seems to have something going on. The thing is, he's got this heavy-breathing thing going, that spit-in-the-back-of-the-throat whisper thing. This guy tonight . . . that sounds like Sam doing his act."

Lucas couldn't think of anything to say for a moment, then blurted out, "An elf?"

"Yeah, you know, everybody gets a little weird and we have a play . . ."

"But it could be him."

"I don't . . . I can't see Sam O'Donnell hurting anyone, for any reason. I mean, he did the karate and all, but that was just exercise. He was really a gentle man, I think."

IF THE KILLER was in Chicago, and he certainly was, then there wasn't much to do except identify him—somebody else would make the eventual bust.

And though they didn't have a hard identification on O'Donnell, if it wasn't O'Donnell, that should be apparent in the morning, when somebody else didn't show up for work.

Nothing to do now, at night . . . Lucas tried to sleep, and sometimes made it, mostly not. If they couldn't make a clear identification, and if the killer ran far enough, interest would fall off . . . he could be gone for years.

He thrashed around, thrashed around, and finally got up at six o'clock. He'd never make it through the day like this, so he popped an amphetamine, quickly felt a lot better, shaved, showered, and dressed. Still early, but he called Sloan anyway. Sloan had Caller ID and groaned into the phone, "Lucas, you gotta get yourself a life. It's not even seven o'clock in the morning."

"Yeah, yeah, listen . . ."

Then, Sloan was suddenly awake: "Jesus: he didn't do another one?"

"No, but he did call Ignace. He was in Chicago when he called."

He and Sloan agreed to meet downtown at nine o'clock. "I'm gonna get Elle to come in. We need some more theory."

TWO DAYS WENT BY:

ON THE FIRST DAY, Sam O'Donnell's name got out as a "person of interest" in the case. None of the cops would confirm that

O'Donnell was the man, and the media outlets were afraid to name him because of libel or slander potential, but most of the newsies knew, and Lucas heard that there were raging arguments going on about when to name him.

On the second day, the lab finished sequencing the DNA. The blood in the truck was Peterson's.

"At some point, Peterson was in the back of that Acura and dribbled a little blood out," John Hopping Crow told Lucas. "There wasn't much, maybe an ounce or two . . . maybe blood that had gathered in her throat after he cut her windpipe and trachea when he gutted her . . ."

"Did you look at it through a scope?"

"Yeah. It was never frozen."

The blood from inside the freezer had been frozen, of course—and the DNA was Charlie Pope's.

"The sonofabitch cut a chunk out of Pope, a finger or something, and stored it in his freezer in case he needed it," Hopping Crow said.

"He knew he was gonna need it—it was part of a plan that went way back before Pope was even killed," Lucas said. "There was a lot of planning, strategy, going on. Like they were doing theory. The fuckers down at St. John's—Lighter, Taylor, and Chase—thought about it for a long time."

"But we know some shit now . . ."

"Maybe. Listen, tell the crime-scene guys to pull anything out of the back of that truck that would carry DNA. We're looking for something besides blood that has Peterson's DNA. There must be hair, there must be something. Spit?"

ON BOTH THE first and second days, Lucas spoke with the Chicago cops and the Illinois State Police.

An investigator had interviewed the desk staff at the Hilton: "There's not much," he told Lucas. "Nobody recognized the O'Donnell mug, but they said probably a hundred people used that phone last night. There were people checking in all the time; this is a major business-travelers' hotel. One guy said the mug looked vaguely familiar, but he couldn't swear that the guy he saw was O'Donnell. Every maid and every staff member will get a copy of the photo when they check in for work, but the way he's been jerking you guys around, I'd say it's a million to one that he'd still be here."

"Taxis? Car rentals?"

"We're covering them with the mug shots. If the Xerox machine don't break down, we'll get them to everybody. Not coming up with anything so far."

"Nobody saw him in the airport."

"A few people said they saw somebody like him, but he's sort of a *type*, you know? The long hair, the earring, sort of an upscale rocker. They're a dime a dozen."

"Yeah."

"But what I'm wondering is, Why do we think he stopped at the Hilton, made the call, and then kept going? Maybe he wants us to think he stayed on the ground. How do we know he didn't hop a ride to the Hilton, make the call, then go right back to O'Hare and fly? He could be in Amsterdam or Hong Kong by now."

ON THE EVENING of the second day, Channel Three named O'Donnell as a "person of interest." The story went network: on the night of the second day, CNN was running O'Donnell's face every fifteen minutes.

Neil Mitford, the governor's top political operator, called Lucas on the afternoon of the second day and said, "We had a press conference this afternoon on the compromises in the aid-to-cities package. Somebody asked if we shouldn't cut our state hospital staff, since we're apparently hiring psychopaths."

"Ah, jeez. Not even the TV people are that dumb."

"Of course not. They were plunking the governor's magic twanger. But we're starting to get a little bleed-through. So, if you don't mind, why don't you just go ahead and pick this guy up and get him out of our hair?"

"Why don't you do it?" Lucas suggested. "The headline would say HATCHET MAN CAPTURES AXE MURDERER."

"I'm just sayin'," Mitford said mildly. "I'm not leaning on you, I'm just sayin': if you're not doing anything else, pick him up."

"You do a swell job of leaning on a guy," Lucas said.

ALSO ON THE FIRST DAY, Elle arrived early, having ditched her summer seminar, and dug through O'Donnell's personnel file. When she was finished, she came and sat in Lucas's office, and said, "I want to interview the staff members down at St. John's. Also, any family members that we can reach."

"I can get you down to St. John's for sure," Lucas said. "Let's do it tomorrow. I'll see what I can do about family members. What do you think so far?"

"O'Donnell has the intelligence and the planning capability. In school, he had nearly a four-point from his freshman year straight through to his Ph.D. That takes more than intelligence, it takes a ferocious *will*. If he ran off the tracks, somehow, he could do this. He is what I expected, except . . . he seems to have been very well liked and respected. That would not be typical. Typically, people with this kind of problem are recognized as being odd, and it shows in their histories."

"Okay: so family and friends should tell us something. I'll see what I can do."

BOTH THE CO-OP and security hospital people had called O'Donnell's parents to see if he'd been in touch. His parents were frantic, not knowing what was going on—they'd gotten the impression that their son might have been a victim of the killer. They agreed to talk to Elle at St. John's.

ON THE MORNING of the second day, Sloan went with Elle to St. John's to interview staff members and the parents. When Sloan got back, he pushed into Lucas's office, and said, "You fucker, you've driven with her before. That's why you didn't go with us."

"Come on, man—if the three of us had gone, I would have driven." But Lucas half laughed, because he knew what Sloan was talking about.

"Sometimes, she'd get out of control and penetrate the forty-five-mile-an-hour barrier," Sloan said. "I thought I was gonna start screaming before we got there. Now I know how Chase feels, down in isolation."

"Maybe you should have offered to drive," Lucas suggested.

"I did. Several times. She said she needed the practice. Going down was a nightmare. Coming back was . . ." Words failed, and he flapped his arms.

"Where is she, anyway?" Lucas asked.

"She stopped in the ladies' room. If she pees the way she drives, we could be waiting for a while."

ELLE SAID THIS: "I talked to his parents, I talked to his friends. There's a very interesting thing that goes on with serial killers. When they have longtime friends, or parents, those people usually aren't surprised by the accusations when they're caught. They *know* that there's something wrong with them. There's often a history of strange violence during their youth—against animals and insects, against other children; and they're usually victims of some kind of violence, usually physical, but sometimes purely emotional. There's often an interest in fire and in general images of destruction. I'm not talking about the interest that you find in game players, but about a kind of fascination with the most grotesque elements of death and dismemberment. Also, there are commonly instances of head injuries . . ."

"And . . ."

"There's none of that in his history. Lucas, I'm coming to the conclusion that he is not our man."

"Then he's dead," Lucas said.

"That may be so."

"Don't tell me that," Lucas said. He was groping: "How about a tumor, or something. Remember the Texas Tower, Whitman?"

"Yes . . ."

"There was a song about him, how he had a tumor in his brain," Lucas said. "Something like that."

"Yes. There was a song, I believe by a person named Richard Friedman. And Whitman did have a tumor, although they don't know if it was responsible for his behavior."

"What if O'Donnell had a tumor?"

"That's a possibility—when you're dealing with the brain, almost anything is possible. However, when there's a tumor involved, there are physical symptoms as well as psychological upsets, and none of his family and friends saw anything like that."

"How do you explain the fact that he took all the money out of his bank account the day he disappeared?"

She smiled and shook her head: "I don't explain it. I leave that up to you."

SLOAN, who had been watching the interchange, said, "Nordwall had a couple of deputies trying to find out where O'Donnell was the night Peterson disappeared. They can't find him. They can't find him on the nights that Larson or the Rices were killed, either—but that might not mean much. He lived out in the woods, and the Rices and Larson are far enough back that nobody really can put their finger on whether they saw him or not."

"Mention the shift problem," Elle said.

"Yeah, the shift," Sloan said. "He worked a seven-to-three shift, but he always came in early, around six o'clock, to get the handoff from the overnight. That means he had to get up around five o'clock, and if he wanted to get eight hours of sleep, he was in bed by nine. So. People wouldn't expect to see him late on the nights of the killings, but it would be absolutely normal for him to be in bed. Legitimately."

"God . . . bless me," Lucas said.

"HERE'S A QUESTION," Sloan said. "He didn't come into work—so presumably he was (a) on his way to Chicago or was already there, or (b) he was dead. Assuming he went to Chicago after work on the day he decided to run, sometime around seven o'clock, he would have been there by, say, nine o'clock. He didn't call Ignace for more than twenty-four hours. What was he doing?"

"Making . . . arrangements," Lucas said. Elle wasn't there at the moment, so he added, "How the fuck would I know?"

"Maybe we ought to call Chicago Homicide, see if they've had anything particularly rude . . ."

CHICAGO HOMICIDE had one murder reported for the night O'Donnell disappeared: a twelve-year-old boy named Terence Smith had run over his uncle, Roger Smith, with Roger's own car.

"They're sure it's murder?" Lucas asked Sloan.

"He ran over him eight or ten times. They said Roger's head looked like a thin-crust pizza."

"Ah."

"What next?" Sloan asked. "Where do we go?"

22

ON THE MORNING of the third day, Lucas, after a restless night, heard the alarm go off, shut it down, waited; and the phone rang.

"Catch him yet?" Weather asked.

"Not yet. Still thrashing around," he said. "How're you doing?"

"Had an interesting case early this morning," Weather said. "A man was shot in the face. I assisted, putting things right."

"That sounds British: *putting things right.*"

"I think I'm becoming British. I like it here."

"Wish I were there . . . sort of," Lucas said. "So: You fixed the guy?"

"Oh, yeah. He wasn't that badly hurt—depending on how you define 'hurt,' I guess. But what struck me as strange was that in the whole time I've been working here, that was the first gunshot wound I've seen. In Minneapolis, as quiet as it is, it's an odd week when we don't have two or three."

"You're starting to sound like a liberal: Want to take away our God-given right to bear arms?"

"No, no. But it's weird: there are no guns . . ."

HE WAS SHAVING, a half hour later, when the phrase struck him: *There are no guns.*

Huh.

He finished shaving, got in the shower, thought about it some more. No guns.

HE CALLED THE airport cops and asked them to round up all declarations of handguns made the night O'Donnell flew. There were only a half dozen: he got the names and addresses, and phoned them to the co-op group, had them check the people behind the names.

When he got downtown, the co-op people reported that three of the men who checked guns were members of a shooting team who were on their way to a match in Virginia. The co-op had talked to sponsors and spouses of all three men, and then to the men themselves.

"They aren't O'Donnell," the co-op guy said.

Two of the other three were going prairie-dog shooting with hybrid single-shot pistols, not the .40 and .45 that Lucas was looking for. The co-op had interviewed a woman in the apartment complex where the two men lived. They were told that neither man looked like O'Donnell, that they lived full-time in the apartment complex, and that they were both members of a gay shooting-sports group that often traveled to Wyoming for prairie-dog shoots. The last guy hadn't been found, but one of the gun inspectors at the airport said that he was a lawyer and a black guy and that the gun he had checked was an antique.

Lucas called Sloan. "Remember when we found that pistol brass in the basement, I think it was .40 and .45, and the gun safe was open, like something had just been taken out?"

"Yeah?"

"If he flew, if he knew he was heading for the airport to fly, what happened to the guns? He couldn't get on the airplane with them. He didn't declare them. The guns weren't in the car. Where are they?"

"I don't know."

"Okay—now try this. What is the great similarity between Sam O'Donnell and Charlie Pope?"

Sloan thought for a few seconds, then said, "They both spent a lot of time in St. John's . . ."

"Something more basic than that," Lucas said. *"We can't find him.* Not only that, nobody's seen him. He's invisible, but everything we've got points directly at him. Just as everything pointed at Charlie—the DNA, the past record, the calls to Ignace. We even had a witness who *thought* she saw him, but now we know she didn't."

"Yeah. But it wasn't like the killer was trying to lead us to Charlie. The lead to Charlie came from that Fox guy, the parole officer . . ."

"That was not quite a coincidence," Lucas said. "A guy who is suspected of killing women after raping them, and who has been treated and released, disappears, and suddenly a sex killer is on the loose. What parole officer wouldn't make a call? Then, because we'd figured that out on our own, when the DNA came in—there was never any doubt. No doubt in anybody's mind, except maybe Elle's, until the cat fisherman brought up Pope's hand."

Lucas continued: "Now, we have the same situation. Guy disappears. Evidence is found both in the refrigerator and in the car. Charlie Pope's frozen blood and Carlita Peterson's blood, not frozen. But *nobody* ever sees the guy. *Nobody* sees his face. Nobody sees him *anywhere* . . . and Elle says he doesn't fit."

"You think we're being conned?"

"I'm forty-six percent sure of it," Lucas said.

"Forty-six percent. You gotta go with that."

"Listen, this is what I think: the guns thing was a fuckup. He's still out there, and he's still got the guns."

"Who?"

"Somebody on the staff," Lucas said. "Somebody medical. Somebody who could get to Pope, and then get to O'Donnell. I mean, the guy was using O'Donnell's play voice *when we were still looking for Pope.*"

"Jesus. I can't even think about that," Sloan said. "All the way back then, he was faking us out on something we might not ever figure out."

"Yeah."

Sloan said, "But."

"But what?"

"But all this only works if it really isn't O'Donnell. Do we stop looking for him?"

"I will bet you one hundred depreciated American dollars right now that it's not O'Donnell," Lucas said. "We'll keep looking—but I think we go back to square one with the staff. Let's get everybody together again and start tearing up the staff backgrounds. There's something in there."

"The guy from California, huh?"

"Yup. The guy from California."

LUCAS HIMSELF CLEARED Dr. Cale, while the coordination staff worked on the other staff members whose records they had. When Lucas was convinced that Cale was clear—he never seriously suspected him, he was too old for a new serial killer—he drove to St. John's, and he and Cale spent two hours in the personnel office Xeroxing staff records for anyone who might have even an indirect connection to the Big Three.

There were eighty files, altogether. Lucas loaded them into the passenger side of the Porsche and hustled them back to the Cities.

"OKAY," he told the group, "This is gonna be tedious. But every single anomaly, I want to hear about it. No matter how silly you think it might be. I want to hear about it."

THEY CALLED REFERENCES listed in the files, and authors of letters of reference, and doctors, and police stations in towns where the staff members had lived, high schools and colleges and psychiatrists. They found minor crimes, alcoholism, drug abuse, altered academic records, mistakes, friends, and enemies.

They found one staff member who had apparently lost his foot in an automobile accident but listed "none" under disabilities and distinguishing marks. They found a woman who'd had an abortion but had listed "none" under operations and treatments by physicians; they found a man who was apparently internationally famous for making box kites.

One man, named Logan, who worked in the laundry and appeared to be immune to embarrassment, sued the manufacturer of a prosthetic pump designed to produce an erect penis, as well as the doctors who surgically implanted the silicone sacs that the pump inflated. He claimed that he'd not been warned that overinflating the sacs could cause his penis to "explode." The suit added that he and his wife could no longer achieve conjugal satisfaction because the surgical repairs had left his penis looking and feeling like a small cauliflower.

"Ouch," said the guy who found the stories about the lawsuit. "Here's a guy who could have stored up some serious bitterness . . ."

He gave a dramatic reading of the news stories, taken from the Internet: but the lawsuit was Logan's only appearance in public print.

Lucas agreed that there might have been some pump-related bitterness but noted that Logan had been given a jury award of $550,000, which might well alleviate it; and he couldn't figure out a way to put Logan and the Big Three together at the critical times.

ELLE CAME IN LATE in the afternoon, to look at the process, at the three BCA staffers with telephone headsets, sitting in front of computers, looking for all the world like a political boiler room.

"The quality of information you're getting is not the right kind to pull him up," she said. "You would have to be lucky to find him. What we need to do is to set up a whole series of interviews and ask each person to nominate his or her top suspect out of a list of suspects."

"The list would include them?"

"Yes. It would work like one of those market polls, where people make bets on the winners of political races . . . All the suspects know one another, and most of them, given their jobs, are intelligent, so you would wind up with dozens of evaluations that would include all kinds of things that you don't get on paper. Personal feelings, rumor, gossip, personal encounters . . . you should probably survey the patients, too. They may have psychological problems, but lots of them are actually hyperperceptive, hypersensitive, to the qualities of other people . . ."

"You might just wind up electing the ten most unpopular people," Lucas said.

"Not really—you'd just tell them not to judge on the basis of popularity. Some people would anyway, but you'd get enough hard, honest opinions that it might be very valuable. How many people are you looking at now?"

"About eighty."

"If you were to give questionnaires to all eighty people, and if the killer is one of them, I would bet that his name is in the top five," she said.

Lucas scratched his chin. "If we go another day or two without a break, I might do that. Why don't you put together the questionnaire, have it ready?"

"Why wait a day or two? If you think this man is really on the staff, and he's still out there . . ."

"Because we'd have all kinds of legal and labor problems," Lucas said. "We're already working through some pretty questionable territory, calling up friends and relatives and asking about these people. We're gonna hear from the unions any time now . . . And the media would go crazy about invasion of privacy and all that. I mean, we *are* on a fishing expedition."

"If he kills somebody else . . ."

"That's why I say I'll do it if we don't get anything in the next day or two," Lucas said. "Right now, I think he's hunkered down. He'll start moving again, if he's like you say, if he doesn't have any choice . . ."

"There's something else. If you let me do this market thing . . . it would be a *wonderful* paper. The *Journal of Forensic Psychology* would be all over it."

The problems of a survey and the labor unions became moot the next day.

THE CO-OP CENTER had pretty much closed down by seven o'clock in the evening. Lucas took home a stack of notes the staff had made on anomalies they'd seen in the incoming data. He read through the notes, sitting in a leather chair in his small library. The anomalies were slight: discrepancies in dates, times, schools; and a few comments by former employers that suggested that this staff member, or that one, hadn't done well at a previous job.

Lucas became interested in a staff member named Herman Clousy. He'd been hired as a medical technician, doing routine lab work, including blood tests on Charlie Pope. To get the job, he'd provided a transcript from a "Lakewood Community College" in White Bear Lake, Minnesota, but nobody could find a Lakewood Community College. He'd also provided three references, and none of the three could be reached at the phone numbers he'd listed. On the other hand, he'd worked for the state for fifteen years, and the references were out-of-date.

The next morning, Clousy was at the top of Lucas's list for almost fifteen minutes. After the daily chat with Weather, he called Dr. Cale, who said that Clousy was an average performer, one of the shadow people whom nobody paid much attention to. He was married, Cale knew, and lived in Mankato. Was there any special reason why Lucas was interested?

"He says he graduated from a Lakewood Community College in White Bear Lake, and there isn't one."

"Really? That would have been checked . . . let me ask my secretary, she used to work for the community college down here."

Cale went away for a minute, then came back and said, "Sandy says there used to be a Lakewood," he said. "She says it's called Century College now."

"Ah . . . poop. Let me check that."

He gave it to one of the co-op staff, who checked and came back five minutes later: "There was a name change, all right. Still can't find the references . . ."

"Take the most uncommon-looking last name in the references and start calling around to all of them you can find," Lucas suggested.

THEY SPENT THE REST of the morning tracking more dead ends: the work was tedious and left Lucas feeling stupid. At lunchtime, he went out for a BLT, then returned to his office and told Carol not to let anyone in, short of an emergency.

He closed the door, put his feet up on his desk, and thought about all the activity in the co-op room. Elle might be right: the kind of information they were getting wouldn't really pinpoint anyone. The other problem was, when you were dealing with so many possibilities, you tended to forget about the facts you already had.

For instance, he thought, somebody had passed the information about Peterson to the Big Three. That was a fact, and they hadn't emphasized it enough. It had to be one of fewer than a dozen people. They were all on tape.

Did O'Donnell make any small specific move, did he touch all three food trays, did he do *anything* that might possibly involve the passing of information? How about the guys up in the cage? Was there some way to fiddle with the time code on the tape, or mess with the tape itself, so the guy in the back could have a little chat with Taylor, Lighter, and Chase and nobody would know?

Lucas couldn't stand going down to the co-op room again, so he dragged out the tapes of the St. John's isolation wing. He ran through them at high speed, the people coming and going in their silent-movie way.

HERE CAME O'DONNELL. Here was the food. He says something to Lighter, and the food goes in. Didn't touch anything that time. He talks to Chase. Food goes in . . .

He couldn't see it. Maybe O'Donnell put the messages in the food in the hallway? Might he have some power over one of the orderlies who delivered the trays?

He ran back and forth through the tapes, watching people come and go, staffers talking to prisoners, interacting with other staffers. Here's Beloit, here's Grant, here's Hart, here's O'Donnell, here goes Sennet . . .

. . .

"WHAT'S HE DOING?" Lucas asked himself.

He was watching Leo Grant. Hard to pick up, if you weren't running the tapes at high speed.

Okay: Grant walks down the corridor, dressed in slacks and a sport coat, hands in his pockets. He's with Sennet. Sennet pushes a button, and they talk to Lighter. While they talk, Grant takes off his sport coat, folds it over his arm.

Lucas couldn't make out what the conversation was about, but watched as Grant turned his back to the window where Lighter was standing. Grant was facing both the camera and Sennet. They talked some more, and then Sennet punched the window release, and the window closed, shutting Lighter away again.

Sennet steps across the hallway. Grant, still with his coat off, steps sideways across the hall, never turning his back fully to the camera or to Sennet. Sennet opens Chases's window. They talk, Grant turns his back to Chase, as they talk. He's facing Sennet. Sennet closes Chase's window. Taylor's window is down the hall. Sennet heads that way, and Grant slips his jacket on, and follows Sennet, his back to the camera. They talk to Taylor, and Grant casually slips his jacket off again. He turns his back to Taylor, but never to Sennet or the camera . . .

Sennet punched Taylor's window when they were finished, and he and Grant walked back toward the camera, Grant a step behind so that Sennet had to turn slightly to talk to him. They disappeared under the camera and, presumably, out the door.

LUCAS RAN THE SEQUENCE several times. Maybe Grant just couldn't get the jacket right. Maybe the temperature was uncomfortable. But maybe . . . could he have had something written on the back of his shirt? Or a piece of paper or cloth tacked to his shirt?

Lucas dug out the anomalies list and found only one short entry for

Grant: a Dr. Peter Baylor, from a clinic in Colorado, had mentioned that Grant had gone to a private psychiatric clinic in Cancun after leaving Colorado. The anomaly was that there were three references from Colorado in Grant's record, but none from Cancun.

Lucas looked up the telephone numbers for Colorado, called, asked for Peter Baylor, and was told that he wasn't working that day. "I'm trying to find the phone number for a former staff member of yours, Leo . . ." He flipped through the paper. It wasn't Leonard, it was . . . "Leopold Grant. He left your hospital and apparently went to Cancun."

After being routed around, he talked to a woman in the clinic's personnel department who didn't have a number, but had a name: The Coetrine Center. After a hassle with the AT&T operator, he got the place. The woman who answered the phone, in Spanish, switched smoothly to English, then forwarded him to another office. The man who answered the phone there, in Spanish, changed to English.

Lucas said, "I need some information about a former employee of yours named Leopold Grant . . ."

"You already have some incorrect information," the man said, pleasantly enough. "Here, you might as well get it from the horse's mouth . . ."

Before Lucas could reply, the man half covered the mouthpiece of the receiver, and Lucas could hear him call out something, but not what he said.

A second later, another phone receiver rattled, and an American man's voice said, "This is Leo Grant. Can I help you?"

23

FOR A MOMENT, Lucas experienced the kind of disorientation he might have felt in a falling elevator.

Then he said, "I beg your pardon? Who is this?"

The Cancun guy said, "Leo Grant. Who are you?"

"Uh . . . Lucas Davenport—I'm an agent with the Minnesota Bureau of Criminal Apprehension. We have had a series of murders here . . . one of the people we're investigating is a Leopold Grant, a psychologist who works at the St. John's Security Hospital. He shows references from the West Bend Hospital in Boulder, Colorado."

There followed a moment of silence, then a crunching sound, as if the man on the other end of the line had bitten off a piece of celery. Then, "How do I know this isn't a stupid pet trick?"

"Do you have a line to the States?" Lucas asked.

"Well, sure."

"Call directory assistance for Minnesota, ask for the number for the

Minnesota Bureau of Criminal Apprehension. Under the listings for the state of Minnesota. Call that number, then ask for me: My name is Lucas Davenport, L-u-c-a-s D-a-v-e-n-p-o-r-t . . . This is critical: do it right away."

"I'll call you right back." There was a final chewing crunch, and then the line went dead.

LUCAS, HIS HEART suddenly booming, stuck his head out the office door. "Carol: run down to the co-op center, tell them we need every speck of information we can get on Leo Grant, the psychologist at St. John's."

"Leo Grant . . ."

"Run."

LUCAS TOOK A COUPLE of turns around his office, thinking about Grant. He was well spoken, soft faced . . . but he'd also hung out with Sam O'Donnell, would have known about O'Donnell's Christmas voice, had worked with Charlie Pope and the Big Three. Could have passed word of Peterson's murder . . .

And going way back, he was the one who said that Charlie was smarter than he looked, that Charlie might go for college girls, that there might be a second man or woman. Jesus. He'd been steering them from the start.

"Ah, man." He looked at the phone: "Call, motherfucker."

A MINUTE LATER, the phone rang. "This is Leo Grant from Cancun."

"Yeah, Dr. Grant. This is Davenport. Are you satisfied?"

"Yes, I guess so," Grant said. "What's going on? Murders?"

"We've got a guy who had access to all the major players in a series of murders. He says he's a psychologist, and that his name is Leopold Grant . . ."

"That seems unlikely . . ."

". . . who did his school at Colorado and then worked at West Bend. He has a set of references from West Bend. Wait, he has a transcript from Colorado that was sent to a 2319 Eleanor Street . . ."

"You've got a fraud on your hands, then," Grant said. "That was my address when I was a graduate student. I've never met or heard of another Leopold Grant. If there was another doc in the field with the same name, I would have heard—if he were legit, anyway. If he contributed to the literature."

"Do you have any idea how this Leopold Grant could have gotten his hands on your files?" Lucas asked. He thumbed through the "Leo Grant" file from St. John's. "There are references here . . . Is Douglas Carmichael a real guy? He's shown here as . . ."

". . . director of psychiatric medicine at West Bend. He's real. It's on letterhead paper, I assume."

"Yes, it is."

"If you've got a transcript and all that other stuff, then I'd say that somebody probably got to the personnel files at West Bend," Grant said. "Have you seen this Leo Grant? What does he look like?"

"He's a pretty good-looking guy," Lucas said. "Six feet tall, dark hair, dark eyes. He's thin—wiry—high cheekbones. He dresses well, he's well spoken. He seems pretty smart. He uses big words sometimes, I thought maybe he was showing off, but it seems pretty natural . . ."

"Oh, boy . . . does he have a tattoo on his upper arm? Like a barbed-wire thing?"

"*Ah, shit.*" Lucas dropped the phone to his thigh and put his hands over his eyes. The hookers at the Rockyard, they'd mentioned the tattoo. He'd never thought about it again. If he'd lined up all the possibilities, had all the men roll up their sleeves, Peterson would be alive.

He put the phone back to his ear and Grant was saying, "Hello? Are you still there?"

"I'm here. I just . . . remembered something. Another witness mentioned seeing a man with that tattoo talking to one of the victims. *Goddamnit.*"

"If it's who I think it is, you've got a serious problem," Grant said. "There was a patient named Roy Rogers at West Bend. Roy Rogers wasn't his real name, but we never found out what his real name was. He killed a man in Denver, a street guy. He'd sat on the guy and nearly cut his head off with a piece of glass. This was over a radio. The cops figured it must have taken five minutes to get the job done: he started around back and sawed halfway through the guy's neck."

"The guy we're looking for has slashed the throats of all three victims . . . You turned this Rogers guy loose?"

"No—he turned himself loose. I ran into one of my college pals at a convention in Chicago, and he mentioned it. Roy was supposedly in a secure area, but somebody left a door unlocked, or ajar, and he walked down through a mechanical area and out the other side. The staff thinks he rode out in the back of a food truck. Nobody's seen him since."

"Is he smart? Any connection with California that you know of?" Lucas asked.

"He's very bright—his IQ, by the old standards, would have been considered genius level. We don't call it that anymore, but he's smart. And he came from California."

"Ah. Thank you . . ."

The Cancun Leo Grant was into it now, his voice intense: Lucas realized that he *sounded* like the fake Leo Grant: "The thing is, whatever his name is, if his story is true . . . Roy's the poster boy for unwanted children. He said he grew up locked in his room—he didn't even have a window. When I pushed him on it, I got the impression that his 'room' might have been a walk-in closet. He wasn't tortured or sexually abused, he was just locked away. His story's a horror, depending on how much you could believe."

"How much did you believe?" Lucas asked.

Grant considered for a moment, then said, "About the growing-up part, I believed most of it. He says the cops came and got him when he was nine or ten—he didn't actually know how old he was—and put him in a foster home. He might have been in the closet from the time he was a baby. He said he ran away from the foster home after a while and grew up on the beach at Venice. The thing about Roy was . . ."

Grant paused again, and Lucas prompted him, "Yeah? What?"

"Roy has no real personality of his own," Grant said. "That's not exactly right, but you can think of him that way. He takes on the personality of the people he's most impressed with. That's how he pulled off this fraud at your security hospital. At West Bend, during treatment sessions, he talked and behaved like a staff member. But if you saw him around the orderlies, he acted and talked like an orderly. Once, in a group-therapy session, with a man who'd been accused of killing his wife . . . I saw him take on the other man's personality in just a matter of a couple of sessions. He picked up the other guy's mannerisms and way of talking, his gestures, facial tics . . . It was like the other guy had been poured into him."

"That explains a lot," Lucas said. "Listen, Dr. Grant, I'm gonna pick this guy up, right now. We'd appreciate it if you'd come up, help us talk with him. The state will pay all your expenses and a fee, of course . . ."

"I can do that," Grant said. "This is a shock, of course. I'd like to talk to the hospital staff up there, and I'd like to see Roy again. Just to hear his story."

"Yeah, well . . ."

"You know where he got the name? Roy Rogers?" Grant asked.

"From the cowboy guy?"

"Nope. Well, indirectly. He got it from a fast-food restaurant. Said it was the best place he ever ate, until he went to jail."

. . .

LUCAS CALLED SLOAN: "It's Leo Grant. I'll tell you on the way down to get him."

JENKINS ANSWERED HIS cell phone and said he was just getting a bite to eat. Shrake was with him. "We're heading down to the security hospital," Lucas said. "I want you guys with us."

"We got a break?"

"Yeah. I'm gonna run over to Minneapolis and pick up Sloan . . ." They agreed to meet at a gas station in the town of Shakopee, on the edge of the metro area.

"Listen, Shrake and me have been talking," Jenkins said. "That list of yours . . . It's gotta have "Fuck the Police," right? NWA?"

THE MINNEAPOLIS CITY HALL was an ugly building, a pile of purple stone almost exactly the color, Lucas had once realized after a hunting trip, of fresh deer turds. Sloan was standing on the sidewalk outside. Lucas pulled up beside him, and he jumped into the truck.

"Tell me," he said.

So Lucas told him, and Sloan was properly astonished. He said, "I forgot all about those hookers, and the tattoo. It all seemed so . . . distant."

"There ought to be some kind of cop computer program," Lucas said. "Like a spreadsheet. You'd put in all the facts that you have, all the suppositions, and rank the suppositions by credibility. Then you'd put in all the suspects, and the program would remind you of what you need to do. If we had something like that, that never forgot anything . . ."

"We'd spend all of our time typing shit into it," Sloan said.

"Yeah, but we would have had everybody rolling their sleeves up . . . Goddamnit."

THEY TALKED ABOUT the details of the case on the way out of town; stopped at Shakopee and waited for five minutes until Jenkins and Shrake arrived, filled them in, and headed south again. Twenty miles out, Sloan asked, "You think we ought to call the sheriff?"

"No. This kind of thing gets around too fast. I want to have Grant on the ground, with cuffs on him, before anybody even knows we're coming."

Sloan looked at his watch. "His shift is gonna be over about now."

"Ah . . . ," Lucas glanced at his own watch. "Call Dr. Cale. Ask him to find out if Grant's gone yet. Tell him not to be obvious about it."

Sloan dialed, got Cale, asked, listened, and said, "Just a minute." He took the phone down and said, "Grant left early—half an hour or forty-five minutes ago."

"Uh-oh. Does Cale know why?"

Sloan asked, listened, then said, "No. He doesn't know why. He just saw him going out through the security wall, and he was carrying a briefcase and looked like he was in a hurry. Cale assumed he was leaving."

"Get a home address. Tell Cale not to mention this, in case he comes back there."

WHILE SLOAN GOT THE address, Lucas pulled out his cell phone and tapped the speed dial for the office. Carol answered: "Carol, check with the co-op guys. When I told them to get every speck of information on Grant . . . did they call the hospital directly?"

She called back: "Yes. They talked to a couple of people. They got the name of a Mrs. Hardesty in Personnel."

Lucas hung up and looked at Sloan. "He might know we're coming."

SLOAN CALLED JENKINS and Shrake in the trailing car, and they pulled into a gas station. The software on Lucas's navigation system wouldn't allow an address to be entered while the truck was moving; he punched it in, got a map, and they took off again.

"Maybe we better call the sheriff now," Sloan suggested, when they were back on the road. "Get somebody looking for his car."

"Do it," Lucas said.

Sloan called the Department of Motor Vehicle Registration, identified himself, and gave them Grant's name and address. A moment later he had the car and the tag number. He caught Nordwall in his office, and Lucas listened as Sloan outlined the situation. Then Sloan said, "I've got the car, tag, and his address. We're coming up on the address, we're just outside of Mankato, now. We're only about a mile out . . ."

He gave Nordwall the description of the car, the tag number, and the address, listened for a moment, said, "Yeah, I can hold. What's going on?"

Lucas glanced at Sloan, who shrugged, then the sheriff came back up and Sloan, suddenly intent, "Uh-huh, ah, jeez, it's gotta be related. We're gonna be there in a minute. See you there."

"What?" Lucas asked.

"There's been some kind of hassle, some kind of attack on a college kid, right there at Grant's address. There are a couple of cars on the way, nobody on the scene yet. The sheriff heard the call through his nine-one-one monitor, less than a minute ago. The address rang a bell."

"Goddamnit . . . Call the city cops. Tell them we're coming in."

24

THE MAN WHO CALLED himself Leopold Grant lay writhing on his bed, pale and naked, in a steaming mix of odors, sweat, semen, tobacco, and bed-sheet starch, plugged into a stethoscope. The black sensor cable led from his ears to a hole in the bedroom wall; in the slanted white light knifing across his body from the half-turned slats in the Venetian blinds, he looked like a movie cyborg recharging its batteries.

He was, in a way. On the other side of the wall, Millie Lincoln was enjoying a visit from Mihovil. Grant was only two feet from her, just on the other side of the wall. With the stethoscope's sensor duct-taped to the back side of the Sheetrock above Millie's bed, he could hear every gasp, groan, giggle, and lick.

He lived for them.

An hour earlier, he'd run out of the security hospital. One of the nondangerous patients, who worked in Personnel, had tracked him down to tell him that they were pulling all the information on him; that they were calling all his references; that the cops had called from St. Paul and asked for every speck of information.

Not for everybody—just for Grant. So they had him.

His first impulse had been to run. He'd run most of his life, it was nothing new. Get back to his apartment, take everything of value, load it into his car, get it up to the Twin Cities, rent another car, run to Chicago, dump the rental . . . He could see himself arriving in Miami, a roll of cash in his pockets, white teeth through a new beard, a new name, a new profession, a Hawaiian shirt.

That had been the impulse; and he'd left the hospital in a shit-faced panic.

But the Gods Down the Hall had gotten to him in some elemental way. They didn't let go; they tried to pull him back. That talk of a glorious Armageddon. And then when he got back to his apartment, that goddamned Millie Lincoln was at it again. Didn't she ever study? Didn't she ever do anything but fuck?

She'd stopped the flight in its tracks, put him on his bed, sweating, writhing, his imagination gone amok.

He'd first heard her three months earlier, and had heard her three or four afternoons or nights every week, with an eager lover, probably another college kid. He thought it was the same guy every time, because the voice had a distinct, baritone vibration.

But it wasn't the guy who did it to him. It was Millie. Millie didn't just have orgasms. She worked up to them slowly, and she gave directions: "Oh, do that again, oh, do that. Oh, oh. Ohhhh, c'mon, slow down, go up a little, oh, oh, God, oh . . ."

Grant had at first heard her only faintly. He'd heard her bed knocking on the wall, a rhythmic *bump-bump-bump* that could be only one thing. He'd pressed his ear to the drywall, and first heard her groans along with some unintelligible words.

He'd tried pressing a glass against the wall, the better to hear. There was some marginal improvement, but not enough. Then, at the hospital, one of the docs had left a stethoscope lying unattended at a nurses' station, and he'd stolen it. He cut a hole in the wall behind the headboard of his bed, and taped the sensor to the wall on the other side. The stethoscope made a major difference. He could hear individual words; he learned her name; and he soon understood that these were modern children, who had an idea of what they wanted and were clear in their requests, which *really* turned him on . . .

He'd gone looking for her, then.

They lived in an apartment complex. Their building had two floors, with eighteen pairs of back-to-back red-brick units on each floor, like an old army barracks but new. Millie's entrance was on the opposite side of the building from Grant's. When he checked the mailboxes, he found four female names.

He watched their doors when he could do it without being obvious. Two of the women were blond, one was fairly dark. The fourth was a bit overweight, chubby but attractive, with fair skin and reddish-brown hair. He thought she might be the one, but he wasn't sure.

Millie . . . Millie was causing him trouble this afternoon. He'd come home, planning to run, and had then heard the bumping on the wall. Ten minutes later, she was pounding away, and here he lay, naked, writhing with her, eyes clenched, ears plugged into the stethoscope, riding with her . . .

Remembering the first woman, Angela Larson:

The first woman hadn't been very interesting. He'd noticed her in an art store six or seven months before the killing and had gone back a few times, just to look. She was a tall, dark-haired woman, but with pale eyes and a kind of wide Slavic forehead and sensuous lips. The first night, while he was still developing into a god on his own, he waited until the shop closed, planning to follow her to her car, and then to her home. The lights went out, and he waited, but she never came out.

The next night, he found her going out the back. He watched her as she walked down to the bar, which had a bigger parking lot than the craft store, slipped into her car. He followed her efficiently, using techniques learned from Robert Ludlum, and was disappointed to find her going into an apartment building. Lots of lights, lots of people around, and since it was mostly students, a lot of awareness.

But that moment in the alley . . . did she always do that? He watched three more nights, and her routine never varied.

On the night he became a god, he'd waited until she started turning out the shop lights, had pulled into the alley that led to the bar parking lot, and then pulled into a space between her and her car. There was some ambient light from the bar, but not much. He could see her coming as he got out: he was humming a snatch of song, which he later remembered as "Danger Zone" from the *Top Gun* movie. And that's what he felt like, like the top gun . . .

He walked around to the back of the car, checking that nobody else was in the alley: *here* was the danger zone, at least for him. He messed around in the trunk, as if he were opening a suitcase or something, and watched her with his peripheral vision. He could see by her hesitant step that she thought about turning, and walking away from him, out there alone in the dark, but that would have been embarrassing, and so she came on, angling a bit away from him, but she was still within a step or two as she went by, watching him out of the corner of her eye.

He let her get another step, to relax just that fatal notch, then with a quick two-step approach, hit her with a dowel rod. The dowel was a little more than an inch thick, sold as a clothes-closet rod, and five feet long. He meant to stun her with it: but in the excitement and fear of the moment, he hit her too hard. She went down, he scooped her up, dumped her in the trunk of the car, tossed the stick in after her, slammed it, ran around to the door, jumped inside, and was rolling.

The first time, he'd been intensely frightened. What if a taillight went out? What if he forgot to signal a turn? What if somebody hit him, an accident, and the cops found the body in the trunk?

All kinds of things could happen.

None of them did.

And then the disappointment: he'd hit her too hard.

When he opened the trunk, she moaned but never seemed aware of what he was doing. He picked her up, and her head rolled, and her eyelids fluttered, and he thought she might be faking. She wasn't.

He was careful, in handling her, to never let her get in a position to slash at him . . . but she never even stiffened as he hauled her into O'Donnell's shed. O'Donnell was in Madison, seeing his mother. The availability of his car shed had been the key to launch the attack. He'd gotten the shed ready before he went after her—had laid down a plastic painter's drop cloth that he'd bought from Home Depot. He'd hung a piece of nylon anchor rope over one of the exposed ceiling beams, designed to hold the weight of an automobile engine. He tied Larson's hands and lifted her with the rope.

She was absolutely slack, all her weight on her shoulder joints, but she never protested, never made a sound other than the low gagging moan.

"Angela," he called to her. He'd gotten out his wire flail. "Angela, can you hear me?"

She couldn't. He snapped the flail at her; the wire cut into her back, and blood seeped out of the cuts. Nothing but the moan, the fluttering eyelids.

He hit her again and then a kind of blankness descended on him, and he began beating her with a fury, hitting her, hitting her, until a misstep sent him skidding across the plastic sheet; he dropped to his hands and knees in the blood, gasping for breath. Looked up at her: she hardly looked human, except for her untouched face. He'd shredded her.

He tried calling to her again, but she was no longer home. Finally, in disgust, he'd cut her throat with a carpet knife. Not a straight razor, but a carpet knife from a Hardware Hank store, stood there and watched the blood pumping out of her throat until her heart stopped, and her blood with it.

. . .

THEN RICE. That had been different; and Peterson . . .

In the room next door, Millie reached a climax and cried out, and Grant cried out with her.

He lay on the bed for a moment: everything was coming down on him now. Everything. He'd never make it to Miami. They'd pull him down, lock him down the hall with Biggie and Taylor and Chase.

Grant staggered away from his bed, sweating, his heart still pounding. Into the bathroom: he felt weird, looked at himself in the mirror. His face was bright pink: his blood pressure must be out of sight, he thought. Had to calm down . . . he splashed a double handful of water into his face, patted his face dry with a towel. Looked at his watch. *What?* He'd been on the bed for forty minutes. It had seemed like only a moment . . .

What to do, what to do . . . He paced his apartment, gnawing on a knuckle until it was raw. They were coming, and he was getting nowhere.

He went into his bedroom again, opened the closet door, pushed away some shoes. Three guns there. Two from O'Donnell, one of his own. One 9mm, one .40, and a .45.

He picked up the guns, looked at them for a moment, then went back to the living room and got his briefcase. The first briefcase of his life. All done now. He poured out the papers inside and threw in the guns. And the razor. Back to the bedroom, he got the straight razor he'd used on Peterson and slipped it into his pocket. He and Biggie and Chase had figured out how to get them inside—as long as he was coming in on a weekday, and on the second shift . . .

Which was where they were now.

And Justus Smith had to be in the control booth. Smith always worked the second shift, on weekdays; but what if he was sick? Or if he'd taken a vacation day? If they were actually going to execute the

Armageddon, they'd always talked of it, Lighter, Chase, Taylor, and himself, as being carefully planned ahead of time, with proper options that would allow them to wait until conditions were perfect.

Now it was all ad hoc. Nothing was perfect . . .

GRANT LOOKED AT his watch. The first shift had just ended. He went to the phone, dialed in to the hospital, and asked for Smith.

A moment later, "Cage—this is Smith."

Grant hung up. "All right," he said to himself. Justus was in the cage, and God in his heaven. He looked around the apartment. He didn't have to pack: fuck all this stuff. He picked up the briefcase, focused now, ready to make his run. Ready to go down with the Gods Down the Hall.

And then it would all be done. No more misery; no more loneliness; no more acid rolling around in his brains, to make him cry at night.

He carried the briefcase down to his car and threw it in, jingled his keys, got into the driver's seat, and thought: *Shit. The coin.*

He went back upstairs, into the bedroom, and opened the top drawer in his chest of drawers, dug around some socks, and came up with the plastic box. Inside was a gold 1866S double eagle. The coin cost him $1,432, but the same coin, in better condition, might be worth as much as $25,000 to $30,000.

Justus Smith was a coin nut.

HE WAS TURNING TO GO when he heard a thump on the wall. Then faintly, a woman's voice. He looked at the door and then at the stethoscope on the bed. There was no time for this, no time. He went over to the stethoscope on the bed and plugged it into his ears.

Millie Lincoln was doing it again. The rush came, as it always did, but this time there was more than lust. This time there was anger and anxiety and Armageddon coming; he'd never even seen her, not for sure, because he had too much to lose.

Now, there was nothing to lose. Millie Lincoln was just getting started when Grant unplugged himself from the stethoscope and ran out the door, letting it bang open behind him.

He didn't know Millie, but he knew where her door was.

MIHOVIL HAD JUST gotten up to go to the bathroom to rinse off when Millie heard what sounded like an explosion; the noise was loud enough, and close enough, that she called, "What was that?"

Before Mihovil could answer, there was another *boom*, and the apartment shook with the impact. She hopped out of bed and picked up her underpants and there was a third impact, and a splintering sound, from close by. Mihovil shouted, "What the hell?" and there was another impact, and Millie picked up her top and pulled it over her head and stepped to the bedroom door.

Mihovil, naked, was standing in the front room, looking toward the outer door. Another *boom*, and pieces of Sheetrock buckled around the door jamb, and then *boom*, and the door flew open. A man came through: he was wearing a white short-sleeved shirt and tan slacks and loafers, and might have been straight-enough-looking, but there was nothing straight about his eyes. They burned straight through Mihovil, and the man said, "Hello, Millie."

Millie shouted, "Who are you? Get out of here . . ." and the man, his face a teeth-bared mask, a lion's face, raised a hand and a razor flashed, a razor like Mihovil's father's razor, and he went after Mihovil like a sword fighter, slashing with the razor hand, trying to punch or grab with the other.

Millie started screaming, never thought of dialing 911 or locking herself in the bedroom, never thought of anything but Mihovil when blood exploded out of his shoulder and he and the stranger went twirling into the kitchen and Mihovil went down under the kitchen table.

When he went down, the stranger turned and came after her. Then she thought of the bedroom, then she stepped back, screaming, tried to slam the bedroom door, but the stranger was right here, flailing with the razor, and then Mihovil was there, too, swinging a kitchen chair.

The stranger saw it coming and fended it off with one arm, but then Mihovil was all over him with the chair, Mihovil himself screaming, bleeding from a terrible wound on his shoulder, not quitting . . .

They twisted and turned around the apartment, breaking furniture and glass, dumping electronics and dishes, Mihovil now completely wild; and then the stranger broke and ran and Mihovil ran after him, stepped in a streak of blood at the corner of the kitchen's vinyl floor, and went down. The stranger went out the door and was gone. Millie grabbed a towel and ran to Mihovil, shouting, "Stay down, stay down, you're bleeding, you're bleeding."

Mihovil, with a sickly smile, looked up and asked, "Who the fuck was that?" and took the towel and pressed it against his shoulder and said, "Call nine-one-one—we've got an artery here."

Millie snatched the phone off the kitchen counter and punched in the number and started screaming. They weren't far from the hospital; she was still on the phone when she heard sirens . . .

GRANT RAN DOWN the center stairwell, out to the parking lot, climbed in the car. *Stupid, stupid, stupid.* Millie's lover had been no kid.

Millie's lover had eyes like he'd seen on the beach at Venice, killer eyes, eyes that had been out on the edge for a long time. The guy would have torn him apart if he'd stayed to fight.

Grant heard sirens as he cleared the parking lot.

Going home, he thought. *Going home.*

25

LUCAS LIKED DRIVING FAST and had gotten in trouble a few times because of it; even liked driving fast in a truck, and now had the Lexus screaming in pain as they roared toward Grant's address. The navigation system put them right into the apartment complex. The fat tires squealing around the turns, the antiroll buzzer beeping in protest, Sloan talking to Jenkins as they tore along a leafy street toward the apartments, Shrake and Jenkins a car-length back.

They turned a corner past a cluster of lilacs and burst into a parking lot, past a swimming pool behind a chain-link fence, and Sloan said, "There!" Lucas looked that way and saw the cluster of expectant bystanders at an apartment doorway—there were always expectant bystanders for the first responding car.

Lucas went that way—he could hear sirens coming in behind them—and he hopped out of the truck, shouted at Jenkins and Shrake,

"One of you guys stay here for the city cops," and he headed toward the door, a half step ahead of Sloan.

A heavy woman with frizzy blond hair, a red bandana, and eyes big with fear, said, "There's a crazy man here. He hurt a man up on two, cut him with a razor."

"Where's the stairway?"

She pointed, and Lucas said, "Show us, take us up . . . Is the guy still here?"

As they jogged across an atrium, she said over her shoulder, "Yes. He's hurt, really bad, there's blood all over the place."

They were in the stairwell, her ass bouncing in Lucas's face as they went up. "He's hurt?" Sloan asked. Shrake was coming up behind them now. "The crazy man?"

"No, not the crazy man. He ran. The other man . . ."

Lucas said, "Shit . . ."

Then they were out of the stairs and running down a hallway toward another cluster of the curious, and Lucas called, "Police, coming through."

The cluster broke, and Lucas went in, found a young woman in underpants and a T-shirt crouched over a man who wore nothing but jeans. The man was awake and talking. Lucas went to his knees and looked at the woman and said, "What happened? How bad?"

The man answered for her, good English, but accented: "A crazy man. We have not seen him before. He cut me with a straight razor, an old kind, and then he went out. He cut a small artery in my shoulder. I'll be okay if they get me soon to the hospital. We must cauterize the artery. For now, we put pressure on it."

"He's a doctor," the young woman said, and Lucas nodded.

"Ambulance is coming," Shrake said. He was on his phone, talking to the 911 dispatcher. "One minute out. The locals are looking for the car."

Lucas asked the injured man and the woman, and then the people jammed into the doorway, "Was the guy's name Grant? Does anybody know if the guy's name was Leopold Grant?"

One woman in the doorway, an older woman with harsh red lipstick, said, "I didn't see the attack, but I know Leo. He lives on the other side of the building."

The man on the floor said, "I have never seen him before this." The woman with him said, "Me, either. He just kept kicking the door. I thought it was an earthquake. He knew my name. He called me Millie . . ."

Lucas said to the lipstick woman who knew Grant, "Show me where Grant's room is."

GOING BACK DOWN the hallway, they ran into Jenkins, with the Mankato cops in tow. Lucas said to a sergeant, "Get the ambulance guys up here quick, we got an arterial. Keep these people isolated, the witnesses. Jenkins, you come with us."

"Where're we going?"

"We're following her." He pointed at the woman who was taking them to Grant's apartment, and they fell in behind her. To get to Grant's, they had to go back down the hallway, through the second-floor lobby, and out the opposite side into another hallway. They'd walked fifty or sixty feet down the hallway, and the woman said, "It's right up ahead. The next door."

"Just about back-to-back with that chick's apartment," Shrake said.

Lucas came up slowly, pulled his gun, pushed the woman back, and pressed a finger to his lips. He could see that the door to Grant's apartment was open an inch or two. He stopped at the door, and Jenkins, gun in hand, went on past. With Jenkins lined up on the other side, Lucas pushed the door open. They could hear a radio—and then Lucas realized that it was coming from somewhere else. From the apartment, he could hear nothing at all.

Jenkins said, "I can't see anything."

"Gonna go," Lucas said. He got his .45 out in front and stepped through, one step, two, three, ready to fire, Sloan right behind him, Sloan's gun tracking to the right while Lucas's gun tracked left. Two bedrooms, two baths. Open-plan kitchen, nobody in that. Cleared a bedroom used as an office, cluttered but not torn up, cleared the master bedroom, the bathrooms, the closets.

"He's a freak," Jenkins said. He'd come in behind them, and he nodded at the bed. Lucas stepped over to look, saw the stethoscope trailing out of the wall.

"Listening to the chick," Shrake said. "They looked like they'd been fucking, the guy must've been over here, must've cracked."

Lucas put his gun away. "All right. I'll call the co-op center, put out a call on the car. It's a snake hunt now."

THEY BACKED OUT of the apartment, not wanting to hack up any evidence: best to let the crime-scene crew deal with it. As they went, Jenkins said, "He didn't take much, looks like his clothes are still here."

They closed the door, got a city cop to come down to watch it until they could get it sealed. As Lucas talked to the co-op center, Jenkins, Shrake, and Sloan went down to Millie Lincoln's apartment. The halls were full of frightened people, and Lucas heard a woman talking about the man hauled away by the ambulance. He went to the lobby windows, finished with the co-op guys, and called Rose Marie Roux.

"We know who he is, but we don't have him yet. He's running."

"But we'll get him," she said.

"One way or another. He could stick a gun in his ear . . . But yeah. It's over."

"When are you coming back?"

"Tonight, an hour or two. There are a couple of loose ends down here."

"Call me . . ."

Lucas rang off and saw the sheriff's car pull into the lot, and Nordwall got out. Lucas looked at the crowd of cops around Millie Lincoln's apartment, decided they had enough help, and walked down the stairs and out into the parking lot.

Nordwall, no athlete, was chugging across the parking lot, a young deputy trailing him. "What happened?"

"We're looking for a Leo Grant. He's a psychologist up at the security hospital. Before he ran out of here, he tried to attack a woman up on the second floor . . ." He told Nordwall about the sequence that led to Grant.

When he was done, Nordwall grunted, scratched his nose, then awkwardly patted Lucas on the shoulder and said, "I knew I was calling the right guy."

"I'm gonna dream about Peterson," Lucas said.

"Yeah, but you know what? I read all those true-crime books," Nordwall said. "Like on the Green River guy. I was afraid we might lose ten people, or fifteen. When we were looking for Pope, it seemed like he was invisible."

"There's that." Lucas's phone rang. He answered, expecting somebody from the co-op center. Instead, he got a voice that sounded like an angry squirrel, high-pitched, chattering, incoherent, frightened.

"Wait, wait, calm down," he said. "Who is this, what happened?"

"This is Cale," the voice shouted. "Up at the hospital. Leo Grant just shot three people, and he's loose in the hospital. He's got guns. We don't have any lights, all the doors are open, we've got a fire in the cage. We've got the ambulances coming, we're calling the sheriff. Jesus, are you coming? Where are you? Where are you?"

26

GRANT WAS HURT: the pain narrowed his focus. Maybe everybody at the hospital knew about him, but it was home. He was wanted there. Needed. He could reach the glory . . .

And the cops had only been asking for information. Maybe they hadn't made a move yet. If they had, it was all over anyway; yet if he was ready, he could still reach the glory, there in the administrative wing, even if he couldn't make it to the Gods.

He screamed out of the apartment parking lot, down through the quiet streets, past a couple of girls on Rollerblades, out to the highway. He turned north and saw, on the other side of the highway, an SUV and a sedan coming south, fast, the sedan with a flasher on the roof.

Was the sedan chasing the SUV? He slowed, automatically thinking, *Cop*, and watched as the two vehicles went past. In the first, in the driver's seat, he recognized Davenport.

They were coming after him. Going to the apartment . . .

"Go," he shouted to himself. "Go, go, go, go . . ."

The odds of getting to the Gods Down the Hall suddenly seemed slimmer. Yet . . . there was no choice, really. Go for the hospital, go for glory, or die on some highway like a dog.

He gripped the steering wheel, focused, saw the Gods waiting for him, as though in a vision, and chanted, "Go, go, go, go, go . . ."

UP THE HILL. Past the reception building: empty parking lot. Flags limp on the flagpole, blue sky behind it, *Postcard of a Nuthouse* . . . Guy mowing yard to the right, lifting a hand . . .

He jammed the car into the handicapped space nearest the door. He had the smallest pistol, a 9mm, in his pocket, two more in his briefcase. He hurried toward the steps . . .

And bumped into Dick Hart coming out. Hart held up a hand: "Hey, Leo, did you see that in-bound file on Mark North? Somebody stuck it somewhere."

Grant shook his head, sidled past. "Haven't seen it. I had to run out . . . Anything going on?"

Hart shrugged. "The usual. Cary decided to pee down the halls again, God only knows what we did."

"Somebody ought to wire that guy shut," Grant said. He turned and started back up the steps.

Hart called, "You coming Saturday?"

"I kind of doubt it," Grant called back. "I've got a lot going on."

HE PUSHED THROUGH the tall doors, and as he went through, the space of the hospital narrowed farther, a tunnel red around the edges, rough, and he was walking down to the mouth of it. One goal, now: the cage. The congenial exchange with Hart spurred him on. They didn't know. He couldn't believe it: *they didn't know.*

He was hurrying down the tunnel of his own vision, passing the various administrative offices, brushing past people, feeling the walls close down, suppressing the urge to jog. He had the coin in his pocket, the gun in his jacket. Right now, he could still turn and run.

But not really, he thought. Because . . . *he felt so good*. He'd been made for this. Yes. Everything would be resolved now. *Everything*. He would break out of the closed room of his life . . . He was free.

GRANT WALKED UP to the outer barred door, pushed the buzzer button, put his ID on the scanner box, and waved to Justus Smith inside the glassed-in cage. The stress was going to his head. He felt as though he were underwater and hadn't taken a breath in too long. He relaxed, took a breath, took another . . .

The outer door rolled open. Instead of walking straight ahead, through the security scanner, he turned right, toward the cage, took his hand out of his pocket, and held it up to Smith. The outer door rolled shut behind him.

Smith looked at the coin through the thick yellowish glass and said, "Hey—where'd you get that?"

"Internet. Could you take a look?" Smith was a big coin investor. He said coins would be good for two or three years, would probably double in price. And he reveled in his specialist knowledge, never lost a chance to show off.

"Yeah. Just a sec . . ." Against policy—but it was done occasionally, the strict safeguards breaking down, especially when the guy outside the cage was a trusted staffer, a professional, a doctor in a white coat . . .

Smith stepped over to the cage's security door, as Grant and the Gods knew he would, and popped it open. Grant had his hand on the 9mm, safety off, finger on the trigger. Last chance to turn around . . .

Smith popped open the door, an expectant eye—raised smile on his face. "Which Web site did you . . ."

. . .

GRANT HAD THE 9MM OUT, eight inches from Smith's heart. Smith's eyes just had time to widen, his mouth to open a quarter inch, and Grant pulled the trigger. The blast was deafening; Smith went down like a punctured balloon, and then Grant was inside the cage.

Marian LeDoux had a husband and three children and brown mousy hair and beautiful turquoise eyes. She knitted when nothing was going on and had once had a brief affair with the manager of the cafeteria. She was at the board, and she swiveled and stood up, eyes widening, reaching for a red alarm button, and Grant shot her in the face from three feet.

Jack Lasker built furniture in his home workshop and always had cuts and nicks on his hands; he was famous for his Band-Aids. He was in the monitoring room, and he fell as he tried to get to the door, to wedge it shut, his watery blue eyes up and looking at the gun, he said, "No, Leo," and Grant shot him in the neck and then, when he went down, again in the chest.

Grant stepped back to the board, breathing hard now, feeling his heart beating against his rib cage. He opened the inner doors, and then unlocked everything in the building. He could see people running on the other side of the outer doors, but nobody with a gun.

Couldn't seem to hear anything except his own words running through his mind: Go, go, go . . .

He ripped all the wires he could see out of the monitoring rooms, and all the monitoring screens went black; and now he had blood on his hands, literally, where he'd torn skin loose. He felt the pain, but ignored it. There were a number of stereolike consoles on a rack, and he threw the rack to the floor, grabbed more connection wires, ripped them loose.

Back in the main room, he physically ripped the control panel loose, reached into it, and began pulling all the wires he could see. Some sparked, but most didn't. What else? He wanted as much chaos as he could get . . .

Somebody was shouting at him, *Leo, Leo, Leo* . . .

He was about to leave when he saw the circuit-breaker panel. He opened it, loosened the two plastic nuts that held on the inner panel, ripped it off, saw the main lines coming through, took the risk: fired three shots into the main lines, the wires sparking, bits of lead and insulation flicking back into his face.

With the third shot, the power went out, and all the lights that he could see. A few seconds later, emergency lights came up automatically, along with an alarm that sounded like an elevator door was stuck: *brenk, brenk, brenk* . . .

Good enough. He left the cage, ran through the open door into the interior of the hospital.

Behind him, a woman shouted, *"Leo, Leo . . ."*

People were coming out of locked rooms, most standing wonderingly in the doorways. He saw two staff members running toward a refuge room, and he continued running himself, past the elevators, into a down-stairway. Down two flights into the security wing.

The Gods should be out of their cells, waiting.

Armageddon . . .

LUCAS SHOUTED TO NORDWALL, "Grant's at the hospital—he's killing people. Get the guys, get my guys up there, get them to the hospital. Get everybody you can up there . . ."

He turned and ran for the truck, jumped in, did a tight circle, and roared toward the street. He was on the north outskirts of town; the hospital was probably seven or eight miles away. Since he'd be slowed going out to the highway and off the highway up the hill to the hospital, just about that many minutes away. Eight minutes: a hundred people could be dead in that time . . .

Past kids on the sidewalk, nearly T-boning a red Taurus, losing it on a turn, over a sidewalk, onto a lawn, off the lawn back onto the street, down a hill to the highway, right, flooring it, the truck screaming in grief, his cell phone ringing, ringing. He ignored it through the set of curves, shifted into the vacant oncoming lane, and blew past a Harley with a bearded old man on it. He picked up the phone on a straightaway. Sloan: "You know what's going on?"

"No, but it's bad. Cale called, he was freaked. Grant's inside shooting, there are at least three down, I'm coming up on it, I gotta go . . ."

"We're two minutes behind you . . ."

Off the highway, up the hill, down the approach road, burning past the entry building, fumbling in the seat console for extra .45 clips. There were two of them, and he put them in his jacket pocket. He topped the last rise to the main parking lot, cut past a man on a four-bottom lawn-mower, serenely chopping grass, and found a sheriff's car and an official-looking SUV parked facing the steps to the main entrance, their doors open.

Lucas jammed the Lexus in beside them and jumped out, ran up the steps, his eyes catching an insignia on the SUV, Minnesota Department of Natural Resources. A game warden . . . and then he was through the front doors and down a dark hallway to the cage.

Cale was there, with a deputy, a game warden, two armed guards, and two orderlies who were opening the outer doors with a manual crank. A half dozen administrative types stood back, clustered, silent. Lucas saw Beloit on her knees in the cage, behind the bars, with another orderly, working over a body—she must have been caught inside. Cale, face white, eyes crazy, shouted, "We've heard shooting . . . all we've got is emergency power, the fire alarms are going off . . ."

"You got staffers in there?" Lucas asked.

"There are a couple dozen of them, we know there are twelve or fourteen in refuge rooms, there are some more, I don't know how many, locked in patient rooms, we've more coming in, they're calling on cell phones, all we got is cell phones, we got people shot, Davenport, we got people shot . . ."

The outer door was opening, an inch, two inches. Lucas pulled his .45, popped the clip, checked it, jacked a shell into the chamber, and asked, "Does anybody know where Grant went?"

One of the administrative types, a woman in a powder blue jacket, said, "He went to the stairs way down on the end. I think he was going down to the security cells. That's what I think."

Lucas said to the deputy and the game warden, "Get all the guys with guns and put them in the stairwells. The elevators won't be working. I don't know whether they're trying to get out or on some kind of suicide run, but we can't let them run us around. We have to move in on them and finish them in a hurry." The two men nodded, and the game warden pulled his pistol and checked it. As he did, they heard two muffled explosions and turned that way.

"Big gun," the warden said. His voice was cool.

Lucas said to Cale, "There are more cops coming in, a minute or two behind us. Get them to seal off all the floors, tell them to be careful, that we're out there."

Cale nodded, and then his eyes went wider: "Oh, my God."

Lucas tracked his eyes, looked down the hall to the right. Black smoke boiled out of a door and began filling the hallways.

"Did you call the fire department?" Lucas asked.

"Yes, yes, they're coming."

"Get some of your office people, go in behind the guys with guns, take fire extinguishers, but be careful. Make sure they stay behind the guns."

Game warden: "I think we can get through."

Lucas said, "Block the stairs, guys. Remember, more people coming. Tell them we're out there."

He squeezed through the slowly opening cell door and heard three muffled *booms*. Beloit was crawling out of the cage, hair hanging in her face, leaving bloody handprints on the floor: nothing he could do, just an image to take with him. He pointed the game warden down to the right, while he went straight ahead toward the shooting. Heard another *boom*, and kept running. . . .

GRANT RAN DOWN the stairs, his feet pounding on the steps, briefcase slapping against his legs, screams ringing in his ears. He burst into the hallway and looked to his left. The door to the security wing was open, and Biggie Lighter was peering around the door frame, a smile wreathing his sallow face. When he saw Grant, Lighter stepped into the hallway.

"Is this it?"

"This is it. That goddamned Davenport got me." Grant reached into the briefcase, saw Taylor behind Biggie, gave Biggie a pistol, and passed one to Taylor. "Is Chase . . . ?"

"He's fucked up, but he's walking around." Biggie peered at the gun. "How many shots?"

"Eight," Grant said. "They jumped me, and I didn't have time to get more clips." He looked past him at Taylor. "You've got ten. Both of them are loaded and ready to go. Push the safety off and pull the trigger."

Taylor nodded. "I'm familiar with this model." They heard somebody talking, loud, and Taylor looked over his shoulder. "Here comes Chase."

Biggie scuttled off down the hall, toward the doorway. "I'm going up to three. I'm going to shoot Morris Knight. See you in hell." Taylor went after him, calling out, "I get Landis. I get Landis." Grant watched them go, took his own pistol out of his pocket as Chase pushed through the door.

Chase stared at him for a moment, his eyes shifting to the pistol. He said, "Good. Give it to me."

"This is mine," Grant said. "Come on with me, and we'll get you one upstairs."

"MINE," Chase screamed, and he launched himself at Grant; Grant wasn't ready for it, and they went down to the floor, Grant's head snapping back against the terrazzo.

Stunned, he struggled to keep the gun, but Chase had it with both hands, Grant had only the one hand, and Chase wrenched it free.

Grant scrambled to his feet. "Give me the goddamned—"

Chase screamed, "Shut up," and pointed the pistol at Grant's face.

"Don't do that . . ." But Grant saw the developing flinch in Chase's eyes and jerked his head away. He was smashed in the face, felt a separate impact when his head hit the floor again, never heard it, never heard the gunshot, then everything went red, and a lightning stroke of pain ripped through his body . . .

LUCAS WENT INTO the stairwell intending to go down to the isolation area, but heard another shot, and it seemed to be up. He went up instead, leading with his pistol. He could hear people screaming, several of them.

At the top of the flight, he got to his knees and did a quick peek both ways down the hall, then a longer look. Two people were lying prone in the hallway, two or three others running away from him, and four or five were either standing or crouched against walls, two with their hands wrapped over their heads.

Two guys were fighting; rolling around, screaming at each other, but were apparently armed with nothing but their fists. The alarms were still belching out the raucous, enervating *brenk brenk brenk*, and he could smell smoke but not see any. Two emergency lights were working far down the hall, but closer by he could see glass from two more, shattered.

Then a shot came from his right, and there was more screaming, and he ran that way. Three people ran toward him, and then past him, shrinking from his gun. He was halfway down the hall when a man lurched into it, seemed to have a gun, was walking in a predatory way. Lucas shouted, "Drop the gun," and the man pivoted into a gunfighter's stance and Lucas fired and the other man fired at the same time, and Lucas went sideways and hit the wall and landed on his face and the man tumbled back through the doorway and out of sight.

Lucas didn't think he'd hit him and kept his pistol on the door, could hear somebody sobbing. Then a woman began a high-pitched keening and then another. A man lurched from another doorway, a slender man in a hospital gown, nobody Lucas had ever seen, and he seemed confused and Lucas began shouting, "Stay back, stay back," but the man continued walking, stepped in front of the doorway where the shooter had been, and Lucas heard somebody yell, "Hey, Don."

The man pivoted toward the doorway and a shot ripped through him and he staggered and went down and Lucas jumped to his feet and ran softly, half crouched, down to the door.

A half second away from it, he fired a single shot at the in-slanted steel door and then did a quick head-peek inside. He'd hoped that the single shot would have jarred the man on the other side, and it had: Taylor stood there in a combat stance but with the pistol pointed at the other side of the door.

The instant he saw Lucas, he lifted his gun to fire, but Lucas jerked back, felt bullet fragments and maybe pieces of wall tile cut his face, dropped, and came in low. A shot banged the door above his head and he pushed his arm and face low around the door frame, center mass, and fired two quick shots into Taylor's body.

Taylor sagged and struggled to control his weapon and Lucas brought the .45 up and fired a third shot, from three feet away, into Taylor's forehead. Taylor went down, dead.

THERE WAS A DEAD WOMAN inside the room with Taylor, and another woman, apparently shot but still alive, huddling under a bed, whimpering. Lucas turned back to the hallway, looked both ways, pulled his cell phone out of his pocket, found Cale's number, and rang him. Busy. He tried Sloan's, got him.

"Where are you?"

"Just inside, Jesus Christ . . ."

"Shut up. Listen to me. The Big Three are out, and they're armed. They have pistols. I just nailed Taylor. I'm on the second floor, right above the stairway that goes down to the isolation area . . . You know where I'm talking?"

"Yeah, we're coming that way, me and Jenkins and Shrake . . ."

"Okay, but Biggie and Chase and Grant are still out there. Be careful, there are guys with guns all over the place. I'm going down to the bottom, down to the isolation unit. Before you come in, tell somebody that there are a couple wounded, maybe dead, in this hallway . . . next floor above the main floor."

"Wait and I'll back you up."

"Can't wait. There are three more guys and they're killing people, we've got to cover as much as we can as fast as we can, we've gotta knock these guys down . . . gotta knock 'em down, be careful, man, be careful. And tell Beloit before you come in that there's a wounded woman in two ninety. In two ninety."

THEN HE WAS UP and running down the hall, the smell of blood in his nose, with the odor of smoke and human waste and the deafening *brenk brenk brenk* . . .

Into the stairwell: he nearly shot a man halfway up the second flight, the man jumping with fear as Lucas jerked his .45 at him, Lucas lifting his finger off the trigger at the last possible second when he realized that he didn't know the man, that the man wasn't armed.

The man curled against the wall, his hands cupped at his temples, and Lucas shouted, "Find a room, lock yourself inside," heard a *boom* from somewhere, then another, couldn't decide where the shots came from, but it felt like they were up again.

He'd thought to go down, but again he went up.

There really wasn't much down below, he realized—not many people. If the Big Three and Grant were determined to do as much damage as possible, they'd be on the first floor, or the second or third. He continued up to three, heard another *boom*. Peeked down the hallway, saw more people down. Two people crawling along the hallway, two lying motionless. More smoke, thin, veiling. Shouting from the left. Doors banging, another *boom*.

His phone rang; he wanted to ignore it, but it could be information. He pulled it out, poked the answer button. Sloan: "We can hear shooting above us, we're on the way to three."

"I'm already there. I went up instead of down."

"We're on the front steps . . ."

"I just came up the back. I'm moving into the hallway, you'll be looking right at me, for Christ's sake, don't shoot me . . ."

Two more *boom*s and a man screaming and Lucas couldn't wait, a shattering of glass, more glass breaking, more screaming, and then laughter. Lucas ran to the doorway where the sound seemed to be coming from, did a peek: a man was battering at a thick glass window with a plastic chair.

In the dim light, he couldn't see who it was, but he thought it might be Lighter. Lucas shouted, "Hey," and the man turned, and Lucas saw that it wasn't Lighter, that he didn't recognize the man at all. Then he saw movement on his right and pivoted and saw a flash, was hit hard in the left arm, taking in the *boom*, felt himself falling and jerked two shots in the direction of the flash and crawled back out through the doorway into the hall. There was crouching, combat-style movement down the hall and he shouted, "Help!"

Sloan shouted back, "Where are you?"

"Down here. I'm hit."

"Ah, Jesus . . ."

Sloan ran to him in the dim light; the smell of smoke was stronger now, and Sloan came up, Shrake a step behind.

"How bad?" Sloan asked.

The pain was coming on. "I think my arm's busted. Left arm," Lucas said. "There's a guy in there to the right. At least a couple people down. I don't think I hit him when I fired back."

SHRAKE DID A PEEK, then put his left arm through the doorway, with his face, ready to fire. Sloan was cutting at Lucas's sport coat with a jackknife. "Let me see . . . ah, man, you got a hole. It's not bleeding too bad, but it's right below your biceps, right in the middle."

"Yeah, that's what it feels like," Lucas groaned. "I can feel a piece moving . . . We gotta take this guy."

"You're out of it," Sloan said.

"I can move okay," Lucas said. He stood up, almost fell, propped himself against the wall. There was smoke now, another fire, the hallways clear except for a man at the far end, dragging a mattress for some reason. "Look: I'll go back down and sit in the stairway, block it off. You guys gotta keep this asshole penned up, or take him. There's somebody in there hurt."

"You know who it is?"

"No. Could be Biggie," Lucas said.

"That motherfucker," Sloan said. "You go on. We'll take him."

"Get some more support up here," Shrake said. "Jenkins went off with that crappie cop, they could hear something down on one."

"Cell phone," Lucas said. "I can't use mine . . ."

"Get your ass down to the stairwell," Sloan said. "We'll take care of this."

JENKINS AND THE game warden, whose name was Deacon, saw the flash of the gunshot and moved slowly down the inside wall of the hallway, closing on the door. They found Chase sitting on the shoulders of a dead man, as though the dead man were a low stool, talking to a woman who had propped herself up against a wall. They could hear Chase's voice before they saw him; a low chatter that continued between the *brenk brenk brenk* of the alarms. When they got right next to the door, they could hear his voice distinctly, as he talked over the racket around them.

". . . is dead, because if he wasn't dead, he couldn't stand it when I put my finger on his eyeball like this. But see, he doesn't even blink. There's still some blood running out, but that's gravity, is what it is. Just like when you cut a chicken's head off, the blood keeps coming for a long time, but the chicken is dead. Have you ever seen anybody do that? No? It's pretty exciting. You get the chicken and you hold it by its legs, and you rub its stomach and it'll get real quiet, then you lay the neck on a block and then really quick, chop, and the head flies off. If you let go of the chicken, the body will run all over the place without a head. It's pretty funny, when you see it . . ."

Jenkins risked a peek. The room was fifteen-by-fifteen feet and the man was sitting with his back to Jenkins, not more than seven or eight feet away. He was pointing a pistol at a woman against the far wall, who sat motionless, head down; she had blood on her blouse. Jenkins was not sure she was alive. He had to assume she was, though, and she was also directly on the other side of the man. If he shot the man, the bullet could go right through him into her . . .

"That's what people mean when they say that somebody's running around like a chicken with its head cut off . . . Anyway, this is what dead is . . . when somebody puts his finger on your eyeball, you don't even blink. I am going to shoot you when I'm finished talking, and you'll feel all your blood run out, and then to make sure you're dead, I will . . . don't move. Just sit there. Just listen, or I'll pull the trigger . . ."

Jenkins pulled slowly back, listening to the beat of the words, checked his gun, turned to the game warden, and put his finger to his lips. He stood upright, carefully slipped off his loafers, took a breath, then took a quick long silent step into the room, then part of another before the man began to turn . . .

Jenkins fired a single shot down through the Chase's skull, from a range of nine inches.

The game warden lurched through the door. Jenkins looked down at the dead man and said, "Fuckin' amateurs."

They both stepped over to the woman. She was a staffer and wore a black name tag that said Bea; she was alive, and she twitched away from him.

LUCAS SAT IN the stairwell, waiting for Sloan and Shrake to make their move on Biggie. The shooting had trailed off—maybe they were running out of ammunition? Lucas tried to think of how many bodies he'd seen in the hallways. Six? Eight? Plus the three in the cage.

His arm hurt; not the worst hurt he'd ever felt, but it was bad enough. He was okay as long as he didn't move . . .

The *brenk brenk brenk* of the alarms suddenly stopped, and the silence was so shocking that Lucas got to his feet . . . and could hear what seemed to be a general, hospitalwide wail, people hurting, people afraid. There was a thump from somewhere below, the sound of feet in the stairwell . . .

. . .

LEO GRANT DIDN'T KNOW how long he'd been on the floor, but it had been awhile, he thought. He knew he'd been shot but couldn't pin down the precise circumstances. His head wasn't working quite right . . .

He tried to push himself up, but his hands slipped. He couldn't see well, but he looked at one hand, then smelled it, and tasted it. Blood, he was covered with blood. He couldn't see very well, there was something wrong with his right eye . . .

He tried again to push himself up, holding on to a window ledge. A door was open next to it, a battery-powered emergency light glowing in the ceiling. He stepped into a cell, then turned and looked at himself in the window—the mirrored inside of the one-way glass. Gaped at himself.

His right eye was gone. The side of his head was a mass of blood . . . he put a hand to it. The eye was gone, and a piece of his eye socket, the outer rim. All gone.

Not much pain yet; a stinging, headache sensation, with little points of pain coming with each step. He started walking, not knowing exactly where he was, or what he was doing. Armageddon, he remembered that. He remembered going into the room with the pistols, and then . . .

Had Chase shot him? He seemed to remember that. Chase had taken the gun and had shot him in the head.

"Crazy motherfucker," he said. He dabbed at his head with his jacket sleeve. Crazy . . . exactly crazy. Why hadn't they thought of that? All the planning, why hadn't they thought of the possibility that one of them might try to kill the others? . . . But that seemed so *unfair*.

He was out of the cellblock now, down the hall, into the stairwell. He looked both ways: a half dozen safety lights provided hardly more illumination than the same number of candles would have.

He could feel the anger rising: he was supposed to be in on this. He was supposed to have a gun. They were *his* fuckin' guns. They were supposed to walk down the hallways, shoulder to shoulder, taking who they wanted, letting other people live, people who begged good enough. Or maybe kill them even if they begged good enough, because it'd be fun to shoot the ass kissers.

Now he didn't even have a gun . . .

He walked past the elevators to the stairway, opened the door, and started up the stairs, hands clenched to his face, trying to hold his head together.

BIGGIE CALLED, "I got four of them in here. Gonna kill them one at a time. You ready? You want to count for me?"

Sloan said to Shrake, "I'm going."

"He'll be ready for you, shooting at the doorway," Shrake said.

"I don't give a fuck, I'm going. Too many bodies," Sloan said.

"Tell me when," Shrake said.

"Now."

They went at once, and just before they got to the door, Shrake vaulted ahead, crossing the opening in an instant; there was a reaction flash and a bullet pounded itself into the wall opposite.

Sloan peeked, saw Biggie across the room, alone. There were no hostages, just the two bodies in the outer room. Biggie now with his hands up, gun on the floor, smile on his face.

"No, no, no, no!" Biggie shouted. "I'm all out. I give up."

Sloan did another peek. Biggie stood there with his hands above his head. "Sloan? That you?"

Sloan turned the corner. "Yeah."

"I quit."

"Yeah, right, Biggie," Sloan said, and he shot Biggie Lighter twice in the heart. One of the slugs went cleanly through, shattered on the wall, and fragments of it ricocheted around the room. A piece of hot metal like the ripped-off rim of a dime hit Sloan in the lip and hung there, protruding from the skin. Sloan peeled it off and flicked it away, tasting the blood in his mouth.

Shrake nodded. "Good shooting."

LUCAS HEARD THE *BOOM* of the gun, turned his head that way. Then he caught the movement coming up the stairwell, turned back, and saw a man coming toward him. The man's head was a mass of blood, and he seemed to be trying to stanch the bleeding with his hands.

Lucas said, "Just sit down, the doctors are . . ." and the man jumped at him, screaming, grabbing Lucas by the broken arm, and Lucas screamed back, swung awkwardly with his .45, and then they both went down the concrete stairs, rolling over and over each other.

Grant, or Roy Rogers, or whatever the fuck his name was. His face was shattered, but Lucas recognized the good half. Grant was soaked in blood, holding to Lucas's broken arm with one hand, swinging with the other, screaming incoherently. Lucas hit the stairs upside down, tumbled, Grant falling over him; he squeezed the trigger of the .45 involuntarily, and the flash lit the stairwell and the surprise and the pain from the broken arm and the recoil pulled the gun out of his hand and he heard it clattering down the stairs.

Grant was underneath him now and they turned again and Grant was on top, scrambling, and Lucas pulled him down and they rolled across the landing and Grant smashed Lucas in the nose; blood flooded into Lucas's mouth and he sputtered, came up close to Grant's face, sprayed blood into Grant's good eye, and they were turning again.

Grant was above him, then, and Lucas saw that he was going for something, the gun, probably, and Lucas managed to tangle up Grant's knees and Grant went down again and Lucas rolled up on top of him. Got his good arm around Grant's neck, got his legs around Grant's body, locked them at the ankles so that he had Grant in a scissors hold.

Grant tried to pull away along the long axis of their bodies, trying to knee or kick Lucas, and they turned again, upside down on the stairs, and he heard the gun clank, thought, "He's got it," and heaved upward as his body weight pushed Grant down.

The gun went off, a flash and a *boom*, then Lucas got his feet braced against a step, groaned and lifted Grant's head up, gave a final desperate jerk . . .

Grant's neck snapped like a tree branch.

He went limp, and Lucas fell on top of him.

Around them, he thought, was nothing but pain and silence: but he was wrong about the silence. In a second or two, when he'd caught his breath and had gotten upright again, he began to hear the screaming, and realized it was coming from everywhere.

27

THE HOSPITAL WAS A SHAMBLES.

A half dozen fires and two dozen fights added to the chaos of the shootings. When the smoke got dense in one wing of the security section, maintenance men used a forklift to break through a locked door to the outside, and frightened, angry, and medicated patients scattered over half a square mile of woods and farmland.

The Big Three, with Grant, killed six people and seriously wounded eight more. The final death toll, including the four killers, was ten.

Of the three people in the cage, one, a woman, had survived because Beloit had gotten to her quickly enough to keep her from drowning in her own blood. The bullet had gone through her cheekbone, her palate, and out through a jawbone, taking along a couple of upper teeth.

The shooting was ending when the fire department got to the hospital, and the paramedics, and three doctors in the hospital itself, quickly got to the other shooting victims.

. . .

LUCAS WAS TAKEN to the hospital in Mankato. Sloan rode with him. Sloan kept saying, "This is not a problem. This is not a problem . . ."

Lucas finally said, "Sloan, shut the fuck up. This is definitely a problem."

THE MORE SERIOUSLY INJURED were flown to Regions Hospital in St. Paul or to the Mayo in Rochester, except for two who needed immediate blood transfusions. They were taken to Mankato to be stabilized.

Lucas was evaluated at Mankato. The bone in his upper arm had been broken by Biggie's bullet. The bullet itself had not gone through but was stuck on the underside of the skin at the back of his arm. With his good hand, Lucas could actually feel the bullet under the skin.

"So what?" he asked. "I'm gonna need a splint or something?"

"More than that," the doc said. "We'll have to go in there to put your arm back together. This will be a little complicated."

After talking with Sloan, Lucas insisted on being reevaluated at Regions. He was flown out with one of the more severely wounded victims who had been taken to Mankato to be stabilized.

At Regions, as at Mankato, he was told that the arm would need an operation to place screws to hold the bones together. He could expect to be in a cast for three to six months; and there would be physical rehabilitation after that.

"Am I gonna lose anything? Any function?"

"Shouldn't," the doctor said. "Maybe a little sensation on the back of your arm."

. . .

SLOAN, JENKINS, Shrake, Del, and Rose Marie crowded in to see him before the operation. Sloan had briefed Rose Marie on the shootings.

"There are already people running around, trying to figure out whom to hang," Rose Marie said, before Lucas was rolled into the OR. "It's amazing. It's like the second reaction. The first is to ask how many are dead, the second is to ask whom we can hang."

THE OPERATION TOOK two hours and was routine, the surgeon told Lucas in the recovery room. He was given additional sedation when he came out of the recovery room and slept through the night, waking at six o'clock.

A nurse came to see him: "Hurt?"

"Not much," he said. "I'd like cup of coffee, is what I'd like. And a *New York Times* or a *Wall Street Journal?*"

"I don't think so," she said. "How about a nice glass of orange juice?"

"How about if you hand me my cell phone? And I gotta take a leak . . ."

Both his arm and his face hurt—his nose had been recracked in the fight—but he was able to walk to the bathroom without a problem, pulling a saline drip along behind him.

The lying had already begun.

He added to it.

WEATHER CALLED AT SEVEN, an hour earlier than usual. She'd heard about the shooting after she'd finished her morning work in the operating theater, and called in a panic. Lucas had kept his cell phone on a bedside table.

"I'm fine," Lucas lied. "But I gotta get into the office. There's gonna be a political shit storm starting about ten o'clock. Soon as the politicians finish their double-latte grandes."

"Were you involved in the shooting? Were you in there?" she asked, still scared.

"Yeah, I was right there," Lucas said. "It's a goddamn mess, Weather. I don't want you to think about it. I gotta talk to everybody on the face of the earth in the next two days, covering our asses and getting the story right. I don't want to have to worry about you, too."

"You sound . . . hoarse."

He was, from the anesthesia. He said, "I spent all yesterday screaming at people. I need a couple of cough drops."

She asked, "What about Sloan?"

"He's bummed. I gotta get to him, too," Lucas said.

"Take care of yourself—don't worry about everybody else," Weather said.

"Hey, I'm fine," he lied. When he hung up, he was satisfied that he'd pulled it off.

Then Weather called Sloan's wife, worried about Sloan's state of mind, and Sloan's wife said, "We stayed for the operation, but Lucas was pretty groggy when he came out of it. They said everything went okay . . ."

"What operation?" Weather asked.

Lucas was talking to the docs about getting out and was being told "No," when Weather called back.

"LUCAS . . . ," she wailed.

"Ah, shit . . ."

Trapped like a rat.

SLOAN AND JENKINS lied about Biggie's death.

Jenkins gave the blow-by-blow. He was a superb liar: "He had his back against the wall. I made a move and he fired at me, six feet away, right through the doorway." He talked with his hands and eyes as much as with his words. "Goddamn, I'm lucky to be here. Sloan came in low, right under Biggie's shot, and shot him twice. It was all so fast, not even Biggie knew the gun was empty. I mean, we're talking *Bam! Bam-Bam!*"

Everybody bought that.

And why not? All the bullet holes were right there. Besides, the reconstruction of events suggested that Biggie's .45 had killed three people and wounded three more, including Lucas.

SHRAKE'S DESCRIPTION OF Chase's death had Chase pointing his weapon at the second woman's face, ready to pull the trigger. The rescued woman was incoherent for two days after the shootings and kept talking about Chase rolling the other body's eyes back and forth with his fingers.

Nobody wanted to know much more about Chase.

LUCAS TOLD THE absolute truth about Taylor and Grant, and blood analysis proved it.

Later analysis also indicated why the shootings weren't more deadly than they were. O'Donnell's guns, used by Biggie and Taylor, were loaded with target loads and cast slugs, apparently homemade by O'Donnell himself, for shooting close range at metal plates. They punched holes in the victims but didn't expand, and most didn't penetrate as deeply as combat loads would have. The third gun, a 9mm that did have combat loads, was used by Chase and had only had two or three rounds fired.

SLOAN, DURING ONE OF his visits, reconstructed Grant's—or Rogers's, or whoever he was—movements after O'Donnell disappeared.

"He killed O'Donnell and dumped him, planted the evidence, and drove up to the airport and left the car where we'd find it," Sloan said. "Then he took a shuttle back to Mankato and a cab back to his place, and went to work the next day. We know about the cab and shuttle for sure. That night, after work, he actually drove to Chicago, made the call to us, and drove back. The next day, he's back at work again."

"Risky . . . ," Lucas said.

"Yeah. He took risks. And there's no way to prove he drove to Chicago, but we checked the stewardesses, and nobody remembers him on a flight. Also, he had an oil change at a Jiffy Lube a week and a half ago and got a mileage sticker on his window. He's driven almost two thousand miles in that time."

"That's good," Lucas said. "You know, if he'd faked a suicide with O'Donnell . . . I don't know that we ever would have broken it out. He got too complicated for himself."

THE CRIME-SCENE PEOPLE believed that Angela Larson was killed in O'Donnell's workshop; they found traces of blood, with indications that somebody had tried to clean it up with commercial liquid cleanser; the cleanser had actually ruined the blood for DNA analysis, but chemical analysis of the concrete dust on Larson's feet matched the concrete of O'Donnell's garage floor. O'Donnell, according to the security hospital records, was working the night that Larson was killed but was not working the night that Peterson was kidnapped. Was he involved? Lucas didn't think so. He thought O'Donnell was probably Grant's—or Rogers's—last line of defense, and had been carefully set up.

THE BIGGEST, MOST complicated lie—if it was a lie, and many people would have denied that it was—appeared in the *Minneapolis*

Star-Tribune four days after the shootings, under the byline of Ruffe Ignace.

LIKE THIS:

The Twin Cities were saturated with media. Reporters were looking for explanations, going to funerals, interviewing people who didn't know anything.

Rose Marie called Lucas and outlined the problem: "The media want a public execution. The legislature is behaving with its usual courage, so there'll probably be one. The only candidates are the Department of Human Services, and us. Some of the DHS guys are semipublicly wondering why you were driving down there to pick up Grant? Why didn't you call the sheriff and have him grabbed earlier in the day?"

They talked about it for an hour, and then Lucas called Ignace. Ignace came into the hospital on the evening of the day after the shooting, armed with six steno pads and half a dozen pens.

"We want to tell the truth before too many innocent people get hurt," Lucas said piously.

"Yeah, yeah, that's what I'm here for," Ignace said.

"You gotta cover me," Lucas said. "I'm not supposed to be talking. So . . . you've got multiple sources, okay?"

Ignace said, "That's fine with me. I've already talked to a couple of people. I haven't gotten much, but I can use them. So, saying I had multiple sources wouldn't exactly be a lie."

Not *exactly*.

LUCAS LED HIM THROUGH the chain of events, from the discovery of Pope's body, to O'Donnell's disappearance, to the call to the Cancun clinic, to the attack on Millie Lincoln and Mihovil, through the fight and the evacuations of the wounded to the various hospitals.

. . .

IGNACE TOOK a full day to write the story. It said, in part:

". . . spent days looking for O'Donnell but couldn't find him," according to one investigator. "We decided we had to look at other staff members. We had the feeling that O'Donnell was another red herring, like Charlie Pope. We also decided that we couldn't really trust the hospital personnel records, so we began researching the records on our own, vetting the staff members."

A BCA researcher eventually contacted a clinic in Cancun, where, he was surprised to learn, Dr. Leopold Grant still worked. "That was the key," said a source close to the investigation. "That's when we knew we had identified the killer."

Asked why they didn't simply call the sheriff's office and have "Roy Rogers" arrested at the hospital, the source said that "when O'Donnell disappeared, everybody thought he must be the killer. The Sheriff's Department was involved in the search of O'Donnell's house, and within a couple of hours, it seemed that everybody in Mankato knew we were looking for him. We didn't know whether the Sheriff's Department was leaking, or the hospital—but there was a big leak somewhere. When it came to Rogers, we didn't want to take any chances. We knew he had at least two guns, taken from O'Donnell's house, and we knew he was a complete madman. We wanted to take him down quickly, and secretly, without any warning. That's why we did it the way we did, why we sent Davenport down with his team. These were all very experienced men, as we saw in the way they handled the firefight. And remember, we were only talking about an hour, not a long period of time. There was no long delay."

Fatefully, when one of the researchers was looking into the "Leo Grant" personnel file, a direct call was made to the hospital. The research request was leaked inside the hospital, and apparently reached "Roy Rogers's " ears, who concluded correctly that he had been identified. He rushed from the hospital, back to his apartment, where the confrontation with Millie Lincoln and Mihovil took place, and the race to the hospital began.

ONE QUESTION POSED by Ignace and left out of the story when Lucas couldn't answer it was "Why did O'Donnell take all of his money out of the bank the day he disappeared?"

Lucas shook his head. "We don't know. We may never know."

IGNACE IDENTIFIED LUCAS variously as a BCA official, an investigator, a state law-enforcement officer, a researcher, a source close to the investigation, a source who asked not to be identified, and a highly placed state official.

Because he actually named Rose Marie Roux, Carlton Aspen, the commissioner of the Department of Human Services, and Jerald Wald, the Senate majority leader, Ignace felt safe in saying that his sources included "police officers, state officials, legislators, and people directly involved in the firefight at St. John's."

ON THE EVENING THAT he finished the story, Ignace spent several hours on the Internet, checking apartment prices in Manhattan.

ROSE MARIE, ON READING the story the next morning, was pleased. "It might not be *the* truth, but it's *one* truth, and best of all, its *ours*," she said. She added, with some satisfaction, "The goddamn DHS is fucked."

. . .

THE MORNING AFTER he talked to Ignace, Lucas woke up, expecting to get out of the hospital, to find an exhausted and angry Weather sitting next to his bed.

"Wait'll I get you home," she said. Her eyes drifted toward a nurse.

"Where's everybody else?" Lucas said.

"They're still back in London. I didn't have time to get everybody here. Lucas, we gotta talk. I'm your wife. You don't get shot and don't tell me about it . . ." Tears started down her face.

The nurse said, "Maybe I better take off for a while . . ."

LUCAS WENT HOME that day. His eye was blacker than it had ever been, but his nose was more or less straight. His arm was immobilized from shoulder to wrist. Two quarter-inch metal rods went straight through his skin from an outer brace: they would be there for a few days, and then another minor operation would take them out.

An orthopedic surgeon was checking out the brace when Weather came back from the bathroom. The doc recognized her and they chatted for a few seconds, and then Weather, with a certain tone in her voice, said to Lucas, "You see these rods going into your arm?"

Lucas looked down and said, "Yeah?"

"That's what orthopods call 'sutures.'"

THE MORNING AFTER THAT, he and Weather were sitting in the kitchen, drinking coffee, reading Ignace's story. Now that Lucas was ambulatory and she could see that his life wasn't in danger, she was talking about getting back to the kids.

"Go ahead," Lucas kept saying, "I'm really okay."

His arm felt like a truck was sitting on it, and his face felt like somebody had driven a nail through his eye. He smiled and suppressed a wince.

"I feel like I'd be ditching you," she said.

"No, no . . . I'm gonna be busier than hell."

She started giving him more trouble about lying to her—although the night before, she'd settled most of his sexual problems, and any that he might have developed over the coming six or eight weeks.

Then the phone rang, and he snatched it up to get away from her eyes. Beloit, the doc from St. John's, said, "I've got to talk with you. Privately. Secretly. May I come up?"

BELOIT CAME UP, and she and Weather sniffed each other's credentials for a few minutes, then Weather went away and Beloit perched on a chair in the den and said, "I think I know why Sam withdrew money from the bank the day he disappeared."

"I'd be interested," Lucas said.

"I don't know how to do this," she said. "I don't want anyone to hear it from me. I don't want to testify. I'd lose my job and so would other people. But I need to get it off my chest . . ."

"So, we'll call you a confidential source," Lucas said. "If there's no way to prove it, we'll just pretend nobody said anything."

She looked at him for a minute, then away, and finally her eyes came back: "We sort of had a social group in the hospital. The longhairs. We occasionally smoked a little dope."

Ah. So that was it. He knew then what she was going to say but let her say it.

"Leo had the connection," she said. "He knew the guy who brought it in from Canada. When the guy was coming by, he'd call Leo, but Leo didn't have much money. So Sam would front the money, and he and Leo would go pick up a can of the stuff—it usually came in one of those big tobacco cans. Sam would parcel it around to the people in our group. We'd pay him our share, and he'd put the money back. He wasn't making money on the deal, he was just . . . facilitating."

"So Leo could have told him the guy was coming through . . ."

"And it was time. We'd been low, or out, for a while," she said. "People had started asking when the guy from Canada was coming."

"Okay. Would you happen to know the Canadian guy's name?"

"Um, Manny," Beloit said, with a tentative smile. "They used to call him Manny Sunshine."

Lucas smiled. "It's always *Somebody* Sunshine."

"You can get this out, without my name?" she asked.

"I'll have our dope guys look into Manny. If we can find him, we'll have a talk. We don't really want to bust a bunch of potheads. But it would be nice if we could explain the money withdrawal."

"Please, please, keep my name out of it."

"I will." He liked her, even if she was a doper. He remembered seeing her kneeling over the woman in the cage, saving a life, as the shooting was going on around her.

"Do you think we'll ever find Sam?" she asked.

"I don't know," Lucas said. "We shouldn't have found Charlie Pope, but we did. So . . . I don't know."

THREE DAYS AFTER Lucas's truth appeared in the *Star-Tribune*, DHS officials, seeing how the wind was blowing, decided to preempt any chance of higher-level hangings by doing a few of their own. Cale and four other administrators were put on administrative leave from the hospital. The word was, they'd never be back, and there might be more heads to roll.

Lucas, Jenkins, Shrake, Sloan, and the wildlife officer were given citations by their various departments, a signal that the departments had decided they were clean.

. . .

THE LEGISLATURE SCHEDULED hearings, and a group of Mankato residents demanded that a monument be built, with the names of the victims inscribed on it, in a plaza, or perhaps a new park. Rose Marie, reading the story, said to Lucas, "You know, it never occurred to me."

"What?"

"That somebody might make a buck on this," she said, as she turned the page.

A WEEK AFTER the shootings, Sloan was gone. He had a lot of accumulated vacation, which he took as a lead-in to actual retirement. His vacation check also helped on the down payment on the bar; he assumed ten years of a fifteen-year mortgage, renamed the place Shooters, and, his wife told Lucas, "The first person he hired is nineteen years old and has tits out to here."

Lucas said, "Huh. He's smarter than I thought."

WEATHER CAME BACK from London with the kids and the housekeeper. The orthopod took the steel rods out of Lucas's arm but left two titanium screws, which would be permanent. The arm ached, and the cast drove him crazy. He found he could scratch his arm with an ingeniously bent clothes hanger.

Letty, his ward, said, "You know, every time you scratch, there's a bad smell."

"Thank you. You do so much to help my self-confidence in social situations," he said.

She was still teasing him when the phone rang. When Lucas picked it up, Nordwall told him that O'Donnell's body had been found in the middle of a cornfield two miles from his home. The body was found by a farmer responding to his wife's complaints of a persistent bad odor from across the road. O'Donnell had been shot once in the forehead.

"Grant, Rogers, whoever he was, must have been looking him right in the eyes when he pulled the trigger," Nordwall said.

THEY NEVER FIGURED out who the killer was. He was buried under the name Roy Rogers, though nobody really thought that was his name. DNA records were kept in case anybody ever came looking for him.

AND FINALLY, a month after the shootings, deep in the bowels of the security hospital, nine patients and a doctor met for a group-therapy session. One of the patients, a man known for his silence, timorously raised a hand as soon as everybody had a chair.

Sennet, who was running the group, suppressed a look of surprise and said, "Lonnie? You have something for us?"

Lonnie, who feared many things—too many things, hundreds of them, a new one every minute—dug into his pocket and took out a tattered roll of yellow paper. "I found this the day everybody got shot. I didn't steal it, it was lying in the hall."

"Okay," Sennet said, encouraging him. "What is it?"

Lonnie unrolled the paper. "It's a list. It says, *Best Songs of the Rock Era.* It has a hundred songs on it."

"May I see it?" Sennet asked.

"May I have it back?" Lonnie looked frightened, as though the list might be seized. "I think about it a lot."

"Sure. If it's only rock songs," Sennet said.

Lonnie passed the paper round the circle of the group, each person glancing at it. When Sennet got it, he scanned the list, then passed it around the rest of the circle, and back to Lonnie.

"Do you have some thoughts about it?" Sennet asked.

"Well, these are the one hundred best rock songs, okay?"

"Okay."

Lonnie's lip trembled. "But, there are no Beatles on the list. Don't you see? *There are no Beatles . . .*"

Lucas Davenport's *"Best Songs of the Rock Era"*

In no particular order, except that, as any intelligent person knows, any decent road trip will start with ZZ Top.

1. ZZ Top	Sharp-Dressed Man
2. ZZ Top	Legs
3. Wilson Pickett	Mustang Sally
4. Crash Test Dummies	Superman's Song
5. David Essex	Rock On
6. Golden Earring	Radar Love
7. Blondie	Heart of Glass
8. Jefferson Airplane	White Rabbit
9. Jefferson Airplane	Somebody to Love
10. Derek and the Dominos	Layla
11. The Doors	Roadhouse Blues
12. The Animals	House of the Rising Sun
13. Aerosmith	Sweet Emotion
14. Aerosmith	Dude (Looks Like a Lady)
15. Bruce Springsteen	Dancing in the Dark
16. Bruce Springsteen	Born to Run
17. Bruce Springsteen	Thunder Road
18. The Police	Every Breath You Take
19. Tom Waits	Heart of Saturday Night

20. Van Halen	Hot for Teacher
21. The Who	Won't Get Fooled Again
22. Gipsy Kings	Hotel California
23. Tracy Chapman	Give Me One Reason
24. Creedence Clearwater Revival	Down on the Corner
25. Eagles	Lyin' Eyes
26. Eagles	Life in the Fast Lane
27. Dire Straits	Skateaway (Roller Girl)
28. Tom Petty and the Heartbreakers	Mary Jane's Last Dance
29. Janis Joplin	Me and Bobby McGee
30. The Doobie Brothers	Black Water
31. Joan Jett and the Blackhearts	I Love Rock 'n' Roll
32. John Mellencamp	Jack and Diane
33. Pink Floyd	Another Brick in the Wall (Part 2)
34. Pink Floyd	Money
35. Billy Joel	Piano Man
36. Eric Clapton	After Midnight
37. Eric Clapton	Lay Down Sally
38. AC/DC	You Shook Me All Night Long
39. AC/DC	Dirty Deeds Done Dirt Cheap
40. The Hollies	Long Cool Woman (in a Black Dress)
41. Bob Dylan	Like a Rolling Stone
42. Bob Dylan	Knockin' on Heaven's Door
43. Bob Dylan	Subterranean Homesick Blues
44. The Rolling Stones	(I Can't Get No) Satisfaction
45. The Rolling Stones	Brown Sugar
46. The Rolling Stones	Sympathy for the Devil
47. Sex Pistols	Anarchy in the UK
48. Grateful Dead	Sugar Magnolia

49. The Pointer Sisters	Slow Hand
50. Eurythmics	Sweet Dreams (Are Made of This)
51. Elvis Presley	Jailhouse Rock
52. David Bowie	Ziggy Stardust
53. Bob Seger	Night Moves
54. The Everly Brothers	Bye Bye Love
55. Jimi Hendrix	Purple Haze
56. The Kinks	Lola
57. Jackson Browne	Tender Is the Night
58. The Kingsmen	Louie, Louie
59. George Thorogood and the Destroyers	Bad to the Bone
60. Metallica	Turn the Page
61. Lynryd Skynyrd	Sweet Home Alabama
62. Queen	We Will Rock You
63. The Allman Brothers Band	Ramblin' Man
64. Led Zeppelin	Rock and Roll
65. Tina Turner	What's Love Got to Do with It
66. Steppenwolf	Born to Be Wild
67. U2	With or Without You
68. Black Sabbath	Paranoid
69. Foreigner	Blue Morning, Blue Day
70. Billy Idol	White Wedding
71. Guns N' Roses	Sweet Child o' Mine
72. Guns N' Roses	Paradise City
73. Guns N' Roses	Knockin' on Heaven's Door*
74. Lou Reed	Walk on the Wild Side
75. Bad Company	Feel Like Makin' Love
76. Def Leppard	Rock of Ages
77. Van Morrison	Brown Eyed Girl

*Yeah, yeah, I know it's on the list twice.

78. Mitch Ryder and the Detroit Wheels	Devil with a Blue Dress On
79. Aretha Franklin	Respect
80. John Lee Hooker, Bonnie Raitt	I'm in the Mood
81. James Brown	I Got You (I Feel Good)
82. The Righteous Brothers	Unchained Melody
83. Prince	Little Red Corvette
84. Chuck Berry	Roll Over Beethoven
85. The Byrds	Mr. Tambourine Man
86. Crosby, Stills, Nash and Young	Ohio
87. Buddy Holly	Peggy Sue
88. Jerry Lee Lewis	Great Balls of Fire
89. Roy Orbison	Oh, Pretty Woman
90. Del Shannon	Runaway
91. Run-D.M.C.	Walk This Way
92. Otis Redding	(Sittin' on) the Dock of the Bay
93. Nirvana	Smells Like Teen Spirit
94. Paul Simon	Still Crazy After All These Years
95. Bo Diddley	Who Do You Love?
96. Brewer and Shipley	One Toke Over the Line
97. Ramones	I Wanna Be Sedated
98. The Clash	Should I Stay or Should I Go
99. Talking Heads	Burning Down the House
100. Dmitri Shostakovich	Jazz Suite No. 2: Waltz 2

**POCKET
BOOKS**

Certain Prey
A Lucas Davenport Thriller

'Sandford knows all there is to know about detonating the gut-level
shocks of a good thriller' *NEW YORK TIMES*

Attorney Carmel Loan is beautiful, intelligent, ambitious –
and used to getting what she wants. When she becomes
infatuated with fellow barrister Hale Allen, she isn't going to
let a little thing like his being married get in the way.

Through the contacts of an ex-client, she hires professional
killer Clara Rinker to get rid of Allen's wife. Smart, attractive
Rinker is the best hitwoman in the business – but things go
wrong, and the shooting of a witness, a cop, brings DI Lucas
Davenport into the case.

Carmel Loan and Clara Rinker team up to clean up the loose
ends – which includes getting Davenport off their backs by
whatever means necessary.

ISBN 0 7434 8419 3
PRICE £6.99

POCKET
BOOKS

Easy Prey
A Lucas Davenport Thriller

'A haunting, unforgettable, ice-blooded thriller' Carl Hiassen

In life she was a high-profile model. In death she is the focus of a media firestorm that's demanding action from Lucas Davenport. One of his own men is a suspect in her murder.

But when a series of bizarre, seemingly unrelated slayings rock the city, Davenport suspects a connection that runs deeper than anyone had imagined – one that leads to an ingenious killer more ruthless than anyone had feared . . .

ISBN 0 7434 8418 5
PRICE £6.99

POCKET
BOOKS

This book and other **Pocket Books** titles are available
from your local bookshop or can be ordered direct
from the publisher.

0 7434 8418 5	Easy Prey	John Sandford	£6.99
1 4165 0231 9	Winter Prey	John Sandford	£6.99
0 7434 8421 5	Sudden Prey	John Sandford	£6.99
0 7434 8419 3	Certain Prey	John Sandford	£6.99
0 7434 1555 8	Chosen Prey	John Sandford	£6.99
0 7434 6869 4	Naked Prey	John Sandford	£6.99
0 7434 8420 7	Secret Prey	John Sandford	£6.99
0 7434 1559 0	The Empress File	John Sandford	£6.99
0 7434 1560 4	The Fool's Run	John Sandford	£6.99
0 7434 1557 4	The Devil's Code	John Sandford	£6.99

Please send cheque or postal order for the value of the book,
free postage and packing within the UK, to
SIMON & SCHUSTER CASH SALES
PO Box 29, Douglas Isle of Man, IM99 1BQ
Tel: 01624 677237, Fax: 01624 670923
Email: bookshop@enterprise.net
www.bookpost.co.uk

Please allow 14 days for delivery. Prices and availability
subject to change without notice